Metropause

Mark Evan and Frank Lulias

Bubble
Press

Bubble Press
Seattle, WA
www.bubble-press.com

First Edition: January 2009

This book is a work of fiction. Names, characters, places and incidents are either products of the authors' imaginations or are used fictitiously. Any resemblance to actual events or locales or persons, living or dead, is entirely coincidental.

ISBN: 978-0-9821078-0-5

Library of Congress Control Number: 2008909543

Printed in the United States of America

For Heloise

Acknowledgements

Our thanks to the following people: Barbara Murtaugh, for her valuable observations and patient edits—a bottle of white is on its way; Pete O'Brien, for his many useful insights; last but not least, Steve, for being our first brave reader and constant advocate.

Metropause

ONE

A San Franciscan would never have to deal with this, Edison thought, slipping off his sweaty T-shirt. Twain was right about the coldest winter being a summer in San Francisco, and Edison had grown accustomed to his cool and foggy summers. He opened window after window in the hot and stuffy second floor of his temporary Seattle home. With the last of the windows open, cool air flowed in around him and he paused to look at the street below. Teens on bikes circled erratically on the street. On the sidewalk, the unspoken war between the stroller people and the joggers raged on, the frozen glares detectable even from his distant vantage point.

He stepped away from the window, suddenly, after catching his reflection in the upper pane. The reflection was his, but he barely recognized himself. Gone was the neat hair and clean-cut look of the thirty-six year-old "Eagle Scout" as his assistant back in San Francisco had called him. Looking back at him was a tall, haggard man with greasy brown hair who hadn't shaved in two days. For all the hours spent in bed the past several days, he still looked exhausted. And was that drool on his chin? he wondered as he wiped it away with his hand. He was usually careful with his appearance, and, while never a great dresser, wore clean and conservatively tasteful clothes. Now, taking stock of both his hygiene and minimal clothing, he was surprised at how fast he had become a slob without being aware of the descent. It troubled him, but the observation gave him no more resolve than to turn on the television.

A shallow macramé bowl on the coffee table was the home for the remotes. Edison had been amused and slightly embarrassed of the macramé creations his mother had mailed him over the years for his very modern San Francisco apartment. Regardless, he had kept each one and had remembered to populate his apartment with them before his parents' visits. After their passing, he had inherited a legion of macramé oddities. They now held a special place in his heart, even though he had no idea what to do with them or even what some of them were.

After finding the correct remote, the television gave a static snap and started to come to life. He gazed at the muted images on the screen. He was about to settle in on the couch, covered by two large macramé throws, he noticed, when the distinctive snap of the front door lock echoed up from the foyer. He froze, his urban sensibilities assuming the worst. The click of heels against the marble floor of the foyer was the next sound he heard.

Edison sighed as he grabbed his shirt and turned to the hallway. Whoever was downstairs was not shy and had a key. The Queen Anne neighborhood where his parents had lived was starting to feel too much like Mayberry. Slipping his shirt on, he walked to the hall and peered over the rail at the top of the stairs. Below, was a wiry and ancient looking Asian woman. She was doing something with a large blue box next to the round table that sat in the center of the foyer. Edison frowned when he saw that she had taken the liberty of tossing some of the newspapers from the table to the floor, as well as his wallet and keys.

"Hello?" he shouted.

The figure ignored his call and in a dramatic sweep of a couture-clad arm, she pushed the remaining papers from the table to the floor.

"What the hell?" Edison muttered as he headed down the staircase. Taking a careful look as he descended, he recognized the brittle makeup and ramrod posture of his mystery intruder. It was his neighbor, Lily Ling, the women he assumed Death forgot or was too scared to collect. She was a loyal friend of his parents and he knew that demanded some respect even if, in the past, she had treated him like the unwashed, which, ironically, today he was. As he padded down the stairs in his bare feet and crossed the foyer to the table, he watched her, noting that she never once looked up to acknowledge his approach.

"Hello, Mrs. Ling," he said politely, eyeing the house key she had placed on the table.

Ignoring him, she poured dozens of paper birds of various colors into a giant crystal bowl that she had produced from the box. Once the bowl was full, she turned and made eye contact with him briefly, only to leave him feeling dismissed and unwelcome in what was now his house.

"The bowl was your mother's and it is Tiffany. The paper hens in the bowl are from an Asian Cultural Center event I attended," she stated flatly, as her eyes focused beyond his right shoulder. "The hens are either for good luck or fertility; I don't know which, since I left the presentation early to have a cigarette." Her eyes fell on him again, briefly. "Whatever the hens bring, it looks like you could use it."

Taking the key she had used to enter the house, she walked away without another word, leaving the empty box on the floor.

Dumbfounded, Edison stared at the back of the slim figure as it passed through the open doorway. The door slammed, leaving him in silence and wondering if he had just imagined the entire event. He reached into the bowl and picked up a delicate paper hen blazing white under the light of the chandelier. As he examined the hen, it seemed to stare back with equal fascination.

TWO

Val pulled into the Whole Foods parking lot and looked for an open space. Crowded as usual, she thought, glancing at her watch. It was just before noon, which meant she would have enough time to catch the last of the Sunday morning free samples before the churchy crowd from across California Street swarmed the store.

She found an open space between a Lexus SUV and a classic Porsche. Looks as if Stacy's BMW will fit in nicely, she thought. She caught a glimpse of herself in the rearview mirror and deciding that her hair was a little flat, she ran her fingers through it a few times to give it enough bounce to be presentable. A few gray strands were among the brown and she noted that her once stylish bob had grown almost shoulder-length. How many months had it been since she'd seen a stylist? She really needed a cut, but she would rather do it herself than be seen at a discount salon that would fit her budget. Maybe she would try one of those $8 haircuts she saw advertised in Chinatown. At least she could pretend it was some sort of wild experiment or that the stylist was an undiscovered genius. Oh, how the mighty have fallen, she reflected.

She entered the store with a cart and saw that the produce section was crowded with shoppers. She spotted an opening near the fresh asparagus and used it to get in range of the remaining pineapple samples. After emptying the tray, she carefully plotted the path of least resistance between her and the next stop on the free sample parade.

She remembered a time not so long ago when she'd bought

only organic produce and made a point of telling this to anyone who would listen. Now, she didn't even look at the expensive organic mixed baby greens or the designer hybrids. Instead, she slinked over to the bins of conventionally raised potatoes, carrots and onions and grabbed a few of each.

She avoided the supplement and personal care section completely, having long ago dismissed the section as a sinkhole for cash. She made her way to the seafood area and saw she was in luck. They were offering smoked salmon on crackers today, and she helped herself to several as she looked longingly at the sushi. These days, she ate her tuna straight from the can, tossing the lids on the ever-growing pile of unopened credit card bills that came with alarming frequency.

At the meat department, she bought beef stew meat and the cheapest cuts of pork. Even the lesser cuts of meat, she had found, would eventually become tender if one cooked them long enough. This was a far cry from the lavish dinner parties she used to host at her Russian Hill flat where one could always count on an excellent filet to complement the best Napa Valley wines. Now, it was just her and the massive LCD TV at Stacy and Dean's condo, where she was squatting, unbeknownst to them, while they were away in Europe for a few months. Dean was on a tour of duty at the London office for his San Francisco-based investment firm and Stacy had gone along for the sightseeing. It wasn't as if she was doing anything wrong, Val frequently rationalized to herself. They had given her the keys to take in the mail and water the plants. So what if she had moved in. It was only temporary and where else was she supposed to go after losing her apartment.

Making her way down the frozen foods aisle, she saw a middle-aged woman had parked her cart horizontally, blocking the aisle, while holding the freezer door open and staring blankly at the pints of ice cream. In the past, Val would have blown her lid at something like this, but with the help of the yoga classes she'd recently been taking, compliments of Stacy's gym membership, she felt more in tune with herself and simply pushed the cart into the woman's expansive backside. She then proceeded down the aisle, impressed with her newfound restraint, not turning back to acknowledge any reaction the ice cream devotee might have to offer.

It was in the next aisle, while she was perusing the salsa and chips, that she saw a woman barreling toward her. Oh, no, not another one, Val thought. She was, after all, just a yoga novice. The woman was tall and thin with a tight blonde ponytail, wearing a sleek black tracksuit. She was simultaneously talking on her headset while pushing her child in a shopping cart, directly down the center of the aisle as if she were Moses parting the Red Sea. Val wasn't about to budge and their carts briefly collided when the woman passed by, causing the child to cry in alarm and the woman to look at Val in horror.

The woman spoke tersely into her headset, glaring at Val, "Suzanne, I have to go. Some bitch just rammed into my cart and Caitlin is crying."

The mother reached over to console Caitlin, but Caitlin was in no mood and took a swipe at her mother's diamond tennis bracelet. Caitlin then looked at Val and screamed, "Bish! Bish! Bish!"

Val turned to the woman. "I'd normally be upset, but I can see by your botched Botox and Rosemary's baby, here," she said, gesturing to Caitlin, "that you've suffered enough." Val pulled away as the woman's jaw dropped open in indignation.

When Val reached the wine and cheese area, she found a moment of peace and was able to recover her composure by practicing some of the deep breathing exercises she'd learned. She pushed her cart forward, wondering who the fools were that had designed this store thinking that narrow aisles and a high-maintenance clientele were a good mix.

She scanned the checkout lines, which were clogged with happy young couples with overflowing carts. "Ugh," she murmured, hoping that all the couples secretly hated each other and were in loads of debt. She avoided the couples by pulling behind a single woman with bad skin and too much makeup. She was surprised when the goth cashier asked to see the woman's ID for the case of chardonnay she was purchasing. Val knew they supposedly required age verification from anyone who looked under thirty, but this seemed a rather liberal interpretation of the policy as the woman looked to be at least forty. The woman's bill came to just over $250, which, Val noticed with envy, she paid with three crisp $100 bills.

When it was her turn at the register, Val readied her ID, figuring that, at just shy of thirty-six, she was several years younger than the rich alcoholic. She was taken aback, however, when the cashier didn't request her ID for the bottle of cheap merlot.

"How come you checked that woman's ID and not mine?" Val asked, not hiding her disappointment. "She had to be older than me."

The cashier looked up at Val blankly, her dyed black bangs making a stark contrast to her ghostly white skin. "Oh, I don't think so," she said flatly. "Paper or did you bring your own?"

"Yes, I think so, *Emily*," said Val, reading the cashier's nametag. "Paper, double-bagged, and be sure to use freezer bags for the meat." Val slid her credit card through the machine, hoping it would cover the $42.14, and was relieved when the charge was accepted. She decided that *Emily* did not merit any further verbal acknowledgement and stared through her when presented with the charge slip to sign.

Back in the parking lot, she got into Stacy's BMW and pulled out of the lot, making a right onto California Street. At Polk Street, she made a quick detour to one of the big name drug stores that seemed to be taking over the city. She hated going into the store, as it was always full of the Tenderloin's finest, but she decided she would brave the downtrodden masses to get some toiletries since she had gone through most of Stacy's.

She found a parking spot near the front door and parked within an inch of the curb on her first try. Her parallel parking skills were superb—an odd skill she had for no apparent reason. She was out of the car and down the sidewalk in no time, worried about leaving the expensive BMW on the streets of the Tenderloin or 'Loin as her friend Edison called it.

What a dump, she thought, when she entered the drugstore with its suggestively Soviet exterior. Inside, the lights were unforgiving and the floor wax scent could only be described as "modern convent." Worse yet, the upwardly mobile homeless loved this store for its no hassle pharmacy and cheap goods. Speaking of which, she mused, turning toward the skin care section, she needed to refresh Stacy's brands with cheap substitutes. She grabbed one of the oddly cheerful red handbaskets and ignored the approving wink the security guard gave her.

Just her luck that Stacy would be the type who would buy the overpriced tampons and have expensive soaps at every sink in the condo. She glared at a family of six ordering ice cream and blocking the aisle ahead of her. She might just lose it today. She had felt her temper go to red at Whole Foods and did not want to have a meltdown in this dump. At least no one would recognize her here at Poverty Plus. She hoped that whatever magic had blessed her credit card at Whole Foods would work here as well … no thanks to the ageist goth bitch cashier, Emily. She would have to send an email to Whole Foods corporate when she got back to the condo. Perhaps she would get some "apology" coupons from the store and have Emily fired and back on a street corner where she belonged.

After a few minutes, her basket was full and her mental checklist was clear. She felt drained and turned toward the cashiers, passing a mechanical laughing daisy that a member of the six-pack family must have activated. She paused just long enough to discreetly snap the flower's stem neck. "Serves you and all you Audrey Hepburn types right," she said to the dead mechanical plant as she daintily touched her throat to ward off a second chin.

Must not be food stamp day, she thought as she walked directly to an available cashier.

"Hello. Did you find everything okay?" the Indian girl asked, clearly eyeing the Chanel scarf she had borrowed from

Stacy. "Nice scarf. It really goes with your hair," the girl said, taking the basket from Val.

"Oh, does it? I dressed so quickly today I forgot all about it." She swiped her card and tried not to tense up as it processed. It was prompt and delivered an electronic DECLINED complete with a sense of shame.

"Do you want to try another card or cash?" the girl asked nicely, as if the card was merely old or broken rather than maxed out.

"Oh, I just brought this one. Let's see, well I do have some cash on me. I'll just take the tampons and the soap." She could feel that her face was aflame and sweat was starting to form on her upper lip.

"Oh, no problem at all," the cashier said moving the other items to a side counter and ringing the two items up in exchange for Val's twenty. "And have a good afternoon," she said brightly, as she held the bag for Val to take.

"Oh, I'll run to the ATM and come back for the rest in a few minutes. Thanks so much for being cool about this," she said, avoiding eye contact then making for the door, grateful for the lack of witnesses. The few people in the store either did not hear or care, as she seemed alone in her humiliation.

"I'll set them aside for you," the cashier said as Val darted out the door for the safety of the BMW.

She was walking uphill to the car when she looked into the windows of the drugstore and saw the cashier drop her items into the returns bin before opening her textbook. "Smart kid," Val said to herself.

THREE

Edison moved quickly out the front door, down the porch steps and onto the sidewalk. He hated being late. The short walk to Brett and Linda's house was still long enough to feel the full force of the summer heat, which felt nice against his freshly showered skin, as did his recently laundered clothes.

He had finally attacked the mountain of dirty laundry and wore his favorite cargo shorts and a clean but wrinkled T-shirt. The odd appearance of Lily and her birds was, in retrospect, a needed reminder that he was sliding into a disheveled despair. Grieving, he had come to realize, wasn't a simple matter of neat steps outlined by someone in a tweed coat with a need to publish for tenure. Grieving was much more complicated, especially when it took something as small as the scoop in the laundry detergent box to bring to a halt any sense of healing. He could hardly explain that he was delayed because he had spent an hour sitting on the laundry room floor alternating between crying and sleeping after realizing his mother was the last one to touch the scoop. San Francisco and his life there seemed impossibly far away now, but it held a sense of hope, hope that the 678 air miles between the two cities would be enough distance to lessen the loss he felt being in his parents' house without them.

In the kitchen, he had found a bottle of wine to bring. It still had his gift card taped to it along with, in his mother's handwriting, the date they had received it and the website of the vineyard. It was a bottle of Schafer cabernet. Linda knew her wine and he hoped she would be as pleased with it as he had been when he had visited the secluded vineyard in Napa.

Crossing the quiet street with its leafy canopy, he could already smell the mix of charcoal and mesquite from Brett's grill and checked his watch. Less than a block away and he was still ten minutes late. Grieving or not, he didn't want to become one of those fashionably late fags he often disparaged. He straightened his shirt and hurried his pace, taking the steep stairs that led up to Brett and Linda's home two at a time. Once on the paving stones of his hosts' porch, he smiled at a familiar but elusive black feline holding court over the flowerpots.

The male cat named Stella had been his parents'. Edison had assumed that Stella was keeping his distance, waiting for his masters to return. Stella didn't budge from the sun-warmed stone and seemed to eye Edison as if he were a servant who had stepped out of bounds. He would mention the idea of adopting Stella to Brett and Linda since his apartment in San Francisco didn't allow pets.

In typical Queen Anne fashion, the front door was ajar. His San Franciscan sensibilities had been challenged repeatedly by the casual habits of his Queen Anne neighbors. Unlocked houses as well as the flowers and cakes left on his front porch made him wonder if a colony of Stepford women had established a foothold on Queen Anne Hill. He rang the bell; he was not going to give up his citified standards, even with friends.

Almost immediately, Linda swung the door open with the grace of a ballerina, a tipsy one, but still a ballerina. Her summer outfit, Capri pants, Italian style sandals and one of Brett's white oxford shirts looked good on her and the extra material clung to her in a flattering way. It also hid Linda's weight gain, which Edison had noticed immediately at the baggage claim where Brett and Linda met him that first horrible night in Seattle. Now, her brown hair was in a ponytail circa 1950, and she was one of the few women he knew that looked younger with her hair pulled back.

"Darling," she said in a faux vamp voice, handing him a martini that would have made Samantha Stephens proud.

"Peapod, thanks for the invite," he said, giving her a peck

on the cheek after stepping over the threshold into the coolness of the house. "I can see your house is still in museum-quality condition," he added, taking in the open first floor with its high ceilings, abundant art and massive flagstone fireplace. The entire house always seemed poised for its "close-up" and left one wondering if the camera crew from *Architectural Digest* was en route. The place smelled like diesel and wood chips, as had their place in San Francisco. He never mentioned it to them and found the smell strangely pleasant.

"Well, I do tend to obsess just a bit with the Windex," she said, leading him into the house.

"This is no surprise from the lady who grew up ironing her sheets," he teased, taking a generous gulp from the martini so as not to spill on the planks that made up the puzzlework floor. He looked again at the room appreciating the set of open French doors that led to the backyard. You'd have to be a Getty to have this kind of home in San Francisco, he thought. He followed her to the heart of the house, the large, bright kitchen with seating for ten and enough technology to support a lunar landing.

"Wine?" he offered, holding the bottle out to her.

"Thank you, that's so sweet of you and so formal. You know you don't have to bring anything over to our place. Oh, it's a Schafer. That's impossible to get up here. Let me correct my previous statement, you can always bring over a bottle of this."

"You've had it before?" Edison asked.

"Yes, your parents brought one over a while back and then we tried to find a bottle locally and couldn't. It is exceptional. We'll open it now so it can catch its breath by the time Mr. Grill out there has things ready." Linda nodded to her tall husband who was visible through the windows, standing in front of the grill, shrouded in a cloud of smoke.

"My parents brought over a Schafer?" Edison asked, confused.

"Easy, cupcake, no drama while I'm holding a full bottle. Is there something special about the vintage? I assumed they turned you onto the wine. Was it the other way around?" She looked at him the way a parent looks at a child who is frequently confused.

"Yes. Well, actually, I don't know. I guess I underestimated them."

"Well, they were a classy couple, but it's usually hard for children to appreciate the finer aspects of their parents. Brett thinks my parents are worldly and I have always thought they were a bit trailer."

Edison took another sip of the large martini and decided not to let the comment go.

"So, are you still in the closet about your roots, Peapod? Does the Queen Anne Collective know that they have a suburban St. Louis girl on their precious hill?"

"Oh, hush," Linda said, dismissing him with a wave. "Don't make me bring up your suburban Seattle roots."

"Truce," Edison offered.

Linda handed Edison the bottle of wine and the wine key, and while he opened it, she fussed with the appetizers. With the wine open and Linda carrying the appetizers, they headed to the French doors at the far end of the kitchen. Once on the brick path that led into the backyard, Edison heard his stomach grumble in response to the smells and sight of the picnic table loaded down with food. Brett was still at the grill cooking even more food and Edison wondered aloud, "Is someone else coming or is this all for us?"

"Just us, and come on, we know you're no stranger to food," Brett said, dexterously opening a bottle of beer for himself and one for Edison. "Now finish that girl drink," he said motioning to the martini, "and have a man's drink."

"Well, I guess there's no reason to put on airs with you two." He took the beer as well as two blackened sea scallops from the sidebar of the grill.

"You look thin," Brett said. In a flash, Brett reached over and tickled Edison's midsection, causing him to laugh and nearly drop his food and drink. "Have you lost weight?" Brett asked. "We'll change that tonight, won't we, L?"

"He's not leaving until he's either drunk or fat, preferably both, speaking of which, come sit by me."

Sinking into the Adirondack chair next to Linda, Edison sighed and relaxed after devouring the scallops. The lawn was green and fresh thanks to the odd summer shower that blew in the previous week from the Pacific. The table was beautifully set, although they would all be eating a bit of pollen given that it dusted the surface of everything. His mother had always put cheesecloth over the set picnic table until the first guest arrived. He would tell Linda if he could do it without insulting her table or sounding like the Martha Stewart queen he secretly feared becoming.

The grill was Brett's baby, and even though sweat streaked the back of his polo shirt, he possessively mastered it and predictably declined any offer to help. Shutting his eyes, Edison took in the pleasant smells and the sound of the air rushing through the tops of the tall fir trees as it raced from the Olympic Mountains to the Cascade passes.

Jerked back to reality, Edison was embarrassed that he had drifted off and woke only when his chin hit his chest. Brett had moved the grilled items to the table and was on another beer. Linda had remained at his side petting Stella, who had taken up residence in her lap.

"Ready for some food, Mr. Sleepy?" Brett asked, openly enjoying Edison's embarrassment.

"Oh, honey," Linda said smiling to Brett, "you know kids need their naps and can't handle their booze."

Edison groaned as he raised himself from the comfortable chair and made his way to the table trying to stifle a yawn.

"How long was I out?"

"Oh, just a few minutes," Linda said, putting Stella on the ground.

Edison doubted Linda's words as the sky had gone from blue to flaming pink and red. Once seated, the behavior of dozens of past dinners took control with rapid conversation and family-style servings. In San Francisco, Edison's dinner parties felt as if they had never graduated past dormitory-level presentation. Even Brett, who never met a Taco Bell he didn't like, could orchestrate a casual meal that would have the guests fat and happy. Brett and Linda had hosted many parties back in their small San Francisco home. Edison remembered the larger parties spilling out onto the sidewalk while inside an endless stream of food and drink flowed from the kitchen.

"So, Eds," Brett said, clearing his throat, looking down at the pyramid of corncobs he had created on his plate. "When can we start the hard sell about you staying up here for good? There are plenty of job opportunities for you and you'll be hard-pressed to find a better piece of property than your parents' house."

"I thought you started the sales pitch shortly after you two moved up here," Edison said, taking another helping of beef filet. "I noticed how both of you would always send something down to SF wrapped in the real estate section of *The Seattle Times*. Subtle, real subtle." Grinning, he filled their neglected wine glasses.

"Well, you cannot blame a gal for trying," Linda said. "I was wondering if you would notice the real estate listings."

"I'm starting to miss the San Francisco life already, though. Dry cleaning alone would break me up here. I was surprised that even the low-end gyms are about the same price as the better ones in SF. I guess there's no competition."

Looking over a large plate of grilled chicken and salad, Linda piped up, "Honey, I have seen how you dress. Unless you have a drag lifestyle we don't know about then I don't know what you're dry cleaning. As for gyms, hell, you could build your own in your parents' house. Just change your locks to keep out Brett in case you have a gentleman caller."

Brett laughed with his mouth full and made a snorting sound. "I'd help you outfit the gym in exchange for visiting rights. As for gentleman callers, you can leave the porch light on and I'll keep my distance. A man needs his own castle, after all, and moats aren't cheap when you live on top of a hill."

"You two are great. I came over here to thank you for your

spontaneous hospitality and to ask you to adopt Stella and you run me over with the welcome wagon. It's hard to picture myself living in that monster of a house. I gotta tell you, it's not easy being over there. Everything I touch seems to have a memory attached to it. Plus, how is a high-maintenance San Francisco homo supposed to find a man up here?"

"Eds, you'd find a man up here easily. Linda tells me our Starbucks barista is gay, and hey, I could always pimp you out to the construction guys at work if you want volume."

"Brett!" Linda exclaimed, slapping his thick wrist with a celery stalk. "Nguor mind him, you'll find a man up her in no time."

Linda's muscular 6'3 husband leaned across the table and whispered loudly, "She beats me, you know, it's just celery in public but it's carrots in private."

"I think there's a support group for you in Berkeley," Edison replied in a loud whisper. "I can look it up and email it to you later." Straightening up, he went back to topic, "A date, yes, I can get that, but someone who helps make the sum greater than the parts is what I want. Anyway, I'm way too sober to be discussing this."

Brett leaned to the side of the table and in a stage whisper said, "I can line up those construction workers if it means you'll stay up here." He grinned at Linda, who pretended to be offended.

"I'll keep that in mind," Edison said, wondering if Brett was at all serious. He noticed the raft of pollen adrift in his wine glass. "Do you think the house will sell?"

"No doubt. The neighborhood has a solid reputation," Brett said, falling into his professional voice.

Edison noticed Brett seemed to be speaking directly to his plate.

"I know someone good if the house needs any work," Brett continued. "If you need to head back to SF for a while, we can take Stella and keep the yard in shape."

With the fading light, Edison couldn't tell if Brett was angry that he hadn't convinced him to stay or if he was feeling the effect of the wine. No doubt to break the sudden silence, Linda passed around the grilled food again, mentioning that her men were not known to pass on thirds.

Taking a large portion, Edison asked, "Brett, would you and your F-150 want to join me for a drive up to Lynnwood? My parents have a storage locker up there that I need to empty."

"Sure, well, I can give you all the muscle you need but let's not use the F-150. She's cherry and I want to keep her that way."

"Don't ask," Linda said flatly. "That truck has higher status than I do. Just rent something." She waved a moth away from the lit candles on the table. "Just remember he would happily give up his right arm for you, just don't ask about the truck."

"Linda, I'm just trying to keep her cherry. Edison understands, right?" Brett said, looking across the table for backup.

Edison smiled at Linda. "I should rent something, regardless; it looks like a sizeable locker judging from the rental statement."

"How's work doing without you?" Linda asked. "Are all those numbers behaving without you there to keep an eye on them? I heard you calling into the office when you were staying here and it seemed like they were a bit needy."

Brett refilled all of their glasses and drank the last bit of wine from the bottle directly.

"The office has been a bit needy but also very understanding. They were cool about giving me as much time as I need as long as I take calls."

Stella had been circling the table and now sat next to Brett, purring loudly with his head resting on Brett's leg.

Brett took the glass cover off the large chocolate cake that had been sitting at the end of the table. It was clearly one of Linda's creations. She had said that in the last year or so since she'd moved up from San Francisco, she had gone from being a master curator to a master confectioner and cake goddess. Brett's slice was just shy of a quarter of the cake. It went without comment from Edison since he was not planning on holding back when it came to dessert.

Linda spoke with a different tone, one suited for discussing something unattractive, like a fallen supermodel. "We had another media person at the door today. It was a station from eastern Washington. I was surprised that they're still trying to piece together a story after all these weeks. Have they told you anything more beyond that it was asphyxiation?"

"No, not really. They have ruled out all the obvious things. There was no sign of a break in and Lily was the only one, apparently, who entered the house, so there are still a lot of questions and few answers."

"Since you've been in the house, does all seem right to you?" Brett asked.

Edison looked at his plate and thought of the haunting laundry scoop and the darkness he felt when he was in the house. "It seems like they're still there on one level, but I imagine this is more my denial. I don't think that they are actually there," he said, looking up from his plate. "I think it's their absence I'm feeling more than anything else."

"That makes sense," Brett said, holding eye contact briefly.

Changing the topic, Edison offered his only interesting gossip. "I had a bit of a surprise today. I found Lily Ling in my house."

"She just let herself in?" asked Linda.

"Yep, I was upstairs and heard a noise downstairs," Edison said with a mouthful of what was one of the best chocolate cakes he had ever tasted.

"She came into our house last year," Brett added. "It was the last time she did that …." He smiled at Linda, who winked back at him.

"She encountered Brett naked in the kitchen preparing a snack to take back up to the bedroom. He was less than pleased and chased her out of the house. She calls now before she comes over," Linda said with a half smile.

"That may be a fine story to tell most people but with Edison there is another piece," Brett said. "Now when we run into each other, she takes a drag off her cigarette and exhales in the direction of," he grabbed between his legs. "The woman isn't what she appears with all that makeup and fancy clothing. She must be related to Mae West somehow."

"So she has a key to your place too?" Edison asked, surprised at the apparent key swapping in Seattle.

"No. No key. The front door was unlocked," Brett said, absently taking another slice of cake.

"You don't lock your doors?" Edison asked, not hiding his dismay.

"Oh, honey, this is Queen Anne, not San Francisco. We don't need to lock our doors all the time. In fact, ours are unlocked now," Linda said.

"I guess it's a Seattle thing. Although, when Lily found my parents, the doors were locked and the security system was activated. Lily came in with her own key much as she did today. I read the police report, and apparently Lily drank nearly half a bottle of scotch in the dining room before she called 911."

"That sounds about right," Brett said. "The police thought she lived there until she Zsa-Zsa-ed a cop and made a run for our booze."

"She really sucked down Brett's scotch but she still didn't seem to be drunk when she was here. She did ding our front door with a flowerpot, though, instead of knocking or using the doorbell," Linda said. "I think she was a lot closer to your parents than we knew and she was certainly distraught. She eventually passed out on the couch in our front room and we tossed a blanket over her. She was up early the next morning and made breakfast for both of us. All that booze and she was better made-up than I was."

"And it was a good breakfast too," Brett added.

They sat in silence for a few moments, eating the last bits off their plates and finishing the wine. The night was calm and far above small clouds rushed between them and the stars.

"I should get home," Edison said. "I have a host of attorneys to see tomorrow and I haven't been sleeping too well these nights. I think it's the silence that keeps me up. I need a good fog horn to usher me to sleep."

He stood up yawning, only to feel his shorts slide down a bit and his shirt slide up over his full stomach. "God, I ate so much, I look pregnant." He burped before he could catch it. To avoid embarrassing himself further, he made a hasty exit, pausing only to offer to help clean up, although he knew Linda always did her own dishes.

She promptly refused his offer and they both gave him a hug at the door under the bright lights of their front hall. Brett said he would call tomorrow about the gym and scheduling a run up to the storage locker. After a final goodbye on the porch, he stepped into the darkness of the lawn and eventually to the silent house, which was now his.

It was only minutes later when he was out of his clothes and with the house dark, he looked from his bedroom window down the street to Brett and Linda's house, ablaze with light. He envied the warm light of their house. He ran his hand from his chest to his stomach, feeling the cold skin. He turned to his bed and fell into it. Knowing that tomorrow offered little promise, he closed his eyes.

FOUR

The fog swirled in the wind as Adam walked down Post Street toward the Financial District, zipping his jacket closed. Typical July weather for San Francisco, he thought. By lunchtime, it would probably be sunny and warm and he would feel like he had dressed for a different season. The warmth would last a few hours, only for the fog to make a grand entrance about the time he left work, billowing over Sutro Tower like a snowy avalanche ready to envelop the city.

He passed by the St. Francis Hotel at Union Square, noticing that the tourists were already out. Some of them were dressed only in T-shirts and shorts, obviously placing more faith in the calendar than in any warning they'd received about the San Francisco summers. The tourists ran the gamut from college students to retirees. By their clothing, many of them looked European, and he envied them for their civilized lifestyles and six-week yearly vacations plus health care. It was a world of difference from his miserly mix of sick leave and vacation, and a health care plan that took a sizeable chunk out of each of his paychecks even though he had selected the cheapest HMO.

As he passed by the long row of stores, he wished that the biggest decision facing him today was how much shopping he felt like doing versus sightseeing. Peering into Williams-Sonoma, he saw a retail queen in a display window positioning some copper pots and pans. Even the life of a retail queen had an air of bohemian glamour, he thought, compared to the stuffy law office where he worked as an executive assistant.

Work promised to be a doozy this week. David Touel, his high-maintenance boss, would be in town from the head office in Seattle. David had made managing partner last year, and, ever since, his ego had grown almost as much as his waistline. Worse yet, David was a closet case, and there was an awkwardness between the two of them that can only occur between two homosexuals who are completely visible to each other yet are not out to one another. At least he wasn't married and never purported to be heterosexual. David, on the other hand, had married a demure Asian woman whose petite frame and intrinsic femininity he, no doubt, had hoped would make him appear more masculine in contrast.

Adam made a left onto Montgomery Street, entering the rush of the Financial District. Unlike the happy, albeit cold-looking tourists in Union Square, his fellow office drones looked mostly somber, returning to the daily grind only in body, not in spirit.

When he reached the lobby elevators of Two Embarcadero Center, he saw by the clock that he was late. He had the uncanny ability to be about ten minutes late to work every day. He was lucky enough to get a solo ride up the elevator and used the time to check his appearance in the reflective surface of the elevator door. In typical fashion, he already had the beginning of a five o'clock shadow even though he'd shaved only an hour earlier. He had good coloring and thick dark hair thanks to his Southern Italian heritage. He could see in the blurry reflection that his khaki pants were starting to look worn. He'd soon have to make a trip to The Gap or Banana Republic in the shopping center downstairs to replace them.

Back to the salt mines, he thought as he stepped out of the elevator onto the 23rd floor, viewing the placard on the wall, "Wilkes, O'Hara and Tarleton, LLP." Entering from the lobby, he found the office was already astir with the Monday morning bustle. People were chattering about their weekends while the non-aficionado coffee drinkers were brewing their morning fixes using the crappy grounds in the kitchen. He made it to his cubicle, which was at the crossroads of all foot traffic, and saw the backside of Julie, the legal secretary who sat in the cubicle directly behind him, and who was busily typing away. He could see her send a disapproving look his way, using her "rearview mirror" that clipped atop her flat screen, probably judging him for his tardiness.

Julie was an adept typist; he'd give her that, though he'd never encountered anyone who could communicate so much anger through her keyboard. Her loud tapping of the keys seemed to be a constant reproach to him or anyone else that didn't type 80 wpm, didn't work the long hours she did, and wasn't immediately won over by her wholesome Nordic looks and false charm.

He smelled the stench of the cheap piña colada-scented shampoo she used on her long blonde hair and he knew that the odor wouldn't fade for hours.

He booted up his computer, which, unlike Julie's sleek new model, was so old he thought it would garner an appraisal on *Antiques Roadshow*. The companywide computer upgrades that had begun with the senior staff hadn't trickled down to him yet, even though he'd been the one who had worked long hours with the Systems department to initiate the upgrades for the floor.

He wondered how many Monday morning "emergencies" in the form of red exclamation points in his email inbox would be waiting for him. After what seemed like an eternity of waiting, he finally logged on to the network when the familiar round and freckled face of Christina, a secretary, appeared in front of his low cubicle wall.

"Adam?" she called in a little girl voice that she always used when she wanted something.

"Hi Christina," he said noncommittally, noticing the split ends in her shoulder length red hair hanging over the wall of his cubicle.

"Thank God you're here! I am so busy this morning and none of my print jobs are coming out of the printer. Can you come take a look at my computer?"

"Um … I just got in so …."

"Oh, no problem, I'll give you a few minutes to get settled."

Christina, like most everyone else in his area, thought he was the goddamn technical help because, unlike most everyone else, he actually knew how to use a computer.

"And I have one more favor," she added in a childish plea that seemed silly coming from a forty plus year-old woman.

"Uh huh."

"Can you plug in my fan? It's always so hot in the mornings and you know how I have trouble bending down because of my bad knees."

No, he thought, you cannot bend down because you are morbidly obese. Christina was perpetually complaining of heat that no one else felt and she was convinced that the fluorescent lights on the ceiling above her were the culprit. At Christina's request, Adam had called the building engineer on multiple occasions, but no matter what adjustments he made to the vents, and no matter how many times he assured her that fluorescent lights emit very little heat, she was never satisfied.

"Okay, I'll try to stop by in a little while."

"Thanks, Adam. I don't know what I'd do without you."

You'd find some other patsy to plug in your fan, he thought.

He opened up his email and was scanning his new messages when his phone rang. He could see by the caller ID that it was someone calling from the phone in the elevator lobby. He picked up his phone. "This is Adam."

"Adam, my man, it's Rod from UPS and I've got a package for you."

"I'll be right there." He had the misfortune of being the alternate contact for all deliveries. "For assistance, call your party or Adam Sirna at 4-2487," the note near the floor directory read in big bold letters. It might as well have said call "Big Loser," as far as he was concerned. He resented the fact that just because the firm refused to pay enough to keep a receptionist, he had to take on the responsibility.

The UPS carrier, Rod, was a tall and lean African-American man in his thirties. Rod had always been friendly in a professional way toward Adam until they'd seen each other at a gay-themed movie playing at the Lumiere Theatre on California Street. The movie had been typical gay tripe with an inane plot, stereotyped characters and so-so production quality, but the allure of seeing some hot guys on the big screen always attracted a large crowd of homosexuals. Ever since then, Rod made a point of chatting him up.

Today was no exception, and as he signed for the package, Rod went on about his night out carousing on Folsom Street. While Rod relayed the highlights, Adam heard the elevator doors open. Looking down the lobby, past Rod, he saw David Touel exit from the elevator. He was dressed in a suit, carrying a briefcase in one hand and lugging a wheeled suitcase in the other. He had obviously just arrived from the airport. Each time Adam saw him it seemed that his dark hair had more gray at the temples and was thinner on top. Today, David had an uptight look on his face, which Adam supposed was meant to convey a measured sobriety, but it mostly made him look as if he had a stick up his ass.

Rod was going on about a "hottie" he had danced with when David appeared next to Rod, eyeing him as if he were a bug he wanted to douse with Raid.

"Good morning, David," Adam said. "Did you have a good flight?"

"Yes, it was fine—at least until we reached SFO. We had to circle due to the fog."

"Yeah, it's thick this morning," Adam said, forcing a smile.

"Well, I'll leave this with you," Rod interjected, probably picking up on David's bad vibe and realizing he had lost his audience for his escapade.

Rod left and Adam held the door open for David with his free hand while balancing the package in his other. He was about to drop the box off in the mailroom when David called after him.

"Adam, did you reserve a conference room for my 10:00 a.m.?"

"Yes, I reserved it on Friday. You have the Oak Room until noon."

"I'm going to be giving a PowerPoint presentation, so why don't we see if the Redwood Room is available since that has the built-in projector."

"Sure, I didn't know you were giving a presentation."

"Don't worry about it," David said, eyeing Adam's pants with a frown. "Julie helped me with the slides and she has it all under control. If the Redwood Room isn't available, we'll need to set up a portable projector in the Oak Room."

"Okay, I'll check on that," Adam said, suddenly feeling naked under David's gaze.

"Good. And while we're at it, why don't we get coffee and pastries for six. And let's use the china. Paper is so tacky. Wouldn't you agree?"

"I hadn't given it much thought," Adam said, thinking that what *was* tacky was that he would not only have to play waiter to these people but dishwasher as well.

Adam looked at his watch and saw that it was nearly quarter to nine. He discovered that Kelly, another executive assistant, had reserved the Redwood Room for someone's birthday party. She wasn't willing to switch rooms, so David would have to make do with the portable projector.

Next, he went to the kitchen to gather the plates and utensils. He passed by Christina's cube several times on his trips between the kitchen and conference room, but he pretended not to notice her looking up at him expectantly.

David stopped by Julie's desk at a quarter past nine to see if the presentation was ready.

"All done," Julie said full of the usual perkiness she reserved for anyone higher up but especially David.

"Excellent. We'll need handouts too, so why don't you ask Adam to make six copies."

"No problem," she said.

"And I'd like you to join the meeting."

"Absolutely."

"Great," said David. He walked past Adam's desk, but turned around. "Adam, were you able to get the Redwood Room?"

"No, it was booked. But I have the portable projector and I'll set everything up in the Oak Room."

"Thatta boy," said David, before walking away.

Adam watched the backside of David, enraged at being called a boy at 33, but took solace in the fact that David's once fit body had changed shape without telling his pants.

"Adam," Julie called out from her desk. "I'm going to email you the PowerPoint presentation. David and I will need six copies for our meeting."

"I'm about to set up the projector. They need handouts too?" he asked, pretending he hadn't heard Julie and David's exchange.

"That's what David requested."

"Would you mind just printing six copies?"

"No, it will take forever on the printer. It will be easier if I send you the file."

"Really? The reason I asked is because I'm swamped right now setting up for the meeting."

"Adam, I'm swamped too, but that's why I'm usually the first one here in the morning. Maybe if you managed your time better you wouldn't be in this situation."

"This isn't about time management, Julie. It's about the most efficient way to do this. All you have to do is click on print."

"Adam, I don't have time for this. I'm busy enough with my own job and I'm not going to do yours as well. Just make the copies," she said turning back to her computer.

He realized it was pointless to continue as he would only say something he would regret.

On his way back to the conference room to set up the projector, he passed by Christina's desk and heard her call out after him, obviously in full needy mode. He went back to her cubicle.

"Do you have time to look at my computer?" she asked.

"I'm really busy right now, Christina."

"Well, do you think it will be soon? It's so crazy today and I have to leave early to take my daughter to her badminton lesson."

"You know, if you're having printer problems, you should call Systems."

"You think I should bother them for this?"

"That's what they're there for."

"Okay, I'll give them a call," she said in a wounded voice, as if Adam had just jilted her. "But can you plug in my fan while you're here?"

Adam relented and entered her cube. Christina rolled her chair over slightly and watched him as he bent down under her desk and plugged in the fan. While underneath, he noticed a mess of crumbs and even saw what looked like a Jolly Rancher that had been overwhelmed by dust bunnies. When he got up, a grimy mix of dust and crumbs covered his palms.

"Thank you kindly, sir," Christina said, turning her fan on medium and aiming it so that it blew through her damaged hair.

Adam went back to his desk and looking at his email saw that Julie had sent him the PowerPoint presentation. He double-clicked on it and waited for it to open, but nothing happened. He tried again, but his computer had froze due to the large size of the file. Goddammit, he thought, he would have to reboot. He looked behind him, but Julie wasn't at her desk.

He walked back to the conference room to finish setting up the projector when Christina called after him.

"Adam, do you have the phone number for Systems?"

He was just about to lose it when he saw Pam, one of Christina's lunch pals, coming down the hall.

"They're having cake in the Redwood Room," announced Pam, poking her horse-like face over Christina's cube wall.

"What's the occasion?" asked Christina.

"It's Tim's birthday."

"Who's Tim?"

"I think he's an attorney. Who cares? It's free cake and I hear it's going fast. Chop, chop."

Christina sprang up from her chair awfully fast, he noticed, for having such bad knees.

"Adam, are you coming?" she asked as she headed off with Pam.

"No, I can't right now."

"Well, hurry up or you'll miss the free cake."

After he finished setting up the projector, he checked the lobby but there was no sign of the coffee and pastries, which were supposed to have arrived ten minutes earlier. He went back to his computer and tried opening Julie's email, but his computer froze again. Julie was still not back and it was twenty minutes until the meeting would start. He searched all over the floor for Julie, then decided to check the Redwood Room and found her with what seemed like half the firm crammed into the conference room eating cake. He could see it was a chocolate cake with a greasy layer of white frosting and a garnish of what looked like canned fruit on the top.

"Hey, Adam, you're just in time. There are still a few pieces left," said Tony, an attorney, whose bellowing voice and senior status always commanded people's attention.

"Thanks, I'm fine. I just need to speak with Julie."

"Adam doesn't eat cake," said Julie. "I hear him munching on nuts and seeds all day like some sort of squirrel." The whole room laughed, as did Adam, feeling his face turn crimson. Julie looked pleased with herself for scoring one at his expense.

"Julie, can I talk to you for a moment about the presentation?"

Julie seemed perturbed that he had interrupted her cake time. She rolled her eyes making a "What now?" face as if he always asked for her help.

When they were outside the room, he explained to her that the attachment had frozen his computer twice and she would need to print out a hard copy from her computer.

She sighed, as if it were his fault that he had a relic for a computer. "I leave for two minutes and everything falls apart," she complained. "I skipped breakfast this morning and now I can't even take a moment to get some food in me before my blood sugar crashes. Come on, I'll print out a copy for you."

He followed her as she walked back to her desk in a hurried manner, the loud tap of her heels seeming to broadcast her sense of indispensability to everyone they passed. How she managed to pull that off on carpeted floors, he wasn't quite certain.

After Julie printed out a copy of the presentation for him, he brought it to the copy room. When he approached the machine, he could tell right away that something was amiss, as a red light was flashing and the digitized display showed multiple paper jams. "Goddammit," he muttered. It was a classic photocopier hit and run. It took him five minutes to locate the jams and he was in the process of making the copies when Christina entered the room.

"Oh, good. You were able to fix the copier," she said. "I tried to find you, but you weren't at your desk."

Adam turned back to the machine feeling too angry to deal with her.

"Adam, you should have had some cake. It was delicious."

"I don't eat much of that stuff," he said, continuing to look at the copier.

"You're so healthy. I really should be eating better. I'm on the company-sponsored weight loss program, but I just can't resist sweets."

"Uh huh," he said, wondering if the toner fumes he was inhaling could cause permanent damage.

"Oh, and you'll be happy to know that I spoke to Systems and it turns out I had somehow changed the settings on my computer so all of my printouts were going to the color printer on 24."

"Uh huh."

"But now the printer near me says the toner is low. I like to print out all my emails everyday, but I can hardly read them because the print is so light. Could you take care of that?"

You print out all your emails? he considered asking, but he didn't even want to go there. He half turned toward her. "I'm busy, but if you just shake the toner cartridge a couple times that will usually do the trick."

"I've never done that. Can you show me how?"

"I'll take care of it in a few minutes," he mumbled through clenched teeth.

"Thanks, Adam. You're a lifesaver."

Five minutes before the meeting, everything was set up in the conference room, but the coffee and pastries still hadn't arrived. He was just about to call the cafe downstairs when his phone rang. He desperately hoped it was the delivery person calling from the lobby, but his caller ID showed him this was not the case. In fact, the name on the display was quite unexpected. He had little time to consider this, though, as his other line rang and he decided to pick up that call. Thankfully, it was the cafe delivery guy and as he hurried to the front door to show him in, he wondered why Val Panos had decided to call him and how she had gotten his work number.

His curiosity was only greater after he returned to his desk and saw that she hadn't left a voicemail. He hoped she would call back since he had no way of contacting her. Perhaps, he hoped, she was riding a wave of success and was cherry picking friends to staff her new venture, whatever it might be. He could see Christina making her way toward his cube and he wondered if he could Google Val's name in a desperate attempt to return her phone call and get a ticket out of this particular hell.

FIVE

Cherie paged through *Parenting* magazine with increasing impatience as she waited for Dr. Tyler to see her. He was already fifteen minutes late and she decided she would wait five more minutes before making a scene. She had an appointment with a client in just over an hour and she, at least, took punctuality seriously. Why Dr. Tyler could never keep to a schedule was beyond her.

She didn't even like *Parenting*, having no interest in it herself, but the double plus size sitting across from her had taken the more compelling *Healthy Woman Monthly*. She could see from the cover that the lead story read, "Top 10 Antioxidant-Rich Snacks—Stop Free Radicals in Their Tracks." She had wanted to read this article but, instead, this woman, who herself looked like a two hundred pound free radical, was reading it and no doubt hoping that a handful of blueberries a day was going to solve all her problems.

Cherie hadn't been due for her yearly physical for another five months, but she'd been feeling rather tense lately and that's why she had come in last week to see Dr. Tyler. He had told her that her blood pressure was high and he had wanted to analyze her blood work, which had now come back from the lab. She couldn't imagine what could be wrong. She exercised regularly, ate sensibly and took several supplements every day. She had been taking medication for depression recently but she hadn't noticed much of a change and, in fact, she thought she felt worse. Perhaps she would ask her shrink to increase the dosage. Or, maybe, the Canadians were back. If so, she would have to go on a special diet to expel the little demons from her body.

A couple of years ago, she had been having gastrointestinal issues along with some other problems and she sought the advice of her friend, Janet, a Christian holistic healer she knew from church. Janet, herself, followed a Bible-based diet whose adherents are only allowed to eat foods that were available during biblical times. Of course, those following the diet are also strongly encouraged to buy the line of pricey "miracle" supplements that are only sold by the author's company.

Despite Janet constantly preaching the wonders of this austere diet, she was quite a large woman ("big-boned," Janet would say), and her complexion was such that, if Cherie didn't know better, she would have assumed she must stand over a deep fat fryer for recreation. More than once, Cherie was certain she'd seen what appeared to be chocolate crumbs on Janet's blouse, but Janet swore she only ate natural sweets such as dried fruit or honey, and she often carried one or the other around with her in a canvas tote.

At the time Cherie had consulted her, Janet had told her she probably had a Candida yeast infection. While Cherie was no stranger to yeast infections, she had never heard of that particular term and thought Janet had said "Canada" infection. Since then, she had always envisioned an army of tiny Canadians hellbent on wreaking havoc in her body while waving their little maple leaf flags and singing *O Canada*. At any rate, she assumed the Canadians had gone back north, or wherever, since her condition had improved shortly after going on Janet's prescribed diet and herbal remedies.

At least she had never let herself go like Ms. Double Plus sitting across from her. She had reached her thirty-fifth year, but easily had the body of a woman ten years younger. She could keep up with the best of the teenyboppers at her gym and the men always paid her a lot of attention, except for the homosexuals. She'd noticed far too many of them at the gym lately—in fact, far too many everywhere, as if they had choreographed it so as to all burst out of their closets in unison. She found she disliked being around men who had no sexual appreciation for a beautiful woman. Once her gym membership expired, she would have to find a gym that wasn't a hotbed of homosexuality.

———————

Forty-five minutes later, Cherie was outside the medical building, walking to her SUV as fast as her heels would allow with two new prescriptions in hand. Dr. Tyler, never shy when it came to prescribing drugs, had checked her blood pressure again and deemed it high enough to warrant her going on medication. He had also said her cholesterol was well above normal and recommended she take a new cholesterol-lowering drug that had recently come onto the market.

She was completely baffled with her test results. Why was this happening to her? She realized she couldn't let herself get frazzled now. She had to hurry back across the West Seattle Bridge for an appointment, and just like the adage from the old antiperspirant commercial, she would never let them see her sweat.

Once inside her vehicle, she took a couple of deep breaths to calm herself down and felt her stomach rumble, reminding her that she'd only had two double lattes and a low-fat muffin to eat today. She rummaged through her purse and pulled out a chocolate soy protein shake, which she quickly downed. Looking at herself in the vanity mirror, she reapplied her lipstick and, after noticing that some dark roots were showing, made a mental note to schedule an appointment for a cut and color. She pulled out a small bottle of mouthwash from her purse and swished it around in her mouth before spitting the contents into an empty latte cup. Despite all she had just learned, she couldn't help thinking, as she gazed at her reflection, that she looked mighty fine.

SIX

Edison sat at the kitchen table paging through the local Queen Anne weekly when he heard the doorbell ring. He had been expecting the realtor, who had said she would be there at 5:30 sharp, but that was ten minutes ago. When he opened the door, he instead saw the familiar visage of Brett, who he noticed looked handsome in his neat khakis and short-sleeved polo shirt, gym bag in hand.

"Hey, Eds. Ready for the gym?" Brett said, flashing him a boyish grin as he stepped into the house.

Edison had seen pictures of Brett when he was a teenager, and, for a moment, he saw that same kid in his youthful grin. If he had known Brett back then, he probably would have fallen hard for him and no doubt end the friendship with some ill-timed, awkward and unrequited statement of desire. Edison had spent much of his life in the unrequited zone and knew all of its dimensions. Fortunately, he was older and wiser and recognized the reality of the situation when it came to men like Brett.

"I'm running a little late," Edison said. "I'm waiting for the realtor who should be here any minute."

"Realtor?"

"Yeah, she's doing a quick assessment of the house."

"I didn't realize you had already contacted a realtor."

"She slipped her card and a condolence note in the front door last week. Crass, I know, but I guess it worked since I called her."

"So you've made up your mind about selling the house and going back to San Francisco?"

"I think so. I love seeing you and Linda on demand, but my life is there. Besides, I've lived in SF for so many years that Seattle seems white bread in comparison. I figure I might as well return to Sodom and wait for the *big one* with all the other sinners."

"Well, there's no place like San Francisco, and the fatalism alone is worth the property prices," Brett said laughing. "We miss it too, but you know Linda and I were hoping you'd consider staying …."

At that moment, Edison heard a screeching of breaks and the blaring of a horn. Both he and Brett stepped out onto the wraparound porch to look down the street and saw Lily's dark green Jaguar at the base of her driveway, half of it jutting out into the street and blocking the path of a large black SUV. Edison stepped to the porch rail to get a better view, just in time to hear the woman from the SUV yell something about "driving while Asian" to Lily. Edison then distinctly heard Lily shout back, "Watch it, you racist bitch!" Lily's voice, while raspy, was forceful in a way that was incongruous with her size. The Jaguar moved out further into the street, narrowly missing the SUV before Lily floored the accelerator, leaving the SUV in a cloud of exhaust.

"What in the hell was that all about?" asked Brett.

"I don't know, but it looks as if we'll find out," Edison said, watching the black SUV, which he now saw was a Ford Expedition, pull into his driveway.

A woman exited from the SUV. She looked to be a bottle blonde, probably in her early 30's, attractive in an Office Barbie sort of way, dressed in a red skirt and a matching red blazer that was open, showing a low-cut blouse. He could tell by the rapt look on Brett's face that her Barbie-like dimensions hadn't gone unappreciated.

She looked to both of them, then turned to Brett and asked, "Hello, Mr. Archer?"

Edison figured that Brett's work clothes had impressed her more than his T-shirt and gym shorts.

"No, he's Mr. Archer," Brett pointed, looking amused.

"Pardon me. Hello, Mr. Archer," she said extending her hand to Edison. "Cherie Cahill, Amsted Realty."

"Nice to meet you. Please, call me Edison."

"Thank you. What a unique name." She extended her hand to Brett as well.

"Brett Gale," he said. "Don't mind me; I'm just the nosey neighbor."

"Well, sometimes those are the best kind," she replied, giving him a flirtatious smile and a wink. "I'm sorry I'm late," she said, turning back to Edison, "but I had an appointment that went longer than I anticipated."

"Not a problem. It looks as if you almost had an accident as well."

"Yes, I regret you had to witness that." She smiled self-consciously looking from Edison to Brett. "She pulled right out of her driveway without looking. Thankfully, I was able to stop in time. I don't know why they let people like that on the road."

Edison let the comment pass, not certain how it was intended. "Well, it's good no one was hurt."

"Exactly. By the way, I'm so sorry for your recent loss, Mr. Arch ... I mean Edison."

"Thank you."

"Have they determined how it happened?"

"No, not yet. But the local press seems to be hinting at supernatural causes now."

"Well, I guess they'll do anything to sell a paper."

"Will this publicity have a negative effect on the sale price?" Edison asked.

"Unfortunately, it's a possibility, but by law there's no reason we have to mention the deaths since they were not violent. As for the curse, my answer is what curse? This is an upscale area so I think we'll get a premium price."

"That's good to hear."

"After all, it's such a lovely house, and I think with some cosmetic changes we can bring it up to its full potential."

"What changes were you thinking of?"

"Well, when I dropped off my card the other day I took the liberty of taking a look around outside and noticed a few things." She pulled a small notepad from her blazer pocket and opened it up with a snap. "The front and side hedges are in desperate need of trimming. Besides being unsightly, they block the natural light, and light is our friend when selling a home. Also, it wouldn't hurt to freshen the flowerbeds with some bright seasonals. They'll give us a lot of bang for the buck. Oh, and she'll need a new coat of paint on the porch steps as well, ASAP. It's the minor changes such as these that can make all the difference."

"Sounds reasonable," he said, noting the lawn was in need of attention.

"Let's see," she said, scanning her notepad. "I'm guessing the house is 4,000 square feet, give or take."

"I think it's closer to 4,500."

"Very good. And the lot I'd estimate to be about a third of an acre?"

"That sounds right."

"Built around 1900?"

"My father had said 1911."

"Wonderbar," she said scribbling onto her pad. "It's certainly a Queen Anne beauty. So you live in the neighborhood too?" she asked, looking up toward Brett.

"Yes, just across the street and down a couple houses. In fact, right across the street from old lead foot in the Jaguar."

"I'm so sorry for you. I certainly hope she's more courteous to her neighbors."

"She's a nice woman, wacky but harmless."

Cherie smiled tersely as if not convinced. "Well, shall we go inside and have a look-see?"

They stepped into the house. Right away, Cherie noticed the crystal Tiffany bowl with the paper hens on the table in the foyer. "What a beautiful bowl and what adorable little birds!"

She picked up a pink one and examined it. "Do you have an artistic little one?"

"No, I don't have any children. They're origami hens from the Asian Cultural Center. My neighbor, the one that you had a run-in with, gave them to me."

"Oh," she said tossing the hen back in the bowl as if it had personally offended her.

Brett picked one up, turned it around in his hands, examined it from every angle and finally sniffed it. "Cute little chickens," he said, placing it back in the bowl upright.

They entered the kitchen after a slow walk through the front room to the left of the foyer. Cherie surveyed the kitchen with an open smile.

"Wow, this is what we like to call a gourmet's kitchen." She drew a finger over a counter top. "Forensic powder?" she asked, turning suddenly to Edison.

"Yes," he replied, somewhat surprised at her knowledge and directness. He felt sweat start to break out on his upper lip and under his arms. Something he could only describe as defensive started to well up inside of him.

"We realty gals see it all the time," she said, smiling and handing him a card from her purse. "Amstead uses this service, and if you present this card they'll give you ten percent off. Have them come in and go over every surface as soon as possible." She continued to look around. "Well, we can make some superficial changes, which will help the salability. For instance, that wooden duck family by the plantation blinds is too tacky for words."

Edison looked at Brett, who winced in sympathy for him. Edison's father had carved the ducks by hand and had made a matching set for Brett and Linda. He knew they kept their set in a place of honor on the mantel of their fireplace.

"I'll be packing up the personal items soon," Edison replied flatly.

"Good," she said, oblivious to the faux pas she was tracking around with every misstep. "And that ceiling fan with the big deco light fixtures screams Home Depot inventory sale," she continued, letting out a rip of laughter. "We'll have to change that. And those plantation blinds must all be open … I couldn't think of a worse way to squander the lovely southern exposure. What an adorable little refrigerator," she said stooping to look at the wine chiller. "Is it for kids?" she asked as she wrote in her notepad.

"Uh, no," Edison replied, "it is a wine chiller." He turned to Brett in time to see him raise his eyebrows in bewilderment.

"But of course, I can be so dense," she said hitting her head with the palm of her hand. "These are great. I know the gays love these along with their big kitchens. At least they always have financing."

Edison noticed that her hair remained dented where her hand had pressed it and decided the sooner this was over the better.

Cherie stepped into the dining room looking down at the hardwood floors. "These floors are beautiful. I'm so glad they didn't make the mistake of covering the entire house with some tired carpeting." She examined the room, taking notes, and then went out to the hallway and headed toward the bathroom.

Edison rolled his eyes and Brett shrugged his shoulders in sympathy as they followed her to the bathroom.

"Faux granite is a burden we all must shoulder," she said, tapping on the vanity top with disdain.

"It's real," Edison said.

"Huh? You know, so it is. The fake ones can be so good it's sometimes hard to tell. Ha!" She turned and slipped past both him and Brett with a flirtatious giggle and murmured something about a tight fit.

She made her way back down the hallway to the living room. She looked about the room, taking notes while voicing her observations. "Floors are very nice. Recessed lighting, excellent and double paned glass is very sensible. Lose this afghan," she said pulling his mother's macramé creation off the large couch. Do people still knit?" she asked the room. "It's so *Little House on the Prairie.*"

"As I said before, the personal effects will be packed next week."

They toured the rest of the house and Cherie seemed very impressed, taking pages of notes.

"Your parents did such a beautiful job of remodeling," she said as they came down the front stairs to the foyer. "I liked that exercise room, so sensible."

"They did put a lot of work into the house," Edison replied.

"Well it shows. Other than those few changes we discussed, it's in very good condition and being the corner lot always helps. I'll run some numbers, but I'd estimate you can get at least this providing the inspections go well," she said, scribbling a figure onto her notepad and tearing off the page and handing it to Edison.

"Great. That's more than I expected."

"I'll drop by with some paperwork later this week. I'd love to be able to sell this house for you, Edison."

"Thank you. I need to finalize my plans but I'll get back to you soon."

"Perfect."

They exited through the front door and headed toward her SUV.

"By the way, I love that porch swing," she said turning around and looking at it. "So quaint and always big with the *Town and Country* set. So, do you boys have big plans tonight?"

"We're gonna hit the gym," said Brett.

"Oh, that sounds like fun. I can see you both must workout. It's a gym night for me too." She looked at her watch. "I can still make my 7:00 spinning class. Where do you fellows workout?"

"The gym on upper Queen Anne Avenue," Brett offered.

"Is it good? My membership is up for renewal and I'm looking for a new one."

"It's a little small but it has all the basic equipment plus some classes," replied Brett.

"How's the clientele? Do you get a lot of freaks?"

"Freaks?" asked Brett, looking a little puzzled. "No, it's a pretty good mix of just about everyone. Wouldn't you say?" he asked, turning to Edison.

Edison nodded in agreement.

"Great. I'll have to check it out. When do you two normally work out?"

"Uh, various times. Mainly evenings during the week and early mornings on the weekend."

"Maybe I'll see you there sometime," she said, giving Brett a playful smile. She turned back to Edison. "You have my card. Please don't hesitate to call me with any questions. You can read my references online at our website and I can put you in contact with them if you like."

"I'll do that," Edison said, wishing she would just leave already.

"It was so nice meeting both of you. I'll be in touch." She got into her SUV and backed out giving them a big smile and wave.

Once she was out of sight, Edison turned to Brett and said, "What in the hell was that crap? Everything is just so tacky. Tacky, tacky, tacky," he gesticulated, imitating Cherie.

Brett laughed as they headed inside. "I tuned out early on, but that was some good talent. If I were a single man …."

"If you were a single man, you would do best to avoid that train wreck. I have to admit, though, I like her drive. I have a feeling that if anyone can get the best price, it will be her. Still up for the gym?" Edison asked, sitting on the bottom stair. He took off his sandals and tossed them to the floor.

"Sure," Brett replied distractedly.

Edison stood and smiled when he saw that Brett was arranging the paper hens so that the ones on the top were positioned to see over the wide lip of the bowl. Once done, he looked up embarrassed.

"Well, they might want to take a look around …" he let his sentence trail off.

Edison smiled. "Is it a chest day for you or arms?"

"Chest," he said flexing in a comic way. "Can I change here rather than schlep home and back?"

"Sure, if you don't mind changing at the house of a known homosexual."

"It wouldn't be the first time," he said slapping Edison's butt playfully as he passed him on the stairs. "I need to wash up too."

He untucked his shirt and pulled it over his head, showing the worn band of his underwear as he went up the stairs. Edison noted that Linda needed to get involved in Brett's underwear purchases again.

"Should we invite Linda to the gym?" Edison asked Brett's naked back as it slipped into the bathroom.

"She doesn't go anymore. She said she is too fat, which is both true and ironic," Brett's voice trailed from the open bathroom door. "Plus, I know better than to interrupt her precious cocktail and Hostess Ho Ho hour when she watches her shows."

Edison raised his eyebrows as he heard Brett's harsh comment. "Aren't you just the bitter pill," he said to the bathroom door.

"Bitterness is the pill that encapsulates my life," Brett replied from the bathroom followed by the distinct sound of his unzipping and relieving himself.

"Hey, that's my line," Edison yelled as he changed into his last clean gym outfit. He wondered if he should defend Linda or let the comment pass.

Brett stepped out of the bathroom in the same gym clothes he had worn when he and Edison first knew each other in San Francisco. Might as well bring that up along with the underwear when he next saw Linda, he thought.

"Ready?" Brett asked, stuffing his work clothes into his gym bag and heading down the hall.

"Yep, remind me to take off forty-five pounds from the bar so you can lift after me."

"Screw you," Brett said as they thundered down the stairs to the front door.

SEVEN

David scanned the gym floor as he entered, enjoying the spectacle of toned flesh. Monday nights were always busy with the post-weekend remorse crowd. It made it a little harder for getting onto the equipment but good for eye candy. He'd been a member of this gym on and off for almost ten years, back from when he was living in San Francisco. When he had first joined, he was in his early 30's, a rising star at the law firm and still single. Such a youngster, he thought, viewing it through the eyes of a different decade. Now, he felt like he could be a father to some of the young hotties he saw working out around him and he would happily play "daddy," if that's what it took, though it wasn't a role that came naturally to him.

Tonight, however, he was in the mood for something more tangible than the standard working out and ogling on the sly. Work had been stressful and he hadn't been sleeping well. Although he'd been in his new position for a while, it seemed to get more challenging by the day and he often felt that his efforts were as effective as struggling against quicksand.

Increasingly, he had been feeling less in control, and desire was getting the better of discretion. Admittedly, when he traveled, desire often got the better of discretion. In a lustful moment, he had even considered going to the Nob Hill Adult Theatre a few blocks from his hotel. Earlier that day, he had walked by the theatre and had eyed a muscle stud in a tight shirt who was standing outside the entrance having a smoke. He had assumed he was a performer, but watching a peep show with common gay trash was out of the question. He preferred to keep his intrigues, as he liked to think of them, private.

It was for this reason that he had phoned his old buddy, Rick, this afternoon from the office. Rick and he had been pals from the days when they were both young professionals living in the Marina. They had enjoyed a friendship "with benefits" that had worked out well, since they had both dated and eventually married women. He hadn't seen Rick for a few years but Rick seemed pleased, albeit surprised, to hear from him and had accepted his invitation to work out and get a drink afterwards. In the old days, this was code for going back to one of their apartments and having an even sweatier workout than the one at the gym.

People used to think Rick and he were brothers since they were roughly the same height and had similarly dark wavy hair and fair complexions, but David could remember being offended that people would liken Rick's broad and rough features to his own finely shaped ones. David had always been leaner than Rick and had much greater stamina during their jogs through Crissy Field. Often, after they had completed their course, he had enjoyed teasing Rick by casually pulling up his shirt to wipe the perspiration off his brow, exposing his muscled midsection with seeming obliviousness, while Rick looked on with a mixture of interest and pain, half doubled over and panting. While David didn't run as much anymore, and his six-pack had gone into seclusion under a healthy layer of fat, he had consistently maintained his three-times-a-week gym routine and wondered if Rick's penchant for beer and doughnuts had gotten the better of him.

Rick had said he might be a little late and for David to start his workout without him. After some warm-up stretching, he went over to the cable machine to do pull-downs for his triceps. He positioned his hands on the small bar, noticing the lighter band of skin on his ring finger. He made a point of not wearing his ring to the gym, not because it interfered with his workout, but because he didn't want to interfere with his options for indiscretion.

Once he began his tricep pulldowns, he spotted a thin young man who was sitting at a nearby machine and looking his way. Must be the ectomorph poster child, David mused. David noticed the guy continue to watch him as he did his ten reps and he couldn't contain a sly smile, sensing this guy was either interested in him or impressed with the weight he was doing. David was pleased that at his age he still seemed to be a hot item at the gym. Although he wasn't as lean as he used to be, he felt bigger built and thought that by greatly reducing his cardio, he was finally giving his muscles a chance to grow. When he happened to read the occasional article in the men's fitness magazines he bought, they were always harping on the point that less is more, and he supposed he was living proof of that maxim.

It was when he was a half-hour into his routine, doing dumbbell curls with the 25-pound weights and focusing intently on his reflection in the mirror, that a man walking toward him from behind caught his attention.

"Dave?" the man asked, smiling and looking him over. "How are you doing, man?"

David turned around to face him. He saw a lightly tanned man dressed in a blue tank top and black shorts who was tightly muscled like a boxer. It was only when he noticed the man's smile that he realized it was Rick.

"Getting a little soft in your climb up the corporate ladder," Rick said to David with a friendly pat to his stomach.

David didn't know how to respond, feeling the sting of the insult, but overcome with wonder at Rick's transformation. "Rick, bud, it's good to see you," he said, trying to gruff it up a bit. "You look great, guy."

"Thanks, I've become somewhat of a fitness fanatic in my old age."

David looked him over and saw that not only was he muscled, but he also had a healthy glow about him. "How the hell did you manage to find the time with your work hours?"

"Oh, I make it a priority. It's very therapeutic, actually. A lot has changed since we last spoke."

"Well, change is good," David said, trying not to stare at Rick's muscle capped shoulders. "And how's Vicki doing?"

"She's doing well, but I guess you probably haven't heard, you see, we split up almost two years ago." Rick edged closer to him and leaned over in a confiding manner. "To make a long story short, I had a little bit of a breakdown a while back and confessed all the sordid details of my bad boy double life. It was all very ugly, but in the end, we had an amicable split. She gets weekday custody of Conner and I get him on weekends. After all, we're WASPs. We don't do drama."

David was flabbergasted. He looked around to see if anyone was listening, but the ectomorph had disappeared and no one else was near. All he could think to ask was "How old is Conner now?"

"He's five, going to start kindergarten this fall. Bright as a new penny. But enough about my dysfunctional life. How are you doing?"

"Doing great," David said, bending over to put down the dumbbells, which had seemed to triple in weight in his hands. "I made managing partner last year so I split my time between the Seattle and San Francisco offices."

"Congratulations. That's what you always wanted, isn't it?"

"Yes, of course."

"And how's Miyuki doing?"

"Oh, good. Couldn't be better, in fact. She keeps me organized … and sane."

"Is she still doing her art?"

"You mean the origami? Yes, she still does that. It's her baby."

"Well, good for her. She's such a talented woman."

David nodded absently in agreement, transfixed by the movement of Rick's Adam's apple on his muscular neck as he spoke.

"Well, shall we get down to business?" Rick asked.

"Sure," David said, thinking he was more than ready to get down to a different sort of business. "What are you working out today?" Rick asked.

"Arms mostly, but I could really use a full body workout," he said, smirking at Rick.

"Great, let's start with arms," Rick replied, apparently oblivious to the innuendo. Rick stepped over to the weight rack and selected the 45-pound dumbbells, and started curling them in smooth arcs with ease.

Not to be so obviously outdone, David picked up his 25-pound dumbbells and placed them back on the rack. He tried picking up the 40's, but had trouble even lifting them and after testing the 35's, finally settled on the 30-pound dumbbells. He started his curls and immediately felt the extra weight. He jerked the weights up and down, trying to impress Rick, who now seemed to be gazing at him via the mirror. David finished half of his usual number of reps and after he set down the weights, Rick turned to him.

"I couldn't help noticing your form and I have a couple suggestions if you'd like to try another set."

"Shoot," David said, trying to catch his breath before picking up the weights again.

Rick edged in close behind David and told him to start the curls. "Now when you're bringing your arms up, try not to swing your shoulders, just keep a controlled movement. It would help if you kept your elbows by your sides and really try to target the bicep," he said, giving David's upper arm a firm squeeze.

Having Rick pressed up against his backside like this and seeing their reflection in the mirror reminded him of a gym-themed porno flick, which had always been a favorite.

"I've got an idea," David said, half dropping his weights to the floor and startling Rick. "Why don't we skip the rest of the workout. I have a suite at the Fairmont. We can buy some wine and catch up. It will be like old times," he added, raising an eyebrow suggestively.

Rick glanced downwards, looking a bit uncomfortable. "It's great to see you, Dave, but I should tell you upfront that I'm in a different place now. I'm with a pretty special guy."

David pictured an underwear model waiting for Rick to come home and felt a pang of jealousy as he remembered when all he had to do was wear a tight pair of shorts to get Rick panting in lust behind him during their runs. "Well, how about you invite your friend over to join us. I'd like to meet him and we could make it a real party."

"Nah, he's not much of a partier and neither am I these days."

"Come on, bud. I can remember a time when you were into many things. I recall a few occasions when we'd gone out cruising to a certain area of town and split a twinkie."

"You mean the Castro? Yeah, I remember that, but that was another life. Boy, we were screwed up back then. Believe it or not, I actually go there during daylight hours now, and sober."

"Well, I'll be damned," David grinned, shaking his head. "I never thought I'd see the day when you'd turn into one of those holier-than-thou activists."

"Activist? Hmm, isn't that just a dirty little catchword for anyone who disagrees with you? Just because I'm in a committed relationship does not make me an activist."

David let out a chuckle. "Committed relationship? I'm sure Vicki would have a lot to say about your commitment skills."

Rick exhaled loudly. "I can see it was a mistake to come here. You're even more messed up than I remember."

"Well excuse me, you self-righteous piece of crap. You're the one who came prancing in here in your tranny gym wear, flaunting your juiced up body. Why don't you just go back to your boy toy in the gay ghetto then? I'm not looking to catch the disease du jour from your type anyway."

Rick's body tensed up and his eyes narrowed looking straight at David. "Dave, let's get something clear. I really don't give a fuck what you think, but just for the record, I'm wearing J.Crew. I live in Cole Valley with my partner, Robert, who's two years my senior, and the body is from good old-fashioned hard work. And while we're on the subject of bodies, you should try taking better care of yours." Rick glanced down at David's stomach. "By that gut of yours, it looks like you're expecting. Maybe you'd have better luck with maternity clothes."

With that, Rick started walking away. Ever the lawyer, David felt a retort coming, but then heard some nearby snickering. Turning to his right, he saw the ecto from earlier laughing at him from the bench press with a well-built friend and the words got lost in his throat. He turned back to the mirror and was momentarily taken aback by the reflection of the flush faced middle-aged man scowling back at him.

EIGHT

Val sat down with her caramel macchiato at the Starbucks near Union Square. She had recently found a $25 Starbucks gift card in the glove compartment of Stacy's BMW and it had been like a godsend. She rarely socialized anymore due to her humiliating financial situation. Therefore, nursing her every other day indulgence at a crowded Starbucks made her feel like she was still part of society, if only for an hour.

Though, even with this windfall, she had been feeling intense cabin fever lately. Stacy and Dean's condo, with its views of Huntington Park and Grace Cathedral, was nice, to say the least, but she was tired of being alone and sick of cheap canned tuna and the endless pasta parade. She needed to get out and be part of the world again.

A few years ago, she had the audacity to believe she was a real player, but like so many prospectors before her, she'd been chewed up and spit back out by this fickle city, her dreams of striking it rich turned to dust. If only she had cashed out her Trident stock options early as her friend Edison had done. This was the big "if" that still haunted her.

She had left a message for Edison yesterday, but he hadn't returned her call yet. She had even called that low-budget homosexual, Adam, under the guise of wanting to catch up with an old friend, figuring he might be worth a free lunch. Although, truth be told, he was never really a close friend, but they had worked many a long night together at Trident and she had pleasant memories of chatting with him over late night pizza at the office.

Adam had been a departmental assistant—a floater, if she recalled his designation correctly—and she had always been friendly to him because she had learned that it paid to treat the support staff well, and perhaps now she could cash in on some of that good karma.

She wondered how long it had been since she'd last seen Adam. A year? Yesterday, when she'd called him at work, he hadn't answered. She didn't leave a voicemail because it seemed too awkward, but she thought she would try him again. On the other hand, she knew Edison would get back to her eventually as he always did, but it might take him a few days. Perhaps, she hoped, Edison had found a new man who was temporarily monopolizing his time.

The last time she'd seen Edison, he had just run into his ex, Russell, on the street and it had become apparent after only one drink that Edison was still bitter over the breakup. Russell had suddenly left him for someone who could better satisfy some very specific sexual needs. Edison, always the gentleman, hadn't gone into any detail, much to her disappointment.

She had never liked Russell—his self-centered chatter always spelled death to an evening—so she had a difficult time understanding why Edison was so heartbroken. Well, it was good riddance to trash, as far as she was concerned, and she had told Edison as much.

She scrolled through her cell's call log for Adam's phone number. Yesterday, she only had the name of the company where he worked, an Irish-sounding law firm. She had Googled the firm's name and obtained Adam's extension from the phone system's directory.

Time to turn on the charm, she thought as she dialed. He picked up after the second ring.

"This is Adam."

"Adam, it's Val Panos. How the hell are you doing?"

"Fine, I'm fine. Wow, this is a surprise."

"Well, I've been thinking about you recently and how it's

been way too long since I've seen one of my favorite people from Trident, so I decided to give you a ring."

"That's nice of you."

"So what are you up to these days?"

"Not too much. I'm still at the law firm, but I guess that's obvious since you called me here."

"Great and how's that going?"

"Oh, pretty good."

"What kind of work are you doing there?"

"Uh, mostly project work and database type stuff."

"Wow, so you're a DBA now?"

"DBA?"

"Database administrator."

"Oh yeah, right. No, not exactly in title, but similar. How about you?"

"Oh, I've been traveling a lot and doing some consulting."

"Sounds like fun. I had forgotten how much of a world traveler you are. Have you gone back to the Andes for another one of your monster hikes?"

"Oh, you know, the Andes, Himalayas, nothing too challenging," she said, quietly lamenting the recent downgrade of her frequent flyer status due to her account's inactivity. She heard Adam laugh on the other end.

"Hey, I know you're at work and can't talk, but the reason I'm calling is because I thought it would be nice to get together for lunch and catch up."

"Sure, that sounds great."

"How does this Thursday sound?"

"Thursday? Yeah, that should be fine."

"Good. I was thinking we should go somewhere decent, and since Boulevard is always dependable, what would you say to meeting there at noon?"

"Boulevard? Sure. I rarely get the opportunity to go there."

"It's a date then. Let's meet at the bar. I'll handle the reservations. Why don't I give you my cell number in case you need to reach me." As she relayed her number, she could hear someone talking to Adam, as well as multiple beeps of what sounded like the scanning of bar codes.

"Val, I need to go. I have someone here at my desk, but I'll plan on seeing you at noon on Thursday."

"Looking forward to it, Adam."

"Likewise. Talk to you later."

"Bye." She hung up. It had felt strange speaking to him after so long. He sounded well, though it was obvious he had gone nowhere in his career. Not that she should talk, since she wasn't even working, but she knew she wasn't cut out for menial work like Adam. She had tried the headhunters and no matter how impressed they all seemed to be with her resume, when it came time to filling a position, they saw her as just another commission and offered her the same crap jobs at slave wages. No, there was no way she was going to be an office drone after being a mover and shaker.

She was looking forward to lunch at Boulevard. She could even handle hearing about Adam's dull life as long as she was bolstered by a glass of wine or perhaps a tasty lobster bisque. This will be fun, she thought. Now all she needed was to find something to wear and she knew just the place to look.

NINE

The westbound 520 floating bridge was a parking lot. Brett looked over his shoulder to the leafy shores of Medina, silently appreciating the architecture of the lakefront mansions and imagining the ease of commute that the Gates' helipad must afford.

The SUV in front of him inched forward only to stop in a flash of brake lights. Brett rolled down the truck window after shifting his manual transmission Ford F-150 out of gear. He thrived on order and simplicity. The random traffic slowdowns annoyed him more than they should, giving him too much time to question the move to Seattle. He and Linda had wanted to escape the hectic pulse of San Francisco for the peace that leafy Seattle offered. His job did prove to be everything promised and the city was truly emerald green, but Linda had not adjusted. She had gone past curvy to chunky and was increasingly distant. She showed no signs of going back to her hard body and high-spirited self and he found himself following links on the Internet he knew better than to explore. He was beginning to long for the shallow chaos of San Francisco. Their many years there had been good, including their intense and prolonged courtship.

The taillights of the SUV in front of him went dark when its driver turned the engine off. The cool lake air moved over his arm as Brett tapped out a random rhythm on the warm metal of the truck door. The Seattle bridge traffic gave him plenty of time to ponder why the hair on his forearms seemed to be growing longer and to stare at the vanity mirror to see if his hairline was receding. He kept himself in shape with the gym and work around the house primarily so he didn't have to watch his diet. Since his twenties, he had not changed much other than the flecks of silver in his hair and a strong desire to be in bed by ten o'clock each night. With Edison's return to Seattle, he had happily fallen back into their old pattern of working out most nights and pushing one another to do more. He could feel his polo shirt was tight against his chest and biceps from the previous night's gym session.

In the next lane, traffic rolled forward and a Mustang convertible pulled even with him, putting him next to a young woman with long, natural-looking blonde hair that caught the light attractively. Brett knew the type well: young, beautiful and, if not blazing a career, then hunting for a husband with Armani in the closet and an Austin Martin in the garage.

She turned to him suddenly, smiling broadly and yelled, "Some traffic today and it's only Tuesday!" Her smile was contagious and Brett remembered this was Seattle, not San Francisco; she was a natural beauty, she could probably change a truck tire in the snow, cook a hearty meal, not to mention pull down a decent salary at Microsoft or Amazon.

"At least it's a nice day to be stuck on the bridge," he said, smiling and raising his hand to shade his eyes, only to put it down again, realizing that he had started to sweat heavily and it was clearly visible on his light blue shirt. "Good day for a convertible too," he blurted out as he eyed both her gym bag and flat midsection, not knowing which pleased him more.

"Sure is. Oh," she giggled, as she pulled ahead, "it looks like I'm in the lucky lane. My name's Kelly and I have the same truck at home!" Her voice trailed off as she drove forward, her hair a blonde tangle reminiscent of a sixties movie. Her lane did speed up and his was at a full stop. She turned one last time and waved, the warmth of her smile still powerful.

Slouching behind the wheel, he pulled at his dark khaki pants trying to get comfortable. Was it two months since they had last had sex? he wondered. Linda, who used to have a gym bag and a convertible herself, was not the same vixen in bed he'd married. He drove forward while remaining slouched behind the wheel like a man thirty years older. He knew he still loved Linda; he could feel it in his heart and felt a longing when he slept alone on the occasional business trip.

Those warm feelings were now starting to fail against his ever-growing desire for sexual satisfaction. It didn't help that besides gaining several pounds, Linda seemed repulsed by his touch the last several months. Sneaking home to have a private moment with Playboy TV when Linda was out was too teenage for a man facing his 39th birthday. Sadly, he was on the 520 because Linda had an interview downtown in 20 minutes and if he ever got off this bridge, he would gladly suffer the dent to his pride for a few moments alone with the remote.

Traffic continued to inch along and soon started to roll forward. He crossed the floating bridge to the far west side only to come to a stop above the arboretum marsh. He saw two shirtless guys playing Frisbee in the sun between the trees on the shore. The sun glinted off their sweaty bodies and he remembered that he and Edison had played with his Aerobe there last year when Edison had visited. Edison had explained that it was a cruising area for some of the rustic gays. Brett had thought he was joking, but after a bit of time he noticed more than a few lingering stares.

Edison was hard to keep up with physically but Brett had managed. He felt his midsection and chest through his shirt with a sense of both satisfaction and pride. Not bad for an old man, and perhaps Kelly would like the muscled older man he was. After all, it had worked for Dennis Quaid, he thought, catching his lecherous grin in the side mirror.

Looking back at the Frisbee players, he thought of Edison and how much time they had spent together over the years. When he first started hanging out with Edison, after Linda's introduction, his drinking buddies had razzed him for spending time with a fag. Funny, how he wasn't in touch with any of those guys now. At first, he'd wondered if Edison was attracted to him as his friends had suggested. No awkward moments ever did happen and when Linda and Russ were not around, they often played a game where Edison pointed out unattainable women for him and he pointed out suitable upgrades from Russ to Edison. It didn't take him long to realize that quality people were a rare find and if Edison liked guys as much as he liked girls, it really didn't matter to him. Linda liked him as well and didn't raise an eyebrow when they returned late, drunk or covered with mud. He also never worried when he came home to Linda and Edison running around the house screaming and laughing like wild children.

He remained hopeful that Edison would decide to stay in Seattle, but the questions around Paul and Ellie's deaths and the weirdness on Queen Anne Hill weren't helping matters. Edison was the one who originally suggested the Queen Anne neighborhood when they announced their move to Seattle. Paul and Ellie had opened their home to them until they could find their own place. The Archers' wide circle of friends quickly made them feel at home and well-connected in Seattle.

Both he and Linda had fallen in love with the neighborhood and when Ellie mentioned a house down the street was going on the market, Paul made the introductions and the house was theirs within days. Paul and Ellie were very firm about not accepting cash or gifts for opening their house to them for over a month. It was then he understood where Edison got both his manners and stubborn resolve.

Both lanes had halted and the glare of the sun was making the cab of the truck feel like a solarium. At least in SF when you were stuck on the Golden Gate Bridge you felt like you were somewhere. Here, well, there were ducks and abundant ugly university architecture. Seattle was an odd place that seemed to have one foot firmly in the future and one nailed in the past. His own seemingly civilized neighborhood had quickly lowered itself to gossip and speculation when Paul and Ellie were found dead. The Seattle legend of the Reaping Widow was all the talk and even got a mention in the more respectable papers.

It had been a bad series of days. He and Linda had been listed as contacts on Paul and Ellie's elaborate home security system. When the police asked about notifying the next of kin, he and Linda volunteered in unison to contact Edison.

Brett made the call and could only imagine the pain that was in Edison's silence on the other end of the line. He had been able to understand Linda's spontaneous sobbing but Edison's silence and flat voice had kept him up that night. At the service, Edison rallied to give a moving eulogy and Linda orchestrated a wake that rivaled Ellie's legendary hospitality. He was embarrassed that he was the one with the uncontrollable waterworks when it came time to bury Paul and Ellie.

Because the house was a crime scene, Edison had stayed at their house initially. It had been satisfying to watch Edison push the television news truck out of the driveway with his rental car on the way to the funeral home. "Nothing parties like a rental," had been the only words said on the way there. With that said, Brett had felt relieved knowing that the Edison he knew was down, but not out.

The car behind him honked none too subtly to let him know traffic was moving. He saw Kelly's convertible exit far ahead on Montlake. He knew he had the real thing at home and he wouldn't exit and follow as his loins directed. Instead, he would go home and exercise his remote control.

TEN

Edison turned on his laptop and sat down in the room his parents had designed for him. It was a spacious bedroom, second in size only to the master bedroom. His parents had furnished it in a minimalist fashion and, to him, it appeared suspiciously like a page from a Pottery Barn catalog. The macramé had crept in, but the room was mostly awaiting a personal touch. It was comfortable and airy for a space-conscious San Franciscan, and Edison enjoyed the luxury of the expensive mattress on the queen-sized bed and appreciated the matching cherry dresser, nightstand and large desk. The walk-in closet was nearly the size of his kitchen in San Francisco and the cedar panels reminded him of his mother's excellent eye for detail.

He found he enjoyed working on his laptop at the desk while occasionally taking in the view of Mount Rainier on clearer days. At other times, he would see the teenage boys across the street mowing their lawn or horsing around, noting their ever-growing tan muscles while ignoring the math, which summed to the fact that he was of a different generation.

However, right now, it was too dark for any view other than the lamp lit street below. Even the long northern summer days had their limits. This evening, Brett and he had worked out at the gym, and after he'd come home he'd been too worn out to cook anything. Instead, he'd finished off a package of smoked salmon along with half a bag of corn chips, throwing a few pieces of lettuce onto the plate to give him the illusion he was eating healthy.

He had wanted to catch up on some email since he'd been

negligent in his correspondence the last several weeks. At least he had called Val back earlier in the day. He had left San Francisco so quickly that he hadn't told anyone about his parents' deaths. She had seemed pleased to hear from him this morning, but shocked to learn about the fate of his parents, as she had met them when they had visited SF. She was profuse with sympathy and apologized for not being in better contact the last few months, saying that it had been crazy for her lately, but she hadn't gone into much detail. He could only assume she was starting another one of her business ventures. He supposed she was one of those people who needed a constant challenge, always jumping from one success to the next with a take no prisoners attitude. It was pretty much how he remembered her from their days working together at Trident.

He logged onto his email account and saw a wall of unanswered email—mostly from acquaintances and coworkers in SF—along with the usual spam. In his post dinner grogginess, he wasn't ready to face the many emails, each requiring, at minimum, a polite response. Grieving people get leeway in their response time, he rationalized, so he opted to check his online dating account instead. He had been corresponding with one nice guy with whom he wasn't interested, but had enjoyed the email banter. He figured a short response was in order to let him know he was out of town rather than just blowing him off. He waited for the service to bring up his account and kicked off his gym shoes.

He had seen some hot guys at the gym this evening and it had aroused some feelings inside him that had been dormant. One guy in an Iowa shirt had especially caught his eye. Working out with Brett was somewhat of a double-edged sword; he enjoyed his companionship and got a much better workout with him, but one of his few social outlets to meet guys was inadvertently sabotaged. Either guys assumed both of them were straight, or possibly that they were a couple, but either way, Brett's company usually succeeded in keeping all but the pushiest queens away. Brett would never have guessed that his rock solid 210-pound frame was acting as a de facto chaperone.

Since his breakup with Russell, he had tried using some of the online services, but they seemed to attract the freak factor and left him even more disillusioned. One persistent posting that had disturbed him was: *I'm on all fours and blindfolded, the door is unlocked and I'm waiting for you.* Edison had imagined the mystery man in his apartment waiting in position with nothing more than the tick of the clock to keep him company. Then there was the one-upmanship. So many people described themselves as *VGL* or *jock* that the terms had become meaningless. Inches were added to one's penis, chest size and height while years were subtracted from one's age. And how could one forget about the attitude: *If you can't fit into my 32-inch waist jeans, you can't get into them either.*

The online dating service he used had initially seemed promising, though he had soon become disenchanted after seeing that many of the same users who were looking to build LTRs in their G-rated ads were seeking quick encounters with X-rated versions. They even had the audacity to post the same face shots on both profiles. But then again, perhaps he was being too quick to judge others, as he'd certainly seen both whore and homemaker in himself.

What his lack of dating options made all the more palpable was his sense of aloneness. Brett and Linda were great, but as good of friends as they were, he couldn't snuggle up to either of them under the covers after a long day. He needed intimacy; he needed a significant other and both had been painfully absent from his life since Russell. What scared him the most was a nagging fear that Russell and their imitation of a relationship would turn out to be the closest he would ever come to finding happiness.

He saw he had seven new messages. He quickly responded to his correspondent with a note mentioning a death in the family and his being out of town. He began reading the remaining six and sat back in his chair to give a little distance between him and the cavalcade of losers he expected from his inbox.

The messages were thankfully short, and as he scanned

each, he reviewed the attached profile. He was amused at how quickly he eliminated them. One guy was far too young, using all hip lingo in his brief note. Another guy was obviously too old, going on about how active he was and claimed that people always mistook him for being ten years younger. The next guy sent a two-liner saying "nice profile" and that his girlfriend was out of town so hit him back for some no strings fun. He remembered that this guy had responded to his ad before, always with the same line, and he marveled at the number of frequent flyer miles his imaginary girlfriend must have. The next guy had a decent body, but it was attached to the face of death and his profile contained too many photos showing him tanned and shirtless with a big drunken smile. He also had attached his travel itinerary, which suggested he did nothing more in life than fly from one circuit party to another. The next guy's picture seemed okay, but his profile was excessively wordy. He used terms such as *pensive, sensitive, emotionally available* and *sarcastic sense of humor* to describe himself, which to Edison translated to a self-absorbed queen with a bitchy streak. He was amused that for people who lived in the city, nearly all of them had mentioned how much they enjoyed hiking. Perhaps that was the new code for going to Banana Republic.

The last email did look interesting. The guy had written him a message that was clear and friendly and showed an understanding of grammar. He had suggested that if Edison was interested, they could chat and then maybe meet up for a drink. He was 37 years old, a professional who lived in Seattle and San Francisco. He was looking to meet guys who were masculine like himself, though he didn't specify what type of relationship he was seeking. He had signed his message "A.," which Edison guessed stood for "Allen" since his ID was AllenRunnerJock. From his picture—obviously taken while hiking through a nature preserve—he was in good shape, but it was a little hard to see any details since he was wearing a baseball cap and the photo had been taken from a distance.

Edison decided to respond to him. He typed a quick email

saying that he would be interested in chatting sometime and asked him what his interests were besides running. Edison saw from the animated icon that AllenRunnerJock was also online. He could instant message him, but that wasn't his style, so he sent the email and waited to see what would happen.

It was just a few minutes later that he received an instant message from AllenRunnerJock. The message read:

ARJ: dude! thanks 4 the email. where r u?

Edison replied:

EDS101:   I'm in Seattle. Where are you?

ARJ: n sf but will be back n seattle this weekend. do u live n sf?

EDS101:   No, I live in Seattle but come to SF for work. You?

Lie number one, Edison thought.

ARJ: what are u into?

EDS101:   The gym and keeping up the house. You?

ARJ: cool. what about sex? top or bottom? kink?

EDS101:   Vanilla guy. Like it simple and to the point.

ARJ: u sound like a take charge kind of guy. i like that.

Great, a pushy bottom, Edison thought. Why am I a magnet for these people? Before he could type, Allen continued.

ARJ: what do u do for work?

EDS101:   A business analyst. You?

Lie number two. Edison frowned realizing he was waltzing down the path to hypocrisy.

ARJ: attorney

Edison felt the IM conversation die and fumbled for a new topic. He hated it when people could not manage the simple volley of conversation.

EDS101:   I am on Queen Anne when I am in Seattle and Pacific Heights when I am in SF. Where are you when you're in Seattle? Do you stay in a hotel when you visit SF?

ARJ: n sf i'm usually at the fairmont. i keep a home in medina, across the lake from seattle.

EDS101:   You live the rough life I see. ☺ Medina is nice. My old college friend Steve lives over there but not lakefront like Bill Gates and the Nordstrom set.

ARJ: such judgment from a man who lives on queen anne hill. medina is nice. the mortgage is steep, though. u rent or own?

Edison paused at the enormity of the simple question. "Well, it's true now," he said aloud to no one other than the macramé owl his mother had placed over the pencil holder.

EDS101:   I own a house on the southwest corner of Queen Anne. It's not Medina but I like it.

The owl seemed to judge him even though one of its eyes was looking up while the other was looking down and to the left.

ARJ: r u near kerry park?

EDS101:   I can't see it but it's an easy walk. You know it?

ARJ   wedding photos for a frat buddy years ago. u want to meet there and then grab a beer at the 5 Spot this weekend?

EDS101:   Sure. That sounds nice. Saturday?

ARJ: a man with a plan. i will meet u there near the ugly sculpture at 2:00 on saturday. i'll have my tight jeans on and a red baseball hat. see ya man.

The jeans comment raised an eyebrow.

EDS101:   I'll be there in a T-shirt, shorts and sandals.

The message was rejected as Allen had signed off. Well, so much for Web manners, he thought, pushing away from the desk. Edison had come down a bit from his hopeful high. The guy didn't do anything horribly wrong in their brief conversation, but he didn't seem to do anything right either. He must be somewhat accomplished, though, if his employer felt he was worth lodging at the Fairmont in SF.

He shut down the computer and walked over to the bed and fell on it face first. Inhaling, he smelled his mother's familiar fabric softener. The sexual and conversational tension over instant messaging drained from him and his muscles relaxed.

Perhaps this could be home, he thought. He pressed his face deeper into the comforter and pulled a pillow over his head to block the lamplight.

He was alone in the house and in life. He felt it deep in his heart and after the funeral, he had felt it grab at each breath and draw at his strength. Alone was not dead, though. He felt the familiar steady beat of his heart through his shirt and the bedding. If there was an afterlife, he knew his parents were close and wanting for him every happiness. He did not feel darkness in the large house. He did not think there was foul play involved, but the questions around their deaths lurked and he wanted to honor his parents by not letting their lives be overshadowed by question marks.

He rolled over on his back and slid under the covers. He pulled off his socks with his toes then reached over to the nightstand to shut off the lamp. The darkness melted the tension behind his eyes. He slipped off his shorts and underwear under the covers and passed his socks with his feet to his hands. He slid them to the side of the bed and let them fall to the floor. The cool sheets teased his warm body all at once like a practiced lover. He slid his shirt off and sent it over the side of the bed as well. The air escaped from under the sheets and comforter, moving over his naked body. He moved his hands behind his head, enjoying the stretch. Awake now, his mind was sharp. He kept his eyes closed and let his thoughts flow.

He chuckled quietly when he thought of his parents haunting the house only to be appalled at his hygiene gaffs and his frequent acts of onanism. His father had talked to him years ago about sex on an impromptu drive to Wallace Falls. They had driven past the falls and had a quiet lunch in the car of burgers, fries and malts. Edison had many questions and his father had answered them all.

Edison had mentioned in the abstract about being gay that day. He learned later that his father had already figured it out. That summer, both his father and mother had sat him down at the picnic table, the one that was now in the backyard, and gave him their version of Gay 101. It was enlightened for the time and from the heart, he remembered. Little did he know that they would be trying to find Mr. Right for him 24x7 from then on out. The closet does have some advantages he had told friends after one of his parents' surprise introductions.

He rolled to his side and rested his head on his shoulder and arm. He looked over to the desk to find the macramé owl looking back at him, lacking judgment from this angle, Edison noted. Sleep was near but he was still alert. He sensed something had changed and in the briefest moment of clarity, he realized that on some level, however transient, he was not alone.

Looking around the room and to the windows, he saw the curtains moving in a draft. The windows were closed against the cool summer night and the stars were shining behind the swaying bows of the firs. He was tired and from deep inside he felt something melt away and allow him to breathe and feel the peace in the rhythm of his lone heartbeat.

ELEVEN

The television across the room was on mute as the Golden Girls suffered yet another senior life crisis. Linda was fascinated by the appalling fashions the old gals sported on the show. Given her ever-increasing bulk, she could hide a lot behind a Golden Girl's outfit. She reclined on her bed among the many pillows and closed her eyes. Her bulk had become a personal hell that she desperately hoped was temporary, but she was starting to wonder when temporary folded into permanent. Brett hadn't said anything but she could feel that he was pulling away since they moved up to Seattle. She wanted to convince herself it was for the best, but she couldn't. Losing Brett was the one thought that could bring her to tears and the one thought she would not allow to become acceptable. Denial may be a vast metaphorical river, but at least the water was warm.

Linda rolled to her side and pulled the comforter over her head to block the late morning light from her eyes. She was spending most weekday mornings in bed, enjoying her power combo of *The Golden Girls* and *Designing Women*. Both shows she had taken up since moving to Seattle. She realized her morning routine was a problem but, sadly, it was the most enjoyable part of her day. When she had worked, she was up before Brett so as not to have to compete for their upstairs bathroom in San Francisco. She would be done in time to cook a full breakfast and enjoy it with her husband. To Brett, a good breakfast prepared by his wife was an act of pure love. To Linda, it was almost embarrassing that it took so little to make him happy. He wasn't the most expressive man, but when it came to breakfast, he didn't hold back the emotional warmth and appreciation for his wife and her omelets.

While she knew she was responsible for their hetero version of lesbian bed death and a growing physical embarrassment to herself, she still was out of bed each morning and downstairs while Brett showered and shaved. In her robin's egg blue sweatpants and matching top, she would throw together a full breakfast and coffee. A few minutes after Brett had left the house, though, she was back upstairs in bed with a snack, catching her shows until she dozed off, finally getting out of bed in the early afternoon. The only positive aspect to her new life of sloth was that she definitely looked rested.

Linda rolled over, and in doing so rolled onto the last of a chocolate Bundt cake and its plate. She assumed either the fork had drifted under the sheets with the napkin or she was just too fat to feel it pressing into her. That whole *Princess and the Pea* character was probably just some anorexic sorority chick that would evolve into a leathery fossil perched at the bar of some country club. She knew the type well from the arts community.

It had been hard to believe that with her museum credentials she hadn't found a job in Seattle despite her best efforts and ever lowering standards. Applying to entry-level gallery jobs had been humiliating, especially when the young person sending out the rejection letters was sitting in the position for which she had applied. They always had names like Chad or Beka. If she had smoked, she would have used the rejection letters as ashtrays. Instead, she shredded them and made them into mulch for her small garden. Her life as a senior curator seemed far away. Right now, she envisioned her life as a bad piece of art entitled: *Big Girl in Bundt—an abstraction of failure.*

Linda roused herself from her gooey nest. One of her secrets would be here in less than an hour. There was another woman in the house not counting the sleazy harem in the *Hustler* magazines from Brett's single days that was exiled to the garage. Linda wasn't afraid of Larry Flint's *Hustler* babes, they were only paper. Real demons took the form of Little Debbie or that tired old queen in the cowboy hat with the lasso, the Twinkie.

The other woman, Carlotta, her clandestine maid, knew and kept Linda's secrets, she mused, as she pulled herself from the tangle of sheets. She walked to the bathroom only to turn back on her heel to the bed. Ignoring the plate, fork and flattened cake, she pulled the sheets back and felt around the foot of the bed for her husband's boxers and socks that he wore to bed but invariably pulled off each night. She used to pull them off him a few minutes after they were in bed with a quip that she wanted to exercise her wifely privileges. Brett never minded being plundered, but preferred, as she had noted over the years, to stake his husbandly claim in the light of day somewhere private but rarely in bed.

Despite their current problems, she knew she would always cook his breakfast and be the only woman to wash his clothes. She didn't like the idea of another woman handling her husband's intimate items, or hers, for that matter. With Brett's clothes in hand, she went to his closet, gathered up the dirty clothes from his laundry basket, carried them across the room and dumped them into her laundry basket. Now she had just enough time to get showered and presentable before Carlotta made her appearance. Then she could avoid reality for a couple of hours as Lily's lunch guest.

Out of the shower, with her damp shoulder-length brown hair in a towel, she applied light makeup and practiced her usual cosmetic voodoo. She felt the growing need to thank someone or something for the absence of gray hair or rogue facial hairs that she noted on other women her age. She gave her face a quick review knowing that Lily could spot makeup errors from 20 paces and was not shy about pointing them out. Lily had once pulled a girl, no more than fourteen, aside at the makeup aisle at Nordstrom and gave her a loud lecture on the importance of applying makeup while sober. Sadly, the girl simply had bad skin. Lily had suggested charity work at a school for the blind after the girl's tearful insistence that she didn't use makeup.

She knew heavy makeup was a waste as it always lost out to her ruddy complexion with its high color. The feminine heart shape of her face provided an odd contrast to the outdoor fresh look of her skin. Long ago, she gave up trying for the milky smooth look so many women took for granted. Fortunately, the natural look was the one Brett preferred so she had used that as her excuse to keep things simple.

Lily's lunches were formal affairs, as Lily never wore anything close to casual. With her voodoo at halftime, Linda went to her closet, pulled down last week's splurge and unzipped it from the Nordstrom bag. The selling point had been that some of the seams looked to her untrained eye as if they could be taken in if she succeeded in losing weight and exited from the Hostess pantheon.

Linda heard voices and cleaning noises downstairs. Carlotta must have let herself in with her key. There was the familiar sound of the kitchen table being moved aside, which signaled the beginning of Carlotta's reign of terror, defeating everything in her path with liberal amounts of bleach and vinegar. Carlotta's sister, Josefina, was the other voice and its echo suggested she was in the main room, no doubt polishing every surface until it yielded to her impossible standard.

When Linda descended the back stairs to the kitchen, she was greeted by Carlotta, who seemed impervious to the wafting bleach fumes.

"Mrs. Gale, what a beautiful outfit. Somewhere special today?"

"Oh, just the usual lunch with Lily," Linda said crossing the kitchen to the pantry. "How are things with you and your sisters? Any good neighborhood gossip?"

"Things are quiet but still very busy. Many families seem to have left for their summer vacations so we're doing some of the special projects like carpet cleaning and floor waxing. The Merkel Mansion remodel is done so we've been working there as a family most nights. It's good for us all to be on one job. Besides, we're one family, one company; we can work fast and furious and enjoy dinner afterwards. It reminds me of when my mother took me on her jobs, many, many years ago."

"Your empire seems boundless," Linda said. "I read in the paper that your company purchased the Millery Building at Lake Union. I was going to stop by but didn't know where to park and figured you would be out working regardless."

"Oh, stop by anytime, someone is always there. It's just a little family business but we're proud of it. The Merkel Mansion is our largest project to date and with the investment in the Millery, we are happy to have the Merkel account." Carlotta took two spray bottles from her smock, attacking the refrigerator with a cloud of vinegar cleaner.

"That building is a good investment. The usual this week?" Linda asked as she reached for her checkbook.

"Yes, Mrs. Gale. Oh, I have your billing summary here with the detail for the supplies broken out by month. Labor expenses are on the last pages. As of this month, we'll be offering limited lawn care service as well. My brother Carlos is out of graduate school for a few months and he wants to put his green thumb to work over the summer. He went back for his MBA after we sisters ganged up on him."

Carlotta smiled in such a way that Linda doubted she was using the phrase "ganged up" in the figurative sense.

"I'll let Mr. Gale know although he is very possessive of his lawn. By the way, do you have room for another client?"

"Mrs. Gale, anyone you would suggest would be welcome. Who is it?"

"Well, you may regret those words. You have heard of the deaths across the street, I imagine. They were the talk of Queen Anne for weeks." Linda noted that Carlotta was absently fingering the Maltese cross that always hung from her neck on a platinum chain. "They were close friends of ours as is their son, Edison, who's living there until the house is sold."

"I knew you were close to Mrs. Archer," Carlotta said. "You have my condolences. I never met Mr. Archer, but Ellie Archer was such a nice woman and her Spanish was impeccable. We saw each other at Pike Place Market and here on the Hill so often that we finally introduced ourselves."

"I didn't know Ellie spoke Spanish. She was as good as they come." Linda looked at the Bundt cake on the counter remembering it was Ellie's recipe and to her sudden horror, she realized she had Ellie's cake platter. She would return it to Edison when she saw him next. Her mind cleared and she was relived that her distraction wouldn't appear flighty but as grieving.

"Would you have time in your schedule to work on the Archer house? I have been there and it needs freshening more than anything else. Edison is a gentleman, and even without the shock of losing his parents, that house would be a challenge for a man to keep clean."

"Angelica has an opening in her schedule. She would be happy to take on another client in the neighborhood. Do you know how they died? Was it a violent death? We are not equipped to deal with anything other than the basic household cleaning."

"Oh, Carlotta, no, not at all. They were found dead in the media room in the basement. There was no sign of foul play or violence. At first, the person who found them thought they were asleep."

Linda remembered the only thing violent that day had been Lily pounding on their door with the remains of a potted plant from their porch. The dents on the door were still there after Brett's attempts to sand and varnish them away. To her credit, Lily had dropped off an envelope of cash with a vague apology addressed to Brett.

"I'll speak to Angelica today and she'll call you for the details. We have a slightly higher rate by $10.00 for newer clients. I trust that Edison Archer will find the rate reasonable."

"I'll speak to Edison tonight and no, I don't think the rate will be a problem for him. Oh, and Carlotta, I feel I know you well enough not to need to ask, but I'm very protective of Edison, especially after what he's gone through recently. He's gay and if that's a problem then there's no need for you to have your sister call." Linda looked for signs of trouble in Carlotta's normally placid face. She saw none and caught the slightest smile forming before Carlotta spoke.

"Mrs. Gale, a few of our clients are, how do you say, confirmed bachelors."

Linda raised her eyebrow at hearing what she thought was a long-retired term.

Carlotta continued, "I wear the cross and I read the scriptures. I also know that God created homosexuals as well as heterosexuals. I judge a man or woman by the content of their character. Anything else is simply ignorance. Did you think I was a strict Catholic because my family is from Colombia or is it the cross I wear?"

"I didn't know for certain, and, as I said, Mr. Gale and I look out for Edison. We consider him family."

"I like to hear that you're protective of your friends. I admire that in a woman. Angelica will be pleased to be working in a house where the man isn't watching her backside. Angelica is the sister who has the best figure. Who knows, perhaps Mr. Archer will see my brother Carlos pick Angelica up after work. He can never seem to find the right man."

"Really," Linda said as she felt a smile break across her face. "So you're a housekeeping and a matchmaking service? Oh dear," she said looking at her watch. "I'm a bit late. I'll speak with Edison tonight and Angelica can call me tomorrow."

"That sounds perfect and here's your statement," Carlotta said, handing Linda an envelope in exchange for the check in Linda's hand.

"Thank you," Linda said, picking up the perfect Bundt cake from the kitchen counter.

"I'm glad you're taking that wicked temptation with you," Carlotta said. "Now that is a sin!"

Linda laughed and moved to the front hall. "Oh," she said, "I'm sorry to say, Mr. Gale dropped some cake in the bed this morning. Men are such pigs at times." Linda paused at the mirror in the front hall to check her hair.

From the kitchen came the murmur, "Mr. Gale, my ass."

Linda smiled and shouted back to the kitchen, "I heard that …" ending in a laugh.

She headed for the door and down the front steps. Crossing the street, she saw the usual sights: kids on bikes and joggers all enjoying the gentle slope her street provided. Two teens approached her on bikes at high speed. The city girl in her rallied and was cool to their last minute skidding stop. She wasn't going to lose a game of chicken to a couple of kids.

"Hey, Mrs. Gale, what are you up to?" the tall lean blond boy asked her.

"Oh, not much, going over to Mrs. Ling's. What are you two boys up to today?"

"Basketball and then Video Isle to return some DVDs," the shorter boy volunteered tugging on his shirt, seeming suddenly embarrassed. Sure enough, one of them had a basketball impossibly balanced on the bike frame and the other had two DVD cases tucked into the back of his shorts.

"Is Mr. Gale going to be taking his boat back to the marina?" the taller one asked.

"He mentioned he was going to return it to the marina now that the slip is repaired. I think it will be happy to be off Queen Anne and in Elliot Bay where it belongs," she said, thinking she would be happy to have it out of the driveway. "You boys look like you could use a quick bite of cake," she added before they could fish about getting Brett to take them out on the water again. She was curious about the gossip in the neighborhood and she had two teenage pigeons before her who would sing for cheap.

"Cake! That's cool Mrs. Gale. What kind is it?" asked the brown-haired boy who she thought was named Brian.

"Oh, it's a classic, chocolate Bundt with vanilla cream filling." Linda sat the cake on the nearest car hood and carefully ripped off two large pieces. "I'll tell Mrs. Ling that Mr. Gale made breakfast out of the cake," she joked as the boys inhaled the cake like wolves, teenage wolves.

"So, what have you heard about the Reaping Widow?" Linda asked, getting down to business.

The blond boy responded, "Mom said that the house is going to sell again once their son carts everything away and the realtor gives the nod that the house is ready for the market. Mom goes to church meetings with the realtor woman." He smiled as Linda rewarded him with more cake.

"So no word yet on what killed the Archers?" Linda asked innocently.

"Mom said it was a double suicide but they did it in some tricky way so their son could get the insurance money. The house told them to do it."

"Oh, so there was a lot of insurance money?" Linda asked, pretending to believe the kids.

"Yeah, millions, according to Mike whose dad works at a bank," chimed in the boy with brown hair.

Linda had no idea who Mike was. "So," she asked, leaning against the warm hood of a black SUV, "would you two spend a night in that house?" She broke off a piece of cake for herself, enjoying the relay of gossip.

"No way, a fag lives there!" said the brown-haired kid.

"No, I mean are you afraid of the Reaping Widow or what did the paper call it, the House of Rapture?" Linda eyed the Archer house radiant in the afternoon light.

"Nah, it's just a house. Who knows why it made them kill themselves. Maybe they were just too old to keep on living," said the taller boy who was growing restless and kept looking at the top of Brett's boat that was visible over the lilac bushes.

"I guess we'll never know," Linda added, not wanting the conversation to turn to her. "You know, if you offer to help Mr. Gale clean the boat Saturday afternoon, I bet he'd take you around Blake Island. We were thinking of taking Edison Archer out on Elliot Bay on Sunday afternoon and there will be lots of food. Have your parents call our house or stop by before then to let us know it's okay."

"Way cool, Mrs. Gale. We'll be over to help at noon on Saturday," the taller one said for both of them. With that, they were down the street in a flash under pedals powered by youth. Down a block, she heard what she had come to expect from Queen Anne kids.

"Thank you for the cake, Mrs. Gale."

Funny how homophobia could be cured with a boat ride when you are thirteen or so, she thought.

She loved kids as long as she didn't have to give birth or be responsible for them. Lily, she knew, would understand her being late and down half a cake in exchange for the neighborhood gossip. She picked up the cake and proceeded to Lily's glass and concrete postmodern nightmare of a home.

TWELVE

I hope they remember me and give us a decent table, Val thought, pulling the silk wrap around her shoulders. She quickened her pace in the cold wind that seemed unaware of the flawless blue sky above. By the tall windows of the Rincon Center, she caught her reflection perfectly centered between two passing homeless men, momentarily creating an image of a gender-confused Janus.

"Not bad, sister," she said, looking again at her reflection in Stacy's Dior ensemble. She smiled, knowing she could neither afford the dress nor the lunch she was about to have. She had spent the morning rummaging through Stacy's closets. It had disturbed Val more than she cared to admit that she had trouble fitting into Stacy's clothes as she had nicknamed Stacy the "big-boned gal from southern Atherton"—the affluent town just south of San Francisco where Stacy grew up. Regardless of the fit, there was no reason that Stacy's clothes should remain closeted just because Stacy was.

Val had her own dresses, some better than Stacy's, but they were tightly packed in dry cleaning bags and she didn't want to disturb them. Plus, Stacy's dresses were new to her, so for the first time in a long time, it felt like she had new clothes. The dress she had selected was fabulous and she felt it flutter attractively around her knees when she swirled through the ever-fashionable revolving door of Boulevard, a San Francisco standard with its large portions of French inspired California cuisine. Once inside, she felt herself relax as the chill of the San Francisco summer melted in the warmth of the bustling restaurant.

Instinctively, her throat tightened when she saw the outline of the Oakland Hills and Bay Bridge through the restaurant's back windows. The *Bridge to Nowhere* was her name for it since she had never seen a real reason to cross it. She had made the requisite excursions to the East Bay in her early years as a San Franciscan, but the allure of cheap housing and the BART train had never charmed her. She had even tried the cuisine of the East Bay, but the weeds and seeds of the hemp crowd were best avoided in her mind. If she wanted to go herbal, she would simply graze the Presidio.

She returned to more pleasant thoughts as she noticed a few male heads turn her way. Perhaps it was more for the blaze of color the Dior ensemble provided or her rushed gait supplied by the slightly too large Chanel heels that propelled her forward. It didn't really matter since this crowd knew money, old or new, and she looked the part. For an instant, she felt her old self rising into form. She had $18 in her purse, so why not have a glass of champagne while she waited for Gay Adam. Hell, looking at the line of fine fellas at the bar, she might even snag herself a husband. Even straight men responded to Dior, she mused, they just didn't know why.

She moved to the bar, but felt a firm hand on her shoulder and a deep authoritative voice in her ear, "Madame, please no unchaperoned women at the bar."

She turned to see Gay Adam dressed in GAP's finest—a button-down blue shirt and khaki pants; nothing could announce "support staff" louder than separates from the GAP, she thought. She felt her smile falter but recover as she remembered she was dining on his card today.

THIRTEEN

Clearly, space age equipment or butter had been involved to cram Val into her dress, Adam thought. Val was not fat, rather the dress was made for a woman of a smaller size. It was a nice dress. Adam wasn't an aficionado of couture but he felt he knew it when he saw it. He was mesmerized by the fit of the dress and realized he was openly staring at the jiggle of Val's backside as they were led to their table by the host. He guessed that she must have purchased the dress during a "leaner" time and the price demanded it get some use even if she had entered a Rubenesque period.

Once seated, Adam was brought back to the reality of the lunch crowd by Val's cheerful voice going on about how she missed the old standards like Boulevard now that she didn't have clients to keep fat and happy.

"What are you up to these days?" Adam asked, realizing he had never really known what Val had done for work since they were both laid off years ago from their shared dot bomb.

"Oh, lots of things," she said pulling half of the bread from the basket a waiter had set between them. "I launched a barter site as well as a survey site. The first one couldn't get its business model ironed out so I pulled out before I lost more capital, and the second one died on the vine when I stepped aside to avoid a nasty disagreement with the founder. Naturally, my cash stepped aside too. Now I'm a consultant for either the investors or the start-ups, whoever has the bigger check. I guess that makes me a size queen," she laughed with a lightness that suggested a carefree attitude in her business affairs that Adam envied and admired. He did note that she pasted nearly all the butter on her bread, leaving little for him, had he wanted any.

Adam quickly reviewed the menu by price. He was relieved to see a variety of prices, as he feared that everything would be expensive. He didn't want to assume that Val was going to pick up the check. Also, he wanted to show he had good business manners in case she was going to discuss employment opportunities. He decided a soup and the lesser chicken course would be the appropriate combination.

"We haven't had good luck with consultants back at the firm," Adam said from behind his menu, trying to sound as if he were involved in the internal workings of the office beyond his step and fetch reality. "The legal community doesn't seem to do well when it comes to external support. In fact, one of the attorneys joked that those who can't do, consult. I bet your experience at Trident is useful, though. You were quite the player there."

"Oh, that was a busy time," Val said. "But don't paint all us consultants with the same brush. I know I earn my pay but I agree there are a lot of frauds out there."

Adam noticed that Val seemed deeply involved with the lunch menu and he waited until she reached for her bread before he asked the question that had been on his mind since she had called about lunch.

"Have you heard from our old VP, Edison?" he asked, trying to sound casual. His long-standing idolization and crush on Edison Archer was something he preferred not to share. Since it was one-sided, and he hadn't seen Edison in months, it felt all the more embarrassing that he was fishing for an update.

"You haven't heard?" Val asked, reaching for the remaining bread, breaking it in two and taking half. "He's up in Seattle. His parents were found dead in their house."

"That's horrible," Adam said, sitting back, stunned. He thought back to the last time he had seen Edison. He had run into him at the Metreon food court where they shared a few laughs as they ate, and the warmth of Edison's smile had stayed with him for hours. He couldn't imagine the loss Edison must be feeling.

"So, he doesn't know how they died? Were there contributing factors?" he asked, instantly regretting his slippage into faux legalize.

Val, with another mouthful of bread, ignored his question, waved a waiter over, and asked for a glass of the Möet and more bread, oblivious to the fact that the man was not their waiter. As he walked away, she hailed him again and turned to Adam.

"Where are my manners? Do you want to split a bottle of champagne or do you want to do glasses?"

"None for me," he said, looking up at the waiter. "I have to go back to the office later."

"Bread?" she offered the basket to Adam with its lone end of bread.

"Oh, no, I don't do well with grains."

"Really? Have you muscled up?" Val asked, giving him a smile.

"You gays and your hot bods. The straight men that come my way are all a little soft in the middle and worse yet, have bird legs. Yuck!" she exclaimed, waving the bread around with her hand and showering the table with crumbs.

Pots and kettles, thought Adam as he straightened his place setting and took a drink of the Pellegrino that Val had ordered for the table.

"So, about Edison. That's horrible. How's he doing?"

"Oh, yes," Val seemed to focus for the first time on the topic of conversation. "I called Edison a few days ago about some silly detail. I had no idea anything happened or even that he was in Seattle because I called his cell, not his landline. Well, he called back and said he was in Seattle to close up his parents' house after their funeral. I was shocked. He seemed very depressed and it was disturbing to hear him blue since he is always so steady. You remember how he was at Trident. No matter what was exploding, he was always calm." Val paused to drink her water and check her cell phone.

"Anyway, he told me that a neighbor, Brett Gale, I think, he used to live down here and knew both Edison and his parents. Brett called Edison and told him that his parents had been found dead by some friend of the family. The police have no clues and there's no sign of a break in or foul play. They were found in the TV room, dead, next to each other on the couch with the television on and tuned to A&E."

"Poor Edison, and not having any idea what happened. It doesn't sound like natural causes ..." he let his sentence trail off.

In the pause of conversation, Adam thought of his parents dying. It had been over a decade since the big freeze. His high Catholic parents had decided to hate the sin, homosexuality, and freeze out the sinner, Adam. He had offered many an olive branch only to have it iced. Adam was fine with the schism. He had enough demons on his dance card. Val waving the empty butter dish at a passing waiter brought him back to reality and the topic at hand, Edison.

"So, is he a suspect?" he asked. "He is the sole heir since he's an only child, right?"

"Aren't you just Colonel Mustard in the library with the candlestick," Val responded with a half smile that had probably attracted many a man.

The waiter came by with Val's champagne and took their order. Adam went with the soup and the chicken breast entrée. Val, he observed, went with the ahi starter and the most expensive item, a filet of beef entrée. She handed the empty breadbasket to the waiter with a look of impatience. Well, he thought, it must be nice to have money and not care about one's carb intake.

"Edison isn't a suspect," Val resumed. "He was in San Francisco at the time. There are no suspects plus they cannot find the exact cause of death."

"How's Edison taking all this?" he asked, still trying to grasp that after what must be weeks, there were no answers.

"He isn't doing too well and it looks like he will be stuck up there for at least a month."

"I can't imagine that being easy for anyone. Did his work give him time off?"

"You know Edison, he moves in VP circles," Val said in a condescending tone.

To Adam it appeared that Val continually glared at his shirt as if it had failed some test. He had checked it out, discreetly using his knife as a mini mirror as he had seen a 1940's starlet do in a movie when checking her lipstick. He couldn't see any stains. Perhaps it wasn't good enough for whatever designer nightmare she had stuffed herself into.

Val continued, "He's on a leave of absence." She paused as the starters were placed in front of them. Then she tapped her empty champagne glass and motioned for another one from the waiter and then tapped her watch expectantly. "These people," she whispered, to Adam, "just because it's lunch they think they can slack off."

The waiter was still within earshot behind Val, and Adam openly winced. The waiter probably made more than he did but he felt a bond, as they were both in the servant class. As if the waiter was a mind reader, he winked as if he fully understood Adam's situation. Adam returned a weak smile as Val continued about Edison.

"It gets juicy, of course. First of all, imagine what his ex is going to think when he realizes he dumped Edison for some Navy sex toy stud and Edison is now worth a fortune. I never liked Russell and told Edison, day one," Val said as if she were addressing a boardroom.

Finally, the trash is at the curb where it belongs, Adam thought, trying to suppress a smile. "His parents were rich?" he asked, realizing he knew little of Edison's origins and had assumed they were modest given Edison's down-to-earth nature.

"Dear, they had to be insured and they lived in a very desirable zip code according to the Internet. Plus, the size of the house alone spells money," Val said in a knowing voice. "It gets more interesting, though, when it comes to the house," she said pointing her fork at him.

Adam was used to Val doing most of the talking, but he was amazed at how she was able to inhale her food and still dominate the conversation. She was done with her ahi starter while he had barely started his soup. Seemingly to emphasize that she ate like a pig, the waiter came by, took her plate and swept away the tribe of breadcrumbs that had gathered on her side of the table. Adam did take some pride in the appearance of his side of the table, which was immaculate, or as he remembered Edison saying, *virginal*.

Val twirled the champagne glass in her hand expertly. "Well, the house, how shall I say it, has a reputation. Among the locals, apparently, it's called the Reaping Widow or what was it, something like the House of Rapture. Damn, I wish I could remember. Anyway, Edison's parents are hardly the first to die in the house and they had only lived there a matter of years ... it's not the house Edison grew up in, is what I mean. Not to sound insensitive, but the Agatha Christie aspect has been on my mind," Val paused briefly, draining her champagne glass, again.

Adam found himself watching Val's mouth move as he imagined what Edison must have looked like in high school— perhaps in a football uniform. He also wondered why someone like Edison went one way and he went another. Was it chance? And then there was Val, who seemed to forge ahead regardless of what went on around her.

The waiter interrupted Val's monologue with the lunch entrées and asked if there was anything else for the table. Both of them nodded in the negative and the waiter disappeared into the rush of restaurant traffic.

The break in Val's monologue was an opportunity, he decided, to extend himself to Edison, and genuinely so, as his mind repeatedly tried to grasp the enormity of Edison's loss. He briefly thought of his own parents' mortality and decided that it was time for him to offer them another olive branch.

"I could check his apartment and take in his mail; I live close so it wouldn't be a problem," Adam volunteered. He was surprised at Val's frozen face in response to his offer.

"Oh, honey, I offered too. I'm on Nob Hill these days at Huntington Park. I'll take care of it. You'd probably be sleeping in his bed with the contents of his underwear drawer strewn over the duvet. I can spot a crush a mile off and you gay guys are so obvious."

"Well, I was just offering to help, not trying to rummage through his drawers. He was nice to me at Trident and I'd like to return the favor," he could hear his own voice trail off. His face reddened and flushed fully when his knife hit the plate and made a ringing noise. The sad thing was, he thought, he proba-bly would look in Edison's drawers. His base high school be-haviors were all too close to the surface and he didn't like that even Val could see them.

Val seemed done with this part of the conversation. "Adam, when was the last time we caught up? It has been a while. And seriously, you are looking very lean and mean. How long has it been, a year?" Val asked as she scraped the plate with bread to capture the last of the garlic mashed potatoes.

Well, she can turn on the charm and on a dime too, he thought.

"No, we saw each other at the MOMA gala. You were with Edison and we went out for drinks afterward. You remember, you hit the cable car guy with your purse and gave us a free show of your commitment to safe sex when your purse came apart. Did the cable car guy ever press charges?"

"Oh that, well, no. He knew he was wrong and backed off," she said both dismissively and defensively.

It was her turn to blush. Like a car accident, Val was some-thing that Adam was drawn to regardless of the well-modulated voice in his head that warned him to step away.

He remembered Val barreling down the halls of Trident. Oblivious of the people in the hall or the papers she was drop-ping, she would charge from one crisis to another, never stopping to hear the voices of criticism or to take stock of the effectiveness of her efforts. He knew she had options that went to zero shortly after Edison left and the company fiscally imploded.

He had often wondered if Edison knew something about the impending corporate collapse or if it was simply dumb luck that he exited before the money did. He knew to the penny how golden Edison's exit parachute was as he had put together the paperwork for human resources. It did bother him since his circumstances were clearly defined by his cube walls.

They continued to talk for a bit about the details of the implosion of Trident and where diasporas rested. Val seemed to know all the dark details and none of the happy endings. The waiter came back with the dessert menus, but Adam declined, and Val, after a moment of hesitation, also declined. Soon the bill came and to Adam's relief Val moved the bill to her side of the table.

"Oh, honey, let me get this one," Val said reaching for the check. "I have the day off so it's the least I can do for someone who has to return to the trenches."

"Thanks, Val. That's so nice of you and I'm glad you thought to call, too. I love this restaurant," he said looking around at the distinctive French décor. "The food was excellent as well. I wish I had the means to lunch here on a regular basis."

Adam watched Val look around the restaurant. "It is nice. I like the Four Seasons too. Both have excellent lunch menus. We should go there next time."

"That sounds great," Adam replied, liking the warm side of Val and oddly feeling like a little kid out on the town with a mysterious relative.

"Oh, no," Val murmured, looking down into her Louis Vuitton bag. "My wallet isn't in here. I must have left it in the car back on Nob."

Val looked up and extended her hand to Adam's wrist, a finger sliding under the cuff of his sleeve. "Adam, could you be a dear and charge this one and I'll pick up the Seasons next time?"

Shit, he thought. He had paid off his credit card only two months ago and was enjoying not seeing charges or interest on the card. But he knew he didn't have a civilized option.

"Sure, no problem, it will wake up my Visa. It's been dormant for a while." He pulled out his well-worn wallet stuffed with an embarrassing number of ATM receipts.

"Thanks, hon. Let's make it dinner at the Seasons with drinks so I can make it up to you."

The waiter appeared, took the bill and again gave Adam a smile. Val excused herself and made for the restroom. The waiter returned with the receipt and Adam's card, leaving Adam in peace to sign the charge. With scrimping, he thought, it would be paid off next month.

On the sunny sidewalk outside, he parted with Val and her effusive promises of dinner at the Seasons. He walked back slowly even though he knew he was two hours into an hour lunch break. A month worth of lunches spent on a chatty woman who couldn't care less about him or the impact of her expensive tastes. If he had forgotten his wallet, he would have been at an ATM within an hour to settle his debt. He hated being poor. He also hated that Val knew just what Edison represented to him, the unattainable.

As he moved into the shadow of the Embarcadero towers, his anger and frustration hadn't faded. If Julie bitched about eating lunch at her desk while he took executive style lunches, he would probably give her a long overdue verbal slap. If he was fired for the long lunch or for barking at Julie, then it would be a bitter party of one at the Four Seasons tonight. He would go down in style.

FOURTEEN

Cherie had parked across the street and half a block down from the gym on Queen Anne Avenue. She had found a good spot in between a van and an SUV so her Ford Expedition blended in nicely. Brett and Edison had said they worked out early on Saturdays and she was going to catch them if she had to wait there all morning.

She had stopped by the gym during her lunch hour on Friday and signed up for a free seven-day trial pass. Compared to her current gym, with its vaulted ceilings and open spaces, this one seemed cozy—at least that's the spin she would have chosen if she were trying to sell it. She hoped its understated nature meant it wouldn't be such a haven for the homosexuals since they were into all things that glittered and had a backbeat. However, for today's purposes, the size of the gym was irrelevant as she had more pressing matters.

Edison Archer's house had the potential to bring in one of her larger commissions to date and there was no way she was going to let Century 21 or some other big name vulture snatch up this high-profile sale from her. True, it was no Merkel Mansion, the account she'd been working on for months, which dwarfed anything she had previously handled. But the sale of the Merkel Mansion was a once in a lifetime event and she had reduced her commission in order to snag it. It was the stately Queen Anne properties, like Edison Archer's, that were her bread and butter, and she wanted to attach her name to as many as possible.

Yesterday, unbeknownst to Edison, she'd posted his home on the Amstead Realty website. While she couldn't physically plant her stake in his lawn, yet, she had staked a virtual claim to his property with specific instructions to contact her and under no circumstances contact the owner per owner's request. She knew if she could come to him with ready offers, there would be no reason for him to choose another realtor. Plus, there was nothing she disliked more than sharing a commission, so whenever possible, she tried to find the buyer for the house she was selling.

Besides, Edison was a hunk and she wanted to make it clear that certain perks were available to him if he chose Amstead Realty. It had distracted her the other day having his similarly hunky neighbor at the house. There was something about a hot man with a wedding band she always found irresistible, though it wasn't just his unavailability that had turned her on. While she oddly hadn't been able to read Edison, she'd certainly felt interest from the married one. She had sensed something akin to raw desire in the way he had looked at her as they toured the house and she would have done him in a heartbeat. She would give Edison first dibs, as a prospective client would always get priority, but she had to admit she was intrigued by Mr. Brett Gale.

The gym opened at 8:00 and she had pulled into her viewing spot a few minutes later, figuring that if by some chance they had arrived at the gym so early as to beat her, more power to them. However, she didn't see either of their vehicles around. Yesterday, when she had dropped off the paperwork at Edison's house, no one had answered the door, though a Prius had been parked in Edison's driveway. Similarly, on one of her drives through the neighborhood, she had spotted a white pickup truck in the driveway of the house where Brett had said he lived—right across the street from the Asian bitch with a death wish. She was aware that they may not show up at all, but it was worth the wait. At any rate, she had brought her laptop and it was the perfect opportunity to catch up on some administrative work, and since she couldn't connect to the office network from here, she wouldn't have email or the Internet to distract her.

She looked at her watch and saw it was now almost 9:00. The cafe down the street was beckoning to her with its promise of a double latte. She would give her vigil another half hour and then she would take a break and surrender to caffeine's sweet siren song.

She reached into her purse, remembering that she hadn't taken her daily dose of blood pressure and cholesterol-lowering medications. She hoped they were working, but all she'd noticed so far was that she had to pee more often and had an unsettled stomach. She had already taken her antidepressant before she'd left home and that didn't seem to be doing anything other than making her more tense and keeping her up at night. Or maybe that was all the caffeine she was ingesting during the day to stay awake due to the sleepless nights. It was hard to tell. Her shrink had increased her dosage, but he had seemed overly cautious, not wanting to raise her to the maximum dose. Perhaps she'd start double dosing and see what kind of effect it had. Fortunately, she had insisted on the antidepressant with the least sexual side effects, so she wouldn't have a forced abstinence. Now that would truly be depressing, she thought.

At 9:25, she was just getting ready to head to the cafe when a white truck passed by and parked on the other side of the street near the gym. She saw Brett get out of the driver's side and Edison from the other side. "Well, well," she said, beaming with pleasure, "the early bird really does catch the worm." She noted with approval that Brett drove an F-150, which solidified for her that he was an all-American red-blooded male. She could already picture her father's nod of approval when he saw her and Brett drive up the lane in the F-150 to her childhood home.

Brett and Edison had both come to the gym dressed to work out, wearing T-shirts and shorts, but even from this distance she could see that Edison's clothes looked new and fit well, whereas Brett's outfit seemed like it had seen one too many workouts.

She kept an eye on them until they went up the staircase to the gym and disappeared inside.

She popped open her compact and saw her face was flawless. Earlier, she had thought she was looking a little ashen—probably due to her lack of sleep—but it was nothing that a little concealer hadn't remedied, giving her that morning glow she used to have naturally. She had worn her lucky sports bra as well as a new pair of spandex pants. She had capped off her ensemble with a dab of her good perfume. She gave them ten minutes and then headed toward the gym.

Checking in at the front desk, she hardly acknowledged the uppity-looking college-aged girl who was folding towels while chatting on a cell phone. As a rule, she despised the younger generation of women—at least the attractive ones—since she saw them as competition and a sad reminder that she didn't have forever to snag her white knight. She grabbed a towel and headed directly to the main part of the gym.

The main room was smallish, just as she remembered it, and because the ground floor was partially below street level, the gym had the feel of a basement weight room. It was definitely a far cry from her gym, she thought, with its floor to ceiling windows providing stunning views of Elliot Bay.

She immediately spied Brett and Edison at the far side of the room, standing in front of the mirrors in the free weight area. Edison was doing barbell curls and Brett was doing shoulder shrugs nearby. Seeing the two of them together, she was able to size them up in a way she hadn't been able to do during the tour of Edison's house. She would have described both men as tall, dark and handsome; although Brett's hair was a lighter shade of brown and he looked to be an inch or two taller than Edison. Both men had broad shoulders and V-shaped torsos. Edison had a deliciously perky ass, and while Brett's may have been nice, it was lost in his oversized cotton basketball shorts. Couldn't go wrong with either, she thought, and she would happily sample both.

Looking around the gym, she saw at most a half dozen other people. They were mainly using the resistance machines and one plump middle-aged woman appeared to be riding a stationary bicycle in slow motion. Certainly more of a homespun crowd here, she thought, as she approached Brett and Edison, but before she could say anything, Brett caught sight of her reflection in the mirror and turned to face her.

"Hey. Ms. Cahill, right?"

"Well hello, Brett. Hello, Edison," she said waving to Edison's reflection and attempting to look surprised. "Fancy meeting you two here. And please call me Cherie."

Edison put down his barbell, turned around to face her and nodded.

"You two are here bright and early for a Saturday."

"Yep. As are you," said Brett.

"Well, I just signed up for a trial membership yesterday and I wanted to beat the Saturday morning rush." She pulled her gaze from Brett and turned to Edison. "You must be blasting those big arms today."

"Yeah, it's an arm day," Edison said with a nod.

"Did you find the paperwork I left in your door yesterday?"

"Yes, I got it. Thank you."

"Do you have any questions?" she asked hopefully.

"No, not right now. I've only had a chance to skim it."

"Well, just let me know if I can be of any help. I included all the necessary forms in the packet, so if you do decide to move forward with this it's just a matter of a few signatures and then we can be on our way to selling your house."

"Okay. I'll get back to you once I'm able to take a closer look."

"Wunderbar! You have all my numbers and email. Just keep me posted and do not hesitate to call me day or night with any questions."

"Thanks."

She noticed him look to his barbell distractedly. "Well, I

don't mean to interrupt you boys, so I'll let you get back to your workout and I'll start mine before my coffee craving gets the better of me."

She moved to a spot very near them and warmed up with some stretching, making sure she bent forward to give them a clear shot of her cleavage. She didn't forget about showing off her own perky ass and spent quite a while doing standing toe stretches. She couldn't help but notice the heavy weights they were hoisting, as there was nothing like strong men lifting weights to get her hot and bothered. She appreciated that they were both relatively silent in their exertions, not making the loud macho grunts the meatheads made.

She noted that the married one stole occasional glances at her and even smiled appreciatively once or twice. Edison, on the other hand, seemed completely focused on his workout and she had even sensed some annoyance in his expression the one time he had looked her way. The strong and silent type had always puzzled her. There was a certain standoffish quality about Edison and she realized that high-pressure tactics would only drive him away. Perhaps he was one of those pretty boys who was used to playing hard to get because it had always served him well. She could play his game and one up him. Better to entice him from afar, than to force herself upon him.

She had just started doing her forward lunges with the five-pound dumbbells—one of her favorite exercises for firming her buttocks—when she heard Edison tell Brett that he was going upstairs to do some cardio. When Brett asked him if he was going to finish his weight routine, he said he couldn't get into it today. Brett said he would finish downstairs and then join him. Cherie watched Edison climb the stairs and it wasn't lost on her that he never acknowledged her with a goodbye. Perhaps she could find out more information from his friend, she thought, who seemed much more receptive to her flirtations.

"Did your workout partner abandon you?" she asked, placing her dumbbells back on the rack.

"Yeah, he went up to do some cardio."

"Well, I hope I didn't scare him away."

"No, I think the force just isn't with him today."

"Hmm, he sure seems like a real athlete. Both of you do."

"Well, thanks. Edison's in great shape and I do my best to keep up with him."

She noticed he was perspiring now and that his roomy shirt was clinging to him, and she could see his muscular chest pressing against the fabric.

"Modesty, I like that in a man. So tell me, which one of you handsome guys is available?" she asked, choosing to ignore his wedding ring which was clearly visible.

He chuckled and wiped some of the perspiration off his upper lip. "Well, I'm married and I don't think Edison is really looking right now."

"That's a shame on both counts. I can imagine it must be a difficult time for him. Still, I'm surprised some lucky woman hasn't lassoed him up."

"Well, I don't think Edison is looking to be lassoed by Wonder Woman. I think Batman or Superman are more his type."

"Huh? No! You're kidding? Edison is a …?" She covered her mouth with her hand, not finishing the sentence.

"He's gay. What's the big deal?"

"I just never in a million years would have thought he was that way."

"Well, now you know."

"But the more I think about it, it makes perfect sense and explains why …" she let her words trail off, realizing it would be tacky to say that it explains why he hadn't shown any interest in her.

"Explains what?"

"Oh, explains why such a hunk is still single. Plus the gays are always in such good shape; it's almost a telltale sign these days."

"Well, I don't think gay men have a monopoly on fitness."

"Oh, I didn't mean to imply that. You're fit and I certainly don't get a gay vibe from you."

Brett laughed, "So how did you sense that I'm not gay?"

"Oh, let's just say it's a woman's intuition." She brushed her hand slowly and sensuously through her hair, having been told on more than one occasion by a man that it drove him crazy with desire.

"So what else does your intuition tell you?" He looked at her with such intensity, almost a hunger, that it caught her off guard.

"How about we grab some coffee this week and I'll tell you then?"

"Uh, I'm not sure I can make it ...."

"Think about it. It's just coffee. Here's my card." She pulled out a card from her sleek side pocket and placed it in his hand. "It could be fun," she added, adjusting the strap on her sports bra.

"Thanks, I'll see what my schedule's like," he said, taking an obvious visual survey of her breasts.

"Well, I best be going. It's almost time for the spin class I want to try. I certainly enjoyed chatting with you."

"Likewise."

"And remember, a little coffee never hurt anyone." She flashed him one of her winning smiles, leaving him standing there to stare after her.

As she climbed the staircase to the third floor, she felt pleased with how she had played her hand. She obviously had to change her strategy with Edison, now that she knew he was a big fruit, but his hunky neighbor had already proven useful. Not only could he help her with Edison, she also felt there was something special about him. There was no mistaking the volcano of passion simmering just beneath his calm exterior, but at least he was a gentleman, so unlike the swine she usually attracted. Maybe, just maybe, he was the one she'd been waiting for all this time.

Unlike other woman, she didn't see a wedding ring as a deal breaker, just an obstacle. While she applauded traditional families and respected the sanctity of marriage, she only cared about the sanctity of her own eventual marriage. She would definitely make it a point to check out her competition and to see if there were any kids in the picture, as she hated complications. She'd Google him when she got home, and if she couldn't find out anything, she'd go on night watch of his house.

She would also seek counsel from her friend at the church, Janet. Of course, she would leave out all the sexual stuff. Her sex life was her business and she kept it private from Janet and her other church friends. She had known from an early age that her needs were strong, but she was certainly no whore. Her brothers had pretty much been expected to have sex before marriage so she never saw why she should have to wait. Having been the only girl, she did the traditional household chores plus the same chores her brothers had done. So, despite her parents' constant admonitions, she had felt entitled to the same privileges that her brothers enjoyed.

She knew she was a good Christian woman and would settle down once she met the right man, but until then, she wasn't going to cloak herself in some self-imposed prison akin to a nun's habit or one of those burqas that were so popular with Muslim women. No, she would enjoy the body with which God had blessed her.

As she reached the third floor landing, a vision came to her that put a smile on her face. She saw her wedding announcement with a stunning picture of the two of them as it would run in *The Seattle Times*: *Ms. Cherie Cahill of Yakima, WA, a successful Seattle realtor, to wed Mr. Brett Gale of Seattle's Queen Anne Hill.* She wondered if her vision was a sign of what was to be, since she knew she could finally settle down and be happy with a man like Brett Gale. And, as for her wedding gown, she would just tell her mother that ivory was the new white.

FIFTEEN

Hookups in Seattle were rare for David. He liked to engage his man to man side in San Francisco or New York, far from his wife and friends who might spot him with a man whose relation he couldn't readily explain. The guy he was about to meet was worth the risk, though. He knew people who lived on Queen Anne, but locals rarely went to the Kerry Park overlook. If they did see him, he could treat this guy like someone he happened upon in the park rather than a gay rendezvous. He didn't have Edison's last name or he would have used his legal databases to research him. The fact that he owned his own home on Queen Anne's expensive southwest slope was intriguing. David wanted a man who was a take-charge kind of guy in the boardroom as well as the bedroom. The picture in his profile had been interesting, a clear shot of a handsome all-American man with the suggestion of an excellent body underneath his clothes. David could respect that Edison didn't put an overtly sexual photo in his profile, but he would have enjoyed seeing all of him. Who knows, with his lucky jeans on, perhaps he would this afternoon.

David turned his car onto Queen Anne Avenue and came to a stop at the red light at the foot of the hill. This guy was worth the risk, he assured himself. He didn't look gay either so he probably was in the closet too. The good guys always are, he thought, as he checked his reflection in the rearview mirror.

Turning back to the street, he eyed the massive hill that lay before him with only the light holding him back from flooring his Mercedes Kompressor convertible. His thoughts turned dark as a man in his forties jogged by looking half his age, though betrayed by a shock of gray hair and a wife who had certainly seen her day in the sun. The man looked like a graying version of Rick, his former San Francisco treat. Rick had gone too far that night at the gym and David was wondering if he had gone too far in teaching Rick a lesson. People like Rick needed to know their place, though, and Rick had crossed the line. David smiled thinking of the tears and gnashing of teeth that must have gone down in Fag Town.

It had been easy. As easy as sliding up Queen Anne Hill in a fine piece of German engineering as he was now doing. He knew enough about Rick's history to set a few demons loose in his personal life. A law school friend who was continually short on both cash and scruples had been happy to call Rick's home midday and leave two carefully worded messages. And given Rick's schedule, it was a good bet that his precious Bobby was home before him to hear the messages first. One was in reference to Rick's old passion for cocaine and the other was a follow-up that mentioned a certain preference Rick had when in bed and a unique attribute that David had fondly remembered about Rick's private parts. The two calls had cost $600 and the coup was that the caller had left a number that would match the caller ID. If either of them called back, David would be alerted, and there was $500 waiting for the holder of the disposable phone to answer in the role of the jilted syphilitic lover and cokehead.

A quick left on West Highland Drive and he was nearly there. He pulled over a block from the park, just past the Ballard Mansion, so he could see who was around and could bail if Edison didn't live up to his online picture. He thought he saw Edison from nearly a block away. He was by himself, leaning on the rail of the overlook, keeping his distance from the large wedding party at the center of the small park. The young couple's smiles were nearly contagious and the photographer was moving them like pawns to take advantage of the Seattle skyline, Mt. Rainier and the islands of Puget Sound in the background.

David doubted they could afford their wedding finery judging from the aged Honda with "Just Married" soaped on the back window.

The irony wasn't lost on him that the last time he had been to this park was for his own wedding pictures. His wife's family wanted pictures and they had the money to demand whatever they wanted. His family, especially his mother, had engaged in a prolonged whispered discussion over why David hadn't found a nice white girl instead of Miyuki, who they had deemed an "exotic."

Miyuki and he had worked out a functional marriage and he did like her steady hand when it came to entertaining and presenting a united front. She also kept a flawless home and a respectable social standing. In turn, David kept up appearances and each month her accounts were flush with cash from a partial transfer of his paycheck. He had no idea if she was saving or spending and she never questioned his hours, travel or finances. If he had to be married, it couldn't have been a better arrangement.

He checked his appearance in the rearview mirror again and turned the car off. Still got it, he thought as he slipped on his favorite Abercrombie & Fitch baseball hat. He hadn't embraced his thinning hair and didn't think that Edison needed to see this aspect just yet. As he had promised Edison in their IM exchange, he was wearing his tightest jeans from Kenneth Cole, and since he was casual, he added his white gym shoes and a short-sleeved shirt. He had stretched the shirt a bit since it had shrunk some and seemed reluctant to meet his belt. "If you've got it, flaunt it," he told himself.

Out of the car, he turned and locked it with the remote. It seemed silly to lock his convertible with the top down, but he did. Putting up the top would spoil the effect and he wanted to impress Edison—especially if they went back to his place for some action. David's spirits soared as he crossed the street and focused on Edison's frame. From the back, he could detect broad shoulders and a well-defined V, ending at what appeared to be a firm ass supported by tan and muscular legs. He liked that he could take this all in as Edison obliviously stared out over the rail at Elliot Bay.

David coughed as he neared Edison and Edison turned to him and stared through him briefly before focusing on him.

David smiled and extended his hand, "Edison, I presume," he said, taking in Edison's appearance. Just what the doctor ordered, he thought. Edison's loose curly brown hair caught the wind and complemented his brown eyes and handsome tan face. He had a unique and intelligent look, and judging from his chest and arms, was in great shape. This wasn't going to be a waste of his time, he concluded.

"Nice to meet you," Edison said, not carrying the conversation forward.

David wondered if he was just shy or maybe not as bright as he looked. "Nice park and the best Seattle view too."

"It is a nice park. Have you been here before?" Edison said slowly.

"Yeah, I'm local or nearly local, grew up on the Eastside. Been to a few weddings up here too," David said, gesturing to the young couple posing for their pictures. He stroked his left hand with his right to check again if he had left his wedding band in the glove compartment. "So, do you live near here, Edison?"

"Yes, I do. I live about eight blocks from here. I walked, in fact."

"It is a nice day. I'm over in Medina, myself," he lied. I had the top down on my Mercedes all the way over, and the way that car moves, I'm surprised I didn't get a ticket."

Again, Edison pulled the conversation down with a death-like pause.

"Looks like you work out too," David said as he lightly clamped his hand over Edison's bicep.

"I get to the gym regularly," Edison said. "I think keeping fit is important."

"Dude, so do I. So many guys let themselves go," he said,

pulling at the hem of his shirt. "It looks like you press a lot of weight, but do you do cardio? I'm a running fiend myself." He had been at one time, he thought.

Again, Edison paused and David thought he must be a mix: a little slow and a little shy. No matter, he needed a *man*, and if this guy had the assets under the hood, then it didn't matter if he was slow. David could do the thinking for both of them.

"I run about three miles a day, five days a week. Tend to run with my neighbor up here to keep an honest pace."

"Sure you're not just trailing him to watch his ass?" David teased. "But seriously, I run about the same amount as you," he lied again. "How many calories do you take in?" David quickly looked down at his shirt. Edison seemed to be staring at either his belt or lower shirt, and, for a minute, David was fearful that he had a stain from the burger he had eaten in the car earlier. Perhaps he was checking out his package. Subtle but provocative. With that, he paid Edison's shorts a heavy glance.

"Oh, I'm not much of a calorie counter," Edison said. "I try to eat organic every chance I get and make sure I stay active. I never seem to gain much weight, but I'm always eating."

"Buddy, you have to count calories if you are serious and want to make it to the next level. It's all about the numbers."

"Oh, really." A smile finally spread across Edison's lips and David was impressed at how it lit up his face. "So, how many do you intake each day?" Edison asked.

David was happy that Edison was taking his counsel on matters both dietary and physical. "Listen, chief, it's not about me, it all comes down to calories consumed versus calories burned." With that, David went into his five-minute summary of how he kept his body in top form. Edison must have been impressed as he nodded and listened, only occasionally checking out his package. David concluded with a conciliatory note about how he believed in Saturday being a "sin" day for calories. It was his impromptu segue to suggesting a beer or two with Edison in a more private setting.

"In fact," David said, "if you like, we can swing by Trader

Joe's and pick up a six-pack and head back to your place. I'd suggest my place except the repairman is working on the Jacuzzi and the water is off on the whole property." A small lie, he thought. The technician would be there Monday to install the new Jacuzzi.

"Oh, my place is a mess right now. I should get a maid or spend more time at home, I guess."

"So, how often are you in San Francisco?" David asked, trying to make eye contact with Edison, who seemed to be focusing more on the wedding party behind him than on the stud in front of him.

"Oh, about one week per month."

"We should hook up down there, man! I'd like to hang with a Seattle dude and chill. I don't like the fags down in San Fran," David said enthusiastically, thinking it would be cool to have a sex buddy down in SF.

Again, David thought Edison was either checking out his package or his shoes. David was getting frustrated with the halting pauses from Edison's side of the conversation and he was becoming convinced that Edison might be one of God's special little people.

Suddenly, to David's surprise, Edison cleared his throat and spoke directly. "Well, it was nice meeting you. I think that wedding party is waiting for us to leave so they can get a photo with the cruise ships in the background."

"Dude, sorry we can't hang for a beer. I'll email you so we can hang out next week and maybe try out the Jacuzzi. It will be a blast, just us dudes so no need for trunks unless you want to be the only one." David gave Edison his best devilish smile.

"Yeah, next time. Again, it was nice meeting you."

David instinctively offered his hand for Edison to shake. The awkward gesture harkened from his corporate life and came across as affected in David's mind given the informal setting. Edison did shake his hand and David decided that he liked Edison well enough to give him a quick hug so he could feel the meat under Edison's shirt. Edison startled and stiffened during the brief embrace and David decided he was more shy than stupid.

"Dude, I'll email you this week, for sure."

With that, he turned and left. He didn't look back so as not to spoil the view of his backside for Edison. Once at his car, he turned back to wave, so Edison would know the sleek convertible Mercedes was indeed his, but Edison was nowhere in sight.

SIXTEEN

Edison stepped out of the shower, feeling invigorated. Brett had phoned earlier in the morning, on his way to the gym, but even with Brett's prodding, he had decided to sleep in, choosing to ignore Brett's somewhat disturbing accusation of him pulling a "lazy Linda." Even so, the day was young, being scarcely nine o'clock, and it looked as if it would be a beauty. What a difference a good night's sleep could make to one's outlook, he reflected.

Yesterday afternoon, after meeting Allen at Kerry Park, he'd felt blue, but even then, he had realized he wasn't truly depressed. He was disgusted by AllenRunnerJock and felt foolish for even meeting him. When Allen had first approached him, he had assumed he was a lost tourist since the man had looked nothing like his physical description. He was certain Allen was several years older than the 37 he had claimed. Worse yet, he had tried to pull off wearing a tight Abercrombie & Fitch Swim Team shirt and his form-fitting jeans had certainly left nothing to the imagination. He had been speechless for most of the meeting, appalled yet oddly fascinated by Allen's stomach that was protruding from his shirt.

Clearly, Allen was neither a runner nor a jock. For all he knew, his name wasn't even Allen. Why the hell someone would blatantly lie about his physical traits when the whole purpose was to meet the other person was beyond him.

The physical part hadn't been the worst of it. Allen had repeatedly used the word "dude" to address him—a word he found wrong in so many ways unless uttered by a surfer or at least by someone under 25. Allen had also asked him about the details of his workout and diet and then had the audacity to dismiss his regimen. Allen then proceeded to tell him what he should do to attain the *next level* of fitness. Edison felt that if someone was going to act as an authority, he should have the goods to back it up. He had encountered Allen's type before and guessed that for all his macho posing, his heels would be tangled in the track lighting in no time. He hoped Allen would not make good on his promise to email him. Oh well, he thought, if anything, it was a reminder that there were worse things than being single.

He finished drying off and wrapped the towel around his waist. After crossing the hallway to his bedroom, he pulled out a pair of briefs from the chest of drawers. He set his underwear down on the desk and reached to close the curtains when he noticed a black Audi sedan parked on the street in front of the house. He could see a man sitting in the driver's seat who appeared to be older, judging by his white hair. The man was gazing up at the house and was writing on a pad of paper. Edison continued to watch him until the man looked up directly at him. The man held his gaze for a second, and then put down his writing pad and hastily drove off.

"What in the hell was that about?" Edison wondered aloud. "Another damn reporter?" He drew the curtains shut and dropped his bath towel to the floor. He had one leg in his underwear when he heard the floor creak behind him. He turned around, startled at seeing what appeared to be one of the undead standing at his bedroom door, and let out an involuntary cry. For a moment, he believed all the talk about the Reaping Widow was true. Then he recognized the corpse standing in front of him, holding a tumbler of scotch as Lily Ling. After the immediate shock subsided, he scrambled to get the towel from the floor to cover himself up.

"You're no Brett and you might want to lose that girlish scream," Lily said, visually appraising him as if he were for sale.

"Mrs. Ling! What are you doing here?!" He could see why he had mistaken her for a corpse as her pale skin made a stark contrast to her heavy rouge and lipstick. Her rail-thin body was draped in a silky black robe decorated with a ghostly butterfly print.

"We need to talk. Pull yourself together and meet me in the kitchen."

She left the room, not waiting for his response. As his heartbeat settled back to normal, a rush of rage swept through him. Why the hell did she think she could enter the house at will? He determined he would no longer put up with her eccentricities and would demand she return the key to the house.

He threw on a shirt and a pair of khaki shorts, still feeling naked; nonetheless, he tried to muster some dignity as he descended the back staircase. He entered the kitchen to see her already seated at the table, petting a contented-looking Stella on her lap. Traitor, he thought, glaring at Stella.

"Lily, you cannot just barge in here …."

"Please call me Mrs. Ling."

"Well, *Mrs. Ling*, I would offer you something, but I see you've already helped yourself," he said, eyeing the tumbler of scotch in front of her on the table.

"Yes, the hospitality around here isn't what it used to be." She took a large sip of her scotch, eyeing him reproachfully.

"Mrs. Ling. As I was saying …."

"Your parents' things," she interrupted. "What have you done with them?"

"What things?"

"Your father's wood carvings and several of your mother's macramé pieces are missing. Where are they?" Both she and Stella were looking at him intently.

"I put them away. Stored them in the basement," he said, suddenly feeling like a child being accused of some misdeed.

"Why did you do that?"

"Because the realtor suggested it."

"Realtor? What realtor?"

"Well, not that it's any of your business, but I met with a realtor to discuss selling the house."

"You mean that blonde bitch who's constantly prowling the street in that monster SUV and snooping around your property?"

"Snooping around my property?"

"I see her all the time. Sometimes she's with other people."

"Well, I hadn't realized she's been around here so much, but, yes, that sounds like her."

"You know your parents weren't renovating this house just for themselves. They were doing it with you in mind."

"I know they put a tremendous amount of work into the place, but I'm not sure it had anything to do with me."

"They meant for you to have this house. It just happened much earlier than they planned." Her eyes became glassy and she pulled out a linen handkerchief from the pocket of her robe, gently wiping her eyes. She then blew her nose, making a honking sound that startled Stella. She folded the handkerchief and put it back into her pocket.

"Is that what they told you?" he asked. "That they purchased this house for me?"

"Sometimes these things don't need to be spoken."

"And sometimes it's a helluva lot clearer if they are. For instance, I don't appreciate you entering the house at will. It is not acceptable."

She stared at him across the table, looking as cold and brittle as a porcelain figurine, causing him to feel momentarily unnerved.

"I expect you to put your parents' personal effects back as you found them. And don't think I haven't noticed that you've moved the furniture around too."

"I've rearranged a few things, but I don't see how any of this is your concern."

"This isn't about me. This is about your parents. They loved you very much. Don't disappoint them."

"Disappoint them? How?"

"Don't get me riled, young man. Just put it all back the way it was. I don't have time for this. My daughter scheduled a mother/daughter makeover at the spa this morning, so I have enough crap to deal with today." She picked up her glass of scotch and finished it in one large gulp. She then lifted Stella from her lap and placed him gently on the floor. She was up from the chair and out of the kitchen before he could say anything, moving surprisingly fast for her frail appearance, her patterned robe making it appear like a flock of phantom butterflies were following her.

Edison followed Lily to the front door, which she had left open. He stepped out onto the porch and scanned the street to see if there was any sign of the black Audi from earlier, but he didn't see it. He stood there for a few moments, enjoying the calm, until he caught sight of a large blue truck that was moving slowly down the street. To his surprise, it turned into his driveway. Three men were squeezed into the cab of the truck and he saw white lettering on the side, but he couldn't make out the words.

The men got out of the truck and the driver, a sunburnt, middle-aged man, waved to Edison as he approached him. "Hello, are you Mr. Archer?"

"Yes."

"I'm Mike Wilcox of M & P Landscaping," he said extending his hand. "We're here to work on your lawn."

Edison shook his hand tentatively, watching as the two other men, both much younger, began to unload equipment from the back of the truck.

"Uh, I think there must be a mistake. I didn't request a landscaping service."

"Nope, there's no mistake. Everything has already been arranged and paid for, compliments of Ms. Cahill."

"Ms. Cahill?"

"Yes, of Amstead Reality. She insisted we get the job done ASAP. We usually don't work on Sundays, but it was the only way we could fit you in. I hope we aren't disturbing you."

"No, it's not a problem. I'm just a little surprised since she didn't mention any of this to me."

"There's no need to be alarmed. We're not making any major changes, just the basics: mowing the lawn, trimming the hedges, putting some seasonals in the flower beds."

Edison considered protesting, but the guy seemed friendly and he had obviously planned his day around this, so he just decided to roll with it.

"Okay, well thank you. Do you need anything from me?"

"Nope. Ms. Cahill already showed us exactly what she wants done. We have everything we need."

"Great," he said, wondering when this had taken place. "I'll be inside if you need anything."

"Allrightee then."

"Thanks again," he said, before entering the house.

Mike went off to join his crew and Edison went back inside, feeling like a pushover now for letting that brazen Barbie doll bulldoze her way into the sale. On the surface, it seemed like a nice gesture, but he was certain her motivation had nothing to do with kindness. He had yet to make up his mind about selling the house and certainly didn't want to feel any obligation to that realtor raptor. He realized that the landscaping needed to be done, regardless, and he supposed he could always reimburse her.

He closed the front door to block out the noise of the lawnmower that one of the landscapers had started. "Boy," he said aloud, peering out the rectangular glass pane at the top of the front door, trying to get a better look at the two younger workers. He then turned to the bowl of paper hens. "It's just a never-ending freak show around here, isn't it?" he said, addressing the hens. They seemed to eye him warily from the safety of their bowl. He noticed that someone had arranged them in a repeating pattern of colors, white, pink, green, red, etc. "Why can't people just mind their own business?" he asked the hens as he inspected the pattern. "Don't people respect boundaries here in

Mayberry? This is my house after all. Yes, *my* house," he repeated aloud, more confidently this time. The paper hens appeared unimpressed, but Edison felt better for having said it. He turned the deadbolt lock on the door, hoping no one had a copy of that key, and went back up the stairs to have another try at his day.

SEVENTEEN

God, this meeting is a real loser, Cherie thought, as she tried to feign interest in Marjorie Jansen's overblown interpretation of the assigned reading. Marjorie looked so smug, sitting there in her neat floral print dress, whose pattern reminded Cherie of a set of sheets she'd had during her college years. She couldn't fathom how Marjorie's husband and children put up with her 24x7. She wanted to take an axe to her head after only a few minutes of her blathering.

The Sunday evening Ladies' Auxiliary meeting was a weekly event Cherie didn't look forward to, but the contacts it had provided her were priceless. Cherie had always been active in the church from the time she was a little girl. Growing up in Yakima, she had sometimes resented her parents' churchgoing ways, but as she grew older, she found a certain comfort in the extended family the church provided. Their views of the world were similar to her own and there was a sense of community that came with being part of this close-knit group. It was only after she moved to Seattle, and got a whiff of the godlessness and unchecked liberalism that she truly realized the value of her church community in Yakima. One of the first things she did upon arriving in Seattle was to find a suitable church.

Not only did she find a church but she had also become quite active in it, singing in the choir, participating in various social events and charities, and helping with the production of the church newsletter. She had undeniably benefited by advertising her realty services in the monthly newsletter, having received many clients and referrals from her fellow parishioners, and she offered them a nominal discount in return.

The Ladies' Auxiliary, however, was where the real connections were made, and when she had been nominated to be the group's treasurer, she had thought it quite the coup. This was why she reserved 90 minutes out of her schedule every Sunday evening to sit in the dank church basement. The bad coffee, uncomfortable folding chairs and this evening's overdone interpretations of predictable Christian fiction certainly made her feel like she was earning the many referrals she got from this circle. One time, she had proposed that their group read the current Oprah's Book Club selection, but some members had objected to it as being too racy so she had dropped her motion.

The Ladies' Auxiliary was far more than a prissy little book club, though. When disasters struck, whether it be a local fire or distant earthquake, the group had held many a fundraiser for the victims. As a good Christian woman, she had done her part for the big Indonesian earthquake relief. Privately, though, she believed these disasters were God's way of decreasing the population and he showed his wisdom by frequently striking crowded third world countries.

She believed that everything happened for a reason and took comfort in this. Just like last December when a nail pierced one of her tires and she ended up replacing all four, two days before a rare Seattle ice storm. She thought that perhaps the nail had been God's way of keeping her safe.

As Marjorie Jansen continued to prattle on, Janet shot Cherie a knowing smile and wink. Janet was President of the Ladies' Auxiliary and someone who Cherie admired for her wise counsel and devout lifestyle. Janet had been one of the first people Cherie had met upon moving to Seattle and she had quickly taken the role of the big sister Cherie never had. Janet had an easy smile and warmth about her that came from a big heart that rivaled her monstrous hips. Like Cherie, Janet was single, though she was a good ten years older and not looking for a husband. She often proclaimed that she was married to the church and that being a pastor would have been her true calling if their church had allowed women in the clergy or if she had been born a man.

Janet followed a rigid Bible-based diet, yet she was a large woman who had oily skin and looked like the kind of person one often sees eating in fast food restaurants—not in the commercials—but in real life. Janet would jokingly lament that she had *big-boned genes*, saying that be it high carb, low carb, or no carb, she was meant to be large. Cherie didn't fault her for her lackluster looks, and had even grown to find them somewhat endearing. She rather enjoyed having a female friend with whom she didn't have to compete, as she was unquestionably the pretty and young one in their unlikely dyad and Janet was always ready with a compliment to help puff up Cherie's ego.

At 8:25, Janet cleared her throat and said they needed to wrap up the meeting, putting an end to Marjorie's exercise in pretentiousness. Usually, Cherie would rush back to her condo to catch her favorite Sunday night soap opera, but summer re-runs were in full swing, and sometimes real life affairs took precedence over the ones on the screen. Tonight, she needed Janet's guidance on what she hoped would be a torrid and lasting affair. She had told Janet that she wanted to chat with her after the meeting, and when the other ladies left, she and Janet cleared away the remaining refreshments.

"These are the most unnatural things ever made," Janet said, staring disapprovingly at the plate of Oreo cookie knock-offs that the church bought in bulk as an all-purpose treat. "Sure, they look tempting, but these things will kill you."

"You mean generic cream-filled cookies aren't allowed on your diet?" Cherie teased.

"No ma'am. I've tried to get Pastor Wilkinson to switch over to something more natural. I've told him what the creator of the diet I'm on always cautions: that a polluted body equals a polluted soul, but he didn't seem too interested. I think he has a weakness for all this sweet crap himself," she whispered.

"Not everyone has your willpower, Janet."

"Well, I try. And I guess that's all one can do. I'm not advocating no sweets. I have a sweet tooth myself, but snack on honey or fruit, for heaven's sake. The Lord provided us with ample sweets. You see me with my bag of dried fruit that I eat during the meeting. It's so I won't be tempted by these devil cookies."

Cherie nodded in agreement, painfully familiar with Janet's fondness for proselytizing on all matters dietary. Best to let her have her say, she thought, before switching topics.

"I hope you're still not living on sugar and caffeine. You have such a pretty figure, but remember you need to eat real food. You don't want those yeasties to come back, do you?"

"No, I've been eating better, *mom.*"

"Good, that's what I like to hear," Janet said, gently rubbing Cherie's shoulder. "Now what did you want to talk about, sweetie? When you pulled me aside earlier, it sounded important."

"Well, how should I begin?" Cherie said, sliding a neat stack of unused Styrofoam cups next to the coffeemaker. "I'll just say it straight out. I've met a man who seems very special and I believe he feels the same about me. The only problem is he's married, although I don't think he's happy."

"Who is this man? How did you meet him?" Janet asked, looking like a mother hen seeing one of her chicks go astray.

"He's a friend of one of my clients. We keep on bumping into each other, almost as if it were God's will, and each time he makes his interest in me known. Is it un-Christian of me to accept his invitation to meet for coffee?"

"And you say he's currently married?"

"Yes, but he doesn't have children. I think he married young and now feels trapped in a loveless marriage."

"Ha. Is that what he told you?"

"Not in so many words, but he's hinted at it."

"Well, honey, this is an easy one. As long as he's married, there is nothing for you to do. No good will come of it."

"But would it hurt to meet him for coffee just to find out what his story is?"

"Are you sure this is just about coffee, hon? If this guy is planning on being unfaithful to his wife, he certainly won't be any better to you."

"Janet, you know I normally would never consider doing something like this, but there's something special about him."

"Honey, you're a grown woman and capable of making your own choices, I just don't want to see you get hurt. You're too good a person and you've taken such bold steps these last few years. You graduated from our Virgin Renewal Program, for one. I don't want you to throw away your newfound purity on some man—especially a married one."

"I don't want to throw that all away. There's nothing more important to me than my secondhand virginity and I promise you that I'm committed to celibacy until I marry. But, as a good Christian, shouldn't I at least give him the benefit of the doubt?"

"Well, maybe you're a better Christian than me, dear, because I would never give a cheating low-life man the benefit of the doubt."

"Oh, Janet," Cherie sighed. "He seems nice, and meeting for coffee is innocent enough."

"Look at me, darling," Janet said, grabbing Cherie by the shoulders. "Be honest with me. What do you want out of this?"

"I just want to know how he feels about me."

"So what if he makes the moves on you, then what?"

"I don't know. I haven't thought that far ahead, but I feel that if I don't do this, I'll always regret not finding out. Wouldn't it be wrong to shun someone who's reaching out to me? Maybe I can set him on the straight and narrow."

Janet looked Cherie in the eyes and slowly a tender smile returned to her face. "I can see you're sincere, sugar snap, and if you really need to do this then go ahead. But just make certain he doesn't reach out and touch that candy apple tush of yours," she smiled, giving Cherie's rump a playful squeeze.

"Oh, stop, you silly girl," Cherie said, pulling away in laughter. "So I have your blessing, then?"

"Yes, but don't give into temptation, no matter how much he sweet talks you."

"I won't. Thank you, Janet. You don't know how much I value your guidance."

"You're welcome, my child. Now come here and give me a big hug."

Cherie hugged her, feeling the familiar comfort of Janet's large fleshy arms around her, gently massaging her backside. She felt relieved at getting Janet's blessing, but already she was imagining that big muscleman Brett having his way with her, reminding her that there was more than one path to heavenly bliss.

EIGHTEEN

Brett stepped off the 2 Express bus, glad to be back on the leafy streets of Queen Anne after being in stagnant air-conditioning all day. He took the express bus to work on days when he knew he wouldn't have to travel offsite, to save unnecessary wear on his truck. The bus reminded him of his yuppie days in San Francisco when he took the crowded 1 California bus to the Financial District.

As an electrical engineer specializing in skyscrapers, he designed the electrical systems for buildings the firm constructed all over the world. Although his firm was a French multinational, his current project was much closer to home. He was drawing up the plans for a proposed skyscraper that would adorn the downtown Seattle skyline within a few years. Once built, it would be the tallest building on the West Coast and a jewel in Seattle's emerald crown.

As he reached the sidewalk in front of his house, he saw the familiar blond- and brown-haired compatriots, Justin and Brian, riding toward him on their bicycles and he waved to them.

"Hi, Mr. Gale," they said, stopping in front of him.

"Hey guys. What are you up to today?"

"Not much," Brian, the shorter, brown-haired boy said. "Just getting some food. Mom came home from work in one of her moods so dinner will be late."

"Well, I wouldn't be too hard on your mom. Moms are busy people. You're old enough to make something for yourself, aren't you?"

"There's nothing good in the house."

"I told you, you can eat at my house," chirped in Justin, the slightly older and more confident-looking boy. "We're having pork chops tonight."

"Well, okay, but I'd rather get a hot dog and nachos at 7-Eleven."

"Whatever," Justin said, looking at his friend dismissively. He turned toward Brett. "Last Sunday was a blast, Mr. Gale. Can we go with you around Blake Island again sometime?"

"Sure, as long as it's okay with your parents."

"Will Mr. Archer be there too?" asked Brian. "He said he would teach us how to cannon ball."

"He did? Well, I'll be sure to invite him."

"If we go on a Sunday, can we leave early and miss church?" asked Justin, looking as if he were trying to suppress a smile.

"I think that can be arranged," Brett grinned, remembering his own childhood aversion to Sunday service back in rural Wisconsin.

"Yes!" Justin exclaimed, raising his hand and giving a high-five to Brian. "I wish my dad did fun things like you and Mr. Archer."

"Well, he's probably tired after putting in a long day at the office," Brett offered, not feeling the need to condemn the father.

"But, I mean, he never plays basketball with us or works out. You must go to the gym every day," he said, eyeing him with admiration.

"Not every day."

"Who's stronger, you or Mr. Archer?" Justin asked.

"Oh, I couldn't say, though I wouldn't want to cross Edison, I mean Mr. Archer," he said in a mock threatening tone. Both sets of eyes widened and they seemed to take this to heart.

"Do you think I can be as strong as you?" asked Brian.

"Yeah, eat right, that means no fast food crap and balance your cardio with some weights and you'll have the body you want. At your age, go for lighter weights and higher repetitions, though. Your bones are growing now, heavy weights might limit your vertical growth and you don't want that. You only get one chance to grow vertically," he added, stretching his hand high above his head.

"How long will it take?" Brian asked.

"Don't know but you're young, so not long. Give it a shot, and if you add in some good grades your parents will be happy. If I see some A's on your report cards and you get your parents' permission, we can go island hopping up in the San Juans next summer."

"Cool!" they said in unison.

"See you later guys," Brett said turning to his front stairs.

"Bye," they said riding off on their bicycles.

Brett watched as Justin did a wheelie, probably for his benefit, he thought.

He entered the front door of the house, still not comfortable that Linda left it unlocked during the day. More than once, he had suggested that she lock it when she was alone in the house, but she had scoffed at the notion that a "hardened city girl" like herself, who had once lived in San Francisco's Tenderloin district, would feel threatened here in *Pleasantville*—her term for the neighborhood. She had added that the only thing that scared her about the neighborhood was all the women pushing double strollers on the sidewalks.

Brett walked through the front hall and heard the clatter of dishes from the kitchen and he guessed that Linda was preparing dinner. He also heard an exacerbated female voice followed by audience laughter coming from the television in the main room. He kicked off his shoes and pushed them over to a corner in the hall, intimidated by the flawless shine of the hardwood floor. One thing he could never fault Linda on was the way she kept up the house. In San Francisco, they had both pitched in with chores, but since Linda hadn't been working, she had completely taken over the domestic realm. As much as he hated to admit it, since he viewed himself as a forward-thinking type of guy, he enjoyed coming home to a clean and orderly home, knowing that a nice meal was waiting for him. If only Linda were more receptive to fulfilling another one of his needs, he reflected, he would be a very happy man.

He went into the main room and saw the hardwood floors were gleaming and the couch and chair pillows looked freshly fluffed. Only an empty King-Size Snickers bar wrapper lying on the couch marred the perfection. He winced as he saw a pouting Delta Burke on the TV screen in all her 80's shoulder-padded splendor.

He entered the kitchen where Linda was at the stove stirring food in a massive stainless steel wok.

"Hi honey," she said turning to him with a smile.

"Hey babe." He bent down slightly to kiss her. "Smells good."

"Just making a chicken stir-fry tonight. Do you want white or brown rice?" she asked, walking toward the freezer.

"White is fine for me."

"White it is," she said, pulling out a box of the frozen organic rice she always bought. "How was your day?"

"Oh, pretty quiet. Paris HQ is in summer vacation mode, so it should be low-key through August."

"That doesn't sound too bad," she said, going back to check on the stir-fry. "Do you think they'll send you to the head office again? I would love to tag along and eat pastry at the cafes after a stressful day at the museums."

"They may send me to Amsterdam in the fall," Brett said, eyeing the shapeless summer frock she was wearing.

"Really?" she said, looking at him hopefully. "We haven't been there since our honeymoon."

"Well, I don't see why you couldn't join me." He thought back to their trip when they had bicycled through the countryside, viewing the requisite windmills and tulip fields, and how Linda and he had also experienced the less innocent but just as requisite Red Light District, sampling hashish in a coffeehouse and then having a passionate interlude in a park. He imagined this trip would be a little different, picturing Linda pedaling behind him with a fanny pack around her ever-widening waistline.

Brett scooted behind Linda at the stove, kissing the top of her head, causing her to flinch.

"Not while I'm cooking," he heard the reprimand. He opened the freezer door and grabbed a pint of ice cream.

"Uh uh uh," Linda said, snatching it away from him and returning it to the freezer. "Dinner's almost ready and I won't have you spoiling your appetite. Why don't you put those big guns of yours to use and open the wine?" she motioned with her head toward the bottle on the counter.

He opened the bottle of white wine, thinking that it was easy for Mrs. King-Size Snickers bar to get all high-and-mighty about spoiling one's appetite.

Linda turned off the gas burner with a *click*. "I'll just microwave the rice and dinner will be ready."

The table was already set and, as he poured the wine, he noticed the placemats were ones he hadn't seen before. On the placemat was a picture of two daisies, one male and one female, he assumed, since one had longer eyelashes. They were both smiling with leaves clasped around one another in a smitten fashion. He pulled out the heavy oak bench that, in lieu of chairs, lay on either side of the large oak table and sat down. Linda called the table her *Under the Tuscan Sun* folly since she'd bought the table on an impulse from a San Francisco antique store shortly after they'd seen the movie together. He had deemed the movie a total chick flick, but it had spoken to Linda, so despite his doubts, he had gone along with the expenditure. While they had found a suitable place for the table in their more traditional San Francisco home, here in Seattle, it looked like an angry relic juxtaposed against the sleek modernity of the kitchen.

Linda brought the rice and stir-fry to the table in two earthenware serving bowls and Brett placed generous portions of each onto his plate.

"It's good," he said to her as he was still chewing his first mouthful.

"Well, as long as I'm doing the '50's housewife thing, you might as well get a good meal out of it."

"So no word from the interview you had last week with that gallery downtown?"

"None. The guy all but leveled with me that I was way over-qualified for the sales assistant position. I tried to convince him to give me a chance, but I guess he thought he was doing me a favor by turning me down."

"You'll find something. It just takes time in a new city," he said, shoveling some more food into his mouth.

"I think *new* turned stale a long time ago."

"So none of your former colleagues have connections up here?"

"Believe me, I've tried. If we were in New York or LA, sure, but Seattle doesn't exist in their world unless perhaps one specializes in Native American pottery or totem poles. North for these people ends somewhere in Napa."

"What about Vera? That woman seemed to have more connections than the Internet."

"Vera said to stay tuned."

"Stay tuned? What does that mean?"

"You've got me," Linda said, sipping her wine. "The last time we spoke, she said she's been busy trying to get my replacement fired, but to stay tuned."

"Well, something will come up."

"On the positive side, I think I actually have fewer wrinkles than I used to because of all the sleep I've been getting." She rubbed the areas under her eyes with her index fingers as if to confirm their smoothness. "How's that for a silver lining?"

"You've gotta take them where you can," Brett said, looking at her and noticing the makings of a double chin, thinking that it was probably the additional weight that had softened out any wrinkles under her eyes.

"Justin and Brian want to go out on the boat again," he said, changing the topic.

"Who? Oh, the kids. They're sweet."

"Yeah, little chatterboxes."

"Any good gossip?"

"Just bitching about their parents."

"What did they say?" Linda asked, perking up.

"Just the usual stuff, moody mom, distant dad."

"Hmm, I think one of their moms stands outside the market with the Jesus pamphlets. I can never remember which kid belongs to which parents."

"I told them we'd take them out around Blake Island the next time we go. I hope that's okay."

"Of course, as long as we don't have to keep them. Could you picture us with our own brood?" she grinned, before stuffing a heaping forkful of food into her mouth.

"Not really," he said managing a smile. He watched Linda chew her overambitious mouthful, noticing a clump of rice stick to the side of her mouth. He wasn't sure he'd pictured this either. He had thought people let themselves go once they had children, but he wondered what the advantages were to an empty nest if it all lead to the same place. "You have some food stuck over here," he said, pointing to the corner of his mouth.

She swiped it with her napkin and then unfolded it to look inside. "My, that must have been attractive."

After they'd both eaten their fill, Linda cleared the table for dessert.

"You'll be the first, well the second, after me, to sample my new creation, a split-level Bundt cake."

"Sounds good," he said, wondering what her fascination was with Bundt cakes.

She took his plate away and he looked back down at the two daisies on the placemat. Where in the hell did Linda get this crap? he wondered. He heard a birdcall from outside and gazing out the French doors, he saw the blue sky framing a picturesque backdrop to the fir trees.

For years, he had dreamt of having a life such as this. He

had a good job and owned a beautiful home in a nice neighbor-hood. It could be perfect if only Linda were the same woman he'd fallen in love with in San Francisco. He had always thought he'd be with her for the long haul, but now he wasn't so certain he wanted to be chained for the rest of his life to a ballooning Betty Crocker who cared more for cake recipes than for him.

Linda finished clearing the table and brought over a cake platter with the split-level Bundt, which, he noticed, had a huge gap in it, making it look like a crescent moon.

"No gym tonight with Eds?" she asked, serving him a hefty slice.

"No, not tonight. He likes to go during the day sometimes and I'm taking the night off."

"How do you think he's doing?" she asked, cutting a gener-ous slice for herself.

"Better. More and more like the old Edison."

"Do you think he's really going to sell the house?"

"It looks that way. I mean, I was over there when the realtor came." He recalled the image of Cherie Cahill bending down in her sports bra at the gym.

"Well, we can't let him leave. We need to start an intense campaign to keep him here."

"I thought that's what we've been doing." He wiped some frosting from his lip with his finger and licked it clean. "The cake's good. If you bring him over one of these, perhaps he'll reconsider."

"Good idea. You know how they say the way to a man's heart is through his stomach."

Brett smiled guiltily, as an image of Cherie flashed through his mind again and he realized that food wasn't the only path to a man's heart.

"Hey, pumpkin. After we're done, why don't we just leave the dishes and go upstairs and have a good old-fashioned roll in the hay? No distractions, just the two of us."

"Oh, not right now," she said, grabbing her stomach with

one hand. "I ate a ton and I feel way too full. I was just going to throw all this stuff into the dishwasher and then watch my show. You're welcome to join me."

"What is it?" he asked, annoyed that she'd rebuffed him once again. If she wasn't feeling bloated or watching her stories, he knew it would have been some other lame excuse.

"A Lifetime original movie: *Bait and Switch*."

Despite the sad irony, he snorted out a laugh, "Oh, Linda. You really need to get out more."

They finished their desserts in silence and after he was done, he left her to clean up the dishes and went upstairs to their bedroom where he stripped out of his clothes and put on a pair of cotton gym shorts. As he adjusted himself in his shorts, he felt a familiar desire make itself known. He had always been very predictable that way—throw some food in him and he became amorous. He thought of the realtor again and, this time, he imagined grabbing her from behind and pinning her down on a mat at the gym and having his way with her.

He stepped into the adjacent room, which served as his office and turned on the laptop at the desk. Once he logged onto the computer, he made certain Linda was at a safe distance, and hearing the kitchen sink running gave him the necessary confirmation. He logged into his email account and typed in Cherie Cahill's email address. He knew it by memory, as he had pulled out her business card more than once during the last few days while deliberating whether he should contact her. He typed up a quick note, saying that he was free to meet for coffee this week if the invitation was still good and hesitated only a moment before clicking on the send button.

NINETEEN

Trudging up California Street, Val was thankful for the red light at Leavenworth. All these years of living in San Francisco and the hills were still a challenge. She watched the cars go by, while twisting the grocery bag handles in her fingers clockwise then counterclockwise. She saw thickening wisps of afternoon fog blowing across Grace Cathedral's central spire. The light turned green and she continued up the hill, chastising herself for snubbing the cardio equipment at the gym. She enjoyed Stacy and Dean's condo, but the downside was that it was always an uphill climb, regardless from which direction she approached it.

She had been to the bank and grocery store after checking her P.O. Box. Today was her thirty-sixth birthday, which was troubling enough, but coupled with everything she'd been through lately, it seemed like the beginning of the end. She couldn't find a job and, apart from the rare perfunctory response, she never heard a peep from the resumes she sent out.

At least her parents and sister had come through with $100 checks, and she had promptly deposited them into her anemic account. She hadn't told her family about her financial predicament, purposely keeping things vague. Early on, there hadn't been much to tell. After Trident had folded, she had relied on her savings to continue her upscale lifestyle. Refusing to believe the boom was over and wanting to be her own boss, she had collaborated with others who were intent on claiming their share of the Internet pot of gold.

First, there was the survey site where people received points for taking surveys. The points would get you crappy prizes and the client companies paid her company for the market research data. However, most companies quickly realized that the people who had the time to take the surveys were not their target consumers. Then there was the bartering website, which was modeled after eBay except for the success. Plus, a home mortgage site, a debacle she would never admit to. Each failure left her worse off than before, and more determined to succeed. Now, only her pride kept her from coming clean to her traditional-minded family. They had always condemned her headstrong ways and, under the guise of wanting only what was best for her, would point out every bad choice she had ever made beginning with her "no good" high school boyfriend and continuing to the present. If she went back home, it would be an old-fashioned shoulda woulda coulda party and she would be the guest of honor. She imagined this was how a piñata must feel when receiving an invite to a birthday party.

To celebrate her birthday, she had picked up a pint of good ice cream at CALA Foods and she planned to order in some Chinese. She had considered going out, but to where and with whom? Edison wasn't in town and she'd already used her *Get Out of Jail Free* card with Adam. The thought of going out alone on her birthday was far too depressing. She would take a long, warm shower and then spend the evening on the couch, wrapped in Stacy's cashmere throw, eating Mongolian beef, followed by some Double Rainbow ice cream, while losing herself in cable TV.

She reached Huntington Park and saw the usual suspects loitering about: people exercising their dogs, parents exercising their children in the playground area and a few older Asian women practicing their Tai Chi moves on a small patch of greenery. Tourists and locals alike were taking in the views of the park, which was flanked on one side by Grace Cathedral—that testament to poured concrete—and on the other side by the exclusive and enduring Pacific Union Club.

She was thankful when she finally reached Stacy and Dean's

sixth floor condo. Even though it was only 4:30, she was hungry for dinner. She knew the delivery would take a while so she called the Chinese restaurant and ordered her food.

About a half hour later, she had just stepped out of the shower when she heard the phone ring. "Damn," she muttered. It figured that the one time they arrived early, she was naked and soaking wet. She grabbed a towel and raced from the bathroom to the phone in Stacy and Dean's bedroom, leaving a trail of wet footprints on the carpet.

"Hello?"

"Hello?" answered a woman's voice. "Who is this?"

"Stacy?"

"Val, is that you?"

"Yeah, it's me. How are you doing?" Val asked, seeing her own mortified expression in the mirror above the chest of drawers.

"Fine. Oh my gosh, how strange. I was just calling to check for messages and I thought I had dialed the wrong number. How are you? Is everything okay?"

"Yeah, everything's fine," she said trying to think on her feet. "Um, I hope it's okay, but my apartment is being repainted and the landlord warned me the fumes would be fierce for a couple days, so I thought you wouldn't mind me camping out here. I would have called, but with the time difference, I didn't want to bother you."

"Oh, of course I don't mind. No, honey, it's Val," she heard Stacy say, along with the sound of her cupping the receiver. "Dean says hi."

"Give Dean a big hug for me."

"Val sends you a big hug," she heard her say to Dean.

"So, how's London? It must be late there."

"Yes, we just got in from dinner and the theater."

"Oh, that sounds so civilized."

"No, honey, I didn't touch the dental floss," Val heard Stacy's half-muffled voice. "I'm sorry, Val. Yes, everyone sounds so civilized here, even the commercials do."

"So you're enjoying London then?" she asked, sensing Stacy's distraction.

"It's great and it looks as if we'll be staying here longer than we thought."

"Really?"

"Well, the London office needs Dean to remain here at least through first quarter of next year."

"That's so exciting," Val said, beaming to herself in the mirror. "So when will I next see both of you?"

"Dean won't make it back until the holidays but, I, on the other hand, am coming for a nice long visit."

"Great," she said feeling her heart drop. "When will you be here?"

"Friday afternoon."

"This Friday?"

"Yeah, I'm so excited and I'm looking forward to telling you all about London. Maybe we can hit the Presidio Golf Course this weekend."

"Definitely, I can't wait," she lied.

"So how's everything with you? Working hard as usual?"

"Oh, you know consulting, it ebbs and flows."

"True. And how are my plants doing?"

"Plants?" Val asked, looking over at the yellowing ficus, remembering now that she had neglected to water the plants the last few weeks. "Uh, I think they miss you. I don't have quite the green thumb that you do."

"I'm sure you're just being modest."

"Not really." As if eavesdropping, the ficus dropped a yellow leaf.

"Oh, Val. While I have you on the line, can you do me a favor and tell me if the answering machine shows any new messages?"

"Sure, just a moment." She ran into the living room with the cordless and found the answering machine buried under a stack of *New Yorker* magazines she had tossed on top of it. She dropped her towel to look under the magazines. "No messages."

"Great. Well, it's after one o'clock here and someone's starting to get cranky, so I better let you go."

"Okay, well, I look forward to seeing you later this week."

"Likewise. And I was completely serious about you staying there. It's absolutely no problem. I remember when we had the condo repainted; we were stranded at the Ritz Carleton for a week."

"I know, the Ritz can be stressful, so thanks for letting me stay here."

"Sure, Val. Have a good night."

"You too. Bye."

Val walked back to the bedroom and placed the telephone receiver on the cradle. She sat down on the bed in a stupor, feeling cool beads of water run off her onto the duvet cover. Her attention focused on the pewter framed wedding photo of Stacy and Dean on the dresser. In the photo, they were both smiling, champagne glasses raised in a toast, but Stacy's smile was rigid and Dean looked tanked. Still, she envied them, their well-funded mismatch.

She was dumbfounded. She had thought she had at least a few more months left to get her living situation in order. Instead, she had two more nights and then she would be homeless. What could she do? Go back and live in her childhood bedroom in Chicago and admit defeat? Her parents nagging her to settle down and marry some nice Greek man from church, so she could drop a litter of grandchildren just as her sister had done. Was this how it would finally end?

Sitting, damp and exposed, she considered her options when the phone rang. It must be the delivery guy from the restaurant, she thought, but she no longer had an appetite. She stood and reached for the phone, catching sight of her wet ass print on Stacy's brushed suede duvet cover. "Just what I need," she muttered. "Happy goddamn birthday to me."

TWENTY

He was just going for coffee, Brett told himself as he crossed Lenora Street and headed into the Belltown neighborhood. There was nothing wrong with meeting a woman for coffee. Was he not supposed to have any female friends just because he was married? He realized there was no point in employing a strategy of self-deception. He was far too honest with himself to pretend this meeting was about making a new friend anymore than it was about having coffee—which he didn't even drink.

He had left work early in order to meet Cherie, but now realized that he had overestimated the time it would take him to walk to the cafe from his office, and, at his current pace, he would arrive conspicuously early, in that window between desperate and creepy.

He slowed down a bit and took in the mix of upscale restaurants and boutiques standing audaciously amongst their less gentrified neighbors, the drug rehabilitation center and the semi-decrepit Ma and Pa shops. He thought it was a strange mix, but he had seen the same fusion of flophouse and fashionable in any number of neighborhoods in San Francisco.

He was getting very close to the cafe and he still had fifteen minutes to kill. He'd already checked for new messages on his cell, but there were none. There weren't many browsing options available on the current block so he decided the custom frame shop would have to do, seeming more promising than either the UPS Store or the Subway sandwich place.

He entered the store and the bell on the door announced his arrival to the older man sitting behind the desk who nodded to him. He saw he was the only customer and quickly regretted not going into Subway, where he could have nursed a soda at a table for ten minutes without any further expectations.

He went to a section of the store that housed the smaller, pre-fabricated frames and looked at the various pictures within the frames. Some of the photos were outdated—pictures of teenagers with braces and feathered hair that reminded him of his own childhood. Other photos showed happy-looking families complete with kids and pets. Something he would never experience, he thought. He and Linda had agreed before they got married not to have children. At times, though, he couldn't help wondering whether the traditionalists had it right, that kids were the glue that held marriages together. In the past, when everything was going well with Linda, he'd readily dismissed this notion as a load of crap, but lately he wasn't so certain.

He continued his search for a frame he didn't want, and seeing a buxom blonde posing in one of the photos reminded him of the one he was about to meet. He considered purchasing a silver 5 x 7 frame to assuage his guilt for using this guy's shop as a temporary hideout, but after seeing the price, he knew there wasn't a snowball's chance in hell and left the store.

When he entered the cafe, he saw Cherie right away. She was impossible to miss in her pink blazer and matching pink miniskirt, which showed off her long tan legs to great advantage. She was peering down at a complicated-looking cell phone, intently entering something into it. The only other patrons were a young, nerdy-looking guy with dark hair and thick black glasses (a "cafe homosexual" is what Edison would have called him) and a woman with purple hair reading a book. As he approached the table, Cherie was sipping her coffee drink with a straw.

"Is that how all the sophisticated ladies drink their coffee now?" he asked, gazing down at her, catching a bit of her lace bra and deep cleavage.

She looked up startled. "Oh, hello," she said donning a smile. "I didn't hear you come in. Oh, and yes, I love coffee, but

I don't like how it stains my teeth so I always use a straw. Listen to me, I sound as if I'm doing a commercial for a denture stain remover."

"Well, dentures are something I would never associate with a pretty woman like you."

"You're too kind. I hope you don't mind, I went ahead and ordered. I arrived a little early and I can be a real piece of work when I'm caffeine deprived."

"That's why I never touch the stuff," he said, catching a whiff of her perfume, the same musky sweetness he remembered from the gym. I ll just grab something and be right back. Can I get you anything?"

"Umm, do you feel like splitting a brownie or something?"

"Sure, that sounds great." He felt a vibration in the front pocket of his slacks. It was someone calling his cell, but he would pick up the message later. He ordered a mineral water and four brownies, feeling hungry all of a sudden, and brought them back to the table.

"My, that's a lot of brownies," Cherie said, putting her cell phone into her purse. She moved her purse onto a free chair and he heard the distinct rattle of pills from inside her bag. She pointed to the brownies.

"I hope those aren't all for me."

"Nah, I'm a little hungry, so I got some extra."

"Well, I like a man with a healthy appetite," she said, looking up at him flirtatiously, her eyes seeming to smile even more than her lips.

"That's me, a regular pig," he chuckled.

He saw her face light up in amusement. She was certainly pretty, he thought, though he wasn't used to seeing a woman so "dolled up"—as his grandfather would have said. Linda had always preferred the natural look unless it was a special occasion.

"You're corporate attire suits you," he said, instantly regretting the pun.

"Why thank you. That's quite a handsome shirt you're

wearing. Let me guess," she reached out and touched his shirtsleeve, "Brooks Brothers?"

"Good guess," he said, surprised at the effect her touch had
on him. He was glad he had worn the shirt as he typically challenged the lower end of his office's business casual dress code.
"How could you tell?"

"It's very popular with the male realtors. Nordstrom as
well."

"So how is everything going in the world of real estate?"

"Oh, there's always something going on," she said, helping
herself to one of the brownies. "Seattle's still an active market,
even though everyone keeps on predicting its imminent demise.
Frankly, I think this whole thing is a fabrication of the liberal
media."

"Liberal media?" he asked, grabbing the brownie he had
been eyeing and eagerly biting into it.

"You know, the National Pinko Radio crowd."

"Hmm, I listen to NPR and I've always thought it rather
center-right."

"Really? By that F-150 you drive, I would have pegged you
as a fellow red person who has the misfortune of living in a blue
state."

"How do you know I drive an F-150?"

"Oh, I think Edison mentioned it." Cherie blushed slightly
and grabbed her coffee, sucking down what appeared to be a
large amount through the straw.

"Don't let the truck fool you. I'm as blue as they come."

"Well, we gals at church have been praying for a giant red
tide to sweep over the country come next election."

He tried to suppress a smile, wondering if these women
knew they were praying for a toxic algal bloom. He wanted to
ask her what drugs she was on, but then he remembered the
rattle of pills from her purse and decided it best not to go there.
She was obviously his opposite on the political spectrum but he
wasn't here for a Poli Sci debate.

"We shouldn't be talking politics. Not unless we're drinking something a helluva lot stronger. Red, blue, maybe one day we'll all be able to get along and create a nice livable purple."

She laughed at this. "You're right, I just get so passionate about politics. I guess I've always been a very passionate person," she added, looking at him pointedly.

He wasn't prepared for this flirtation and instinctively deflected it. "Well, passion is good. I'm sure it helps you sell all those houses. Speaking of which, do you think there will be a lot of interest in Edison's house?"

"There's plenty of interest. The ball is in Edison's court, though I get the feeling he's having second thoughts."

"Really?" Brett said, picking up another brownie, happy to hear this piece of news.

"You're friends with him, maybe you can find out why he hasn't committed to anything yet. He's been so vague with me and lately he hasn't been returning my calls."

"Sure, I'll talk to him." He smiled, realizing that he and Cherie were on opposing ends of Edison's house sale, as well.

"That would be great. So, how funny was it that we ran into each other at your gym?"

"Yeah, that was a coincidence. So, you're thinking of joining?"

"We'll see," she said with a playful smile. "You certainly were moving around some heavy weights."

"Well, I've gotta keep up with Edison."

"He's such a handsome man. I never would have pegged him for a fruit."

"He's not a *fruit*. He's just a guy who likes guys."

"Oh, I know, live and let live, blah, blah, blah. It just seems like such a waste, for a single gal like me to see all these guys who are either gay or mar … unavailable."

"I guess I can understand, but a woman like you must not have much of a problem finding a man."

Cherie smiled. "Well, it's more an issue of quality than quantity, and when I do find quality, I go after it."

Brett felt his face turning red. Maybe Cherie would get her wish after all and he'd change into a red person.

"An attractive woman like you certainly deserves the best."

"You are very kind," she said, gently playing with the pearls of her necklace.

Brett took a long sip of his water and then wiped the perspiration from his upper lip with a napkin. "So, what was all that talk at the gym the other day about your womanly intuition? Do I get to learn the details now?"

"Oh that," Cherie said smiling. "Let's just say a girl gets certain vibes when a man is interested, and that's why I didn't think you were gay."

"Hmm, well I have to admit my Spidey sense was tingling as well."

Cherie let out a girlish laugh. "So where does that leave us?"

"Do you have plans for this evening?" he asked.

"Nothing special. Would you like to come over to my place for drinks? I live just a few blocks down the street."

"Sure. That would be nice," he heard himself say, ignoring the voice inside that was screaming, *You are married, you idiot! Run, don't walk!*

"Are you parked around here?"

"No, I took the express bus to work today."

"Great, we can go in my SUV. It's parked right outside. I just need to brush my teeth in the ladies' room if you don't mind. They say sugar is highly corrosive to one's teeth."

"Please, brush away," he said, suddenly feeling self-conscious about his own dental hygiene.

She got up and headed to the bathroom and Brett couldn't help but look at her long, beautiful legs that were attached to an ass that wouldn't quit. Before entering the restroom, she turned around unexpectedly, catching Brett shamelessly in mid-stare, and gave him a knowing smile as she pushed open the restroom door.

What in the hell am I doing? he thought. Have I gone out of

my mind? He knew that nothing good would come of this. Cherie knew where he lived, where he worked out … even what he drove … and a few moments of pleasure were not worth sacrificing everything he had with Linda. Still, he sensed it was futile to reason with himself because reason wasn't what had brought him here.

He felt the vibration of his phone, reminding him of his new voicemail. He reached into his pocket and took it out, and dialed in to retrieve the message. "Hi, honey," he heard Linda's voice, sounding like she'd just woken up from a nap. "Can you pick up some heavy whipping cream and parmesan cheese on your way home? I'm making Fettuccini Alfredo and am running a bit short. Oh, and some Chunky Monkey ice cream would be great too. Maybe get two pints, but surprise me with the second one. Love you."

He pictured Linda stretched out on the couch, perhaps watching one of her shows before making dinner. Just like that, as if someone had flipped a switch, he felt his desire diminish and a tenderness well up inside his heart. He realized that he couldn't go through with this. How could he ever face Linda again? But what would he tell Cherie?

As if on cue, Cherie stepped out of the restroom, approaching the table with the confidence of a model on a catwalk.

He stood up. "I just got a call. Something's come up at work and I have to go back. I'm sorry, but I won't be able to have drinks tonight."

"Oh no," she said, her entire face seeming to collapse. "You're sure it can't wait?"

"I wish it could, but I've got to head back."

"Well, at least let me drive you there," she said, reaching down to collect her purse from the chair.

"No, it's a quick walk. I can burn off some of the brownies this way."

"Don't be silly. I'll take you there." She took his hand and led him outside the cafe. He politely tried to pull away, but she tightened her grip on him like a vice. Once on the sidewalk, she led him to her SUV, which was parked in front of the cafe. He knew this was his last chance to get away.

"Really, I'll be fine," he said, pulling himself free. "I'm sorry about this, but I guess it's what I get for sneaking out of the office early. Thanks for the coffee. I had a nice time."

"So did I. Let me know if anything changes." She gently rubbed her hand over the top of her blouse. "I'll be in all night."

He parted from Cherie feeling like a gazelle who had narrowly escaped the jaws of a lioness. Part of him still wanted her, but he knew that that ship had sailed.

He now wanted to rush straight home to Linda, but he had a paranoid sense that Cherie was following him, making sure he headed back downtown. He didn't dare turn around in case she actually was, but headed back in the direction of his office. He would catch a cab from one of the downtown hotels to avoid her seeing him waiting at a bus stop.

He knew he wouldn't be contacting Cherie again, as long as he was with Linda. He had no doubt that sex with Cherie would have been hot, but that would have been it. While he and Linda had their problems, and his affair with Playboy TV wasn't a long-term solution, at least it was a form of cheating he could accept. Right now, he just felt an overwhelming sense of relief that he had managed to come back to his senses before it was too late.

TWENTY-ONE

Well, it could be worse, Val thought, tossing her bags on the bed. The small bed sagged briefly and then collapsed without further hesitation. Well, now it is worse. A heated exchange with the front desk manager left her and her bags out on the sidewalk. She was not too worried about the threat of the manager to charge her for the damage since the credit card she had used for an imprint at check-in had been maxed out a month ago and declined across the city.

She took comfort in having hit rock bottom. The acting days for this girl were over, she mused. She escaped Stacy and Dean's condo with her dignity intact and, as far as she knew, Stacy had thought she'd only been there for a matter of days. She wasn't happy with the marathon cleaning session she had to pull to return the place to Stacy's meticulous standards nor the precious cash she had to spend to replace Stacy's expensive household supplies. She did end up going cheap on some items hoping Stacy would think they had gone stale while she was in London. It had been more than she wanted to spend, but her conscience was clear and that was worth something.

Her plan was to call Edison and see if she could camp out in his hip Pacific Heights apartment until she got back on her feet. She could benefit from his sound counsel as well as his legendary discipline. She had trusted his calm sensibility in the past and now she knew she was willing to ignore her pride and get down to business. She should have done this originally, if for no other reason then good fortune seemed to shadow Edison. Well, at least professionally. His family didn't seem to fare too well when it came to Fortune's hand.

She had called Edison and left a message when she made her exodus from the condo and she was tempted to call him again. Earlier in the year, she had splurged on the latest cell phone that required a full year paid in advance in order to get the unlimited minutes and a huge discount. Now, with no credit and almost no cash, she felt very attached to her phone and its comforting blue glow.

After walking up Sutter Street a few blocks, she put down her bags less than halfway to her destination. She needed a rest and the other hostel was still both vertically and horizontally distant. Her bags were very handsome, but even when empty they were heavy. Her reduced life was now in them and she was already wondering what else she could part with to lighten the load.

Stepping over an empty champagne bottle, of exceptional vintage she noticed, she stacked her bags on a clean piece of sidewalk. Her cell phone beeped, alerting her of a voicemail, and she saw that she had missed a call. A call from Edison! "God damn it. Just God damn it all," she fumed, causing a passing group of Asian businessmen to stare at her. "Oh, go fuck yourselves," she said not giving their silent judgment any ground.

She turned away from them and stared at the traffic while dialing her voicemail. A quick calculation from the message's timestamp told her the call must have come when she was yelling at the manager of the hostel. She made a mental note to keep her ears open when yelling at others.

Edison's message told her two things: he was not going to be back in San Francisco any time soon and the tone of his voice suggested that he was not tap dancing through the steps of grieving. She had listened to the message twice and it drove home how much she had depended on Edison to be his steady self. He was clearly suffering and not in any condition to help her piece together the shambles of her life.

The gravity of both their situations drew at her last energies. She stood watching the Sutter Street traffic whiz by and fought the tears welling up in her eyes. Who and what she had become was so far from where she wanted to be. It shamed her that she was thinking of Edison's apartment and the good counsel she hoped he would give her and forgetting that he was in a situation much worse, much more real than her financial folly. She could go home to Chicago if she had to and it would devastate her ego, but she would manage.

It was time to focus, she decided. First, she would get her bags to the next hostel and then she would go to a cafe where she could iron out her two options: return home or camp out at Edison's place until she secured whatever work she could get. Perhaps she could request a fashion consult from Gay Adam so she too could master the separates from GAP. Her humor and resolve faded a bit when she remembered she had luggage to lug up another damn hill.

She kicked the champagne bottle to the gutter and the irony wasn't lost on her that she used to order the same vintage by the case. She carried her bags the remaining blocks, noting that not one person offered to help her with them. She wasn't too hard on her fellow San Franciscans, though, as she knew she had never offered a hand to anyone toiling away under a burden.

At the front of the hostel, she was sweaty and short of breath. She knew she had blighted karma and wondered how long it would take to repair. The handle of her well-worn Louis Vuitton case gave way at that moment and that was answer enough for her.

The hostel had looked clean from the street and her room appeared secure as it took two keys to open the door. She did like the sight of the two young men walking down the hall with towels wrapped around their firm bodies en route to the communal showers.

Once in the room, she knew she wouldn't last long. To her right, she could hear an amorous young couple discussing birth control in French. To her left, she heard what she could only assume was a male prostitute returning calls from prospective johns. It concerned her that she could even hear the tones of his cell phone as he dialed.

She saw the bed sheets were stained and the dark crud on the surface of the dresser could have been from the fire of 1906. The legions of dead roaches were the most troubling for her. If they had died, how was her fragile species expected to survive? She would ponder that at Starbucks until it closed. The lock on the door was serious, but as she examined the door, she realized it was so flimsy even she could probably punch through it without breaking a nail.

She laid out some of her older clothes on the top of the bed and made a nest to nap in, taking care not to touch any part of the bed sheets with her skin. She blocked the noise and smells around her with a cashmere scarf over her face dabbed with Chanel No. 5. She was tired, and with her eyes shut, she recalled pleasant images of her suite at the Peninsula, Hong Kong from years ago and drifted to sleep.

Two hours later, she woke suddenly to what sounded like a gun shot, but she preferred to assume was a car backfiring followed by a police investigation. She stood and arranged her few items and felt a strong premonition that Fate was about to cast a die in her direction. In her mind, Fate was not terribly interested in whatever the die read. She had always pictured Fate bored, sitting at a craps table, Vegas-style, with a drink order pending.

Leaving the dank room, she passed through the clean and homey lobby that gave no suggestion to the dark cells they called "budget accommodations." There was a Starbucks two blocks down toward Union Square and she thought it a good time to use the rest of Stacy's gift card and distance herself from the dead roaches that littered her hostel cell.

Maneuvering down the busy sidewalk and through the doors of the Starbucks without luggage gave her a sense of lightness and agility. Once seated in a quiet corner, she decided to see if her sudden good mood would come across in the supportive message she wanted to leave Edison. She dialed and waited for the call to roll over to voicemail while trying to place the passing tourists with their home countries. She was startled by Edison's live voice on the other end.

"Oh, Edison, it's Val. I had assumed I would get your voicemail so I was sort of in a zone waiting for the beep."

"No problem. I know that zone. How are you doing?"

"Oh, I'm fine, about the same, really. I'm at a Starbucks near Union Square. But screw that, Edison, how are you doing? What is it like up there? When are you coming back? Can I crash on your couch this month?"

"What? Wow. That was a lot of questions. Is this an inquisi-tion?"

"Well, are you going to stay up there? I guess that's the big question. I can't keep your seat warm at Scala's forever, you know. Without you here to wolf down their mashed potatoes, they're going to be facing bankruptcy."

"I'm sure they'll manage given their waitlist. As for San Francisco, well, I'm not sure. I have engaged a realtor but I'm having mixed feelings … no, it's more that I can't seem to make a decision. It's odd, I mean, this house, it feels like home even though I didn't grow up here." He hesitated, leaving a silence that caused her to look at her phone to see if the connection had dropped.

"What kind of property is it?" she asked, suddenly aware she knew very little of Edison's family in Seattle.

"Oh, it's a house in Seattle proper with all the possessions that go along with a middle-aged couple. Not to mention a cat, a full garden and a lawn.

"So you're not going to be down here anytime soon to par-ticipate in the collective drama of all of us self-absorbed urban-ites? You know, we have real problems too, like is sushi a flex vegetable in the troubled vegetarian's diet?"

Edison laughed for the first time, Val noted.

"I do miss San Francisco, and things up here are hardly fun. It helps, oddly, that there's no choice in the matter. Brett and Linda have been great, though Linda has increased in volume since you last saw her. I think she has fully embraced the snack cake culture."

"Oh, my," Val said, eyeing her diminished caramel latte in sympathy with Linda. "How is Brett? He seems like he would do well up there in the land of polar fleece."

"Better than Linda, but as much as I like spending time with him, it's as if I have a little brother following me around. I think he's lonely and sort of attached himself to me. It's weird, though, he often comes here immediately after work, even before he sees Linda. Any other circumstance and I would be flattered."

"Oh, Edison, people like to spend time with you. You should be flattered. Hell, if you need some help with stuff, I'd come up and eat your food, drink your wine and camp out in one of your spare rooms for a while."

"I thought you wanted my couch in SF?" Edison asked, clearly eating something and holding the phone distant. He continued, "You'd come up for a few weeks? You could catch up with Brett and Linda, there's plenty of room and I could use the help, frankly."

"It sounds like you need a good dose of Val and a *Nick@Night* marathon. I will burn some miles and be up sooner than you can say *Mary Tyler Moore*." Val tried not give voice to the glee she felt as she visualized her unexpected San Francisco escape hatch.

"What about your work?" Edison asked, sounding closer to the phone.

"Not a problem, believe me. Don't ask. Oh, that dime store fag, Adam, has muscled up. You interested? He still thinks of you as the good daddy he secretly wants to please."

"Ah, well, no thanks. If anything, I think I will try to find myself a shut-in with good teeth, low expectations and a penchant for Napa wines. Adam's a cute kid, there's no reason he shouldn't have gentleman callers knocking down his door. What about you?" he asked, again with food near the phone.

"Oh, I've been having a complicated relationship that's going to end soon with a caramel latte. It's all too sordid." Her phone interrupted with a loud low battery warning. "Rats! Edison, I gotta go, my cell battery is low. I'll see what I have in frequent flyer miles before the airline cancels its mileage program like they did their food service and civility. I'll forward my itinerary. You still at the same email address?"

"Yep. Cool. I'll email my street address," Edison said quickly. "You okay down there?" he asked, sounding very much like a parent.

"Yeah. Nothing too bad but nothing seems to measure up to the champagne and glitter of our yesterdays. Gotta go," she said, as the battery alarm alerted her to its impending shutdown.

"Bye," was the last thing she heard before the connection was lost. She sat back in the comfortable chair and realized she may have just forsaken San Francisco for a new nest in Seattle. Well, she mused, at least it isn't the East Bay.

TWENTY-TWO

Edison drifted in and out of sleep while sitting on the third step of the front staircase, waiting for Brett to show up. He had been there for about 25 minutes, listless, listening to the noises of the house and the birds outside.

The summer sun and the bird chorus reminded him that life was moving on. He could imagine his father telling him the same thing, but each time he tried to move forward, he lost traction and slid deeper into the gloom. A Seattle winter would be the ideal environment for his mood, he thought, as he moved his sandal-clad foot out of range of the Sun's beam o'cheer shining down from an upper window in the foyer.

Brett wasn't late, but Edison didn't have the motivation to do much more than sit and let his thoughts go round and round. Since the funeral, his mind had been less focused and more driven by emotion, his thoughts tangential and uncontrolled. The inconsistent sleep didn't help any; he felt himself becoming less and less rational, and the fact that he was actively avoiding a sunbeam summarized his mental state pretty well, he concluded.

One recurring and irrational thought involved Brett. In San Francisco, they were nearly inseparable, and while Brett was a handsome guy, Edison hadn't viewed him sexually—more of a best buddy or brother who happened to be good-looking. Brett was one of the few people he was open with and he had always taken any criticism from Brett to heart without raising his usual defenses. A few days after the funeral, he and Brett had gone to the gym like old times and Edison felt a peculiar shame when he caught himself eyeing Brett in a sexual way. He had naively hoped that it was a one-time thing or some confused emotion caused by all the stress.

Emotion wasn't something that came easily to him, as Russell, his ex, had often told him. He knew he wasn't dead inside even though he had joked with Linda about feeling that way after going with her to a chick flick. He felt a lot of things, but at his own speed. He was surprised at how much he resented the realtor's comments about his mother's interior selections, but was more concerned about his sexual thoughts and urges in response to seeing Brett's muscular legs and mischievous grin. He didn't want to jeopardize his friendship with Brett, and, by extension, Linda. He was resolute in his decision not to make an ass of himself.

In apparent agreement, the paper hens shifted as the sunlight hit the bowl. The room started to glow as the lead crystal bowl refracted the sunlight into hundreds of broken rainbows. One of the rainbows landed on his upper thigh and he could feel the heat relax the muscle. He relaxed further and started to drift off until he heard the door click open.

He knew it was Brett, but he still wondered why these Seattle people never knocked. Without grace, he sat up and tried to focus on the bright rectangle of the doorway. No one was there. He stood unsteadily and wiped the sleep from his eyes. Although Brett was a big guy, he moved with little sound and a surprising fluidity. He had come in with Stella resting on his shoulder, then moved to the center table, where he was teasing Stella with a blue paper hen from the bowl.

"You do sleep in a bed at night and not on the stairs, right?" Brett asked without taking his eyes from the game of cat and hen that he was playing with Stella.

"Yeah, I do make it up the stairs occasionally," Edison said, wondering if he had embarrassed Brett with his sprawled stair nap.

"I like the big window seat in our guest bedroom, but Linda

prefers that I avoid it since her silk pillows are endangered by my alleged drool and crumbs." Brett seemed to speak to Stella more than to Edison, which gave Edison a second to kick the dirty clothes on the floor into a smaller heap.

Brett put Stella on the floor and Stella walked back out to the porch, having been defeated by both the hen and Brett.

"You planning on a warm day?" Brett asked, gesturing to Edison's shorts and T-shirt.

"You think it will be cold?" He wondered if there was some weather coming he didn't know about.

"No, just seemed cooler this morning," Brett said, now eyeing the pile of abandoned clothes at the foot of the stairs mixed with takeout boxes.

"I'll take a sweatshirt just in case," Edison said as he grabbed a moderately clean one from the pile of clothing on the lower stair. Edison pulled on the sweatshirt and was startled to find it was still wet from his run a couple nights before. He pulled it back off and with it, his T-shirt. He separated the two quickly, knowing Brett liked to keep things moving and didn't suffer fashion delays well.

"You gay guys and your ripped abs," Brett said in mocking condemnation. "Impressive after all the eggs you usually eat for breakfast." He rubbed his own flat stomach through the Carhartt button-down shirt he was wearing and proceeded to extend it and rock the protrusion as if it were a baby.

"Now, that's disturbing," Edison said, nodding to Brett's faux baby.

"Linda packed us a few things for the drive up to Edmonds so you don't waste away." Brett turned to the door and walked out onto the porch.

"Linda has really gone domestic on you," Edison said, giving up on the hope of clean clothing and grabbing a different sweatshirt from the floor.

"She's taking on the role of house frau, as she calls it. She does keep the place up, but she needs to spend more time out of the house and far from the refrigerator."

Edison couldn't see Brett but his voice and the sounds of his pacing steps on the porch were clear enough.

"You straight people, you're all so complicated," Edison echoed Brett's earlier tone, then reached for the rental car and house keys that were under the watchful eyes of the hens. Once out the door, the blazing sun promised a warm day but the damp and cool air still dominated the shadows under the trees and on the porch. They proceeded down the porch stairs toward the rental SUV parked at the curb. Edison felt a hand go around his shoulder and simultaneously felt a pleasant electricity race through his entire body.

"I've been worried about you, buddy. Don't know what to say but I'm here." He pulled Edison closer to him, "I mean, we are here, Linda too. You know and I know I don't have any answers, but I'm a good listener. And all kidding aside, we're serious about wanting you to stay up here since we both miss you. We won't push you much more but you gotta tell me, any chance you're going to stay?"

Edison barely heard the words as he felt the warmth from Brett's arm through his shirt. He hated that so much of his life was wasted on wanting the unattainable like Brett or trying to look past the damage of the Russells of the world. Brett's fingers gently pressed into his shoulder causing Edison to move under his arm as if it were a wing. How long had it been since he felt like this? And why now? Damn, he felt a rush of tears pour from his eyes and down his face at an alarming rate. At the sidewalk, Brett moved his arm from his shoulder to his upper arm.

"You okay, buddy?" he asked, looking puzzled at the waterworks on Edison's face.

"Yeah, I'm okay; it just sneaks up on me at times." Before he could react, Brett used his shirtsleeve to wipe the tears from his cheeks and then ruffled his hair.

"It will be okay, buddy. It just takes time." Looking past Edison, Brett eyed the rental SUV and laughed. "Can you imagine the mileage on this piece of tin? Sorry we can't use my truck; I didn't want to ding her."

"No problem. The rental is cheap and, as I always say, nothing parties like a rental." Edison tried to turn the conversation light before he gave into the flood of emotions. "I think we should visit a few drive-through places on our way and make sure there are French fry grease prints on every major surface of the rental."

"Sounds like a plan, and there's a Krispy Kreme on Aurora if we need backup."

Brett crossed to the passenger side as Edison unlocked the doors. Once in, Edison picked a CD case off the driver's seat and tossed it to the backseat. He'd mixed a CD of mutually acceptable music, fearing that Brett would tune into his acid rock favorites and ramble on about the tragedy of Kurt Cobain.

"So, your parents' house, I mean, your house now. It has a ton of space. Why did your parents rent storage space up in Edmonds?" Brett asked, opening the brown paper bag he had taken from the hood of the truck.

"When my grandmother died a few years back, my parents didn't want to spoil their remodeled spartan splendor with the fussy furniture my grandmother left behind so they stored most of it and only brought back a few treasured items to Queen Anne. I guess they thought they had plenty of time to sort through everything but, well, looks like I get to instead."

"Edmonds or bust, then," Brett said, over the first track of the CD, *Black Coffee in Bed* by Squeeze. Brett broke off a huge piece of a homemade croissant and popped it in his mouth. He nodded to the bag, indicating one for Edison. Edison declined and absently slid the truck into drive. He was about to make a crack about the crumbs Brett was leaving on the dashboard when he saw the familiar SUV of the nutcase realtor pull in directly behind him. She wouldn't recognize the rental, he hoped, as he pulled away from the house abruptly. He didn't notice until he turned left onto West Highland Drive that Brett had stopped eating, his attention focused on his side view mirror.

TWENTY-THREE

The weather had been promising since Adam stumbled out of bed, with clear blue skies and no sign of fog. By lunchtime, a warm breeze had replaced the cooler morning air. Even Julie had made a point of announcing that she was going out for lunch today, because "she just needed to take some time for herself."

He ate outside at his favorite spot at Four Embarcadero Center, though whenever the weather became warm, a lot of the fair-weather lunchtime crowd came out of their cube farms and became free-range, taking over the tables and benches in his usually quiet spot. After eating, he had taken a brief nap on the grassy hill at Justin Herman Plaza and became so comfortable in a dreamlike state that he went over his lunch hour.

He had been bringing bagged lunches to work ever since his unbudgeted expense at Boulevard. That day, he was too stunned to do anything but politely pay the check. He doubted Val would ever make good on her offer to treat him to dinner at the Four Seasons. He wondered how she had become so tactless and supposed it was the price one pays for success. He guessed that Val had reinvented herself so many times that she had unwittingly discarded her better traits.

He had to admit, though, that the expense of the meal had been partially worth it since Val had relayed the latest news on Edison. He had been shocked to hear about Edison's parents, though Val's news about Edison wasn't all tragic. He'd had to suppress an ear-to-ear grin when Val had told him that Edison was no longer with Russell—the guy Adam begrudged for keeping Edison off the market. Adam had always thought of Edison as the one that got away, but that assumed Edison had once been his, which was hardly the case. Back at Trident, Edison, from all accounts, was happily coupled and, as a lowly assistant, Adam had felt way out of his league. None of this had stopped him from having elaborate fantasies that usually involved Edison professing his secret love before freeing him from his clerical shackles. Adam usually tossed in an "ever after" ending, including a large Marin home.

Back in the office, reality was waiting for him in the form of a note stuck to his computer monitor. The note was in Christina's telltale curlicue handwriting and said to call David ASAP on his cell. The note had a time of 12:35. Damn, he thought. It figured that David would call with an urgent request right after he had left for lunch. Before calling David, he checked his messages and saw he had an email marked as high-importance from David as well as a voicemail. Well, he thought, he had better put out this fire before he got burned and he dialed David's cell.

"David Touel," he answered after the first ring.

"Hi David. It's Adam in SF; I just got back from lunch and …."

"Adam. Thank God! I've been trying to reach both you and Julie, but no one was around except for Christina."

"Yes, I was out to lunch and I think Julie must be too."

"Well, I'm all for you two taking your lunches, but we'll have to talk about coverage in our meeting next week. I need you two to support me and just because I'm not always down there, doesn't mean my expectations are any different. Christina's a nice lady, but she's useless. It's just like in the Tour de France," David continued, "we're all on the same team, but there can only be one top dog in the yellow jersey, and the rest of the team has to work together to help their leader."

"Uh huh," he said, surprised at how hollow he sounded to himself, marveling at David's implicit self-comparison to a Tour de France cyclist.

"I need you to send me two files from my computer down there. I have a three o'clock meeting, so I need them pronto."

"Okay, I'll call you right back from your office."

"Good." Adam heard David hang up and he opened his drawer to get the key to David's office. As he turned to leave, Christina waddled over to his desk.

"Adam, did you see the note I left for you?"

"Yes, thanks. I just spoke to David."

"Oh good!" she said, moving a hand to her bosom in relief. "He sounded so stressed and both you and Julie were gone. I told him I would try to help him, but then I didn't know where you kept the key for his office and he just hung up."

"Well, I'm helping him now. I need to call him back from his office."

"Where do you keep the key, so I'll know for the future?"

"In my top drawer where I've always kept it. Remember, we've gone through this before."

"Oh, that's right. I must be getting Alzheimer's," Christina said, turning and smiling at a woman walking past them. "Hi Beth. Jamba Juice in five?" Beth said she would meet her in the lobby and disappeared down the hall. Christina turned back to Adam. "So what was I saying? Oh yeah, sometimes I think I have Alzheimer's. Can you believe that? A 42 year-old with Alzheimer's?"

"Yeah, strange world. Well, I need to call David," he said, stepping away.

"Oh, when you get back, I have a teensy weensy question about an Excel spreadsheet I'm trying to print out so it fits onto one page."

"I may be a while …" he said, as he continued to move away.

"Not a problem, I'll wait," he heard her call after him.

Adam reached the other side of the floor where David's office was located, the executive side. He always felt like he was in a different building when he crossed the elevator lobby and entered the "plush zone" with the rich carpets, gallery quality art and tastefully furnished offices in contrast to McCubeland where he sat. Once inside David's office, he closed the door partway to deter the busybodies from looking in and then turned on the computer. While he was waiting for the computer to boot up, he saw Tony, one of the senior attorneys, wave from the hall as he passed by the office, then walk back and poke his head inside the door.

"I like your new digs," Tony said with a smile. "Did you get a promotion?"

"No, just helping David with something."

"Is he here this week?" Tony asked looking a little surprised.

"No, he's in Seattle, but he needs a file from this computer."

"Well don't let those fascists from Systems know that you logged onto his computer. I found out the hard way that it's against firm policy to give out one's password."

"Well, I'll say I was just following orders."

"Yeah, isn't that what we all do around here? Especially from Herr David," he said, clicking his heels together and giving a mock salute, causing Adam to laugh.

"Well, I'll see you later. I've got to go answer Mother Nature before my two o'clock gets here."

Adam waved. Tony always cracked him up. With all the macho posturing on the floor, Adam found it refreshing to talk to a man who was secure enough with his sexuality to be friendly to an assumed homosexual.

He called David back. "Hi David, it's Adam."

"Are you at my computer?"

"It's all booted up. I just need your password." David relayed his password and Adam logged on. "Okay, I'm in."

"Now what I'm looking for is a Word document that should be named something like 'Harrison Case.'"

"Okay, where do you save your Word files?"

"What do you mean?"

"Is there a certain folder you save your files in?"

"No, I just save them."

Oh boy, Adam thought, recalling David was second in the office only to Christina in lack of technical skills. "Do you know when you might have last opened it?"

"The last time I was down there."

"Okay." Adam sorted the documents by the date they were last modified.

"Any luck?"

"Yes, I think I see it," he said, spotting a file named "Harrison Notes" three up from the bottom. What caught his attention, though, was the file on the very bottom of the list that was named "Edison." He had only ever known one Edison and he wondered if *his* Edison could somehow be a client. "Okay, I found a document called 'Harrison Notes.'"

"Sounds right. Can you send it up to me?"

"Sure." Adam opened up David's email and attached the file and sent it to David, seeing it arrive in David's inbox. "You should see it in your inbox."

"Great, I just need one more file ...." Adam heard a ringing in the distance and David said, "Hold on, I've got a call on my landline."

Adam heard him pick up the call and talk on his other phone. While he was waiting, he felt tempted to open the "Edison" document. He could hear David in the background and from what he could make out, it sounded as if he was talking about his upcoming meeting. It was then that he heard David say, "No need to worry, I've got the little faggot helping me now."

That asshole, he thought. Screw it, he decided. He double-clicked and opened up the "Edison" document and saw what appeared to be an instant message exchange that had been saved into a Word document. The exchange was between an EDS101 and someone named ARJ, which he could see from the ID at the top of the page was AllenRunnerJock. He guessed ARJ was David since he always boasted about how much running he did. Also, he knew from ordering David's business cards and letterhead that David's full name was David Allen Touel. He began reading the IM banter and was at the point when ARJ was asking whether Edison was a top or bottom when David came back on the phone.

"Adam are you there?"

"Yes," he said, stifling a laugh.

"Now I need you to do the same thing for another file, probably called 'Stewart Litigation.'"

"Okay." He found the file, seeing that it was sandwiched between files named "Ken" and "Jeff." He emailed the file to David.

"Thanks, Adam. I see them in my inbox. You're a real team player."

"Glad I could help."

"I've got to run. Talk to you later."

"Bye."

Adam hung up the phone and pulled up the "Edison" document. He looked toward the door, but didn't see anyone in the hallway. Still, he could feel his heart racing.

From what he could tell from reading their IM exchanges, Edison and David were planning to meet at a park in Seattle. The IMs were over a week old so Adam guessed that they had already met. He was positive that EDS101 was Edison Archer, since all the details seemed to fit. He wondered what Edison could possibly see in David, though he quickly remembered that this was the online world, where David could say anything he wanted. He wished he could print it out as a keepsake, but it was too risky with the busy shared printers.

He had gone this far and felt compelled to find out more about David's double life. He closed out of the "Edison" file and opened the one named, "Ken." Once open, he saw it was similar to the other file in that there were a number of IM communications, but this time it was between an AllenSubJock and MasterKenXXX. The IM's with Ken made the exchange with Edison seem Disneyesque in comparison. David may have been the big boss at work, but from what Adam could gather, he preferred to take orders during his off hours. Right then, he heard a noise at the door and he turned to see Julie's cascade of blonde hair as she entered the office.

Adam quickly minimized the "Ken" document and switched to the legal document he still had open. He felt himself get flush in the face as he turned to confront an inquisitive-looking Julie.

"What are you doing in here?" she asked.

"Just helping David with something."

"Your face is all red. Is everything okay?"

"Yeah, I just got a little too much sun at lunch."

"You and your long lunches," she sighed. "What did David want? I tried calling him, but I just got his voicemail and then Christina told me you were here." She walked toward the computer to look at the screen.

He quickly closed out of Word. "He needed me to email him some case files."

"Hmm," she said, sounding dubious. "Which files?"

"Harrison and Stewart."

"Well, David sounded upset in the message he left me. We need to talk about coverage. Why don't you let me know when you go to lunch from now on so one of us is always around?"

"We should wait until next week to discuss this when David's here."

"Well, I'm going to run my idea by David today. I don't like to be made to look bad when I've done nothing wrong. I hardly ever take my full lunch, and then the one time I do, this happens."

"Well, that's your choice."

"Of course it's my choice and I'm going to call him right now."

"Okay," he said rising from David's chair, realizing she had misunderstood him.

Julie stormed out and Adam shut down David's computer and closed up his office.

Even with the near miss, he couldn't help smiling at what he'd learned. He felt as if he had hit a voyeur's jackpot. He had always suspected David of being the kind of guy that jumps at the chance to pick up the soap in the men's shower, but to see such clear evidence of it was startling.

And what about Edison? He was tempted to warn him about David, but what would he say? That he had been reading his boss's instant messages? No, he didn't think that would look particularly flattering. Perhaps he could have a little payback fun with David, though. He could find a photo of some handsome jock from one of the lesser-traveled muscle sites and create the perfect dominant stud to court AllenSubJock and get the little chameleon to show all his colors. Adam thought this would be right up his alley since lately he seemed to live online during the weekends. At least this would give him a mission, and he couldn't think of a more deserving victim than David.

TWENTY-FOUR

It had felt like three nights in purgatory, but Val was finally free of the hostel of the damned. During the days, it hadn't been so bad because she spent time in cafes or running pre-departure errands, and had even taken the Muni train to Ocean Beach on a sentimental whim to see the Pacific Ocean. However, the nights were a different story. The French lovebirds next door had spent only one night before flying the coop. They were replaced by a man who drank cheap booze, judging by the empty bottles he left outside his door, and who bathed in even cheaper cologne. The man's odor wafted out his window, only to ride a vengeful air current into her room. Of course, this had all happened during an unusual San Francisco summer heat spell, so it was either shut her window and roast or open it up and gag on the stench.

What was more disturbing was that his headboard was directly on the other side of hers; the thin wall separating them might as well have been a piece of Kleenex for all it did to drown out his crazed, drunken muttering and wild boar of a snore. She had switched positions on the bed, putting her head near the base, but that only brought her closer to her other neighbor, the male prostitute, who, apparently, like a convenience store, was always open for business. During the rare times there was a moment of tranquility, it was usually interrupted by the ceaseless fire trucks. Did every damn fire truck in the city have to use this street? she wondered. And where were all the fires?

Val had seen the filthy underside of San Francisco and had survived, a little frazzled for her time there, but now that she had checked out of the place that cleanliness forgot, she felt the worst of her ordeal was finally over.

Walking down Powell Street to catch the BART train that would take her south to the airport, she felt like she was in an oven; the sea breezes that normally provided a natural air-conditioner were still conspicuously absent. She had worn a short-sleeved powder blue silk top and black pants in an effort to look presentable for her arrival in Seattle, but already she noticed sweat stains forming under her arms. Now, she wished she had worn shorts like everyone else around her. She wasn't even certain she owned any shorts, since she had purged most of her casual clothes in an attempt to squeeze her nicest outfits into her two suitcases.

Taking in the view of lower Powell Street, she was surprised she didn't feel any nostalgia now that she was leaving, but she didn't have many memories connected to this part of town. Other than occasionally frequenting a few of the nicer restaurants, she had habitually avoided this area with its crowds of tourists and shoppers. And lugging her heavy bags through this throng of people certainly didn't lend itself to reminiscing.

Today, however, was the beginning of a new chapter in her life. She was leaving this god-forsaken city, and once she was safely in the air, it could be hit by an earthquake and crumble into the Pacific for all she cared. Any place that couldn't recognize and reward her talent was officially dead to her.

As she approached Market Street, she made her way through the line of people who seemed to be permanently waiting at the cable car turnaround. Heading down the BART escalator, she ignored the interchangeable homeless men who peddled *Street Sheets* near the underground entrance. She thought that her recent brush with homelessness would have made her more sympathetic to their plight, but if anything, it had hardened her. She was tired of having the fiscal challenges of others shoved in her face at every street corner, as all she had to do was look in the mirror to see the face of poverty.

Once in the station, she purchased a one-way ticket to the

airport, happy that it only set her back a few dollars. Her phone started chirping like a hungry baby bird and she admonished herself for not charging it fully. She checked for messages while she still could, but there were none, so she descended a second escalator and waited for her train.

She only had to wait a few minutes before her train showed up. Once onboard, she found an empty row of seats toward the back of the car in which to sit and place her luggage. The doors closed, and as the train sped south, the gentle rocking and steady rhythm of the wheels did its magic and lulled her to sleep. The train ride to the airport was relatively speedy and she felt refreshed from her brief slumber. The precious minutes of sleep on the train had seemed more restful than all the nights at the hostel combined.

She found her way to the terminal without much difficulty. The lines weren't very long and she checked her two large bags. The line through security was likewise short and other than the graceless manner in which she stumbled while removing her shoes, she was through it without incident.

She felt so relieved to be checked in that she decided to throw caution to the wind and celebrate her exodus from San Francisco by paying the exorbitant airport markup for a caramel latte. She even decided to splurge on a muffin, since her appetite had returned for the first time in days, and she thought it was a sign of her improved spirits or maybe just relief at being in air-conditioning.

With drink and muffin in hand, she found a gate with open seats and positioned herself away from the monitor playing the insipid airport news program. Things were certainly starting to look up, she reflected, sipping her drink and removing from her bag a *New Yorker* magazine she'd swiped from Stacy's condo. Perhaps Fate had absolved her of her past transgressions.

Boarding began just after 1:30 and if everything went well, she would land in Seattle just before 4:00. Edison had said he had an afternoon appointment, but that it would be over by the time she landed, and he would meet her at baggage claim.

Once onboard the plane, she sat down in her window seat and tried not to get irritated after a heavyset man sat next to her and she saw his flab flow over the armrest into her space. Compared to the last several days, this glorified cattle car felt luxurious and she was determined to make the best of it. She practiced her deep breathing while ignoring the flight safety video, and soon became drowsy again.

It wasn't until the plane took off that it fully hit her that she was leaving San Francisco. She pressed her head against the window and felt her eyes get misty as she saw the Bay Area recede further and further away under a picture perfect blue sky. How had she let it come to this? Spotting the parched Marin Headlands, she suddenly felt as if she were on the losing end of unrequited love. She had given San Francisco the best years of her life, but other than granting her some early success, it had been hard and unyielding in return.

As she continued to peer out the window, watching the details of the landscape become more and more unfamiliar, she broke free from her maudlin thoughts. Maybe she wasn't the one who had failed; maybe the City had failed her. Sure, she had made her share of miscalculations, but perhaps her biggest one had been in always giving San Francisco the benefit of the doubt, thinking of it as an enchanted place at the end of the rainbow where anything was possible.

She regained her composure, wiping her eyes, and pulled the window shade shut. Well, unlike the song, I won't be leaving my heart there, she resolved. "Good fucking riddance," she muttered, loud enough for the man next to her to hear and glare disapprovingly.

"Don't judge me until you can fit into your own seat," she said, not in the mood to be sneered at by a failed armchair critic. He turned away in a huff.

Gradually, she settled into a slumber, only to wake when the woman in front of her reclined her seat. "God damn you," she said, kneeing the seatback once in retaliation. The plane was feeling more and more to her like a cattle car with wings.

She closed her eyes and vaguely sensed the beverage service roll past. When she woke up, she looked at her watch and saw that it was 3:30. She opened the window shade and could see that the sky that had been blue over California was now overcast with grey clouds. She thought Edison had said summer was the dry season, but perhaps it was relative. As they descended toward the city, the captain announced Seattle was 72 degrees with scattered rain showers. She started to get excited about seeing Edison, but she remembered that she needed to temper her excitement due to his loss.

Upon disembarking from the plane, she saw she had a message from Edison, and quickly found out that he would not be meeting her at the airport. Apparently, he was stuck in a meeting with his probate attorney, and in a long message peppered with multiple apologies, he requested she take a taxi directly to his house. He left her detailed instructions on where to catch a taxi along with his address, and told her there was a spare key on top of the light fixture near the back door.

Leave it to a gay man to stand up a woman, she thought. She knew she was being unfair since Edison was one of the most dependable people she knew. He couldn't have known about her dire financial predicament, but how was she supposed to get to his house with little cash and no viable plastic? As if in answer, her phone gave a final spiteful chirp before its blue screen went black.

Her mood, like the weather, had turned foul, and after a short train ride, she reached baggage claim. Looking around, she felt like she had arrived in the land of white people. As she waited for her bags, she quickly tired of all the happy couples flaunting their reunion bliss and walked to the nearby information booth to find out her options for getting downtown. There was a door-to-door shuttle, but that cost almost as much as a cab. Besides that, a hotel shuttle went downtown for much less, and there was a bus option. She knew she should investigate the bus, but she had taken enough mass transit for one day. She had enough to cover the hotel shuttle and decided that if she could just get downtown, Edison's place couldn't be too far.

After her bags arrived, she made her way to the shuttle departure area. When the driver asked her where she was going, she named a major hotel chain that, fortunately, was on his route.

Once they were underway, she looked out at the landscape, which was drab under the gloomy sky, and she couldn't help feeling that she had regressed from the Technicolor world of sunny California to an earlier sepia-toned one.

As they approached the city, however, she became more hopeful when she saw the skyscrapers and felt once again like she was entering civilization. Her hopes were quickly dashed, though, after seeing the skyline was much less impressive than she remembered it from the few times she had watched the sitcom, *Frazier*. What have I gotten myself into? she wondered, recalling now that this was the place where dotcommers went to pasture.

The shuttle went to two hotels before stopping at hers. When paying the fare, she gave the driver exact change, her profuse apologies doing little to soothe his offense at not being tipped. The bellhop immediately pounced on her, trying to help her with her luggage, but she shooed him away and quickly moved from the hotel before he could launch a second attack.

Now what? she considered. The showers had stopped, though the sky still looked threatening. She contemplated setting up camp in a coffee shop until perhaps she could get a ride from Edison, but she had spent the better part of the day sitting around and was anxious to reach his place.

She looked at her watch. It was just after five and rush hour was obviously in full swing. She wasn't sure where she was going, but went downhill to Third Avenue, only because it was easier than going up. She considered calling Edison from a payphone, but at that moment, she looked down the street and saw a bus that said *E. Queen Anne* on its front. She knew Edison lived in Queen Anne and hurried with her luggage to the next bus stop, thankful that no one she knew would witness her in all her *Grapes of Wrath* glory.

Once the bus arrived, she followed the people who were boarding through the backdoor, figuring she would have to pay later. The bus was packed and there were already people standing in the aisle by the time she got on. She wasn't certain why she had thought taking luggage on a bus during rush hour was a good idea. No one offered to get up, and, instead, she got vicious stares from several of the passengers for blocking the aisle.

The bus proceeded through the downtown area and people continued to pack on. The driver caught sight of her luggage through his mirror and said she needed to find a seat or get out as she was creating a hazard. Val looked around helplessly and finally a young man in the back of the bus offered to give up his seat so she could rest her luggage on it. She recalled Edison's address and asked the man if the bus went to it. He told her she needed the bus that goes to *west* Queen Anne. He explained to her that they were currently in Belltown and that she should get off when they reached the top of Queen Anne Hill, though she would still have a long walk to her destination.

When the bus stopped near the summit, she dragged her luggage to the front of the bus, not turning back to acknowledge the grumbles from the people she swiped with her bags. She barely had enough money left to pay the fare. The bus driver looked annoyed and told her that next time she might not be so lucky if she tried to bring all that luggage onto the bus.

"Believe me," Val said, mustering the last vestiges of her dignity, "there won't be a next time."

Once off the bus, she felt as if she had been magically transported to the heart of suburbia. Large older houses, grassy lawns and trees of all sizes surrounded her as far as she could see; all of it was in stark contrast to the celebration of concrete she'd known in downtown San Francisco. The showers had started again and she didn't see a soul, though two luxury SUVs had already sped by on the street.

According to the helpful young man on the bus, she needed to head due west to reach Edison's street. She was already getting soaked and, looking down, she noticed that her silk top had now become transparent. Her hair, which she had never bothered to have cut, being too scared to risk an $8.00 Chinatown surprise, felt like a wet animal on her head. Her luggage wasn't faring too well either. Though her largest bag had wheels, the other one didn't, and she could feel the handle, which she'd repaired with some duct tape the night before, was starting to come loose.

She set out on a westerly course for Edison's house, deciding that if she found an actual person on the deserted street, she would ask for directions. If she found a phone, she would call Edison collect, as tacky as it may seem. She could always pretend she'd lost her wallet, though she realized—even if she wasn't quite ready to face it—that she would have to fess up to him sooner than later about her reduced circumstances and the true nature of her "visit."

When she came to a crest in the hilly street, she looked south and got a view of the city skyline in the distance. She saw the Space Needle prominently in the foreground, that tin relic from the 1962 World's Fair. Was that the best the city could do for a claim to fame? she wondered. "A city of relics," she said aloud. "That's just so goddamn fitting." She wiped away some moisture from her eyes, realizing it wasn't from the rain, but from tears. "God damn it all," she said, and she continued up the street.

TWENTY-FIVE

"Hey Miss Linda, welcome to Squalor Central," Edison said warmly, holding open the front door for Linda and her split-level Bundt cake. Linda walked past him, stopped just inside the door and surveyed the foyer.

"Oh honey, this place is a mess. How are you going to sell it with all your gym clothes and take out bags on the front stairs?" she asked, moving a pair of gym shoes and socks out of her path with her foot.

"I know, I know. The realtor vulture left me a yellow sticky note on the front door saying as much. I'm just so used to coming into my apartment in San Francisco after a run and ditching my clothes, but here, the bedrooms are so far from the front door it's ridiculous."

"My tears fall for the poor man with such a big house," Linda said, a mocking sympathy in her voice. In her normal voice, she cut back to her familiar line of interrogation that Edison knew she used on everyone except Brett. "So, how are you doing in this house anyway? No weirdness, real or imagined?" she asked, putting the cake down on the table next to the bowl of paper hens.

"There have been a few cars driving by slowly or parking and looking in as if this place were a tourist destination. No reapers, thankfully, although I wouldn't be surprised if these birds from Lily were up to something." He went to Linda's side, scooped up two handfuls of hens from the bowl and poured half into her hands.

"Odd," Linda said, "they have eyes. I wouldn't be surprised if the eyes were printed before they were folded. No room for error if that's the case. I've seen these gals before. Oh, yes, Lily has a few in her living room sitting in an ashtray. Lily's birds look angry and a tad desperate; these look pretty happy and prosperous given their numbers." Linda placed her birds back in the bowl delicately. Once she was done, Edison poured his handful of hens into the bowl, watching them bounce.

"Now, Edison, don't manhandle the birds just because they are from Lily. She must like you or she wouldn't have brought them over. Oh, by the way," she said before Edison could respond, "this cake platter and cover are your mother's, so when we're done, I'll leave them in the kitchen."

"Please keep it. I don't bake much and maybe you'll feel obligated to bring one more cake over before I head back to San Francisco."

Edison noted that Linda was stacking the birds, and, with her artist's eye, she arranged them in a cascade of complementary colors. After she finished with the birds, she turned to him and with an unexpected rawness asked, "So, when do you think the house will sell?"

"Well, there's a lot of stuff both here and in storage. An estate sale agent will deal with whatever I don't take. I'll invite you and Brett over as there are a few items I want you to have and you can let me know if there's anything you two want."

"Well, we'll take a look, but we're bringing a checkbook too. Paul and Ellie had excellent taste and we wouldn't feel right not paying you something. I'll take this cake platter back, though, so I can make a new cake style for you. My inner Betty Crocker is roaring these days."

"Inner Betty Crocker? Leave her at home, but I'll take the cake. Seriously, though, your money is no good at Chez Archer."

Linda picked up a paper hen and tickled Edison's neck with its beak, causing him to laugh while gently trying to fight her and the hen off.

"Don't be telling me what is what. I may be yesterday's bitch but my husband's money is good," she said breaking into laughter with Edison.

"Okay, okay, uncle! Let's keep this civil. After all, we have a special guest arriving today and we need to keep up appearances." He paused to look over at the pile of papers and clothes on the staircase. "Well, perhaps I can distract Val with all the food and drink I bought and she won't notice what a dump this place has become. My mother may just return as the Reaping Widow with a mop if I don't start cleaning. I guess it's too late for Val, though. She's going to cab here this afternoon and walk into this mess."

"You aren't going to meet her at the airport? I thought you were Mr. Manners."

"I wanted to pick her up, but today's probate meeting was going to go long. Once I got there, though, I noticed the address of the house on the paperwork was wrong so the meeting ended early. I had already called Val and told her to take a cab so I took the time to set the table for us instead. Brett's still coming later, right?"

"Yes, he's looking forward to it. He's going to come home and shower and then walk over with his appetite."

"Good. I went a little crazy on the food and drink and I was planning on him eating his usual share. I know you and Val are the types to peck at your food while hiding behind your dainty silk fans."

"Me peck at food? Yeah, right. And by the way, just where is my drink, boy?" Linda said as she playfully swatted Edison on his butt.

"Don't bruise the fruit, lady," Edison said laughing, as he motioned Linda to follow him though the front rooms to the kitchen. He continued, "I brought out the formal bar service I found in the dining room. It looks well used. I thought we could sit outside even though it looks like some nasty clouds are stacking up on Mt. Rainier."

"This sounds like a different Edison from the one I knew in

SF who had the *fancy* paper plates for when he wasn't eating over the sink. Remember when you first had Brett and me over to your apartment on Telegraph Hill? We all sat on the floor and you were short plates for dinner. And then you had to order Chinese after Brett ate the main course thinking it was an appetizer. Funny, I remember that as if it were yesterday. We had a lot of fun down there at your place, eating takeout, watching movies and playing all those board games until the wee hours."

After stopping in the kitchen to put the cake in the pantry, they continued to the side porch by way of the back door.

"I forgot. Why did we stop game night?" asked Linda

"One word," Edison said smiling, "Russell. He didn't like board games."

"Oh no, I remember, he didn't like losing at board games."

"That would be more accurate," Edison chuckled.

They stopped on the back porch while Edison ran a garden hose, testing the water temperature with his fingers. Once cold enough, he filled Stella's water bowl. He dried his hands on his khaki shorts and looked out over the lawn wondering if it would brown before he sold the house.

Linda broke the silence, "You know, I was always afraid that Brett was going to drink too much one night and say something to Ms. Russ that we might all have regretted."

"I wish he had. It could have saved me some time. I can just imagine Brett yelling at dear Russell. But enough talking about trash." Edison put his arm gently around Linda's shoulder. "I'm hungry and food is not used to waiting at this house."

They walked the short distance to the side porch and turned the corner to the table he had set. It was lavish by Edison's standards. He'd laid out the silver and china he'd found in the house. His parents had frequently entertained and, with Val arriving, he felt a respectful obligation to keep to their standards.

"Edison, this is amazing!" Linda exclaimed as they turned the wide corner of the porch. "Why, if I didn't know better, I would think that you're trying to woo me."

"Oh, baby," Edison said, in the lowest and sexiest voice he

had. "This gay thing is all a front." With that, he nuzzled the back of her neck with a dry kiss and some heavy breathing.

"Oh, stop that, you big tease. I haven't been hit on since I became the Depressed Pillsbury Dough Girl of Queen Anne. I will need that fan and a hoopskirt to go with my blushing, you flirt, you."

"Then allow me to seat you at my table of sin and don't worry, the drinks are alcohol-free, really."

"You sound like all those guys at Berkeley who used to ply me with wine coolers, telling me that they were not really alcoholic." She sat with a sigh in a large wicker chair.

Edison mimicked Linda, plopping down into his chair. He reached over and started to mix Linda's favorite martini to her familiar specifications.

"All this food, you are no good, Edison. You even have wine out for later!"

"You can join me and your husband at the gym tomorrow if you are feeling guilty."

"Oh honey, Brett already thinks I'm hopeless. I don't need to prove it to him at the gym. As you can see," she said, pinching an inch at her side, "I have become more than I was since leaving San Francisco."

She paused and looked across the street while Edison stirred her martini. He could see she was looking down the street at her house with a detached stare, which Edison noted was not too far from a glare.

Linda's next words came in a voice that was tired and solemn. "I cannot accept that I'm depressed; it's more that I feel powerless."

Edison was surprised to see the change in Linda's face. Her eyes looked angry and her face held an expression that hinted as to how she would appear after twenty years of hard living.

"I'm sorry for the drama, but you are one of the few people I have to talk to these days. You knew me before … now I'm just so damn mad and frustrated."

She was visibly fighting an urge to cry, and from Edison's perspective, she had won.

"Damn it," she said. "I'm not going to be that woman who cries and I know you're not good with tears. Neither one of us is built for emotion, as I remember. Where's my damn martini?" she asked in a rusty voice.

Edison smiled, "I know we have judged others for turning on the waterworks indiscriminately." He handed her the martini and continued, "But lately it seems I have switched ranks. I started to cry yesterday when I found my dad's hunting knives in a macramé reindeer holder my mom made for him. I won't even go into the laundry scoop of tears. Perhaps we were a bit hard on others in the past." Edison leaned back in his chair. "I'll tell you my woe if you tell me yours."

"Oh Edison, your grief is real. Mine is nothing compared to what you've had to deal with. I'm not a good friend at all, crying over my stupid self when you have lost so much."

Picking up his scotch, he raised his glass to her martini glass. "Things may not be good but we are not alone." They sat in silence. Edison noticed that Stella was on the front walk moving with purpose.

Linda spoke from behind her martini glass. "I don't know what's wrong with me. I really tried to make things happen up here. I was honest in my approach and critical when I reviewed my failures but nothing has worked out. In SF, I never worked this hard and I was always at the top of my game." She sighed and drank from her glass.

Edison sipped his scotch and put it down. It was too early for scotch and not a good idea on an empty stomach. He had put out the cabernet glasses and had a bottle of Schafer open and breathing for later. He offered Linda some wine and she waved him off. She was smiling at Stella, who had arrived on the side porch, no doubt smelling the smoked salmon. Edison poured himself a glass as they watched Stella stake out a vantage point to stalk the salmon.

"So," Linda asked, "you looking forward to going back to the inevitable city?" Her voice had an air of defeat and he wasn't sure if it was for her or for him.

He raised an eyebrow over a sip of wine to signal a question.

"You know, SF, the inevitable city, because it's inevitable that one ends up there. Brett always jokes that it's not the city at the end of the rainbow but the city at the end of the slippery slope."

"I don't get it," Edison said putting down his wine glass.

"It's the city where people with expectations and dreams go. I'm beginning to think that *Seattle* is really a typo for *settle*." She slouched in her chair and focused beyond the porch rail. "Damn, instead of hitting menopause, I've hit metropause."

"That's a little harsh," Edison chuckled. "One, I think you are a bit young and two, Seattle is hardly a slum." Edison gestured with his glass at the leafy street behind a very poised Stella sitting on the porch rail.

Linda was quiet for a moment and then blurted out, "Edison, it's not going well. I think Brett wants to leave me and I don't blame him. He wants the girl I was in SF and that's not happening up here. I just eat and watch my failures stack up. If I get any bigger, small objects are going to start to orbit me." She wiped a tear from her cheek and reached for the last of her martini. "I love Brett but I don't think I can be what I was in SF up here in Timber Town."

Edison paused, not knowing what to say, "Have you talked to him about it?"

"No, we don't talk anymore."

"Well," Edison said, sitting back in his chair, "that has got to change. Assumptions thrive in silence. Do you want me to talk to him?"

"No, I know you're right. I'll talk to him. I just don't know what to say. He kept his side of the bargain and more. His job is great and he likes it, and we even landed a house that exceeded our imaginary dream house. It's just that I've developed the touch of death since moving up here. Oh, sorry, that was rude."

Edison smiled, "Don't worry about it. Hungry?" he asked as he lifted up a plate of lamb salad.

"Oh yes, I need something to absorb the martini before it absorbs me."

They passed the food, and when they were both ready to eat, Edison noted that Linda's plate, while full, was laid out as if it were prepared for a photo shoot. His plate looked like a three year-old who had returned from his first buffet. He was turning into a slob and it was one of many behaviors he wanted to change. He made a mental note to make a mental checklist.

"What do you want to say to Brett? Do you want to move out of Seattle or perhaps not try to replicate your professional life of SF up here? Get him involved in something you would like to do, perhaps?"

"No, I don't want to move. Brett is happy up here and I don't want to be the one that takes that away from him. I could talk to Brett if I just knew what I wanted. Damn, it's complicated. How is your woe by the way? No reason to talk about my circular problems that I can't even articulate," Linda said peering into the martini shaker.

Edison noticed that Linda always became the host no matter where she went. She refilled his water and wine glasses and then set about freshening her martini.

"I did hear from the County Coroner," he said, embarrassed that his voice seemed a bit perky given the subject. "The cause of death is asphyxiation as they had earlier presumed. How they asphyxiated is the question. The only good news is that it is unlikely they suffered. The question of foul play is still out there since half of Queen Anne apparently has keys to this house. I'm a little worried about Val staying here. I'm going to put her in an upper room and have her keep the windows open until we know for sure what happened. The report is public record, so I fully expect Val to see the hordes of Reaping Widow fans on the front lawn when it hits the press. I'll tell her they are the Queen Anne Welcome Wagon whose theme this month is the occult."

"Hmm, not the best news, but it's something. I heard Lily

threw a phone at the homicide investigator when she thought he was being impertinent. She is so gracious, normally."

Edison put down his fork, stunned. "What?!" he exclaimed. "Lily? Hardly! That woman and her chorus line of cigarettes is hardly gracious."

"Oh, Edison, be nice. She is a delightful woman with such manner and poise. I feel like a philistine when she has us over for cocktails and dinner. That woman has more linen than Cleopatra, by the way."

"Lily entertains?" Edison asked. "I thought she spent her leisure time searching for baby carriages to use as ashtrays."

"Oh, you heard about that baby carriage incident? But seriously, Edison, your mother wouldn't be happy to hear you speak ill of Lily. Both Paul, I mean your father, and your mother were so close to her."

"Well, if you like her, I'll consider giving her yet another chance."

"She's such a kind and caring woman, I cannot believe you have any quarrel with her. It must be a male thing, although she and Brett get along just fine."

"I guess I'm the one with the problem," Edison said scraping his plate clean with a piece of sourdough bread. "If I seem distracted, it's because I keep looking for Val's cab. It should be here soon."

"I do remember Val, now. She was the curvaceous cover girl type who was the queen of the dotcoms way back when?"

"That's her. I don't know what she's been up to recently but it sounds like she could use a break from SF."

"Oh, I almost forgot," Linda said with a mouthful of salad. "The lady that sometimes helps me with my cleaning can take an extra client if you want some help."

"Can she start today?" Edison asked as he held up a dirty dish. "Give her my number and she can take a look at the house to see what she will charge."

"You'll love her, I promise. The house will sell at a better rate if it's gleaming from top to bottom."

"Agreed. It's going to be a busy time, so an extra set of hands would be a good investment, and I have a feeling that Val is a stranger to domestic tasks as I remember her office being a bit chaotic."

Dark clouds were starting to take over the sky but the air remained warm and Edison felt himself relax. Linda, with feet up on an empty chair, had taken Stella into her lap and the cat was purring loudly.

"He never does that with me," Edison remarked, pointing at Stella.

"Perhaps you don't fit into his reality yet. It takes time. Or maybe he knows something about you we all don't," Linda said, raising an eyebrow in mock suspicion.

"I know something you don't know," Edison said in a sing-song voice. "I met someone at Kerry Park."

"Really," Linda said, her face lighting up as she reached for Edison's wine glass.

"Yes." Edison smiled and served himself another helping from the various plates and bowls in an attempt to build the suspense. "And in case you were wondering, SF-style trash can float up to Seattle. There must be a hidden canal."

"Do tell," Linda said as the rain began to fall on the warm street.

TWENTY-SIX

Val turned the corner and looked at the number on the house nearest her, relieved to see that she had finally reached Edison's block. She had walked up what seemed like every god-damn staircase known to man, not understanding why so many of the streets here ended in staircases. And the hills seemed ten times worse than any she had encountered in San Francisco. Wetter and wearier for her travels, she had found it necessary to stop repeatedly along the way because of the weight of her suit-cases. She had seen very few people on the streets, mostly just passing luxury cars. Several times, she had felt like hurling something through the windows at the passengers who stared out at her as if she were some sort of alien. She had never felt as low as she did now, and all her preparations to make a good impression on Edison seemed like the farce that it was, as trans-parent as the soaked front of her silk blouse.

As she continued down the block, she caught sight of a man and a woman seated at a table under the protection of a wrap-around porch. She could see a large side table with dishes and heard a woman laughing. As Val got closer, she could tell right away by the man's brown wavy hair and profile that it was Edi-son. She tried to get a better look at the woman, but only saw her backside. She wondered what was going on. Edison was supposed to be in a meeting with his attorney, but instead he was lounging around while she had just been through the train, plane and automobile combo from hell.

They hadn't noticed her, and as she approached the front of the house, she felt a surge of resentment. Objectively, she knew

Edison had done nothing wrong, but her thoughts turned dark. Why did she come up here? Why hadn't she just pushed for Edison's couch in SF?

She confirmed the street address was indeed Edison's, crushing any hope that her eyes had deceived her and that the person sitting there so carefree and oblivious to her misery had been a stranger. When she approached the stairs leading up to the front porch, Edison caught sight of her and did a double take. The woman with whom he was talking turned around and gave her a puzzled look. She proceeded up the stairs, yanking up the dead weight of her suitcases, step by step, feeling the weariness in her arms. As she neared the top of the stairs, she yanked her luggage up from behind her and the duct taped handle came completely off her suitcase. She watched helplessly as it fell down the stairs with several loud crashes, opening up and spilling its contents on the wet pavement.

Edison rushed over, looking startled at the sight of her. "Val, you're soaking wet. What happened?"

She must have looked as if she had just washed ashore from a shipwreck, judging from the concern in Edison's eyes. Edison, on the other hand, looked better than ever. It was only now, seeing him in person, that the full enormity of his situation hit her. She felt her anger dissipate and something else began to well up from deep within. She looked down below at her worldly possessions lying in the rain, then back at Edison, and tried to speak, "I ... I ...." Then, the emotions she had been holding back from the last desperate months in San Francisco came pouring out of her. Initially, her mouth started quivering and then, to her horror, she heard a low sob rise from within.

"Val, are you okay?" Edison asked, putting his arm around her.

She tried to control herself, but now that the floodgates had opened, she felt the tears pouring from her eyes and she started to convulse uncontrollably. Against her efforts, her sobbing became louder and she felt tremors rip through her body. The woman hurried over to them, who she now recognized as a doughier version of Edison's artsy gal pal, Linda Gale, from San Francisco.

"Honey, are you okay?" Linda asked in a concerned voice.

Val tried to speak, but she couldn't stop sobbing, and, as they helped her up the final step, she noticed they both looked panicked.

"Here, come sit down," said Linda, leading her to the table on the side porch and pulling out a wicker chair with a pillow seat for her. "Eds, why don't you get her suitcases and clothes out of the rain."

Edison hurried down the steps, clumsily retrieved her clothes and luggage and brought them up to the shelter of the porch. He came over and kneeled beside her, taking her hand in his. She tried to speak, but she had no control over her facial muscles, which were quaking wildly.

"Val, what's wrong. Are you hurt?" Edison asked.

She tried to answer, but the words didn't come.

"Honey, you're soaked. I'm going to get you a robe," Linda said before going through the front door and disappearing into the house.

"Just take it easy, Val," offered Edison, rubbing her shoulder. "You don't have to speak, but can you nod your head?"

She shook her head yes.

"Are you hurt?"

She shook her head no.

"Were you in an accident?"

She shook her head no, fearing that an unattractive bout of hyperventilation was about to set in.

Linda appeared and wrapped a robe around her. "We should get her inside," Linda said, wiping Val's face dry with a hand towel. "Val, honey, are you able to get up?"

She nodded that she was, and Linda led her inside through the front door and Edison trailed behind with her bags. They brought her into a front room and sat her down on a large couch, positioning themselves on either side of her like worried bookends.

She sat there for a moment, feeling mortified as she imagined what kind of damaged goods she must appear to them. Prior to the past week, she hadn't cried in ages, and she had oftentimes wondered if she had any real emotions, but just like that, she had completely broken down and turned into the kind of person she hated. Perhaps, she mused darkly, now that she was homeless and pathetic, she could take advantage of her new penchant for tears and send in an audition tape to that television show that builds houses for down-and-out people—where they focus on the people crying on the lawn rather than the crap construction they do. Hearing someone enter the room broke her from her reverie and she turned to see Edison glaring toward the kitchen.

"Oh, Mrs. Ling, just help yourself and come right on in," he said.

Even in her current state, Val detected sarcasm in Edison's voice. An older Asian woman in a colorful pantsuit entered carrying a heaping plate of food. Val noticed it was the same chinaware and food that she'd seen from the table outside and couldn't imagine what this rail of a woman intended to do with it. The woman said that she had heard a loud wailing and was hoping that Stella had finally put an end to that nasty Johnson child.

"I wanted to make certain that dear cat was okay," the woman added.

"No, both Stella and the Johnson boy are fine," Edison said, taking a sideways glance at Val.

It was only now that the woman seemed to notice her.

"Oh, dear," she said, moving to Val, putting her plate down on a wooden tray that rested on an ottoman. "You look like you've been through hell." Lily pulled out a linen handkerchief from her jacket pocket and wiped the moisture from around Val's eyes, and Val caught the scent of lavender. "It looks as if you can use a drink," she suggested, leaving Val with the handkerchief and turning her gaze to Linda. "Linda, dear," the woman said, gently grabbing Linda's hand. "How nice to see you here. Can I get you anything?"

"No, I'm fine, Lily, but don't feel you have to play host here. Just have a seat. Edison or I will be happy to get you whatever you want."

Val looked over at Edison who was rolling his eyes.

"That will be the day," Lily said, glaring at Edison before disappearing into the kitchen.

Val heard the sound of a cabinet opening in the kitchen and the clinking of ice in glasses. Lily reappeared a moment later with two tumblers of scotch and handed one to Val. "Just drink it down, dear. It will do you good."

Val wasn't a big scotch drinker, but, instinctively, it seemed right and she cupped her shaking hand around the glass and took a sip.

"By the way, Val, this is my neighbor Mrs. Ling," said Edison. "Mrs. Ling, this is my friend Val Panos from San Francisco."

"All my friends call me, Lily," she beamed maternally at Val.

Gradually, Val felt better and was able to regain her composure. She described her ordeal, starting with her trip to Seattle, and to her amazement, she didn't stop there. In a monologue, she recounted her downward spiral in San Francisco from the loss of her options at Trident to her recent flirtation with homelessness. The words just poured out of her as the tears had flowed earlier. After keeping her string of failures a secret for so long, she found this unlikely confessional to her friend and two near strangers liberating. Edison and Linda listened with concern, while Lily gazed on from across the room, alternately drinking her scotch and eating, watching Val as if engrossed in a real-life docudrama.

"Val, I wish you had told me about all of this earlier," Edison said, after she was done, putting his arm around her shoulder. "That's what friends are for."

"I know," she said. "Please don't take it personally. I haven't told anyone, including my family. I just kept thinking I'd get back on my feet. I've always managed in the past."

"Believe me, honey, we've all been there," said Linda.

"People don't like to advertise their bad luck. They just learn how to cushion the blows," she said, patting her stomach.

There was a moment of silence, which was interrupted by the clatter Lily made placing her empty plate onto the wooden tray. She squinted down at her watch as if trying to make sense of a new high-tech gadget. "Oh dear, I need to leave for a dinner party I'm attending at my daughter's."

"I hope you'll have some appetite left," Edison said, and again Val heard the sarcasm in his tone.

"It's better not to have one when dining at my daughter's. She dresses like a prostitute," Lily added flatly, as if in explanation. She walked over to the couch and placed her hand on Val's shoulder. "Dear, you've obviously been through a lot. I live two houses down if you need anything. I'm glad you're here. You've got spirit and people like him," she said, pointing to Edison, "are in dire need of it." She kissed Val on the forehead as if giving her a blessing and told her to keep the handkerchief. Lily turned to Linda and gave her a warm hug goodbye, mentioning something about high tea later in the week. She was out of the room before Val knew it.

"What a nice woman," Val said after she left.

"So, by nice woman, do you mean neighborhood menace?" asked Edison.

"Oh, Eds," said Linda. "You can't expect Lily to warm up to you with that attitude."

Linda took her leave next, saying she should check on Brett since she couldn't imagine what would be more pressing to him than food. They saw Linda to the front door and before leaving, she turned to Val and told her that she and Brett had plenty of extra space at their place if she ever needed a vacation from Chez Edison.

Val thanked her, genuinely touched by the offer. She hated feeling like a charity case, but at least she was a charity case with options.

Once Linda had left, Edison closed the front door and turned to Val, looking serious. "Val, I had no idea you were going through all of that, but I hope you know you are welcome to stay here until I move."

"Thank you, Edison," she said, feeling another bout of tears coming. Now that they were alone, Val realized she had yet to express her condolences to him. "Edison, I show up here like a train wreck but it's all my own doing. I'm so sorry about your parents. From the first time I met them, I wished they were my parents." She opened her arms to embrace him, and they stood hugging for a while until Edison made a crack about them being bad entertainment for the birds.

"Huh?" Val asked, prying loose from Edison, only now noticing the dainty paper birds in the expensive looking crystal bowl. "What in the hell are those?"

"They are origami hens. Lily Ling, the drunk whom you just met, brought them over. I think she stole them from a lecture she attended at the Asian Cultural Center."

"They're pretty," she mumbled as she stared into the bowl and plucked out a scarlet hen near the top.

"She said they're either for good luck or for fertility. Apparently, she skipped the details to have a smoke."

"She sounds like a character, but she seemed rather gentle to me," Val said, feeling a wave of lightheadedness hit her, causing her to wobble.

"Are you okay?" asked Edison, grabbing hold of her.

"I think I'm just a little hungry. Is the buffet out on the porch still open?"

"Yes, and there's plenty more in the fridge. Why don't we go and get some food in you."

"I should probably change, first," Val said, gesturing to the robe draped over her wet clothes. "This soggy castaway look is so *Gilligan's Island*."

Edison chuckled, pointing to the corner of the foyer where he'd set down her luggage. "I kept the clothes that fell out of your suitcase in a separate pile since they were a little wet. Fortunately, most of them were wrapped in plastic. There's a bathroom just down the hall to your right," he continued. "I'll fix you up a plate of food while you change. Just holler if you need anything." He headed toward the kitchen, picking up the scotch glasses and plates in the front room.

She reached back toward the bowl to return the scarlet paper hen, but something compelled her to hold onto it. She looked down the hall and, with Edison out of sight, slipped the hen into her purse.

Rummaging through her suitcase, she pulled out the most casual outfit she could find: a summer skirt and blouse. As she went down the hall to the bathroom, she turned around one more time to look at the bowl, and felt an odd guilt as she saw the dozens of other hens seeming to glare at her for abducting one of their own.

TWENTY-SEVEN

Adam closed the door to his studio apartment, breathing a sigh of relief as he put down his keys and Mexican takeout near his laptop on the desk. He had walked home in a hurry, anxious to start his weekend, and had worked up a sweat even though the cool ocean breezes had returned to town after an extended hiatus. Friday after work was his favorite part of the week since the whole weekend was in front of him. And this weekend, he had determined, was going to be different.

While taking in the familiar clutter of the apartment, he kicked off his shoes and emptied his pants pockets. The futon was unmade as usual, barely ever in the upright couch position except on weekends when he cleaned. It was a large studio, with a decent-sized main room, a walk-in closet and a separate kitchen with room for a table. His studio was on the top floor of a six-story building and had a southerly exposure, which provided plenty of sun and an unobstructed view of the city beyond. The building had been built in the 1920's, so it had all the quality detailing of the period, including stained glass windows at the building's entryway, a marble floor in the lobby and high ceilings in the apartments. The downside was that the longtime owner hadn't kept the building up, which could be seen by the peeling beige paint on the ceiling and walls, the worn cockroach-colored carpet, and appliances in the kitchen that harkened back to another era, when terms such as "icebox" were used. If he had been more ambitious, he supposed he could fix it up, but he suspected that it would still be a dump regardless of whatever cosmetic futility he exercised. It was a dump but at least it was a rent-controlled dump.

He pulled off his corporate casual ensemble and threw it into the laundry basket. His socks were tight and it felt good to liberate his feet from them. He went to the bathroom sink to wash the perspiration off his face. Afterward, he stretched for a moment, stifling a yawn, before collapsing onto his futon.

It had certainly been an interesting week, he reflected. The glimpse into David's double life via his office computer had been a shocker. Adam had seriously considered joining the online dating service and having some fun with the hypocrite, but after he thought about it, he decided he didn't want to go there. He had seen enough on David's computer to realize what the inner David was all about and it wasn't attractive.

More troubling to him was how David's online life had hit a little too close to home. During the week, Adam had a regimented routine of work and the gym, which didn't leave much free time. The weekends were a different story, and not a pretty one, given his current and socially isolating online rut. He had friends, but nothing like the close friendships he'd had during school. And while he had met a few guys at the gym, they were never the ones he had his eye on.

He could go out to the bars, but his few experiences had been negative. He didn't drink much, didn't like the loud music and found all the attitude overwhelming. Therefore, he usually spent several hours of each weekend online trying to meet someone, but rarely connecting with anyone, because once he weeded out all the frauds and creeps, there weren't many people left. The last time he had met someone interesting was on a warm winter day while reading in the park. Luc, a handsome 24-year-old who was visiting from Lyon, had sat next to him and started a conversation. It hadn't been lost on him that he'd met Luc simply by getting out of the apartment and joining the ranks of the living.

He also knew that time was not a friend in the youth-oriented gay community and that there was already a new generation making him feel like yesterday's news. It was one thing to be bitter from the sweet, but he felt bitter from the lack of it. He'd never had a long-term relationship, only the occasional bad date, which never seemed to blossom into anything but a couple more bad dates. He only dated people who approached him or that he found online, and, more than not, he was the one who ended up calling it quits.

So, barring that his dream man came knocking on his apartment door to rescue him like some reclusive princess in a fairy tale, he realized nothing would ever change unless he took action. After all, he didn't want to turn into David, still trolling the personals ten years from now. Though he had to admit that even that reject had at least managed to have a successful career, which was more than he could say for himself.

He needed to make things happen, so he had decided to skip the online world this weekend. He wanted to dive right into his new life by arranging a sure thing and rationalized that an erotic massage was the answer. He knew it wasn't ideal, but he thought it would at least fulfill the basic need of being touched and perhaps touching an attractive guy.

Once he finished dinner, he searched through his canvas bag and pulled out a *Bay Area Reporter*, one of the local gay weeklies. He had picked up a copy on his way home from work knowing that the back section contained a comprehensive listing of massage ads. He liked the fact that many of the masseurs had photos so he could easily assess their physical attributes. However, he knew to be wary of the Father Time factor since he'd noticed some of the photos hadn't changed in years.

As he paged through the massage ads, he wondered why the selection of men wasn't better for being in a gay mecca, but there tended to be at least a few promising ads. When he turned to the last page, he thought he had found his man. His name was Phil and the ad gave his stats as 6'0, 185, 31 y.o., blond/blue eyes, with an in rate of $100. There was a black and white picture of him standing shirtless in a pair of jeans and his chest appeared smooth and nicely muscled. His arms, which were folded below his chest, were also nice-sized and his midsection looked lean and muscled. The feature that really sold Adam, though, was his face, which had a cute and boyish grin. He looked wholesome, as if he were fresh from stacking bales of hay on a farm. In reality, he probably smoked three packs of cigarettes a day and referred to people he didn't like as "Mary," but at least he looked good in the smallish black and white photo. He determined that if Phil was a dud, he'd try someone else next week. And why not? he reflected. He was the new Adam who got out and did things—even if he couldn't afford them.

He decided to call and make an appointment for tomorrow afternoon. As he picked up the phone to dial the number, he was overcome by nervous excitement. His heartbeat was racing and his hands had become cold and clammy. Relax, he told himself. You're just making an appointment for a massage. It's no big deal. He took a few deep breaths and dialed the number. After only one ring, it went straight to voicemail, the message saying: "Hey, this is Phil. I'm not available at the moment, but leave your name and number and I'll get back to you."

Phil's voice sounded okay, more gruff than anything else, but not like the Queen Mary he had feared. Adam left a message conveying his desire for a Saturday afternoon appointment. He used his online alias "Dan," and left his phone number. He hung up the phone, relieved that it was over. Lying back down on the bed, he felt slightly apprehensive as to what he had set into motion, thinking how scandalized his high Catholic parents would be, but he was pleased that he had taken decisive action.

He had just drifted off into a post meal slumber when the phone rang, bringing him back to reality. "Oh crap," he said aloud, feeling the new Adam run for cover, but he calmed himself down and reached for the phone.

TWENTY-EIGHT

Cherie pulled into her condo's underground garage and eased into her parking space. The commute from the realty office was less than four blocks, but she chose to drive anyway, rationalizing that because she was often out meeting clients, she needed her vehicle to be on hand. Even on days when she wasn't meeting clients, she preferred to drive, despite the fact that parking around her office was scarce, leading to frustrating drives around the block, all of it taking much longer than if she had just walked.

She stepped out of her SUV and walked to the elevator bank. Once inside the elevator, she pressed the PH-1 button to go up to her twenty-third floor penthouse. She was relieved Friday had finally come since it had not been a good week for her. Seeing her less than dazzling image in the reflective surface of the elevator door confirmed this. She knew there was something wrong when even her concealer couldn't hide the dark circles under her eyes.

Her once promising Queen Anne sale was looking less and less likely. It wasn't for lack of interest from prospective buyers, as she had received numerous inquiries since she had posted the listing on Amstead Reality's website, but she'd had to stall them because of one very large obstacle: Edison Archer. Apparently—and she could only speculate since she was never able to reach him—Edison wasn't ready to commit to the sale. She had pulled out all the stops on this one and even her complimentary landscaping ploy hadn't had the desired effect. Instead, Edison had sent her a rather terse note acknowledging her efforts, but making it clear that he did not want her pulling a stunt like that again. He had also included a check for the exact amount to cover the cost of the landscaping.

This was another reason she didn't like dealing with fruits since they had immunity to her full arsenal of charms. It would take drastic action to revive this sale and she was prepared to take it, if only she knew what to do.

Her efforts with Brett had proven just as unsuccessful. He had completely blown her off since their coffee date. She had emailed him soon after, but he didn't return her messages for days, and then, when he did, only to say that his schedule had become very busy. She had tried to catch him at the gym on a few occasions, but she hadn't had any success and she was now suspicious that he had changed his schedule in order to avoid her. She called his listed number twice, but on both occasions, a woman who she could only assume was his wife had answered and she had hung up. She had spotted his frumpy hippo of a wife a few times on her night watches, and couldn't fathom what Brett's attraction to her was. Perhaps, she mused, Brett was one of those types that liked a charity case for a wife. She had considered doing at least a drive-by this evening, if not a full park and watch, but she simply didn't have the energy.

She wouldn't beg for this sale, she reflected as she stepped out of the elevator and walked down the hallway, nor for some man who seemed to prefer a manatee to a mermaid. She was not about to give up on the Archer house or Brett just yet. But for now, she had bigger things to worry about such as putting the many pieces of the Merkel Mansion sale into place.

She reached her condominium door and unlocked it. She had bought the condo a few years earlier in the aftermath of a friend's vengeful divorce settlement. She never learned all the details of the split, but hadn't cared much as she knew a bargain when she saw it. She had since grown enamored of vertical living for the views it afforded and the distance it put between her and the trash on the streets.

She walked through the front hall to the kitchen and put her purse down on the counter, seeing she had a new message on her answering machine. She was about to check it when she heard a noise behind her.

"Hello, Miss Cahill. How are you?"

Cherie turned around in alarm, relieved to see it was just her maid approaching, carrying a bucket of supplies. "Oh, Carlotta, you startled me. I didn't realize you were here."

"Yes, Miss Cahill. I just finished. It took longer than usual."

"Well, it looks as if you've been very busy, Carlotta," Cherie said, admiring the kitchen in all its brushed aluminum glory and the hardwood floors of the main room which gleamed. The early evening sun shone through the balcony doors, infusing the rooms with a saffron glow. "I may have mentioned this before, but my father used to hire your people to help pick the fruit on our farm. I remember one or two in particular that I got to know quite well," she added, hoping her smile didn't betray the nature of her memory.

"My people?" Carlotta asked, looking perplexed.

"You know, Mexicans." Cherie saw what appeared to be a look of annoyance flash across Carlotta's face.

"Miss Cahill, you must not remember, but we spoke about this before. My family is from Colombia."

"Well, I didn't remember the exact city, but I knew it was from somewhere in Mexico."

Carlotta laughed. "Colombia is a country in South America."

"Well, color me blonde," Cherie said, twirling a bit of her hair in her fingers. "I never pay much attention to that part of the world. Say, how's that handsome brother of yours, Carlos, doing? He never comes by to pick you up anymore."

"He's fine. He's back in school for his masters but he's been helping with the business over the summer."

"I'm glad to hear he's trying to better himself. Is he the first one in your family to go to school?"

"No, I have a degree in marketing and my sister Josefina has a degree in accounting and Angelica is going back for her MBA part-time this fall."

"Oh, how nice," Cherie said, suddenly feeling less self-assured about the communications degree she had earned from a college known throughout the state as "the party school."

"Miss Cahill, I got the coffee stain out of the master bedroom carpeting. I arranged all of your medications alphabetically and put them on the top two shelves of the medicine cabinet. I ran two full loads of dishes through the dishwasher and did the rest by hand. And it turns out that the odor from the guest bedroom was a carton of Chinese food that had fallen behind the headboard."

"Well, it was probably from when my brother visited last month. You know how messy men are," Cherie said, knowing none of her brothers had ever visited and that she had passed out more than once in her guest bedroom after a night out. "How much do I owe you? The usual?"

"Actually, it will be an additional $30.00 due to the extra time."

"$30.00? If your prices keep going up like this, I'll need a second job," Cherie said, forcing a weak laugh. "I must be personally subsidizing your family's higher education."

"May I suggest that if you keep things a bit tidier, your charges will be as before."

Cherie met Carlotta's steady gaze, and, for a moment, she felt like shoving her into the wall and beating her repeatedly with her bucket of supplies; instead, she smiled coldly as she took her purse from the counter and fished out several bills from her wallet. "Well, don't spend it all in one place."

"Thank you, Miss Cahill. Have a good evening," Carlotta said, as she headed toward the door.

"Adios, Carlotta. Hasta … next week," Cherie replied, the small amount of Spanish that she'd picked up on the farm failing her. As she was closing the door, she thought she heard Carlotta say something from the hallway, but when she peered out, Carlotta was gone.

She walked back to the kitchen, still seething at the nerve of that uppity Latina. On the farm, what she had just paid Carlotta would have been the equivalent of a hard day's wages. "Tidier my ass," she fumed, scanning the kitchen. Sure, she'd been a little lax lately, but she was under a lot of stress. She marveled at Carlotta's impudence suggesting that she, the employer, should clean up the place for her, the maid.

The blinking red light of her answering machine caught her attention and she pressed the play button. "Hi, honey, it's Janet," she heard her friend's husky yet warm voice. "Just wanted to see if you could come a little earlier to the meeting on Sunday to help me with setup. It should be a good one. We're going to organize some protests over the next couple of weeks. One will be at an abortion clinic here in Seattle and the other will be at the state penitentiary in Walla Walla. Some anti-death penalty group will be protesting the execution of a convicted murderer and we're going to stage a counter-protest. Hope you can make both as we need as many people as we can get. Oh and I'm bringing my famous coconut, date and honey clusters that you liked so much. Okay, hon, I'll talk to you later. Bye."

"Yuck," Cherie said loudly, remembering the sticky little nightmares she would forever associate with a violent case of diarrhea she developed after eating them. She would call Janet later as she didn't have time for activism right now. While she liked capital punishment well enough, the abortion issue was more complex for her. She played along, of course, that it was murder and all that, but she knew no man was going to tell her what she could or could not do with her body. She would be damned if she'd ever carry an unwanted pregnancy to term just because some Johnny one-nighter's seed got lucky. She had never felt the maternal instinct so many other women claimed to possess and, even in the best of circumstances, she couldn't envision devoting twenty years of her life to raising some brat who would probably grow up to resent her as much as she did her own parents.

She turned on the TV, switching to FOX, as she found it the most trustworthy news source besides her talk radio shows. The lead stories were all too familiar: more bombings in the Middle

East and one in Europe. Where had all the terrorists come from? she wondered. Maybe these really were the warning signs of the end of days as some of the women at church were convinced. America was a lone beacon of hope in a crazy world. But even here, she worried that the God-fearing people like herself were gradually becoming the minority. It was all too much for her to think about right now and she muted the TV.

She went into the master bedroom and stripped out of her work attire, tossing it on the floor. She opened a chest drawer and took out a pair of cotton pajama bottoms and a tee that Carlotta had washed and neatly folded. Moving to the adjacent bathroom, she opened the medicine cabinet and saw that Carlotta had been true to her word and had alphabetized her medications. Of course, Carlotta didn't see all of them, since she also had a second stash in her SUV.

She used to carry all her prescriptions in her purse, but it had become so heavy and cluttered that she had felt awkward walking around sounding as if she'd just swiped an aisle of medications from the drugstore. Her SUV glove compartment now served as her portable pharmacy. She located her desired antidepressant and took out a double dose.

She had been feeling worse recently and had taken it upon herself to increase her dosage, but so far, she hadn't noticed any improvement. She alternately felt tired or wired, but never at the appropriate time of day. If it wasn't for her daytime crutch of caffeine and her nighttime dose of sleeping pills, she was convinced she would be a total zombie.

Once she sold the Merkel Mansion, she planned to spend a long weekend at her cabin in the Cascades. She actually found nature quite dull, but after having spent much of her life on a farm, she did find she missed the quiet at times. Well, she reflected, if those Middle East terrorists ever started bombing this place, she would be off to her mountain cabin in a flash. She kept an emergency survival kit in the back of her SUV and she had stocked the cabin with a host of supplies. Though it wasn't a cabin in the rustic sense. She'd furnished it with all the modern amenities such as a kitchen full of new appliances, a satellite dish, plus a generator, and had plenty of comfort foods on hand. If the end of days were truly coming, she would pray for salvation, but in the meantime, she intended to do whatever was necessary to survive.

She shut the medicine cabinet and, in the bright vanity light, noticed that the dark circles under her eyes were worse than the polished steel of the elevator door had revealed. Tonight she would sleep well, she decided. She cupped the pills in her hand, went to the kitchen and poured herself a glass of white wine. She popped the pills in her mouth and took two deep gulps from her glass before refilling it. With glass in hand, she sat down in front of the TV, turned the volume up and watched for signs of the end of days.

TWENTY-NINE

Running late as usual, Adam thought, putting his fare in the Muni turnstile. He had only ten minutes to get to the Castro and to find the masseur's apartment to make his 4:00 appointment. Descending the stairs leading underground, he heard the familiar chimes designating the approach of a train, followed by the recorded female voice announcing that an outbound K would be arriving in two minutes. It was perfect timing since K was one of the trains that would take him to the Castro. By the time he was down the stairs, he heard the roar of the incoming train and felt the draft of forced air blow through his hair.

The station was packed, which wasn't surprising for the Powell Street Station on a Saturday afternoon. People were already positioning themselves to get onboard, and he saw several older Chinese women with pink grocery bags stealthily maneuver to the front of the crowd. Eyeing the swarm of people, he regretted not just shelling out the extra money for a cab.

Once the train came to a stop and the doors opened, he merged with the throng of bodies positioning themselves to get on, hardly giving the disembarking passengers a chance to exit. By the time he boarded, it was standing room only. He held onto the overhead rail and felt the bodies squeezing in all around him. While he didn't enjoy being in the crowd, somehow, today, it was all part of the experience, and it was better than sitting alone in his apartment in front of the computer.

The car started with a jolt and he bumped into the man standing next to him. Adam turned to apologize only to see that the man was smiling at him. Adam smiled in return, noticing how cute the guy was in an unconventional kind of way. He was a little taller and leaner than Adam and looked to be slightly younger. He had pale skin and his dark brown hair was cut in a retro '70's style suggestive of Peter Brady. He had multiple piercings in his ears, which Adam never considered a turn-on, but on him it worked. The man was wearing headphones and listening to an iPod that was attached to his belt loop.

As the car started again and they entered the tunnel, Adam gazed straight ahead at his reflection in the train window, though he couldn't help looking at the cute guy's reflection, which he could see was grinning at him. Adam smiled, though his self-consciousness got the better of him and he averted his eyes.

Their reflections vanished as the train entered the light of the Civic Center Station. A few people squeezed on the train before it departed. As the train went back into the tunnel, Adam looked straight ahead and saw the cute guy was still looking at him, though now he was mouthing words to his music. Adam tried to play it cool, but he suspected his occasional uncontrollable smile gave away any pretense of casualness.

He was trying to figure out what to do, and as they reached the Van Ness stop, the dilemma was solved for him. They were pushed together as outgoing people squeezed past. The mystery man pulled off his headphones and turned toward Adam, donning a self-assured smile.

"Pretty crowded today," he said.

"Yeah, is something special going on?"

"Who knows? Probably just a delay. I'm Ben, by the way," he said, extending his right hand.

"I'm Adam," he said, shaking hands.

"So where are you headed today, Adam?" Ben asked in an officious tone that was offset by his smile.

"The Castro. How about you?"

"Same," he said, giving Adam a knowing look.

Adam tried not to be too obvious as he looked Ben over. He

was wearing a mod dress shirt and dark jeans, the kind of clothes that could just as easily be designer label as from a thrift shop, and the kind that Adam never purchased. Looking down at his own clothes, he now saw how bad his untucked short-sleeved polo and tired jeans looked in comparison. And who wore topsiders anymore? he considered, eyeing his brown boat shoes that looked as if they belonged in a Molly Ringwald movie from the 1980's. Ben, on the other hand, had hip leather shoes with three fancy racing stripes on the sides.

The car started again and they proceeded through the tunnel. Adam looked at his reflection, trying not to show his excitement at the flirtation that was apparently in progress, but Ben seemed completely relaxed and just smiled as if he saw right through him.

At the Church Street stop, people struggled to get past him and he lost his spot next to Ben when a woman with short grey hair and wearing a leather biker jacket, apparently exiting, decided to stay on and squeezed in between them.

At the Castro stop, Adam saw Ben get out ahead of him and walk toward the stairs with the exiting passengers. Ben didn't turn around or show any indication that he was looking for him. Adam thought he might have missed his big opportunity—whatever it had been—but after Ben went through the turnstile, he stepped out of the exiting crowd and stood to the side. Adam approached him, pleased but anxious.

"Hey," Ben said.

"Hey," Adam said, not able to hold back a smile.

"What's so funny?" Ben asked, grinning.

"Oh, nothing," said Adam, embarrassed that he lacked the skills to play it cool.

Ben looked him in the eyes. "You have a nice smile."

"Thanks, so do you."

Ben grinned. "No, mine's more naughty. You heading up?"

"Yeah."

They walked up the stairs that led to Castro Street, Ben climbing the steps two at a time with the agility of a dancer.

"Ah, fresh air," said Ben, taking a deep breath after they reached the top. "Something smelled foul in that car."

"Yeah, I thought maybe it was the creepy looking man in the Dinah Shore Golf Tournament jacket with bullet holes in it."

"That was a woman," Ben said laughing. "So I take it you don't live in the Castro?"

"No, I'm just here for an appointment, I mean, I'm meeting some friends. How about you?"

"I'm going to work. My shift starts in a little while. I'm a server at a restaurant down the street."

"That must be interesting—I mean to work in the Castro."

"Yeah, it's kind of intense, but I only do it part-time. I'm a grad student at the Academy of Art."

"Oh, I see their buildings all over the city. I think they're taking over my neighborhood."

"Oh yeah? Where do you live?"

"Nob Hill."

"Cool. Do you work in the city?"

"Yeah, at a law firm downtown."

"What do you do there?"

"I'm a project manager," Adam lied, not feeling the need to reveal that he was basically the office version of a waiter.

"Nice."

There was a pause, and Adam looked at his watch and saw it was already after 4:00 and he still had to find Phil's apartment.

"I was going to grab some coffee before I start my shift," Ben said, before Adam could speak. "You're welcome to join me if you're not in a hurry to meet your friends."

"I wish I could, but I'm already late."

"Cool. Well, I work at Nirvana, just down the block." Ben pointed down Castro Street past a woman with a pink Mohawk. "Are you familiar with it?"

"No, what kind of cuisine?"

"It's Asian fusion like every other restaurant in this city, but it's good. You should come check it out. I'm there most evenings and I'll give you an appetizer on the house."

"Thanks, I'll do that."

"Well, see you around," Ben said, nodding his head.

"Yeah, it was nice meeting you."

He watched as Ben walked away, slipping his headphones back on. Adam waited at the corner for the green light and when he turned back toward Ben's direction, Ben had already disappeared into the crowd on Castro Street.

Phil's apartment was just a couple blocks from the Castro Muni Station. Once the light changed, Adam crossed the street, noticing all the men and feeling the heightened sexual charge in the air. He wondered why he didn't come here more often. It was like a live version of the online personals.

He was able to locate Phil's building easily. The building was a three-story Victorian and Phil had said that he lived on the second floor when they spoke on the phone. Their conversation had been brief, as Phil had seemed a man of few words. When he rang the bell, the buzzer sounded and after the front door unlocked, he climbed the stairs to Phil's apartment.

He was now ten minutes late, and when Phil answered the door, he looked annoyed, but then a smile flashed across his face. Adam noticed right away that Phil's hair looked brown as opposed to the blond he'd advertised. Adam guessed he was one of those people who had once been blond and had never stopped seeing himself as one.

"Hi, I'm Dan, your four o'clock," Adam said.

"Come on in, Dan," Phil said looking him over.

Phil appeared older than he had in his ad. His face was lined and it looked as if he spent a good deal of time in the sun. Adam now doubted it had been a recent photo, though he supposed it was possible he'd seen what he wanted to.

"So, make yourself comfortable," Phil said.

Adam saw there was a massage table set up in the middle of the studio apartment. There was a bed in one corner, a small couch in another and a desk with a laptop computer in front of the window. The entire wall behind the massage table was covered with large mirrored tiles. Turning around, he saw a tiny alcove that made up the kitchen. Everything was crowded, but very neat.

"Feel free to undress in the bathroom if you like," Phil said, still eyeing him.

"This will be fine," Adam said, noticing the armband tattoo around Phil's right bicep. He could see that at least Phil was fit and that he looked good in the tank top and gym shorts he was wearing.

Phil closed the mini blinds near the desk, turning the room a butter yellow color. He pressed the remote control for a Boise CD clock and new age music filled the apartment. Adam noticed there were a couple of candles lit near the table that were giving off a scent that reminded him of last year's Pottery Barn.

"I wasn't sure if you were going to show," Phil said.

"I'm sorry. I was running a little late," Adam said, as he took off his polo shirt. "I would have called if I couldn't have made it."

"Well, that would make you more courteous than some," Phil said, letting out a cackle.

"Oh, before I forget, this is for you." Adam offered Phil five $20 bills he had pulled from his jeans pocket."

"Thanks." Phil took the bills, examining them briefly before putting them down on the desk.

Adam stripped off his jeans, leaving on his boxer shorts.

Phil grabbed a clear plastic bottle from the massage table. "You don't mind me using oil, do you? It's unscented, non-greasy and hypoallergenic."

"No, that's fine."

Phil poured some oil into his hands and rubbed them together, looking over at Adam. "You can take off your shorts, honey. You'll be more comfortable that way."

"Okay," Adam said, wondering how he had become *honey*. Adam took off his boxers and Phil directed him to lie face down on the table.

"Are you comfortable?" Phil asked, once Adam was lying down.

"Yes."

"Now just relax."

Phil started to rub his back and his touch felt firm but nice.

"You're tense, just relax."

"Guess I'm just a little nervous," Adam spoke into the open headrest, his voice muffled.

"Well, I don't bite—at least not until I'm asked," Phil said, breaking into the same cackle. "You have a nice body. I can tell you must work out."

"Thanks, so do you."

"Well, thank you."

"Do you work out a lot?" Adam asked.

"Yeah, almost every day. How does that feel?"

"Good," Adam said, feeling a tingling pleasure as Phil's hands traveled down his back.

"Feel okay?" Phil asked.

"Uh-huh," Adam said, wondering why Phil kept on asking him that. He noticed Phil's voice had a completely different quality in person and he wondered if this was the same person he had spoken to on the phone.

"So what kind of work do you do, Dan?"

"I'm an attorney," Adam said, deciding since it was a day of lies, he might as well upgrade.

"And how do you like it?"

"It's good. Uh, busy, but good."

"Do you live in the city?"

"Yeah, in Pacific Heights," he lied again.

"Do you own or rent?"

"I rent, but I'm thinking of buying."

"In the same area?"

"Possibly. So, have you been doing massage for long?" Adam asked, trying to change the topic.

"For about six years. I used to work in finance, but I hated it."

"That's great. How do you like doing massage?"

"I love it. I don't have to report to anyone, I get to pick my own hours and I can take time off to travel whenever I want."

"It must be nice having all that freedom."

"Yeah, and I can work anywhere. I've lived in Miami, LA, Hawaii …."

"Wow," Adam said, realizing the source of Phil's sun damage. "How was Hawaii?"

"At first, it was great and I thought I could live there forever. Then it felt a little claustrophobic when I realized I was trapped on a rock in the middle of the Pacific. Plus, everything was so expensive there and the locals aren't as friendly as they appear in the sugarcane commercials. Although I did get laid a lot," he said, with a loud cackle.

Adam laughed politely at the pun.

"The only downside about this job is you never know who you're going to get for a client."

"Yeah, that must be weird."

"So what do you do for fun?" asked Phil.

"Oh, just the usual kinds of things. How about you?"

"Well, I go out sometimes, but not as much as I used to. There's so much trash out there."

Adam listened as Phil went into a long tirade against the bar scene.

"So, do you have a boyfriend?" Phil asked, after he finished talking about the bars.

"No. How about you?"

"Well, I just broke up with mine."

"Oh, I'm sorry," Adam said. "Were you two together a long time?"

"It was four … no, going on five weeks."

Adam smiled, thankful his face was hidden from view. Phil went on to tell him what he called the *Reader's Digest* version of his love life. He ended by explaining the symbolism of the tattoo around his bicep, saying it was a metaphor for the barbed wire he'd put up around his heart because it had been broken so many times.

"Why don't you turn over now," Phil said, taking a break from his monologue.

Adam had felt his interest completely disappear during Phil's ranting and he saw Phil appraise him, looking a little dissatisfied.

"Would you be more comfortable if I took my clothes off?" Phil asked, grinning.

"Sure."

Phil took off his tank top and Adam saw he was smooth and muscled like his picture had shown, though his tan skin was heavily freckled around the shoulders and various-sized moles dotted his torso. He dropped his shorts and Adam noticed the absence of tan lines.

Phil smiled, as if he was used to being admired. "So what made you choose my ad?"

"Um, I liked your picture," Adam said.

"But *what* did you like about it?"

"I thought you had a very nice face and body."

"Well, thank you. You're such a sweetie," Phil said, smiling at Adam and then looking at himself in the mirrored wall. "You can touch my chest if you like." He bent down toward Adam and Adam reached up and rubbed his pectorals while Phil flexed to make them bigger. "Feel nice?" Phil asked, smiling at Adam and then looking toward the mirror.

"Yeah," Adam said, wishing he could block out Phil's voice, which was sounding more and more like Paul Lynde from *Bewitched.*

Phil stood upright again, rubbing Adam's chest and arms for a while, and then he eased lower toward his waist. He bent his head down, massaging Adam's upper legs and started kissing the inside of Adam's thigh. Suddenly, Adam felt uncomfortable and gently pushed Phil away.

"Uh, I'm sorry, but I'm not really cool with that."

"You know, I don't do this for everyone, but you're a hot guy and it's been a while."

"Wow, I would have thought that in your line of work you'd get some clients that would make good fantasy material."

"Well, sometimes, but I also get plenty of trolls. I told you, I don't usually do anything with my clients. It's not like I'm a whore," he said, cackling loudly.

Phil started massaging him again and gradually he made his way to Adam's groin.

"I'd rather you not go there," Adam said firmly.

"Suit yourself, honey," Phil said, sounding annoyed.

Phil went back to massaging his legs and Adam felt that the spell had been broken. After a while, even the massage no longer felt pleasurable and the rubbing was just making him irritated.

"I should probably get going," Adam said, propping himself up on his elbows.

Phil glanced at the clock. "You have ten more minutes."

"Oh, I need to meet my friends soon."

"You don't want me to finish you off?" Phil asked, sounding a little needy.

"No, that's okay. Thank you for the massage, though. I really enjoyed it. I'll get dressed in the bathroom."

"There's a shower and an extra towel in there if you need it. I can join you if you like."

"Oh, maybe another time," Adam said, realizing how stupid he must sound. He made for the bathroom and dressed quickly, rinsing his hands and face and combing his matted hair with his fingers. When he came out, Phil was wiping himself with a towel.

"Thanks again," Adam said, heading toward the door.

"Sure, honey, don't be a stranger." Phil followed Adam to the door.

Adam hurried down the stairs, turning around once to see Phil watching naked from his doorway.

Back on the street, he shivered in the cool breeze and saw that a blanket of fog now shrouded Twin Peaks. He walked away from Phil's building feeling stupid for pissing away a $100 on Mr. Tropic of Cancer.

By the time he arrived at the Muni station, he felt thoroughly defeated. Seeing that he only had a few quarters, he put a dollar bill into the change machine and got a Sacajawea dollar coin in return. Feeling like a failure with his failure of a coin, he paid his fare and went through the turnstile. He descended the stairs and waited for the next inbound train. It wasn't long before it was announced and he heard it coming down the track. He watched the train approach and it dawned on him that he was reverting to his old self. What had he been expecting anyway? That a completely new and exciting life would emerge for him after one adventure to the Castro?

The train stopped and he quickly debated whether or not to board. No, he decided. He couldn't go back and face his shabby apartment. He wouldn't give up this easily. The train departed and a thought came to him that made him smile. Perhaps he could find Nirvana, he mused, and he headed back up the stairs to take Ben up on his appetizer offer.

THIRTY

With Janet off the phone, Cherie settled into what was becoming the most enjoyable part of her day. It had started with a simple daily detour by Brett's house. Back then, she could even claim that she had business on this street before the deal with that fruit, Edison, had spoiled on her. Now, she gave up all pretenses and enjoyed her park and watches in front of Brett's house. She took notes on what she saw and even included Hippo sightings. She liked that Brett took the time to talk to the neighborhood kids as it gave him the respectability of a family man, which was important, if she took him back to meet her parents. The Hippo must not be able to give him children, she concluded, which would be a good wedge issue. Cherie was very confident of the vitality of her loins, which had always been more of a nuisance than an advantage.

She turned on the interior lights just bright enough for her tasks but not too bright to attract attention in the twilight of the tree-lined street. It was just another reason she was satisfied with her choice of tinted windows, contrary to the SUV dealer's warning about tinted windows in the Seattle rain. With the lights adjusted to a soft glow, she noted the time on the console clock and wrote it down next to the date on her pad. While she liked her condominium high above Belltown, she found her park and watches on this quiet street very relaxing. Who knows, she thought, if she got Brett in her sweet embrace, she might like living on this street. It was odd that while Queen Anne was certainly her turf, she didn't remember Brett's house going on the market, and she knew Brett and the Hippo had moved to Seattle in the last couple of years. She made a note on her pad to look up the property records when she got home.

Her nightly routine had become predictable. She would leave here after about an hour, pick up some takeout and then input what she had seen on the street into a spreadsheet. She had even made codes for certain events so she could sort by date and show frequency.

With nothing going on in the street, she reached into her leather day bag and fished out her pill-splitter and Bible. She opened the glove compartment and took out a bottle of antidepressants from her portable pharmacy. She found pill splitting a pleasant way to pass her park and watch evenings. She wasn't happy with her antidepressant dosage, but going up in full pill increments past a double dose had made her edgy and forgetful, so having the option to add a half pill was very empowering.

On her twelfth pill, she nearly dropped the splitter and the Bible it was resting on. Brett had come by the side of the truck, oblivious of her presence. She saw him clearly, still in his gym clothes. He had come from the direction of Edison Archer's house. He was tossing his keys in a wide arc from hand to hand. Sexy and coordinated, she thought, tapping a half pill to her lips. She put her night vision binoculars to her eyes and took a closer look as he neared the steps that led up to his house. Tan, hairy, muscular legs as she remembered from the gym. She smiled as the pill perched between her lips slipped into her mouth. She enjoyed the chalky bitter taste mixing with her sugar-free teeth-whitening gum. She moved up his legs and focused on the clinging fabric in the front of his shorts, taking in the contours. This was only to be outdone by the even split of his backside as the loose material cupped his muscled rump. She moved her gaze up over his flat stomach, and almost as a gift, he raised the material of his tank top and wiped his face. She took a quick penetrating look at his muscled midsection under a light forest of dark hair. She could feel heat rising from her own body. Sexual side effects my ass, she mused, chomping on her pill and gum mix. At the last minute, she caught his handsome face and muscular neck before he disappeared behind a large holly bush.

"Damn bush," she said, frowning. She sat back and dropped the binoculars in her lap. She felt very alone as the binoculars slid between her hose clad legs to the floor. She was going to have to be more aggressive. God did not intend for women to be sexually frustrated. It was against nature. Like many things, she thought, looking at Edison's porch light in her rearview mirror. She would have to bring that fruit back to the straight and narrow ASAP. She was determined not to lose the Archer house from her portfolio.

Her heart leapt in her chest as the adrenaline hit. Her primal urges for Brett were gone, replaced by a sudden rush of terror. She saw her own eyes round with fear in the rearview mirror. They were fixed on the unfriendly red dot of a laser targeting scope. It held steady on her temple. Since her teens, she had subscribed to *Gun Totin' Ladies*, the magazine for the discriminating lady gun owner. She knew that someone had a scope focused on her temple and if he had that steady of a grip, he probably didn't bother with the safety.

Her hands flew into action. She fired up the truck and threw it into reverse. The truck hit something hard that made a crumpling sound with a tinkling of shattered glass. She cranked the wheel to the left and threw it into drive, clipping the car ahead of her even though it was not that close. The steering wheel moved like putty under her shaking hands. In the rearview mirror, she was horrified to see the steady red dot was still with her but now on her neck. She sobbed and floored the truck.

She was down two blocks before she could look again. No dot, but she didn't let up on the accelerator. She did see the traffic circle with its shrubs, carefully placed flowers and reflectors in front of her, only to see it disappear beneath the hood followed by an awful noise. She slowed down, turned onto a narrow street and parked. She never heard a shot, but with hands shaking, she got out of the truck and walked around it, looking for damage and bullet holes. The damage was significant. Whatever had been behind her was silver and judging from the hood ornament embedded in her bumper, it was a Mercedes. She was relieved to see that there were no bullet holes in the truck and no sign of activity in the streets around her.

She climbed back in and knew she needed to focus on getting home and hiding the damaged truck in her underground parking. She turned on the exterior lights now that it was dark. She reached in her day bag and pulled out the silver flask she kept loaded with whiskey for emergencies. She took a deep drink and put the flask out of sight in the bottom of her bag. With the truck in drive, she headed home, careful to obey every speed limit and law so as not to draw attention to her shaking hands or damaged truck.

The laser targeted on her forehead was disturbing, but what chilled her more was that she had underestimated someone significantly. And on Queen Anne too, she thought. Clearly, she didn't know the lay of the land. How was she to win in this world if she couldn't tell the sinners from the saints? Perhaps these were the end of days after all. She wished she hadn't put the flask back in her bag.

THIRTY-ONE

Brett slowed his truck and signaled to turn into his driveway. Even though the street was quiet, he had learned not to roar up his steep drive since the neighborhood kids gravitated to the boulders and large ferns that made up their vertical excuse of a front lawn. The kids were no doubt attracted to his wife's generous hand when it came to cake as well. He'd often heard Linda referred to as "Cool Mrs. Gale." He smiled, thinking of Linda's domestic side. Kids did seem to like both of them. Perhaps they were too quick to condemn their few parental notions. He turned the truck into the drive and accelerated, only to slam on the brakes, sending the contents of the cab bouncing to the floor.

Ahead of him in the drive was a white van. It looked like a service van, but nicer. He put the truck in neutral and set the emergency brake before stepping out into the bright sunlight. Walking around the side of the van, he wished he had put on his sunglasses as the sun forced a strong squint. He could already feel the sweat running down his back and collecting at the belt on his khaki pants. A shower and a change of clothes were in order, he thought, wiping his upper lip with his shirtsleeve.

The van had a sign on it for *Three Sisters' Maid Service*. Odd, he thought, Linda hadn't mentioned calling in cleaners. They had discussed having the hall on the second floor waxed by a professional rather than renting the equipment. Well, he thought, pulling his shirt from his pants, perhaps she had gone ahead without mentioning it to him. Maybe she was "showing initiative." He grinned, thinking of the phrase, having just spent the morning giving performance reviews to summer interns. One of the nubile female interns had caught his eye. In his younger, single days, he would have enjoyed the chase and showing the intern some of his more intimate expertise. He roguishly adjusted himself for his own humor as he walked back to his truck.

His thoughts went back to Linda and one particular thought he shared with no one. Had he pursued Linda simply because she had appeared unattainable? Linda hadn't been in his circle of friends and their courtship had been like an elaborate game. He had wondered if Linda qualified for what his grandmother had often said about his youthful fantasies: *be careful what you wish for.* He pushed the thought from his mind as he reached the truck door.

Leaving the truck in neutral, he let it roll down the driveway, braking in time to check for kids and traffic, then he let it coast the rest of the way to the street, where he dexterously steered it to the open curb and parked far from the other vehicles on the street.

Betty, his truck, didn't need to be crowded by the glitzy Porsches and BMWs. Passing the front of his truck, he patted it on the hood giving her a parting "atta girl" before turning to his house.

He entered the front door and was immediately aware of people moving about in the front room. He kept his boots on since they were clean and he didn't want to be walking in socks around strangers in shoes. He stepped forward in the front hall and saw two maids in uniform cleaning the front room. He waved and they said in unison, "Good afternoon, Mr. Gale." Not knowing what to say, he walked into the kitchen looking for Linda, wanting to joke that there were women on her turf and, worse yet, using her wood polish. The sunny kitchen was open to the backyard, and even with the summer air blowing through the house, the smell of bleach and wood polish was strong.

On the kitchen table, a lone piece of paper sat with an orange as a paperweight. He went over to it thinking it odd that Linda would leave the house while strangers were there or, for that matter, leave him a note since she wasn't expecting him home. He quickly saw that the paper wasn't a note for him, rather an invoice from the Three Sisters' Maid Service for this week's cleaning. On the back was a neat itemization of the prior weeks dating back over six months. He scrutinized the dates and saw that one of the weeks that was missing was when he stayed at home with a sudden cough and a new Xbox as well as all the time that Edison had stayed with them.

What else was going on behind his back and how was she paying for all this? He dropped the invoice on the table and a breeze caught it and sent it to the floor. He picked it up and folded it neatly before putting it in his back pocket.

He stepped out onto the patio and saw that Linda wasn't in the backyard. He went back into the house and looked into the dining room, gleaming in the afternoon light. No dust in there, he thought, before retuning to the kitchen and taking the back steps two at a time.

On the second floor, he saw that the floors were clean but not freshly waxed. So that assumption was wrong, he thought, pausing and listening to the Spanish downstairs. The master bedroom door was closed, which was unusual, but today everything in the house was unusual. In a fluid movement, he turned the knob and pressed forward, and to his surprise, he collided with the door, making contact with his nose. He knew the door had a lock but he and Linda never used it.

His shock was replaced by the underwater sensation from his nose as a hot fluid streamed down his face. He touched the ridge of his nose delicately and was relieved that it wasn't broken. The blood made a quick matter of splattering the white door, the planks of the floor and the runner as well as his shirt, pants and boots.

He tilted his head up to ease the bleeding only to feel the blood run down his neck and into his shirt. "Goddamn it," he muttered. He rolled up the bottom of his already ruined shirt and held it to his nose. He moved gracelessly down the hall to the next door, the master bathroom. Reaching for the knob, he heard the lock click from the other side.

When he turned the knob, it slipped in his hand from the fresh blood.

"Goddamn it, Linda, let me in!" he said, now bleeding profusely. He waited and listened, hearing nothing but the faint sound of birds chirping from the open window at the end of the hall.

A horrible thought flashed in his mind and went to what he had assumed was an impossible place, that Linda was not alone on the other side of the door. He heard nothing but the blood dripping from his nose and his pounding heart. In an instant, his anger went to deep despair. Linda pulling away from him more and more, her disinterest in everything that involved him, the disappearance of their sex life. He had worried it was depression or perhaps the onset of a chronic illness. Now it was clear, she had moved on. He knew he had no facts. Probably some suave guy, he thought. No doubt from her museum circle that spoke the elite arts language he had never bothered to learn out of a dismissive stubbornness. He knew Linda could leave him, he knew he couldn't stop her, but he could scare the hell out of the guy who stole her.

His despair vaporized in the heat of what he could only think of as rage. He felt his chest muscles tense up and the rational voice in his head retreat to the sidelines. Without thinking, he raised his boot and with surprising precision, hit the door immediately to the left of the knob. The heavy door flew open sending the splintered doorjamb deep into the bathroom. The upper hinge broke, dropping metal to the floor before his feet like an offering. He strode into the bathroom wishing he had something more to kick.

Halfway across the large bathroom he picked up the biggest piece of the doorjamb and weighed it in his hand like a club.

What the hell, Linda had left him for another man without him even realizing it. He didn't have a lot to lose now, did he? he thought, feeling the heavy wood hit against his palm. He might as well make the other man pay, pay dearly. He could afford a good attorney and another man with his wife in his house would be just cause in any courtroom.

"My house," he muttered as he slammed the wood against the marble counter top. He pivoted toward the sliding door that led to their bedroom. "No lock on this one, asshole," he said to no one. As he reached for the door, the reflection of his blood-streaked forearm caught his eye and he looked into the side mirror.

He saw a man with a large piece of broken wood in his hand. The white enamel paint on the wood had flaked onto his face and hands. He looked smaller than normal. His skin seemed thin over his muscles giving him an aged look. He looked into the eyes of his reflection and saw something cold, but more alarming, he didn't see himself. He dropped the wood to the tile floor. If someone else made Linda happy, then so be it. He'd always wondered if he was the better man and as the despair rushed back to replace the fading rage, he knew he was and it felt like crap.

He kicked the wood back toward the center of the bathroom and ran his hand through his wild hair. How had his life become so laughable? He smiled weakly at the mirror, comforted that his old self was back. The dried blood cracked on his skin and he could see tears well up in his eyes and then recede. Well, he thought, I might as well get this over with.

He slid the door open to the master bedroom. Linda lay face down buried in two collapsed piles of clothes, not moving.

"Linda?" Brett asked, wondering what was going on. He crossed the room wondering if the other man had snuck out the bedroom door. His hand was bloody so he picked up a sweater and used it to tap Linda on the shoulder. She jerked up, surprised but sluggish. She pulled a wireless earphone from her right ear and then her left, becoming more alert. She turned and looked up at him. Brett could see her surprise grow as she raised herself up.

"Honey, were you in an accident? Are you okay?"

"Yeah, I'm fine," he said, scraping some of the dried blood from his face and watching it fall onto the white bed cover. "So," he said, settling on the bed, keeping his distance. "I think we should have a talk."

"But Brett, what happened to you?"

"I slammed into the door because you locked me out of my own bedroom."

"Our bedroom, Brett, and I didn't know you were going to be here this afternoon," Linda replied coolly.

"Apparently," he said, reaching to his back pocket, taking out the invoice and tossing the neatly folded paper at her. It hit her square in the chest and bounced to the bed. She picked it up and looked at it briefly.

"Apparently," she said back at him with a calm defeat in her voice.

"And then you locked me out of the bathroom."

"I didn't even know you were there! I thought it was them," she said pointing to the invoice that lay between them. "I wanted to listen to my music and nap undisturbed so I locked both doors to keep them out and make it quiet in here."

He heard the creaking of the broken door and footsteps on the tile floor behind him. Before he could think, he turned toward the bathroom and shouted, "We want privacy. Everything is fine. Deseamos aislamiento. Todo está muy bien."

He heard the footsteps retreat but didn't hear them pass by the closed master bedroom door.

"Brett, they speak English," Linda said, sounding embarrassed.

"I think you should be less worried about what they speak and more worried about why I don't know about them."

"They help me clean, Brett," she said directly.

"I can read a goddamn invoice, Linda," he said in the coldest voice he could muster. "What in the hell else goes on around here when I'm gone?"

Linda moved off the bed. "Well, perhaps if you spent more time around here you'd know."

"I'm here plenty. All I can stand, in fact," he yelled, standing up. He could feel the blood start to drip from his nose and then stop. Two drops had hit the white bed cover. "I just love being here with a woman who won't touch me and makes only polite conversation like some sort of fat mannequin."

"Oh, that's classy. Look at what I have to work with," she said gesturing with both hands toward him. "You're like a hotel guest here. Never adding anything to this place!" she yelled waving her hands around. "Hell, I have to find out from Edison what's on your mind. His parents are barely in the grave and you're over there like a teenager wanting to hang out. How do you think that makes me feel back here? Why don't you just move in with him? He'd probably love it since he has horrible taste in men."

Brett tried to calm down, but he could feel his hands shaking in what was now a familiar state of rage.

"Don't bring Edison into this," he snapped. He could see Linda step back from him as he stepped forward. "Just answer me one question and I will leave you in peace. What else is going on around here that I should know about? It will be a lot easier for us both if you tell the truth so we can walk away from this with some dignity." The coldness in his voice chilled even him.

"Brett, no, no, there isn't anything or anyone." He could tell from the shortness of her breathing that she was about to cry and his heart told him she was telling the truth.

His rage was again gone. "Then what the hell is wrong with us?" he said in loud frustration. "Linda, I just don't know what to do anymore." He kicked the side of the bed harder than he meant to and the mattress flew about a foot, sending the piles of clothing to Linda's feet. He was on his knees and Linda was in his arms before his mind could cut through the fog of emotions.

"Honey, honey, I don't know what's wrong. I can't keep it in anymore," Linda said, hoarse with a deep sobbing that made Brett instantly want to protect her.

Choking on her words, Linda continued, "I want to go back to what we had in San Francisco. I'm so miserable up here. I know you're happy, but I want my old life back and I'm taking it out on you and myself." She recovered. "I'm sorry about lying to you and getting the maid service. I can't keep this place up. It's all I can do to fake a smile and make you two meals." Linda pressed her head into his chest and was silent, her breathing ragged.

"Why can't we ever have sex anymore?" he whispered, directly to the top of her head where his chin rested. His blood and tears were falling into her scented hair and he was too spent to do anything but watch them.

"We can, honey, but I put on so much weight. I know what kind of women you like and, right now, I'm not that kind of woman. I don't even like seeing my reflection in the mirror."

"You *are* the kind of woman I like," he said slowing his words, trying to keep his composure but failing. Pressing his face into the top of her head, he held her tightly and rocked them back and forth. He felt like a child sitting on the floor with his wife. He listened carefully to her frustrations and his mind raced for solutions but he only voiced supportive suggestions. He promised her that he would be home more often and they would go out at night or she could meet him downtown for drinks and dinner as they had in San Francisco.

"I need to tell you something so you know everything," he said after a silence. "Edison's realtor is attractive and we had a coffee date, and while I had the option to go back with her, I didn't and I never want to see her again. I'm sorry, honey. I betrayed you. I don't have an excuse."

Linda pulled away from him and, like a cat, her eyes held his unwavering. "Nothing happened?" she asked.

"Nothing. Not in a Bill Clinton way, either. Nothing, nada, zero," he said, returning her gaze.

"Okay," she said, pulling him close. "Let's start over. I don't want this hanging over us like a sword to be pulled down every time we fight."

"Me too," he said rubbing his nose gently against hers.

"I want to give Seattle another try," she said, taking a fallen shirt from the floor and wiping his face with it.

He saw the white shirt turn red and brown. He heard footsteps moving away from the bathroom, pass the bedroom door and fade down the stairs.

"I want you to keep the maid service," he said. "This place is huge and I don't want us to have secrets. I love you too much not to know all of you."

"I love all of you," she responded, leaning close and massaging his shoulders and delicately kissing his bloodied nose.

"Linda, what, what would you like," he said speaking to her chest more than to her, "if you could have Seattle your way?"

She was still, and dropped her hands to the tops of his thighs and gently massaged them. "I don't know of any gallery here that is worthy of me," she said caught in her own laugh. "I guess I would want my own small, ultra-edgy gallery. Something that would make New York and SF wonder why they are buying plane tickets to Seattle to see what's truly innovative."

"We should do it then. If we need to, we can take out a mortgage on the house."

"Let's think about it and run the numbers together," she said, stroking his chin.

"Absolutely," he said with the solemnity of a wedding vow.

"So, you don't mind a fat chick?" she asked, unbuttoning the single button of his polo shirt.

"You are no fat chick, you are my chick," he said and then gently slid his dirty shirt over his sensitive nose.

"I've missed you so much," she said, opening her blouse for his waiting hands.

He eased her on her back and undid his belt and pants with

one hand while sliding the exterior of his knee against the interior of her thigh.

It was hours later when the rumbling of his stomach woke both of them up. The room had a distinct but pleasant smell to it, strong enough to penetrate his damaged nose.

Linda naked, left his side and found the cordless phone near the bed. She returned to his side and dialed.

"Who are you calling?" he whispered in her ear, while pressing up against her to see if she was interested in more.

"Delivery pizza," she said, smiling and pressing back against the hair on his chest, making them both giggle.

"You know me too well," he said with a kiss to her neck. With the hold message audible to both of them, Linda reclined against the heap of clothing and Brett took this as his signal, only to hesitate for his stomach to quiet before tenderly kissing his wife.

THIRTY-TWO

Seeing Pauli and Greg outside the restaurant had genuinely raised Edison's spirits. Both were from his old neighborhood up in the northern suburb of Edmonds. In high school, Edison had drifted from them as he became aware of his sexuality and felt out of place with their girls, sports and more sports mindset. He had lost contact with them completely when he moved out of the Northwest. Pauli and Greg had attended the funeral service, though Edison was embarrassed that he didn't remember seeing them or their parents there. He did remember his labored eulogy and fragments of other speakers, but little else. Tonight they were friendly and warm when they spoke on the busy First Avenue sidewalk.

Now, seated at the table for four in Arcadia, he wondered about Greg and Pauli. They moved together like a couple, but to be fair, they had been inseparable best friends for more of their lives than not. Still, it was interesting that two handsome and good-natured guys who were in their mid-thirties were still single. Not that it mattered, he thought, taking a deep drink of his Lagavulin scotch with two ice cubes. He was envious of the open warmth of their relationship and wished them well. Greg had given him his card before they had separated and they had agreed to meet up in the old 'hood for a beer. He would call tomorrow. Normally, he would wait a day so as not to appear too eager, but something in him changed after meeting that glam fag Allen. He was tired of the games and bullshit. He would call tomorrow.

Relaxing in his chair, he surveyed the restaurant. It was trendy with clean lines, light woods, modern fixtures and blinding white table linens. He had arrived early to hold the table since he knew Val was delayed and Linda was always fashionably late back in San Francisco. Looking down at his scotch, he was surprised to see that it was nearly empty, though the rush of heat in his body indicated exactly where the scotch was. The restaurant crowd was thickening and the private party that had reserved the bar area was clearly having a good time. Edison had worn a sports coat and tie as a precaution and given the formalwear around him, it had been a wise choice. He thought of calling Val to warn her, but instead he decided to flag the waiter for another scotch.

When the waiter returned with the scotch, he hesitated just long enough to replace the bread and seasoned butter while Edison polished off the last drops of his first scotch. With the second scotch quickly dented, he had one piece of the bread from the second serving and reviewed the wine list. The list looked like it belonged in San Francisco with its preference for Napa and Sonoma wines at the expense of Washington and Oregon vineyards. He sipped his scotch and determined it was better to drink ice water for a while. He had already decided he wouldn't be driving back home after dinner and that he'd pick up the Prius tomorrow after the walk of shame down Queen Anne Hill.

The bar section of Arcadia overflowed with the well-dressed members of what Edison guessed was an Irish company given its name of Wilkes, O'Hara & Tarleton, which was listed on the "Reserved" sign behind the velvet rope that circled the beaux arts bar. To Edison's amusement and the staff's obvious frustration, the well-watered faux Irish had started to stake claim to the restaurant tables beyond the bar's perimeter. The party attendees were better dressed than he thought Seattle was capable. Perhaps the city was on the San Francisco track after all, he thought, noting his favorite Napa cabernet on the wine list.

He kept an eye on the entrance and sipped at his scotch only to look down into his glass and see that it was half-empty. He could feel the heat rise in his cheeks as the alcohol moved through him. Drunk before his own dinner party, he mused. This was going to be an interesting night. Perhaps after another few glasses he would have a Bette Davis moment and start throwing cocktail glasses into fireplaces in an emotional meltdown. Hysterics were better watched than expressed, he thought, putting the glass down. Looking again to the entrance, he saw Brett's head above the others near the front door. He waved and Brett waved back from across the long restaurant.

"Has your party arrived?" asked the waiter, who seemed to have the ability to appear out of thin air.

"Yes," Edison said, looking at his watch, "better late than never."

"Yes, sir." The waiter smiled as he expertly cleared the table of breadcrumbs and replaced Edison's water with a new glass. "Another scotch, sir?"

"Sure, why not. Tonight's a celebration and I don't think I'll be driving back to Queen Anne."

"We can always call you a cab when you are ready, sir. And if I may, what are you celebrating tonight?" he asked, placing water glasses at the empty seats.

"Oh, it's complicated," Edison said, smiling as he leaned back in his chair and looked up at the handsome waiter who could pass for 25 or 35. "I guess it's best described as old and new friends around the same table. It's hard to put into words."

"Sounds like the stuff life is made of, sir. Your next scotch is on me."

"Thank you. That's very kind of you. My name's Edison, yours?" he asked offering his hand.

"Joe. Nice to meet you. That's an uncommon name."

"Yeah, my parents must have been having a creative moment."

"I like it. I think I have the most common name possible."

Another waiter passed by and said something to Joe that Edison couldn't hear.

"I need to go help the new guy."

"No problem, you're working and I'm just working on being a lush."

"I'll bring that scotch and come back when your friends are seated."

"Thanks," Edison said, feeling suddenly awkward.

Brett and Linda had made it halfway across the restaurant floor. They were stalled as Linda, with her fake smile cranked up to maximum, spoke with an Asian woman in a dress that looked as if it had been pulled from Eva Peron's closet. Brett was standing at Linda's side but clearly not paying any attention as Edison followed his eyes to passing trays of food and drink.

His scotch arrived with a smile, and the waiter was gone. Edison was worried that he, in his alcohol buzz, was being overly friendly. He'd cool it and give Joe a break. There was no reason to entrap the poor guy at his workplace.

His thoughts were interrupted by Brett and Linda's boisterous greetings. Edison stood up, giving Linda a hug, happy to see her dressed in something that didn't resemble a sack. He extended his hand to Brett and referred to him as "Mr. Gale."

Brett laughed and grabbed his wrist, pulling him forward roughly and giving him a bear hug. "You know how I feel about formalities, Eds," Brett said in a mockingly stern voice as he pulled out a chair for Linda.

With Linda seated, Brett and Edison took their seats and Edison planted his elbow on the table. Brett responded by putting his hand in Edison's in a rogue's game of arm wrestling.

"Boys!" Linda exclaimed, putting one hand on Brett's bicep while fanning herself with a napkin. "Don't fight over my virtue," she gushed. "Brett made me a woman just this afternoon."

"Really?" Edison asked, feigning shock. "I thought you were a virgin in perpetuity."

"Oh, that was just my fragrance. Now I wear Big Easy Girl."

"I'd call your fragrance *Best Wife*," Brett said, looking straight at Linda.

"Well, you two seem like the happy couple. Did you start a Big Pharma lifestyle of happy pills or is something in the water?"

Brett started to say something but Linda gently slapped his wrist. Then they both started to say different things at once, which confused Edison to the point of incomprehension.

"We had a fight. A big fight," Brett blurted out.

Edison noted Brett's expression had turned serious.

Brett continued, "Linda has been having a hard time in Seattle and as it started to take a toll on her, I retreated into my work and just expected her to do the bootstrap thing. I wasn't there for her when she needed me most." Brett looked at Linda again, his hand on the back of her neck with his fingers gently rubbing the skin beneath her pearl necklace.

"And I flirted with your realtor," Brett added, looking at Edison briefly before looking down at his place setting.

"That tramp?" Edison asked, quickly realizing the scotch was talking.

"Is she a tart?" Linda asked. "I have to admit I'm curious about her in a sick sorta way."

"A tart?" Edison considered, "well, her clothes are well tailored, but a bit short and tight. She clearly puts on her makeup with a spatula. All she really needs is a purse to swing and some chewing gum and she is ready for a street corner near you."

"Hmm," Linda feigned deep thought, "I could go to Cross Dress for Less and get some modern whore clothes, cake on the makeup, pad the bra and meet you at the front door after work with a stiff drink," she said to Brett.

"I want you just the way you are," Brett said, putting his arm around Linda. "Don't change a thing."

"But call me if you want help with that outfit," Edison said, knocking his water glass against Linda's.

"Oh, great, a dyad. Some reward I get for being honest," Brett said, pretending regret.

"There's plenty of responsibility to share in our unhappy chapter," Linda said, pulling apart a piece of bread and giving half to Brett. "I came up here without a plan and after failing for months, I didn't change my game. Never told Brett how bad it was going and decided to fill the void with Little Debbie and Hostess products while filling my days with sitcom reruns. Then, get this, I hire a maid on the sly to cover my duties around the house and go frigid and ignore my man. All because this bitch cannot get the job and life she had in San Francisco."

"So, big fight, lots of making up, any resolutions?" Edison asked, sipping some scotch and handing the glass to Brett.

"For my part, we are going to be a team. If my girl is down, then we'll solve whatever it is together." Brett took a drink of the scotch and passed it to Linda.

"I talked it over with this guy here," Linda said, putting her hand on Brett's and taking a sip of scotch then putting it down before quickly picking it back up and taking another sip. "We've looked at our savings and I've decided if I can't join their game, I'm going to beat them at it. Did I mention I hate losing?" She gave the scotch back to Edison and continued.

"We're going to look at buying a space; I mean a storefront property in Belltown or Capitol Hill and convert it to a gallery specifically for those artists who are too small or inconsistent to be shown in the usual galleries. Hell, it's the crazy, unpredictable artists that are the on the edge and that's where art happens. Oh, and I signed up at the gym at the base of the hill and I'm filing for divorce with Little Debbie."

"And I'm giving up realtors," Brett piped in, "and we're going for walks at night for joint cardio."

Edison was about to add that he was giving up realtors too, but was interrupted by the waiter.

"Looks like you're all almost here. Would you care for drinks?" he asked Linda and Brett, eyeing Edison's diminished scotch.

"Well, perhaps a large bottle of Pellegrino for the table," Linda said, "and I'll have a glass of champagne."

"I'll have what he's having," Brett added, pointing to Edison's scotch.

Edison turned to the waiter, giving a quick smile. "The lady isn't allowed to have champagne by the glass due to a nasty arbitration with Liza Minnelli. Could we get a bottle of Veuve-Clicquot Grand Dame and four glasses?"

"Certainly, Edison," the waiter said, nodding and departing.

"They know you by name already?" Linda asked.

"Did you get his phone number?" Brett asked in quick succession.

"No, nothing like that. I got here a little early and we spoke as I sucked down a couple scotches."

Brett picked up Edison's glass and sniffed it. "What are we having?" he asked as he swirled the remaining scotch under his nose and then took a sip, which lowered the scotch to almost nothing.

"Lagavulin. You like it?"

"Nice," Brett said, passing the glass to Linda. "It's good to have a scotch man in town."

Linda passed on the dregs of the scotch and returned it to Edison. "No more firewater for me. I'll stick to the virgin's preference, champagne."

"My little virgin," Brett said, nuzzling Linda's neck after pushing her hair away.

Linda giggled and to Edison's surprise blushed scarlet against the white silk collar of her top.

Edison noted that since they had arrived, they'd been in almost constant physical contact. He felt very much an island on his side of the table. Draining his scotch, he was aware that Brett's lips had touched the same glass, and then the crush part of his crush interrupted his thoughts just long enough to remind him that he would probably die alone. The ice cubes hit his nose as he finished the last of his drink. He put down his scotch and took the napkin from his lap to dry his nose. He may die alone but he had standards.

"You okay, Edison?" Linda asked, shoeing Brett away from her neck.

"Yes, just drinking on an empty stomach. I like your house where the booze and food are always in proportion." Edison reached for a piece of bread and saw that where there had been six pieces just a minute ago there was now one. Linda's place setting was immaculate, but Brett's looked as if there had been a bread war and the bread people had lost. Odd, he hadn't even seen Brett reach for the bread, let alone eat it.

The waiter appeared with the champagne, and after Edison's nod, he opened it for the table with a loud pop that turned heads and brought smiles from the nearby tables. With all the glasses poured except Val's, they decided to review the menu while waiting for her.

Edison knew what he wanted almost immediately and decided he would pick up the bill tonight if for no other reason then he could order as much as he wanted. He was hungry and had news for the table. Val already knew, so perhaps he wouldn't wait.

He looked toward the door and instantly focused on Val storming through the reception area. She moved across the restaurant floor without grace and did not hesitate to push past clusters of people. She made good time and was soon at the table. Edison stood to pull out her chair.

"Oh, thank you," she said calmly, despite her flushed cheeks from her speedy clip across the restaurant and, perhaps, from the car, judging from her windswept look. "Can you believe what a gentleman this one is?" Val asked directly to Linda.

"Hey, I'm a feminist," Brett said, taking Linda's hand. "I rise for no one who is not this one."

"I bet I could get a rise out of you here and now," Linda said in a low seductive voice.

Edison wasn't surprised to see Brett's nostrils flare slightly as he moved closer to Linda and Linda's hand moved out of sight under the table.

"Those two are going to make me sick," Val said, pouring herself a glass of champagne and looking at the menu.

Edison noted a new and pleasant confidence in Val's demeanor. Her outfit was stunning and when seating her, he had noticed more than one man taking note of her.

As if she could read his mind, Val put down her menu and spoke to the table.

"Pardon my Madame Butterfly look."

Her dress was on an Asian theme with discreet black chopsticks in her hair and a mix of red and gold silk wrapping her suddenly hourglass figure along with black stiletto heels.

"Edison, I hope you don't mind, I parked the Volvo on the street. I had to nose a meter maid cart out of the spot. It was hardly worth it since it was over three blocks away. The parking here is no better than San Francisco."

"Nice outfit, Linda said, putting her menu down. "I'm guessing by that woven open stitch on the sleeve that you're wearing something that has never seen a rack."

"Good eye. This was one of my indulgences from long ago. When I bailed out of SF, I mainly packed designer clothes and left the crap back in an SF dumpster. Edison is going to take me up north to the outlet stores. Perhaps you two can come along."

"Ricky, we could play some blackjack at the casino while Lucy and Ethel shop," Edison chimed in speaking directly to Brett.

"Then we can all head back to the Tropicana Club after we smoke a carton of cigarettes and drive with open beverages," Brett responded.

"Sounds like a plan to me, boys," Linda said, not missing a beat.

The waiter appeared and freshened the glasses, and when the bottle was emptied, looked to Edison, who nodded for another bottle of both Pellegrino and champagne.

"Oh," Edison said, "this is my treat so please order whatever you want."

"I'm the only straight guy here; shouldn't I be buying to assert my masculinity?" Brett asked, gently kicking Edison under the table.

The waiter exchanged smiles with Edison before they placed their orders.

"Edison, you don't have to treat," Linda said. "You're a guest here, we should be treating."

"Well, I do have an agenda," he said, suddenly nervous around old friends. "I have some news." He paused for effect and to enjoy the moment. Val had turned in her chair and was smiling, waiting to hear what she already knew. Brett was staring right at him in open curiosity and Linda was more childlike with an eager anticipation clear on her face. Edison saw the champagne glasses were full so he raised his.

"First, to my parents, who are around this fine table in spirit and I don't think they will ever be far away when there are friends, laughter and, of course, champagne." They toasted. "And another thing," Edison added. "I'd like to introduce you all to the newest permanent resident of Queen Anne Hill. Edison Archer, formerly of San Francisco."

"You're moving up here?" Brett asked before anyone could say anything.

"Yep," Edison replied.

"Yes!" Brett shouted loud enough to turn heads.

He raised his hand to high-five Edison from across the table. Edison rose in his seat slightly to meet Brett's hand and as Brett's legs hit the table, the glasses slid into Edison's lap and onto the floor. They sat back, laughing, as Edison wiped the liquids from his lap. Both Val and Linda could afford to laugh since they had rescued their glasses at the first sign of trouble.

"Buddy, you're really staying up here for good?" Brett asked loudly, clearly animated by the news.

"Yep. It's a done deal, neighbor."

"Edison, this is wonderful," Linda said. "I didn't think you were going to stay. Oh, it will be like SF. With Val here, we can do bridge again and hearts all winter!"

The waiter appeared with new champagne glasses and extra napkins.

Linda slipped her credit card into the waiter's hand and told him that she and her husband were paying tonight and that his, pointing to Edison, money was no good.

"Oh honey," Val said, putting a sisterly hand on Linda's wrist, "if his money is no good, can you imagine what that makes mine?"

Brett had been quiet and Edison briefly made eye contact with him, too drunk and shy to hold his gaze. He tried again and Brett smiled at him.

"Damn," he said, "I got my main man and my best gal back in the same city. I am one happy man. And some hot chick with a Moulin Rouge outfit to boot," he added, nodding to Val.

"Tell them about your work thing," Val said excitedly.

"Well, the senior staff met and decided that since I was staying up here, it was a good time for the firm to finally switch the herd of contractors in Seattle to a staff of full time actuaries. It's a challenge but also very do-able and a great position for me."

"Congratulations! Do you need a perky curator?" asked Linda.

"Or a dot bomb princess?" Val offered.

"What I need," Edison hesitated, "is a bathroom, and I hope no one notices that I'm wearing my drinks."

THIRTY-THREE

Evenings like these were always trying, David reflected, as he pretended to be amused by one of Peter O'Hara's animated stories. His boss was a bore, and looking at his flush and fleshy jowls shake with laughter, he wondered how long it would be until the overweight drunk succumbed to a heart attack or some nasty cancer. He was well into his sixties, after all, and watching him stuff food into his mouth, David could imagine his arteries clogging up in real-time.

There were six of them at the table, two of the three founding partners of the law firm plus David, along with their spouses. Peter O'Hara liked to take the firm's senior staff out to dinner two or three times a year and, this evening, he had reserved the bar of an upscale restaurant in Belltown. About two dozen of them in all, including spouses, were seated at tables in the fashionable bar. Miyuki was at his side, quiet as usual, but reliably gracious. David knew his wife was not the timid flower she appeared and was not to be underestimated. She had worked the politic admirably to attain her job as Executive Director at the Pan Asian Art Museum and had made a name for herself with her unique and exquisitely crafted form of origami.

He certainly didn't mind the assumptions others made about their relationship and he played right into them. More than once, his male colleagues had openly admired the neat figure Miyuki cut, who always carried herself with poise and dressed impeccably, favoring classic designers. They envied him for finding such a "traditional" wife whose seeming submissiveness offered a refreshing contrast to whatever ailed their own unhappy unions. And for his part, he would discreetly hint that Miyuki was a tigress in the bedroom. This was especially laughable since they slept apart.

Miyuki had come to the U.S. from Naha, Okinawa for postgraduate studies in Art History at Berkeley. When she spoke, one could tell she wasn't American-born, but her reserved manner and slight accent were deceptive since her grasp of English was near perfect and it was he who often turned to her for help in editing his casework.

A mutual friend had introduced them several years earlier at a San Francisco art gallery and they had soon discovered they each possessed something the other wanted: Miyuki desired stability and the fast track to citizenship in order to pursue her artistic aspirations and David needed a bride to appease his family and to bolster his career. To the outside world, it had been a storybook romance, but in truth, it was simply a marriage of convenience. Overall, it had worked out better than expected, with neither of them questioning the other's personal affairs. Of course, he wasn't *out* to Miyuki, and while he was certain she knew little of his private life, the issue remained comfortably unspoken.

Tonight, he was sitting across from Peter O'Hara and felt like a matador, deftly reacting to his boss's bullish conversational thrusts. Even so, he was conscious of the prestige in sitting at the head table and wouldn't have had it any other way. The other three members of the table, Elizabeth O'Hara, John Tarleton and his wife Eleanor, had formed a triad. This was par for the course for Elizabeth O'Hara, who mostly ignored her husband at these events and never made an effort to talk to Miyuki or to David beyond the obligatory greetings. He could only guess that his position at the firm wasn't high enough or that Miyuki wasn't white enough. This came as no surprise from the woman who, in confusing herself with another Elizabeth, had worn a large tiara to the firm's Christmas party.

The most interesting aspect of the evening had been the sultry Latin waiter. He sensed the waiter had been checking him out all night. Of course, he was used to such attention, as he was at his best in formalwear, and he realized he especially stuck out at this table of dinosaurs. Nevertheless, David ignored the waiter's flirtations. In another place and time, he would have loved to bed this piece of working class meat. He enjoyed giving himself up to these service industry types and the ethnic twist added yet another level of excitement, but with the head partners and his wife at the table, he kept his desires in check.

"How about those Mariners?" shouted Peter O'Hara across the table to David, breaking him out of his thoughts.

"Having a helluva year," David said, trying to match the rowdy banter of his boss. "Maybe this will be the one," he added with false animation. He was indifferent to sports, but made it a point to watch the local teams and to stay abreast of the professional and college games. Sports, he had long ago realized, was the great common denominator among men and he might as well have had a stamp on his forehead that read *sissy* if he declared his genuine disinterest.

"What do you think the odds are of them going all the way, Touel?" Peter asked through a mouthful of bread.

"About as good as Anderson's firm beating us at the annual golf tournament."

"Ha, ha ha. Well, we shall see. My-o-kay," Peter bellowed, slaughtering her name as usual, but neither she nor David bothered to correct him anymore. "What do you think about our team this year?"

"Oh, I don't watch baseball," she said, shaking her head as if the idea were disagreeable. "I only see it when he's watching and then I go to another room."

"But the Japanese, I thought they love baseball," he said, a piece of bread shooting from his mouth, flying across the table and landing near Miyuki's plate, where she ignored it.

"Yes, it's very popular."

"Well, you come from a fine people, very industrious."

Peter started telling a story from his father's service in the Pacific during World War II. "It was the last good war," David heard him say to Miyuki. David knew immediately to tune out when Peter begun his WWII ramblings. He had heard these stories so many times he could recite all the monotonous details. He gulped down the rest of his wine and scanned the bar for the hunky Latin waiter, but he was nowhere in sight.

He tuned back in to the discussion to hear Peter probing Miyuki as to whether she thought the use of the atomic bomb had been justified in Hiroshima and Nagasaki. David turned to his wife just in time to see her faintly concealed mortification. He knew he should probably intervene, but let her squirm in the hot seat for a while, he decided.

He looked around the restaurant and a man sitting at a far table caught his attention. He was part of a foursome, strapping in an oblivious sort of way, and showing a great deal of affection for a woman seated next to him. He abhorred such displays of public affection and certainly didn't want to be subjected to it in a restaurant of this caliber. Nevertheless, looking at the man's broad shoulders he felt a familiar awakening in his loins and shot the woman a wrathful look of envy. The world certainly wasn't fair, he mulled, when chunk tuna such as that could hook up with such a prime specimen of man. He peered at the other man at the table who was looking down at his drink, a tussle of brown hair covering his forehead, and almost gasped when the man suddenly looked up and he saw Edison Archer.

He was thankful that Edison hadn't been looking his way and that he seemed engrossed in his little quartet. He was wearing a sports jacket and David noted that the formal attire suited him.

Just like me, he mused, the kind who you could take to the theatre and then the leather bar afterwards. But who were the other people at the table? He could only assume the woman next to him was his girlfriend or wife and as he tried to get a closer look, he saw her silky kimono and the chopsticks in her hair, and was floored that Edison had also married rice. Quickly, though, he noted her wavy brown hair and Caucasoid facial features and realized he had been fooled by her geisha girl

getup. Though this would certainly explain Edison's elusive behavior, he considered. Perhaps Edison and the geisha girl's relationship was not the accommodating type that he and Miyuki
enjoyed. Well, I'll be damned, he thought. We're like as two
peas in a pod.

He now refocused his attention on the other stud at the table. Could he be the reason Edison stopped returning his email?
But no, the way the man was nuzzling the puff pastry next to
him seemed too genuine to be an act. David knew firsthand
what phony affection looked like, and the man had the sort of
self-assured masculinity he had always associated with heterosexual men. It was a behavior he had studied and tried to emu-
late—quite convincingly, he liked to think—his entire life.

David turned his gaze back to Edison, who he saw had his
champagne flute raised in a toast. He had done some detective
work on Edison since their fateful meeting at Kerry Park. It had
begun a few days after their meeting when he read an article in
The Seattle Times about the infamous curse of the Reaping
Widow of Queen Anne. In it, there was mention of the latest
victims' surviving son, Mr. Edison Archer of San Francisco. He
did some Internet research and quickly found an Edison Archer
listed as a VP on a San Francisco-based company's website. The
matching photo had confirmed that the two Edisons were one
and the same. The discovery had given his fixation on Edison a
new lease on life, since prior to that, he had reached an informa-
tional dead end.

Thereafter, he began regularly driving by the house, and
sure enough, on his second visit, he'd seen Edison sitting outside reading on his front porch. He'd visited on numerous occasions, since then, initially just driving by and then working up
the courage to park his car and walk back and forth along Edison's block. One evening, when he was feeling especially randy,
he had been tempted to knock on Edison's door, but now seeing
the wife, or whoever the hell she was, he was glad he had managed to contain himself.

His mood darkened as he reflected on how his growing obsession with Mr. Archer had come at a heavy price. Only this past weekend, he had been undergoing a little night viewing near Edison's house when he was startled by the sound of a nearby crash and looked just in time to see a dark SUV speeding off, his new Mercedes Kompressor the victim of a hit and run. It had all happened too quickly for him to get the license plate number. He had been enraged to see the front of his car bashed in and the hood ornament completely gone. His rage had quickly turned to panic as he realized the neighbors would soon come out to investigate, so he had hurriedly driven off, rather than stay and file a police report. Not wanting to deal with any questions from his insurance agency, he had brought the damaged Mercedes into the dealership that Monday and had traded it in for a new Jaguar convertible. He had taken quite a hit for Edison and he was now more determined than ever to collect his recompense.

Stealing another look at Edison, he saw him and the other man give each other a high-five across the table, but then there was a mishap and it looked like Edison was on the unlucky end of some spilled drinks. The table seemed to laugh it off in good spirit, though. They certainly seemed like a happy bunch, he reflected, so unlike his own table with demure Miyuki plus the senior center crowd who looked as if they had all penciled in appointments with Death.

He glanced over at the festive foursome again and saw Edison stand and head toward the restrooms. Opportunity waits for no one, David thought. He stood up and excused himself from the table.

"Don't be too long," shouted Peter O'Hara, "or I just might steal My-o-kay from you." David gave an obligatory smile and turned to Miyuki, who appeared to be wincing more than smiling.

He headed to the restrooms and as he walked down the secluded corridor, he spotted Edison at the far end of the hallway, waiting outside the men's room. He had forgotten that the restrooms here were single-occupancy and Edison was waiting for the men's to become available.

He decided to go for breezy as he approached him. "Hey, stud," he said, noticing the wet stain on Edison's pants and giving him a sly smile. "Have an accident or are you just happy to see me?"

Edison stared at him, not appearing to recognize him. David couldn't tell if this was feigned or real, but he decided to help him out.

"It's Allen from Kerry Park," he offered. "I forgot that you've never seen me in my *GQ* threads."

"Yes, I remember you," Edison said, turning back to the bathroom door.

"Hey dude, we really ought to get together. I think we have a lot in common if you know what I mean."

"Uh, I'm sorry, but I thought I made it clear in my emails that I'm not interested."

"Look, Edison, it's cool. You don't have to pretend with me. I have a wife too. I understand how it is. In fact, I prefer guys that are married."

Edison looked confused, but then seemed to comprehend what he was saying. "Listen, don't presume to know anything about me."

"I know more than you think, Mr. Archer." This seemed to get his attention and Edison looked at him inquisitively.

"Hmm, that's odd, I don't recall telling you my last name."

"Let's just say I have friends in high places."

David heard a toilet flush from inside the bathroom and then a moment later the door opened and out came a silver-haired man, thankfully not from the law firm, he observed. The man disappeared down the hallway, and as Edison turned to go into the bathroom, David grabbed him by the shoulder.

"Maybe I can help you clean that mess up," he said, looking Edison up and down, as he licked his lips sensuously.

Edison's face turned menacing and he grabbed David's hand in a painful grip and wrapped it around his backside. David heard his voice, low and direct, as he felt a sharp pain in his arm.

"Look, all you need to know about me is that I'm not interested. You got that?" he said, pushing him away, so that David almost fell down.

David turned back around, grasping at his arm and trying to shake out the pain. "You just made a very big mistake," he said in the most intimidating voice he could muster.

"Stay the fuck away from me, you low-life queen," Edison growled, pointing his finger and taking a step toward him.

David backed up, feeling a rush of fear, but even now, he felt its close cousin, arousal, surging through him. Against his better judgment, he wanted Edison more than ever. He looked on silently as Edison went into the bathroom and shut the door.

David looked down the hallway and saw a woman approaching, holding her young daughter's hand firmly and heading toward the ladies' room. He wondered how much she had seen and as he flashed her an embarrassed smile, the harsh and suspicious gaze she returned answered his question. He now wanted nothing more than to escape his shame, but he knew he had to buck up and return to the table.

He peered down at his suit and straightened the creases out with his hands. He realized he couldn't very well wait for Edison to finish up in the bathroom, so he pulled out a handkerchief from his jacket pocket, and, using the reflective surface of the nearby payphone, wiped the perspiration from his brow and straightened out his hair.

Edison Archer would certainly pay for this, he seethed, as he tried to make himself presentable. Maybe he'd let the Geisha know what hubby was up to online. Still, his desire for Edison hadn't diminished, rather, it was stronger than ever.

Once he regained his composure, he headed back to the table. After taking his seat beside Miyuki, he planted a kiss on her cheek in an uncustomary show of affection, giving his best rendition of an adoring husband.

THIRTY-FOUR

The trashcan was starting to look like a better idea, Linda thought. The pile of junk food before her was gaining in size, as was her embarrassment. She had hidden food all about the house so as not to draw attention to her obvious problem. Originally, she was going to give the booty to Edison, but she decided he would be fine without it. She pulled the trashcan out from under the sink and set it on the table. Her mother's disapproving voice went through her head as she dumped a handful of Zingers into the trash.

The ring of the kitchen phone interrupted her thoughts. "Probably another job offer or the lottery," she said for her own amusement. She was still amazed at the lack of response to her resume. Though, after the fight with Brett, she knew it didn't matter, but her ego was still bruised.

Her mood brightened when she saw the caller was from the 415 area code, San Francisco. She reached for the remote and muted the small kitchen TV.

"Hello," she said in her best Donna Reed voice, knowing that she would hang up on any solicitor without a second thought. A cough came through the line and a familiar voice swearing at someone regarding luggage.

"Vera, is that you?" Linda asked into the phone.

"Yes. Linda, could you hold on for a second?" Vera asked from what sounded like the other end of a very long tin can.

"Certainly," Linda replied, putting the receiver a few inches from her ear as a tirade of expletives was launched about luggage, occasionally broken by the sound of what Linda could only guess was the cell phone being slammed repeatedly against metal.

Vera, her former co-worker, wasn't known for her patrician ways. Her distinct whiskey strained voice made Lauren Bacall sound like Maria von Trapp. Linda heard Vera shout "Hello?" into her cell phone as if she were yelling down a mineshaft.

"Linda, I have to make this short. I have wall-to-wall losers here. Can you meet me for lunch Friday?"

"Vera, dear, you do remember I'm in Seattle, don't you?"

"Of course I do. Alice sends her regards by the way. I'll be up Friday. Things down here have been total shit since you left. I've had my hands full getting your latest replacement fired. She's gone now, as are all the office supplies that bitch could pack into her purse. Incompetent and a klepto, can you imagine that?"

"Oh, do go on," Linda said, sucking in her stomach as she caught her reflection in a kitchen window. "I could use the ego boost. This timber town wouldn't know art if I stapled it to their woodenheads. It's all so sad. Did I mention I'm obese now? Some girl scout asked me if I was having a boy or a girl."

"You're fat?" Vera asked in such a way that it sounded more like a statement than a question. "They still make girl scouts?" was Vera's next question followed by her yelling the F-word at someone as both a verb and noun. "So, fat and depressed in timber town is what I'm hearing."

"I prefer the word curvaceous."

"Yeah, right, Delta. Listen, I have just the thing to keep you out of the cookie jar. Meet me for lunch Friday at Sazerac. The reservation will be in my name for noon."

"You have work up here?"

"Yes, new project with a couple of your local billionaires. I'm on a sabbatical from the museum for the next year. First, I have to go down to L.A. to slap around some of the Getty trash that forgot that Los Angeles is strictly second tier. You'd think they would have read the memo by now."

"That sounds great, Vera. Should I invite Brett?"

"No, lunch is business. I need 100% of your attention. Perhaps we can have dinner with Brett one night when I'm up there, but business before pleasure."

"Absolutely. Do you need a ride from the airport?" Linda offered, thinking of Val's trek.

"No, I have a town car scheduled. Linda, I have to go, there's a situation developing here."

Vera's voice went off for a moment, then to static before it came back with "and the horse you rode in on, pussy boy."

"Are you okay?" Linda asked, concerned.

"Oh, things are fine. I'll see you at lunch on Friday at Sazerac."

"Okay, looking forward to both the business and catching up with you."

The line went dead and Linda wondered if it was Vera's limited tolerance for small talk or a dropped connection.

Linda hung up the phone and considered what Vera had said. Possible work with Vera in Seattle was great news and it would get her back in the game. Her luck was changing, as she knew an opportunity when she heard it. She headed up the stairs, leaving the girls of Eastland Academy alone and muted in the kitchen to sort out the facts of life. She would need Edison to tell her which outfit was best, but first she wanted to share the good news with the man who thought Carhartt was a designer label.

THIRTY-FIVE

Edison marveled at the beauty of the chandelier as he slowly turned the dimmer switch from low to high and back to low. He saw the moody bordello look in the lower settings and the stairway to heaven effect, as Val had referred to the steps, when the chandelier was turned to high. He could only guess how it must look to people on the street who could see the lights dim and brighten from the windows of the upper foyer.

Carlotta had been the one to suggest cleaning the chandelier and her experience had been valuable, as she had quickly found the small crank in the hall closet that lowered the chandelier to the floor. Her younger and very shy brother, Carlos, had been on hand to steady the heavy chandelier while Edison lowered the glittering monster. Later, as Edison had sorted papers in the adjoining room, he listened to Carlotta and her sister banter in Spanish and was surprised to hear them speculate whether he and Carlos were a good match. Carlotta said she would check with Mrs. Gale to see what type of men "Señor Archer" dates.

Their conversation continued as they discussed various matches for their two single siblings, and it ended abruptly when Carlos returned to help raise the chandelier to its roost high in the foyer. Edison had wondered where Carlos had gone while his sisters were cleaning and why he was there in the first place, since one person could easily raise and lower the chandelier.

Edison smiled to himself when he noticed that Carlos had slicked back his hair while he was gone and was now wearing cologne. Edison asked him if he wanted a beer when his sisters were out of earshot, but Carlos declined and quickly left. He did enjoy the assumption by Carlotta that he was just another monolingual gringo.

Edison turned the lights to maximum and looked about. The house was clean enough to meet even his mother's standards. The disorder and dust had been banished under Carlotta and Angelica's reign and, with Val in the house, Edison had decided it was time to stop living like a stereotypical bachelor. He even folded paper towels for napkins at meals as he'd seen Val do when she ate at the kitchen table.

He had started to toss or recycle his parents' items like medications and reading glasses from the cupboards and counters, room by room. His grief was changing slowly. He accepted they were gone and found himself regretting the easy shallow conversation that had passed between them over the years. He made a resolution not to always rely on there being a "tomorrow" to catch up with friends. While he did call a few people he wanted to catch up with and it had been heartening, he decided it was time to cut some baggage loose too. Russell had sent a Hallmark card with just his initials under the printed message that was actually for the loss of a child. Unlike the rest of the cards and notes from his parents' many friends, Russell's card was shredded and mixed in with the eggshells in his mother's compost pile.

He had shut the door on the past as far as Russell was concerned but had opened it in other ways. He had called his old friend Greg the day after seeing him and Pauli outside of Arcadia. It wasn't awkward after the first few moments and he appreciated the immediate invite for a game of basketball and dinner up at Greg's house. Greg even invited him to breakfast the next day at his parents' house if he wanted to drink a few beers with them and not worry about driving back to Seattle.

He had asked Brett and Linda to fly down on his nickel to SF and help him pack up his apartment and then drive up

Coastal Highway 101, taking detours to the national parks along the way. Linda had hesitantly declined since she had committed time to Vera, but with Linda's blessing, Brett excitedly agreed to come and had talked Edison into including a week in Yosemite. How he and Brett were going to pull off a moving trip and a week in Yosemite was beyond him, but he knew they would have a good time no matter how it played out.

He looked about the rooms one last time and was amused that Carlotta and Angelica had moved the furniture back to where his parents had placed it. It signaled the end of his efforts to arrange items to his liking. He imagined Lily sneaking out to Carlotta's van and bribing her to execute her furniture agenda. Not certain that it was entirely in his imagination, he reminded himself again to change the locks on the house.

The front door was wide open to let in the cool evening air. It had been a warm and flawless summer day. Edison decided to sit out on the porch and wait for Linda and Brett rather than perch on his usual step on the staircase. Once out on the porch, he heard Linda's giggle from the street and then saw her race up the front walk with Brett close behind her. Smiling, Edison waved from the porch. Almost immediately, Linda was behind him, using him as a foil to keep a sweaty and laughing Brett at bay.

"Edison, keep this beast away from me! You would not believe what he did!"

"I think I could guess," Edison said, as he smiled knowingly at Brett.

Linda used Edison's shoulders to guide him and keep him between her and Brett. Brett tickled Edison's ribs making Edison laugh and duck to protect himself. Brett kept Edison distracted in one move and then tagged Linda. While laughing, she moved with lightening speed and tagged Brett back just under his arm, which sent his head slamming into Edison as he laughed.

"Truce!" Edison called as he stepped aside.

"Truce," Linda replied, and Brett muttered something that started with a T mixed with a lot of panting and laughter.

"Edison, you would not believe what he did," Linda repeated, pointing at her grinning husband. "My loving husband played that frat boy trick of unhooking my bra with two fingers on the sidewalk while walking over here. I looked like a trailer park escapee!"

"Edison doesn't care about these things," Brett said, catching his breath.

"Perhaps, but the Miller twins certainly noticed when they biked by us."

"Well," Brett said, again laughing, "maybe you shouldn't run across the street screaming if you don't want attention."

"What in the hell is going on out here?" Val asked, stepping onto the porch. She was smiling but with a hands on hips mock stance of anger. "And you, young lady," she said, pointing to Linda who was backed up against a porch pillar. "Why aren't you wearing a bra?"

"Oh, damn, people really can tell! Excuse me," Linda said running into the house.

"You going for ice cream?" Brett casually asked Val.

"No, making some calls to Chicago. They have two hours on us so I need to call before it gets too late, but I'll be happy to bury you fools in the board game of your choice when you get back."

"Uppity little thing for being so perty," Brett said to Edison in a faux cowboy aside.

"When will y'all be back?" asked Val in her own cowboy drawl.

"We're going to take the long way by the Merkel Mansion and sneak a peek since the scaffolding is down and they finished the topiary work with the fancy lighting," Edison said, looking inside for Linda. "We'll come back on West Highland and circle up. I'd say about an hour."

"Perfect. I'll make my calls and do my yoga so I should be ready to show you all the dark side of Monopoly." Val hesitated, "I wasn't too harsh with Linda and the bra thing, was I? I don't know her all that well."

"I don't think so," Brett said. "Anyway, she likes you so it doesn't matter."

"Ah, so I'm winning friends in Seattle. Why did I ever stay in fog city for so long?" She paused, tapping the cell phone against her chin. "I had better call Chicago before they all go to bed." She nodded to Edison and saluted Brett, then slipped inside and pounded up the staircase.

"She sounds like a side of beef going up those steps," Brett said stretching his hands above his head.

"Never mind her, I take it things are continuing to go well between you and the Missis?"

"Edison, it's great. She's like a kid, well, no, more like a naughty co-ed. We were almost late tonight for a very good reason," he said, smiling.

"You poor thing," Edison teased. "You know, you look younger. Perhaps you two have found the fountain of youth."

"It feels like it," Brett said, again stretching and cracking several vertebrae in his back. "We need to get you laid before you slip into permanent chastity mode."

"You still have those construction workers you wanted to pimp me out to last month?"

"I lost my big felt hat and they all went astray. What about someone from the gym or maybe one of those guys over on Capitol Hill?"

"Sad that the straight guy is giving the homo man-to-man advice," Edison said. "I think it's like the gypsy, Carmen. If one pursues, she darts away. If you ignore her, she'll be lurking in your bushes and putting your pets in the Visionware."

"Well, that's a bit twisted," Brett said, stepping away from the door as Linda came out of the house looking much more put together than the woman who ran up the sidewalk a few minutes before.

"Honey," Brett said, "we need to find Edison a man."

"I've already had an inquiry about his availability," Linda said.

"Well, tonight," Edison said, "I'm only interested in ice

cream and lording over you all with my stunning Monopoly victory."

"Dream on," Brett and Linda said in unison, then laughing at their verbal jinx as they headed down the front walk.

THIRTY-SIX

Fanciful thoughts of grandeur went through Val's mind as she quickly ascended the front staircase. The staircase was wide and the curve gentle enough that many a girl would be happy to descend it to meet her guests or perhaps a groom. The top landing would be an ideal place to toss a bouquet to all the strays and losers waiting below. She had often been in the crowd of desperati trying not to care about the bouquet but darkly superstitious when it landed in a bevy of younger bridesmaids. Edison clearly had different thoughts when it came to the signature staircase. He had mentioned that the upper landing would be a great place to defend the house with a machine gun. Gay or straight, men were hopeless, she concluded.

She paused on the first landing to look at the glittering chandelier. Edison had certainly been fortunate in his inheritance. Her first night here she had been envious of both his good business fortune as well as his inherited wealth. The next morning she hadn't felt as envious when she happened upon Edison in the garage with a tear-streaked face as he put his father's clothes in boxes for donation.

She had kept her family at a distance to avoid their lectures and, more recently, to minimize the lies she had to tell to hide her fiscal woe. Once up in Seattle, she had called Chicago to let them know of her new location and had given them the sanitized version of her emergency exit from San Francisco. She told them she was living with a man, a gay man. She had braced herself for the lecture or, worse yet, the silence. In truth, with first her mother and then her father she found no judgment, just questions and then, surprisingly, an offer of a plane ticket home and the coveted bedroom over the garage that she and her sister had fought over in the past. Her mother was quickly on the tangent of decorating the room and remodeling the bathroom when Val, to her own amazement, calmly explained her position of both needing to stay to help her friend Edison and to try to make a go of it in Seattle. Her father had spoken up from the extension that he'd like her to come home for Thanksgiving on their nickel and he would be sending a check to Edison's address to help her get on her feet. It was after that call she had a clearer idea why Edison was not to be envied.

Val continued upstairs to the hall and passed the exercise room, filled with weights and miscellaneous equipment that was suited for the senior set. Edison had mentioned the room might become a home office that would be more private than the study downstairs. The weights were easy for Val, so they were a joke for someone of Edison's build. She did want to try the mini-trampoline before the lot went off to whatever charity Edison had selected. She rolled the trampoline to her room, the formal guest room. Edison's room was at the far end of the hallway and she was surprised to see that he had left the door wide open. Earlier, she had noted that he usually closed the door when he left the room, which was contrary to her upbringing. Aside from their different habits, she was growing to like living at the Archer Hut, as Edison called it. Edison was quiet and went about his own affairs and the size of the house allowed them each a large degree of privacy. She did have a desire to explore every room of the house including the closed media room where his parents had died as well as the attic with its dormers and cut glass windows.

She finished rolling the trampoline into her room and let it settle on the rug. It was an odd house, she noted, no carpet, just Persian and other types of rugs over endless hardwood. It must be a Northwest thing, she concluded, moving quickly back down the hall. At the stairs, she peered over the banister and saw the empty foyer with just the bowl of birds to judge her indiscretions. She continued down the hall enjoying the drama of it all.

The light from the foyer was enough to show the contents of Edison's room. It was a nice room, with a row of identical windows looking out over the front yard with enough privacy from the trees to create an air of seclusion rather than showcase. The bed was unmade and there were piles of neatly sorted paper around the computer on the desk. The desk appeared new and, looking around the room, she realized that all the furnishings looked as if they had been purchased as a set.

She picked up a paper with Edison's creepy block letter handwriting. She read his "to do" list, which even by her standards was confusing. She put it down and gently stroked the macramé owl that stared with one eye on her and the other on the pillows on Edison's bed. She had noticed a lot of macramé around the house and had wanted to make a snide comment, but had checked herself when she remembered Edison's box of macramé at his San Francisco apartment and how he would march out all the items before his parents visited.

She walked over to the windows and looked out at the street scene. No sign of Edison, Brett or Linda, and other than Stella on the sidewalk, there was no activity. The stars were just starting to show in the sky, something she had missed when she was in San Francisco. She looked to the street and then smiled. Red Shorts, as Edison had named him, ran by the house. He had become a pleasant distraction for Edison. Harmless and unattainable, the man ran by the house daily. Evening was a new time for him but his outfit was similar, red shorts and a shiny blue shirt. Red Shorts disappeared from view after detouring around Stella. She turned from the windows, "Well, this room's a bust," she said to the empty room. She looked around once more before heading to get her purse from the kitchen. This house is a cardio workout, she thought, too many goddamn stairs.

The shock was not her falling but that the floor was rapidly nearing her face. Her first thought was that the Reaping Widow was back and had a quota to fill. Then she hit the floor, catching most of her weight with her hands but still too much with her chest. She struggled to breathe and to kick her foot free from whatever had hold of it. Her mind flashed to what a Reaping Widow would look like. She came up with Bea Arthur holding a scythe. She quickly rolled to her side and grabbed one of Edison's shoes to hit whatever had hold of her. She looked down, hoping not to turn into a pillar of salt after making eye contact with the Reaping Widow, and saw Edison's black gym shorts caught on her ankle and pulled tight against the foot of the bed.

Her heart was pounding even though she let out a sigh of relief and felt the tension leave her limbs. The floor was cool and surprisingly clean given Edison's bachelor tendencies. Her hair was tangled beneath her head and smelled of the Aveda shampoo Edison's mother had stocked in the guest bathroom. It was a pleasant change from Stacy's endless Neutrogena products. She relaxed in her ridiculous position. Her foot free, she kicked the shorts under the bed, flipped her head to the side in a "quarter Exorcist," and looked under the bed. Odd that Edison would have crumpled Kleenex under his bed, she thought, since he didn't seem to have a cold. Perhaps it was just allergies. What surprised her more than the stray Kleenex was the large amount of dirty laundry under the bed, especially since there was a washer and dryer just downstairs. Well, if this was his Achilles' heel, then she could help. She may not be a mover and shaker anymore, but she did know how to wash and fold. She got up on her knees and then feet and realized she had no business being in this room.

Out in the hall, she straightened her hair in front of the wall mirror and went downstairs to get her purse. At the base of the steps, she saw the front door was ajar and closed it. Not that it mattered since the tall front windows that opened out to the porch were wide open.

In the kitchen, she looked at the microwave's clock and realized she only had time to call her sister. With purse in hand, she made a deliberate and wide arc around the cake Linda had dropped off earlier. Heading to the front steps again rather than the dark back stairs, she dug through her purse for the slip of paper with her sister's number and stopped at the foyer table to sort out the mess.

Under the bright light, she saw a slightly dented scarlet paper hen in her purse, the one she'd taken for good luck. She felt bad for it, all alone in her purse away from its clutch. She smoothed it out and put it back in the bowl. She looked in the bowl and remembered that birds sleep at night. She collected her purse and phone, went to the wall switch, and dimmed the lights slightly. "You gals get your sleep," she said, heading up the stairs, painfully aware of the irony given all the homeless she had ignored on the streets of San Francisco.

She did have news for her sister. She had come up with some ideas on what to do for their parents' anniversary when she visited in November. She also wanted to let her know that she had some fiscal peace. With Edison's guidance, she had found all her credit card accounts and canceled them as well as put out a fraud alert since some of them had activity she didn't recognize. Once they were closed, Edison had suggested that she roll them into one card with a low interest rate and he would back it with his signature. She was uncomfortable with this arrangement, but when she calculated the interest, fines and penalties, she knew she didn't have a choice. Who knows, perhaps she could get a good job in Seattle. If nothing more, she could do Edison's laundry.

She reached her room and closed the door halfway before stepping on the trampoline. Once on, she felt exhilarated by its spring. She kicked off her shoes and dialed her sister trying not to giggle. Dialing was impossible between the laughter and springing motion moving through her body. She tossed the phone on the bed, pulled Edison's MP3 player from the pocket of her Capri pants and decided she could call her sister tomorrow. The trampoline waits for no one.

THIRTY-SEVEN

The Merkel Mansion was a coup, but two on Queen Anne would be a true coup de gras. It would silence the naysayers back at the office too, Cherie thought. While the Archer house was no Merkel Mansion, it was certainly a grand dame of Queen Anne Hill. She slipped on her gloves and slid an envelope in her new stealth purse, slim and black, and fitting the latest look she was sporting after a recent trip to Barneys. Her ensemble was all black and, while stylish, very functional down to her soft-soled flats from Milan. Her mother had maintained that Italians were suspiciously dark and disapproved of their attempts to pass for white, but they had both found the shoes unparalleled. Instead, they focused their concerns on the Greeks being unquestionably questionable given their geography and dark features. She and her mother had few tolerable moments, but their post church discussions over the map of Europe with coffee had always been a pleasure.

She would drive over the mountains with a new map with larger print for her mother once she settled things on Queen Anne. She would treat the drive to Yakima as a victory lap. "Nice thoughts," she said to herself, putting on a black beret and adjusting it to a seductive angle. Double-checking her pockets for anything that would make noise, she took a moment to adjust the automatic 9mm that rested above her heart. It was a gun show special and, while unregistered, she loved it just as much as her other guns. The cool metal was comforting as its bulk pressed against her chest through the black silk top she had on under her trim coat. If someone targeted a gun scope on her to-night, she was prepared.

It was time to send Mr. Archer back to Sodom where he be-longed so a family or someone deserving could move in and remove the Archer name from Queen Anne Hill. Hell, she thought, thrusting her shoulders back in a dramatic show of de-termination, if she could have timed things right, she and the handsome Mr. Gale could have moved into the Archer house and made it a real home, free of any hippo dust his current home might have.

She stepped out of Janet's cheap car she had borrowed for the evening and brushed herself off, sending dark crumbs into the street. She always found crumbs on her clothes when she drove with Janet and it didn't matter whether she was a passen-ger or driver. She shivered despite the heat radiating from the street into the evening air. She looked down the street and saw the glint of broken glass on the pavement near Brett's house. That horrible day was past and best forgotten, she concluded.

She made her way across the street, keeping to the deep shadows provided by the canopy of trees. She did not like feel-ing unwelcome on her own turf. She needed to put an end to many things on Queen Anne, she thought, as she mounted the front steps of Edison's house.

Light streamed though the large windows, bathing the porch in a pleasant glow. She paused before the front door and then abruptly pivoted to the left and walked past the windows and around the corner to the side porch. She stopped, startled, as a black cat sitting on the porch rail hissed at her. She took a swing at the cat with her purse making full contact, sending the cat into the shrubs beyond the porch rail. The shrubs she had paid to be trimmed. The ungrateful fruit, she thought, not caring about the check he had sent her and that she had cashed. "It was the principle," she said to the empty porch.

She continued around the porch to the side door that opened into the kitchen. As she expected, the door was unlocked. She walked inside and noted that someone had both cleaned and spruced up the kitchen. There was even a cake on the table and fresh flowers for a centerpiece. There was a smell in the air, she knew it, but couldn't place it. The answer came from deep in her memory; just like her father, someone had been smoking Marlborough. Perhaps he was more of a man than she thought. "But not man enough," she said to herself. She went to the butcher's block near the refrigerator and selected a knife big enough to do the job.

The last time David had been on Edison's street he had stood in disbelief as a crazed SUV driver smashed his car. That had been a bad night but at least he had recovered in style with an upgrade to a Jaguar. It was the first time he'd seen his wife raise an eyebrow at any of his expenses. She knew better than to say anything, but to be fair, he raised her allowance without comment.

Tonight, though, wasn't about money; it was about making someone pay. He'd held himself calm that night at Arcadia. To be honest, he was taken off guard by Edison Archer's aggressiveness and his own emotions toward Edison. Tonight he needed to stay cool. His revenge would be perfect and he would satisfy his more base desires as well. Once Edison learned his place, perhaps he'd give him another chance. David looked at Edison's house from his car. Damn, he thought, easier commute than Mercer Island and screw the Reaping Widow, he could grow to like the Archer house.

He pulled the neatly addressed envelope from the glove compartment with his gloved hand. He had done enough criminal defense work to know not to use his laser printer and paper or leave any fingerprints. The printer in the library at his club in Bellevue had proved both useful and sufficiently anonymous.

From a distance, he'd seen Edison and a woman he presumed was his wife leave the house with their friend. Lucky for him, they'd left the front windows wide open. Now, with no one in sight, he saw an easy opportunity to slip in and leave the note somewhere intimate where only Edison would find it and slip out. The note was clear, meet him at Kerry Park again and accept his terms.

In exchange for his silence, he would not expose Edison's sexuality to his wife, the Failed Geisha, as he liked to think of her. All Edison would have to do is be on call to perform light sexual duties. He loved the fact that Edison knew nothing about his identity, and now he couldn't even identify his car. With no one in sight, he stepped out of his car and walked casually to the front of the Archer property, only to pause briefly to check for signs of activity before continuing up the walk to the porch stairs. He strode up the stairs but tread lightly on the solid planks that made up the large wraparound porch.

The lights are on and no one's home. How typical these simple gay boys are, he thought dismissively. The sheer summer curtains blew out from the windows on the porch and played with the light hypnotically. On a lark, he tried the front door and found it unlocked, and as he stepped into the house, he saw the security panel to the right of the door. To his relief, the flashing light showed that the entire system was unarmed. Stupid faggot, he thought, pulling the envelope from his shirt pocket.

He stepped forward, looking at the expansive foyer and up the steps to the second floor. Nice, he thought, as he knew he had nothing like this to inherit. Edison had a lot to protect, which made his plan even better. In front of him was a bowl of something colorful. He stepped closer only to step back in shock. Miyuki's hens? He remembered seeing her making hundreds of them on the back deck when he'd returned from New York in June. How did they get to Edison's house? In his research, he had found all of Edison's details in San Francisco, but he was certain the hens were made after Edison's parents died, given the date on the obituary.

After a moment, he decided to have a look around instead of going upstairs to the master bedroom as he had planned. He headed left into a room his mother would have called a parlor. The large fireplace with its marble mantel dominated the room.

The windows that opened out to the porch made him feel exposed so he moved quickly to the other end of the room toward what he expected was the kitchen.

He paused at the piano and noted an atrocious macramé throw that covered part of it. He looked at the framed pictures on the piano for any signs of children since there was no mention of them in his research. There were a lot of old people in the pictures, but a persistent trio of Edison and his parents was the theme. One picture caught his eye. A teenage Edison holding a surfboard with a piece missing from it. He was shirtless and in swim trunks that he had clearly outgrown. David put the framed photo into his pants pocket and forced it in even though the edge scraped his leg painfully.

All his pants seemed to be shrinking in the dryer these days. Perhaps it was time to replace the appliances. Looking back at the bowl of hens under the foyer light, he thought it might be time to replace his wife too. He scolded himself for not monitoring Miyuki as he had when they were first married. The details of her life had been so boring he had stopped in fear that the dullness would rub off. Well, that couldn't be helped now, he thought turning to the next room. The Rice Plate, as he often thought of Miyuki, had served its purpose. It was time to move on and perhaps play the pitiful divorcee card for a while.

He turned and froze. He felt his right foot brace and dig into the rug as his body's momentum was denied by a paralyzing terror. He wasn't alone. Before him was, was something. He blinked repeatedly; it didn't go away. It was horrible whatever it was. He had never really thought the Reaping Widow was anything other than a nickname for the house. One last blink and it was still there, now moving slowly toward him. The dim bluish backlight from the kitchen hid the face in shadow, thankfully, but the glint of the large knife it held was clear and very real. He tried to turn but only his head moved. It held something else in its other hand that he couldn't make out. When he heard the rattle of its walk, he felt a hot stream run down his leg. The figure lurched forward another step.

The back stairs would do nicely, and while Cherie had seen them on her visit to the house, they had used the front staircase on the tour. She expected to see the steps in disrepair or cluttered; instead they were neat and without a squeak. It was a narrow staircase and the walls were perfectly white. The staircase turned on a landing and, to her pleasure, high above was a small chandelier otherwise identical to the massive one in the front of the house. She momentarily forgot her mission as she marveled at the precision duplication of its massive twin. She would have to think seriously about selling the house to herself. She knew she didn't have the cash, but she never underestimated her ability to get what she wanted.

She continued to the broad open hall of the second floor and, once there, paused. One room had a light on but it wasn't the room she had seen Edison using when she had toured the house. She quietly went down the hall, turning to look in the lit room as she passed. The backside of a woman bouncing up and down on some sort of trampoline was not what she was expecting to see. She was startled, but strangely mesmerized as she watched the form jump up and down. She shook her head in disgust and decided that since she had gone this far, she might as well continue to Edison's room and do the deed.

It smelled like a man's room, even with the windows open. She had enough brothers, and hell, lovers, to know the scent of male sweat. He did look like a real man, she credited him, which is what had fooled her at first. She looked around the room at the stray pieces of clothing. She wondered how many years it took for a physically fit man like Edison Archer to convert into his opera loving sissy destiny. A disturbing picture on the desk caught her eye. *Her* Brett and the Fruit on a beach, both tan, shirtless and each holding an end of a large fish. She picked up the photo, deliberately knocking some papers and a macramé mouse to the floor. She stared at it, taking in Brett's form and eyeing the pattern of hair on his chest down to the point where it entered his sagging shorts. He won't be needing this, she thought, sliding the frame neatly into her pants pocket so Brett would be close to her flesh. She would pay handsomely to have a professional remove Edison from the picture.

"Now to remove Edison from this picture," she said aloud to the room. She adjusted a pillow on the unmade bed and pulled up the sheets slightly. With the pillow in place, she tossed the note down on the pillow top and raised the knife. She brought it down hard and as it cut through both the note and the feather pillow, she heard a woman scream from downstairs. She released the knife, startled by the scream and the cloud of feathers that settled onto her black outfit. She looked down at her handiwork, pleased that the knife remained upright with its tip no doubt in the mattress. Apparently, gay men's pillows scream like women, she thought, concerned by the noise from downstairs.

She moved to make her exit but felt a shift of weight within her pants as the sharp edges of the heavy picture frame cut down her upper leg until resting painfully above her knee. She tried to reach down her pants and pull the frame back up but she only managed to wedge it in more tightly and cut her leg again.

"This is ridiculous," she said, kicking off her flats. She lowered her pants, easing them down and around the bloody picture frame. She was troubled by the amount of blood but then remembered that one of her blood pressure medications had anticoagulant properties. She pulled at the frame and heard the glass crack as her thumb pushed against it. A sudden pain from her thumb made her gasp and she lost her balance and fell forward. Her gun slid out from her coat as she went down and it bounced under the desk and disappeared. She reached for the desk only to twist and catch her lip on the desk chair before she hit the floor. She looked up and saw gentle white forms floating above, feathers, she thought, no, angels, angels to guide her to heaven. She couldn't focus on the heavenly messengers and turned her head slightly as the room dimmed. Her eyelids fluttered and, for a moment, things were clear again. She stared at the macramé mouse, alone in the red glow of the power strip, its gaze falling over the 9mm that pointed at her. Not again, she thought before the room went dark.

———————

David heard his own scream the second time. The first time it didn't sound like his, more like a gasp of one of Wagner's Ring gals. The apparition moved another step closer and again there was a rattle or tinkling but that was the last he saw of it. His legs were his own again and he bolted across the room toward the foyer. The note slipped from his hand as he sprinted to the front door. He saw the hens out of the corner of his eye as he skidded past the door, hitting the wall lightly, before turning and running out the door. He slowed down, as the porch was slick under his shoes. A black object darted behind him and hissed. Was the Widow a shape shifter? was his only thought as he ran to his car.

It was in his car that his shaking hands gave him pause to smell the scent of fear in his wet pants. He locked the doors and closed his eyes with his forehead resting against the steering wheel. Once his hands stopped shaking, he slid the key into the ignition and drove down the back streets of Queen Anne. He drove slowly in the fast car, trying to make sense of what he had just seen.

———————

When Cherie came to, her mind was clear. A macramé mouse was staring at her over the gun muzzle and she knew it was no doubt Mrs. Archer's idea of a mouse cozy. She had a trashcan full of macramé every time she returned from a family gathering. She eased herself up and deftly pulled off her pants and slid the picture frame from her pants leg. She sat briefly on Edison's bedroom floor in her panties and delicately touched her swollen lower lip. What the hell was going on? she wondered. Clearly, this all must be from missing her 6:00 p.m. double espresso and double antidepressant dose. She would not make that mistake again. She turned her pants right side out and put her hand into the pocket. The stitching was ripped. "Damn child labor," she grumbled. Well, she would return the pants after Carlotta got the blood out. She quickly dressed and, upon standing, realized her copious bleeding was no easy cleanup. She turned on the desk lamp and looked about her. The knife was perfect but the floor looked like someone had slaughtered a cow on it. She sighed and wondered why things had to be so hard. She slipped the picture in her purse, shut the light off and walked out of the room.

The hall was still quiet and she took the front stairs, noting she was still dripping deep red blood. Well, she thought dejectedly, it made for a good dramatic effect and, if nothing more, she wasn't lacking iron.

At the base of the stairs, she peered quickly into the dark rooms on either side of the foyer and didn't see any signs of activity. She stepped into the center of the foyer and halted. The door was open. Someone had entered the house. She was about to make a run for it when something moved behind her and hissed. She spun around to see the same black cat jump from the floor to the newel post.

It had been a bad night, but she was not going to back down from a housecat. She took a hard swing at the cat with her purse but slipped on her own blood. Missing the cat, she let the swing follow through to keep her balance. The low arc hit the glass bowl of paper hens dead on, sending them to the floor in an explosion of shattering glass and color.

This place is cursed, she thought, righting herself and heading to the door without concern. She stepped firmly on several hens as she walked out, suddenly realizing a glass shard had come through the bottom of her flat. She felt the blood become sticky between the flat and her foot. It was all just too much. The table was within her reach and she flipped it over to complete the scene.

"Goddamn fruit!" she said loudly as she left the house limping, making it down the steps and walking to the car. Once inside, she took off her flats and drove off slowly. At West Highland Drive, she stopped to let the pedestrians cross. She looked up to see Brett, Edison and the Hippo pass in front of Janet's car. She froze, hoping not to be seen. She caught her reflection in the rearview mirror and realized her beret was still at Edison's. A quick and needless check of her holster told her that the gun was also in Edison's room under the watchful eye of that macramé mouse. Other than running them over with Janet's crap car, there was little she could do. She looked into the mirror again and saw that the blood had mixed with her makeup and formed a crust. With the intersection clear, she put it in gear only to have the gears grind and the car stall. From the distance, she could hear Brett's laugh, and when she finally made her turn, she saw in the side view mirror that Brett had his arms around both the Hippo and Edison. She wanted to blink away what she thought was a tear but instead felt her false eyelash bounce down her cheek into her open blouse.

THIRTY-EIGHT

Getting Edison and Linda to walk more quickly was impossible, Brett concluded. Even the frequent reminders of melting ice cream, as he waved the two bags he was carrying, were ignored. Now, at least, they were climbing the final section of the hill on their street before it flattened at Edison's corner. Linda and Edison were trailing behind him by several steps arguing about the Golden Gate Bridge tower height. If they had bothered to ask him, he could have told them that it is about seventy stories from top to high water bottom. But why would they bother to ask the engineer in front of them? He sighed and picked up his pace to pull away from the armchair engineers.

He turned up Edison's walk, not wanting to wait anymore for the ice cream's sake and his own desire to open the chocolate marshmallow. The rich veins of marshmallow he saw when the boy scooped the quarts of ice cream had been on his mind since they left the store. He was hoping he could spoon into Linda's share now that she was on a diet and clearly serious about the gym.

Halfway up Edison's front walk, he saw Lily in a wicker chair, pulled from the side porch, sitting near the front door. Brett sensed trouble but not from the frozen expression on Lily's shadowed face. It was more that trouble seemed to hang in the warm, unstable air all around Edison's house.

"Lily," he said loudly, "you're in the right place for ice cream." He lifted the two bags of ice cream for her to see.

"None for me, dear," she replied, lifting her familiar cocktail tumbler, shaking the cubes.

"Is everything okay?" he asked, as he approached the house.

"No dear, it has been an eventful evening. A few curious visitors to Paul and Ellie's house since you all went out for ice cream."

On the steps, he paused, looking back to see Linda and Edison coming up the front walk. Turning back to Lily he saw that her face was its usual inscrutable self but her body and posture, while normally rigid, now appeared taut like a rubber band that was about to snap. Stella was under her hand but without the usual high-volume purring. Lily's cigarette shook slightly, which was a first, he noted.

"Are you okay, Lily? You look a bit stressed," he said softly.

"I'm fine dear, thank you for asking. The scotch is a bit low in the house but what can you expect from this new generation? No offense to you, dear. Linda keeps your house in perpetual spirits, which is admirable. It's that type that fails us," she gestured at Edison who was now behind him.

"Lily, I see you found the scotch again and let yourself in as well," Edison said, passing Brett on the porch.

"You don't want to go in there just yet, boy," Lily said, raising her cigarette for a deep drag, speaking more to the street than to Edison.

Edison stopped and looked to Brett and then to Linda for help in dealing with the clearly inebriated Lily.

"It seems like he only has guests when he's gone and none of them have keys," Lily said with a deep and suggestive voice as she continued to look out at the street.

Stella jumped off her lap, and after making a quick pass at Brett's bare legs and the bags of ice cream, went down the steps and under the bushes that sat before the house.

"So, Lily," Brett said, thinking again of the ice cream. "How about we discuss these mystery guests over another glass of scotch and some ice cream?" Brett emphasized the distressed state of the ice cream by raising the two bags in what had been a useless gesture throughout the evening.

"Oh, yes dear. Ice cream for you all does sound like a fine

idea and perhaps I'll freshen this one up," she said, shaking the ice cubes in the glass. "It's a warm evening; we should get those to the freezer before you have to drink them."

"We don't want to get between Brett and his ice cream. It's a dangerous place," Linda said as she came up behind him and rubbed the sweaty fabric of his polo shirt.

"Or Lily and my scotch," Edison added, opening the front door.

"We should all mind our step once inside. The floor is a mess with broken glass and desperate hens," Lily said, rising from her chair.

"Broken glass?" Edison asked, taking a bag from Linda.

"Oh, and you, dear," Lily said to Linda, clearly ignoring Edison, "should be careful with those thin-soled shoes. One woman already cut her foot on the crystal. You can see the bloody tracks on the porch. I think a weak bleach solution will clear that up but not damage the wood."

"What woman?" Edison asked, stepping inside.

"Your realtor, the big slut, of course," Lily said, walking past Edison, turning and looking directly at Brett before extending her hand to Linda. "Come dear, look at what happens when something cheap like that realtor woman touches something tasteful like Ellie's crystal."

"I had nothing to do with this," Brett said, putting both bags in one hand and then taking Linda's hand in his.

"I know. That's in the past," Linda said as she walked with him past Edison. "Clearly, the tart doesn't understand the word no." Linda smiled at Brett. "If I ever meet her, I have a few ideas how to drive the point home."

They all stopped, side by side around the edge of the foyer, silent. The chandelier above them was dialed up to its brightest. Brett could see the trail of blood down the side of the stairs and continuing to the front door. The bowl of his hen friends had been shattered with great force. Pieces of crystal were all over as they must have ricocheted against the near wall and slid back on the marble floor. The paper hens were scattered across the floor in dramatic positions. Despite his rational notions that they were just paper, he felt bad for them and stepped forward to right the toppled table and put the nearest hens on it. Edison and Linda followed his lead, and Edison moved the table over the lone black tile, crunching crystal underneath his sandals.

With two fists of hens, Edison looked as if he was about to say something, but then he froze for a second before turning away from Brett, making a sniffing sound.

"Do you smell that?" Edison asked.

Brett inhaled and smelled only the musty odor of the paper bags he was holding, dampening with the condensation of the ice cream quarts. Then it hit him. Any frat house was incomplete without it.

"Your suitor needs adult diapers," Lily said from near the front door. "His wife Miyuki must have his diaper size. If you plan to continue your relationship, I'd suggest giving her a call. In fact," she said, taking out a very modern cell phone from the pocket of her jacket, "we can call Miyuki now and put in a request for hen repair too."

"Allen?" Edison asked. "You know about him?"

"I know about everything on Queen Anne. I am old, not blind. Those hens are his wife's creation. I'll give you his number if you'd like to call him. He might respond better if you use his real name, though. It's David, David Touel."

Brett felt the need to lean against something solid and walked to the wall that divided the foyer from the parlor.

Lily crossed the foyer, not waiting for a response from her audience. "Next time you pick up trash at Kerry Park, perhaps you should use a pseudonym as well so it doesn't come looking for you here on our street. You know, you're not the only one who lives here." Lily glared at Edison and Brett watched as Edison returned the favor.

Brett moved toward the source of the scent. Lily and Edison followed him and Linda trailed behind in silence. They all stopped around the obvious wet spot on the large Persian rug near the piano.

"I guess it's time to start locking the doors and using the security system," Linda said, looking at the spot on the floor with a form of disgust Brett rarely saw in her.

Edison took the bags of ice cream, went to the kitchen and placed them in the large freezer.

"Eds," Brett yelled. "Get some baking soda while you're in there."

"Damn, that stinks," he said to Linda, moving behind her and rubbing her shoulders while watching Lily pull a bottle of scotch from behind the pictures on the piano. She poured long and filled the glass she had from the porch and then offered the glass to Linda who smiled and accepted it.

Lily offered the bottle to Brett and, after a second, he took it. "It looks like it's going to be an interesting evening," he said before taking a drink directly from the bottle and passing it to Edison, who was at his side with a box of baking soda. "I learned this from my college days," Brett said, taking the baking soda from Edison and opening it. Stepping back, he motioned Edison to join him on his side of the wet spot. He sprinkled the baking soda over the spot with steady precision. "It kills the smell and is easy to vacuum up, too."

"You have a practiced hand," Edison remarked, smiling.

"Not from personal experience," Linda said laughing, "I hope."

"No, no. Just a lot of drinking buddies who passed out and wet themselves or mistook the living room for the bathroom. All done and all out," he said, putting the box on the macramé cover on the piano. He motioned for the scotch bottle from Edison. "Damn, Eds," he said, looking at the lowered scotch level. "You and Lily have one thing in common." He took one more hit and handed the bottle to Lily.

"So," Edison said to Lily. "How about you tell us what happened here and ..." Edison stopped. "What about Val?"

"Val? Who's Val?" asked Lily.

"She lives here," Edison said with exasperation in his voice. "You met her when you invited yourself over for food and drink when Linda and I were on the side porch a couple weeks ago."

"Oh, I thought I imagined that," Lily said, refreshing her glass after Linda returned it to her.

"Val!" Edison yelled, heading to the front stairs, skirting the debris on the foyer floor.

Brett followed close behind. The blood on the stairs had his attention, the higher the stairs went, the bigger the drops were. And where was Val in all of this? If something had happened to Val, then Edison would be moving and he'd help him pack. He caught up with Edison at Val's bedroom door.

"Val?" Edison asked apprehensively as he knocked on the door.

"I hope this is the Archer Ice Cream Delivery Service," came Val's voice from the other side.

Edison sighed, putting his forehead on the wall near the door. "Yes ma'am, we aim to please."

Val opened the door with her hair wet and wearing khaki shorts and a blue top. "Hope you don't mind, I took you up on your offer to wear your mother's clothes. Fits well enough, at least for Monopoly."

"No, no problem at all," Edison said.

Linda and Lily came up behind them.

"Such an audience. I thought we were having ice cream and games?" Val asked, looking at Edison.

Brett turned to Edison and saw his brow furrow and that he had started to sweat heavily from either the alcohol or nerves. Brett sensed that the evening had turned very personal to Edison.

"I think we had better go down the back stairs and talk in the kitchen," Brett said, looking at Val.

Val came to Edison's side and ruffled his hair. "Damn," she said. "I thought all the drama queens were left behind in SF. Perhaps they found that hidden canal you mentioned."

"Oh, you heard about that canal, too?" Linda asked, guiding Lily by the elbow.

"And here I thought it was trash specific but apparently it

has a drama channel as well," Val said, heading to the stairs next to Edison.

Lily's voice, amazed, followed Val's. "Oh, she is real." Lily tried to touch Val's shoulder but missed as Val and Edison walked toward the back stairs.

Brett turned to the front of the house and could see that the trail of blood appeared to head toward Edison's bedroom. He looked back to see Linda steady Lily as they descended the back stairs. He turned and went down the hall, careful not to step in the drying blood. As he went past each room, he checked for signs of activity.

Everything seemed as it should until he entered Edison's room. Feathers floated in the air, caught in the current from the open windows. He flipped on the room light and immediately saw a large knife in a bed pillow. He circled to the right of the bed to make sure no one or no thing was lurking in the shadows.

The knife had cut through a piece of paper before it sank into the deflated looking pillow. He picked up one of the other pillows and knocked the knife free from the stabbed pillow. He pulled the note from the knife, relieved to see that no blood was on the knife. As he unfolded the note, he briefly wondered why Edison slept with four pillows on the bed. He focused back on the note long enough to see that it opened with the salutation of "Sodomite." Brett folded it in half; Edison could decide whether to share his hate mail.

He slipped off a pillowcase and then dropped the knife and note into its opening. Looking back at the bed and the four pillows, he wondered if Edison had a bed buddy or if he was just a guy who liked pillows. Looking around, he saw a black beret on the desk chair, which he doubted belonged to Edison. It looked like it belonged in a French cafe more than a man's bedroom in Seattle. Walking around the bed, he made for the beret, but halted when he saw a pool of blood on the hardwood floor.

He squatted near the edge of the blood, and while it looked like a lot, most of it was smeared with one central pool. He picked up the hat and turned it around. The label read *Henri Bendel — New York* and there were a few long blond hairs on it and a familiar perfume. He had hoped that this was a past and brief chapter in his life but, clearly, Cherie had staying power. He tossed the hat on the bed, looked down again at the blood under the desk and saw the nose of a gun in the glow of the power strip.

From bad to worse, he thought. But why was it here, and apparently not discharged? His knees were starting to hurt and he didn't want Edison coming up here out of curiosity. He picked it up and put it on the desktop, carefully checking the safety. Looking under the desk again, he saw more blood splatters and a macramé mouse. He reached down and took the mouse out from under the desk. Ellie had made him one too. Two, actually, he remembered, one for the home computer and one for the office; the one in the office had become very popular with his coworkers.

"Little guy," he said softly to the mouse, "wish you could talk." He looked in its eyes, which looked back at him, almost with the suggestion of hope. He put the mouse on the desktop and collected the odd items he had found. He decided to take the booty downstairs in the pillowcase. A knife, a gun, an odd cap and a note with a hint of Old Testament homophobia, enough clues to create a unique version of Queen Anne Clue. He regretted touching anything in case the room was a crime scene, but knowing Edison, he would want to review the facts before deciding to include the police.

He walked down the hall and sighed, stopping at the top of the back stairs to double-check the gun's safety. Once sure it was secure, he looked up at the miniature chandelier, seeing its ornate chain disappear into a black stone circle in the ceiling. He remembered the sunny fall afternoon when he and Paul had installed the chandelier with Ellie and Linda holding the scaffolding steady. Funny, he thought, they had installed a brushed aluminum fixture where the chandelier met the ceiling, not a black one. He looked over to the sconce holding the discreet hall lights and saw the familiar brushed aluminum. He could not imagine Paul installing a new fixture without help.

Animated voices from below reminded him of bigger mysteries and, for the moment, he decided to put aside all questions and tried to remember if bourbon went with ice cream.

THIRTY-NINE

At a different time, Val thought, she would tell Edison that she liked his hair longer, as it was now. She was looking at the back of his head as she followed him down the steep stairs. His hair was loose and curly when it was longer which gave his face a less serious look. Both Brett and Edison seemed tense since returning from their walk. She wondered if there had been an incident with one of the Reaping Widow devotees that frequented the sidewalk in front of the house.

Once down in the kitchen, she decided to play hostess rather than speculate on the current weirdness. After pulling the box of assorted booze Edison had purchased at the liquor store from the pantry shelf, she asked the three in the kitchen what she could mix for them. Lily wanted vodka with an ice cube, a lime wedge and a dash of seltzer, but as Lily said this, she started to mix the drink herself. Linda said she would have a Cape Cod and that Brett usually wanted a bourbon and Coke.

"I'll have what Brett's having," Edison muttered, walking to the far end of the kitchen. He flipped lights on as he went and when he was at the entry to the parlor, he stopped and stared at the parlor floor.

Val busied herself with the drinks and Linda set out dishes for cake, moving about the kitchen as if it were her own. Val noticed that someone had already taken a serious slice out of the cake since she had been to the kitchen to fetch her purse.

"Edison! Did you already have some cake?" she asked, teasing him for his gluttony.

"No dear, that was me," Lily replied before Edison could answer.

"And you were here why?" Edison asked Lily directly, not hiding the fact that she was unwelcome in his house.

"Watch your tone, little man," Lily said walking toward Edison. "You need to know what I know before you start acting like the new little bitch of the hill."

"Stop it, you two, or no cake," Linda said, obviously familiar with the role of peace broker.

Lily turned toward Val and Linda, smiling lightly. "Just sparring, dears; I won't pull out the big guns out of respect to Paul and Ellie. Or at least not until I finish my drink."

"I'll keep your glass full for our sake," Val said.

"I knew I liked you." Lily turned on her heel toward Edison. "You have such nice friends, young man. I hope they will be an influence on you. So, have you figured out what is missing from the piano? Your suitor took something dear to you."

Edison walked to the piano with Lily hovering like pestilence. Even Val could spot what was missing, the picture of a teenage Edison on a beach with a broken surfboard. Edison had explained to her that his father had kept the shark bite photo on display for years against Edison's protests that he looked emaciated and ludicrous in the too-tight swim trunks.

"The Hawaii photo," Edison said.

"Yes," Lily responded, sounding satisfied. "He spotted it and pocketed it in no time." Reaching in the pocket of her silk jacket, she pulled out an expensive-looking cell phone. "How about we dial his wife and ask her to run the picture over tonight. She can have my ice cream in compensation for any inconvenience. She is very sweet, you'd like her."

"No, I'm not up for that kind of game tonight. Plus, my mother has the negative, and after Allen touched it, I don't want it."

"His name is David Touel and he has been lurking in your shrubs for a couple of weeks now."

"Wow, a stalker after one date," Val said, coming up from behind Lily with a cocktail glass and a large slice of cake with a generous scoop of ice cream, only to stop suddenly. "Yuck, it smells like a cheerleader on spring break."

"How did you come up with that comparison? I don't see you having pom-poms in your closet." Edison continued, "Linda on the other hand …."

Val was happy to see that Edison could crack a joke regardless of the evening's downward spiral. Val asked again, feeling the need to catch up, "so what is the smell if it's not wet cheerleader?"

"The date I mentioned broke in, stole a picture and then pissed on the rug," Edison said with resignation.

"You know how to pick them," Lily said, pushing between Val and Edison to return to the kitchen.

Val handed Lily a second drink as she passed, briefly forgetting that Lily had made her own.

"Never a problem," was Lily's quick reply holding both drinks and taking a seat at the head of the kitchen table. The room turned to the back stairs as Brett thundered down the steps causing the dishes in the near cabinets to rattle.

To Val's eyes, Brett looked worried, and his casual dopey air she had grown to expect was gone. He went to Edison, who was closest.

"Sit, buddy," was the only thing Val heard him say before he put a white cloth bag on the table. He went to Linda, who handed him a plate of cake, and then he cleared his throat, putting the untouched cake on the table, away from the cloth bag.

"Val, could you sit down? We need to focus for a minute. This is worse than we thought."

The room went silent as they took seats around the table. Val noticed that Lily's posture was perfectly straight like a schoolgirl's, and her eyes held steady on the white cloth bag.

Watching Brett display one item after another from the bag, she felt her own breath move to a quick inhale when Brett placed a knife followed by a gun on the table. With a steady smooth movement, Lily reached for the gun. Then, with a clearly practiced hand, she released the clip, slipped the round into her jacket pocket and put the gun back on the table.

Brett sat down to the right of Edison with one hand on his shoulder and the other holding the empty bag. "Eds, these were in your bedroom with a splattering of blood. This note was stabbed into your pillow." Brett handed a ripped note to Edison.

The silence took root as Edison read the note without showing emotion. Val envied the stiff drinks poured around the table and wondered if Chicago might be a better option rather than staying here with the Reaping Widow and her house of drama.

Edison put down the note. "Hmm, interesting. Apparently the Reaping Widow has a laser printer, but needs a proofreader."

"Is the note something that you can share, Edison?" Val asked, reaching for the vodka and mixing herself something stiff with a wedge of lime.

"Oh, it's not personal, it's just hate. I guess I have officially left the city at the end of the rainbow."

"Eds, it's not the city, it's just some nutcase," Brett said. "I'll ring that bitch's neck the next time she slinks onto the hill."

"Oh, dear, no," Lily said, "I have a gun that will do nicely and, I promise, these new hollow tips leave minimal splatter. No messy clean-up."

All eyes went to Lily.

"So, I've heard," she added, adjusting her hair.

"Well, here it goes," Edison said.

Sodomite:
Go back to Sodom before your next to see my wrath. Atone for your sins in your own land. Do not disgrace your family name by sinning where they dwell for eternity.
Reaping Window

"Fucked up, just fucked up," Brett muttered. "Lily, what did you see tonight?"

"Quite a bit, dear, and none of it pretty. Would you like me to start with the Daughter of a Thousand Whores or Mr. Tinkle?"

"How about Mr. Tinkle so we can break up the Old Testament theme? It's too warm to be biblical," Linda said, sitting up straight and reaching for a fork.

"Good choice, he's the more amusing of the two," Lily said, lighting up a cigarette after fumbling with the lighter that clanked against the clip in her pocket. She continued, "I saw Linda cross the street with a cake earlier today, which in the past meant Ellie and Paul were going to host an open party. See, I used to be welcome here," Lily said, turning to Val.

"Oh," Val said, looking to Edison, who was looking down at the note, not giving Lily's comment any response.

"Well, since it was like old times, I came over later and helped myself to the scotch in the kitchen cupboard. Ellie and I would always share a glass when Paul and Brett or whoever engaged in some talk of sports or computers. Since they have been gone, the scotch hasn't been refreshed, so I went into the dining room and found the last bottle of single malt. I heard someone go up the back stairs and I thought it was him," she said, pointing to Edison. "So, I went back to the kitchen, poured myself a drink and had a sip or two before getting a knife to cut the cake. I did notice that the largest knife was missing and it wasn't in the sink or by the cake. Ellie's knives are too nice for the dishwasher so it couldn't have been in there." Lily took a sip of her drink and a drag of her cigarette and continued.

"I cut myself a piece of cake and heard a noise in the parlor, so I got up, with the knife in my hand, to put it in the sink. I must have startled the little man as he was stealing your homoerotic photo. I came toward him with the knife in one hand and, of course, my scotch in the other. He must have thought I was a ghost because he looked affright and then made that mess on the rug." She smoothed her hair and brushed invisible lint from her immaculate jacket.

"Brett, I think baking soda is a good try, but when my children had issues on the carpet, Mr. Ling and I found a little salt would kill the odor and prevent a stain from setting. Anywho…" Lily went on before anyone could respond, "that little man ran out of here like he was on fire. My hair is a mess but I can't be that bad. Oh, he left this, or rather, he dropped it when he ran for the front door." Lily reached into her jacket, pulled out an opened envelope and passed it to Val, who handed it to Edison.

"Great, just what I need, another note."

Val watched as Edison read the note and Linda shoed Brett away from Edison's side so he could read it privately.

"Oh, don't worry, I don't have any secrets at this table," Edison said, scanning the note. "Clearly, though, I don't have any idea what's going on in this house." Edison paused, "Val, I'm sorry you have to see this; I had no idea when I invited you up."

"Not a problem, you should have seen the neighbors I had my last few nights in SF. They make these halfwit note ninnies look like amateurs."

"Even so," Edison continued, with a slight break in his voice, "I bet there's a peaceful bed at Brett and Linda's house."

Lily spoke up with surprising clarity. "I have extra bedrooms and fresh linens galore, so you're welcome to stay over at my place and I have enough firepower to take out a legion of this trash." She gestured with her drink to the two letters in front of Edison. "Oh, and a low-stress breakfast served at eleven-thirty. Morning light is so unforgiving."

"Our door is open to both of you," Linda said. "No reason you can't camp out at our place."

"There's a rockin' breakfast babe at our house," Brett said grinning mischievously at Linda. "The food is good too."

"If Edison stays here, I'm staying here," Val said politely but firmly. "Not that it's any of my business, Edison, but I think you should move into the master bedroom. I am the guest here, not you. Plus, Note Ninny One knows where you sleep."

"You know, Val," Edison said, drinking from his glass for the first time, "I think you're right. "It's my house and it's time to stand my ground."

"The man of the house, it suits you, buddy," Brett said, reaching for Linda's unfinished ice cream. "So, Lily, what else did you see?"

"Why Brett, you don't know? It's the lady who watches you. And Linda for that matter. She's the one who hit the Mercedes of the Mr. Tinkle—I mean David Touel, and left all that expensive glass out on our street."

"Someone has been watching us?" Linda asked, anger rising in her voice.

"God, what's with this town," Val said, quickly regretting her outburst at a table of locals.

"Well, I guess I'm the only one watching over the street at night with my binoculars." Lily went on, "the woman that nearly clipped my Jaguar with her tank of a truck. The Barbie Doll gone bad …."

"Cherie Cahill, the human mattress," Edison said, sharing a smile with Linda. "So, the Reaping Widow is a realtor by day. The widow rumor would be a good idea if you want to move the house at an artificially low price."

"How unattractive, both in form and function," Linda said dismissively.

"Frightfully, dear," Lily agreed. "And anger issues for days … those poor hens."

Val noticed a tear race down Lily's cheek and a quaver in Lily's hand as she pressed it to her lips.

"That woman must have entered from the back when I went to get a fresh bottle of scotch. I think I would have noticed the knife missing the first time around. Ms. Cahill must have been upstairs doing her evil while Mr. Tinkle was down here wetting the carpet." Lily drained her glass and took Val's drink. "After Mr. Tinkle ran out, I followed him and saw him drive off in a different car, a new Jaguar, like mine, actually. The smell in the parlor was dreadful so I went into the dining room to check if all the furniture was as Ellie had it."

The table was quiet and Lily seemed to drift off. Val looked down the table at Brett and saw that he was looking at Edison with one eyebrow raised, and Edison returned his look with a shrug.

"I do miss Ellie so, and Paul too," Lily said with a deep sigh. "As I was saying, though, I was in the dining room with the lights off since the foyer lights were on. I heard footsteps on the upper landing, then her muttering. Then I heard dear Stella hiss and I saw her purse swing and hit the bowl of hens. I imagine she was aiming for Stella but got the hens instead. Those brave little birds never had a chance." Again, she faded, looking at the stairs behind Edison that led down to the basement media room.

"Ellie and I bought that bowl together," Lily's voice stopped in a choking cry. Before Val could react, Linda was at Lily's side whispering soft words. Linda guided Lily through the kitchen and out to the side porch. Brett and Edison were silent, and when Val looked back at the two of them, they were both eating cake. When she heard the distinctive click of a lighter from the side porch, she decided to have cake as well.

After a few silent moments, Brett suggested that they look over the rest of the house so there would be no more surprises. They all agreed and got up from the table. Brett motioned them to wait for a second as he moved stealthily to the porch. He moved well for such a big guy she thought. Perhaps he has a brother. Her thoughts surprised her after months of a silent libido. Looking out the window to the side porch, Val watched Brett whisper something to his wife and then he returned to the kitchen.

"Basement up?" Edison asked the two of them.

"Eds, if you don't want to look in the basement, I can," Brett offered.

"I'm not worried about my parents' ghosts. They would be on our side. It's the realtors and low rent fags that scare me."

He smiled, showing them he was okay, and they all headed down the broad stairs to the well-lit basement. Val was still tempted to grab a knife but decided the Nancy Drew in her would have to take a backseat.

Room by room they looked for signs of intruders and found

nothing new. In the high attic with its steep dormer windows, they paused to take in the moon over the mountains. Val asked Edison why there was a black circular stone insert above each of the windows that faced north, south, east and west.

"I have no idea. I never noticed them when I visited in the past, but now I see them everywhere in the house." He reached up to touch the one above the south window.

"Sort of like realtors," Brett joked. "It is nice up here," he continued, taking the north window seat.

"Too nice for Reaping Widows," Edison said, taking the south window seat.

"Are you going to stay, Edison?" Val asked as much for herself as for Edison.

"Tonight only cemented my resolve."

"That's my man," Brett voiced from the northern shadows.

"I think it's the right choice," Val said, taking the eastern seat, finding the old cushion on the window seat cozy. They sat in a comfortable silence for a minute before Brett stood up, straightened his shorts and said that they should get downstairs so Linda doesn't worry.

They headed to the kitchen and reported to Lily and Linda that they had found nothing new. Val glanced at the second note on the table long enough to see that it demanded a meeting at a specific time so as to keep his silence. His silence about what, she wondered.

Linda asked when Edison was going to call the police and how involved he wanted them all to be and if he had thought about the press.

"No. No calls, especially now that I know who they are. I'll change the locks and learn the security system tomorrow."

Edison sat at the head of the kitchen table and reached for the second note.

"Val, David Touel thinks we're married. He saw us all at Arcadia that night and thought we were a table of couples."

"Clearly, he does not know a hag when he sees one," Val quipped, pretending to be offended for not having her status recognized. "He wants to blackmail me. His silence in exchange for sex on demand."

"Damn, no wonder you're single. He makes Russell look like a prize," Brett said, taking a seat to the right of Edison.

"Brett!" Linda exclaimed, hitting his shoulder playfully. "Think it, don't say it, like we talked about."

Edison picked up the other note and smirked, "Cherie just wants the sale and no doubt a piece of Brett. Your people, always a disappointment," Edison grinned, looking at Brett and Linda.

"Well, I've had enough for tonight," Lily said, taking the gun from the table. "I'll put this with the rest of mine for now. If she comes back, you don't want her to find it. If she comes to my place, I'll just use mine. My magnolias could use the fertilizer. I have your shovel still, Brett, dear," she added, leaving the room.

"For roses," Brett said to the table, smiling. "Really."

Edison sat down again after rising for Lily's exit and Val went to his side.

"Well, this makes Clue look rather casual. Can I get you anything, Edison?" she asked, clearing Lily's glasses.

"Anyone hungry?" Edison asked.

"Sure," Brett responded.

"I could heat up some pizza," Edison said.

"I'll toss a salad," Linda offered.

"Sounds like a plan," Brett said. He looked to Val, "How about we clean up the front hall and then get the Clue game from the study. We could try to piece together a timeline of tonight's events from our clues and the game board."

Liking the inclusion, Val agreed, leaving the kitchen just in time to see Edison toss both letters in the recycling and hear Brett's expletive after stepping in Mr. Tinkle's last stand.

FORTY

Valet parking, how civilized, Linda thought as she pulled up to the Monaco Hotel. It was something she assumed she had lost when she left San Francisco. Brett was pleased with the lack of valet parking in Seattle, being possessive of all their vehicles, but Linda loved tossing the keys to someone else and letting him deal with the parking. The smile of the young attendant was flirtatious. He must have a mommy complex, she thought, entering the tall double doors of the hotel.

The restaurant was just beyond the lobby, a hard left on the shiny floor. She remembered it from going out with Brett's co-workers at one of their frequent events. At his work functions, she enjoyed making Brett proud by playing the perfect wife and then diving into a catty recap once they were safely in the car. The one at the Monaco's Sazerac restaurant had been a wild one. Neither of them drank much at these functions and that night they ended up being split apart at the end of the evening to serve as impromptu designated drivers. Linda had two couples squeezed into their car. The first couple she dropped off on Mercer Island, having to wake them up to find their house. She was tempted to leave them at the foot of their steep driveway, but instead she got them into their house and left them on a bench just inside their front door. To their credit, they had sent a large bouquet of flowers with several pricey gift certificates to local restaurants among the stems.

The other couple seemed to wake up on the ride over Lake Washington, and when she got to their home in Issaquah Heights, they had asked her to come in for a nightcap, and although nothing was said, it seemed they wanted more. When she picked Brett up at his last drop-off in Bellevue, they detoured to an IHOP in the University District and laughed nonstop over a late-night breakfast. They stood in sharp contrast to the much younger, drunker crowd in their casual bar clothes. She smiled at the memory and made a mental note to remind Brett of their IHOP night. She pushed through the large upholstered door that led to the restaurant, enjoying the feel of her business attire on her body rather than the sweatpants she found herself wearing too often.

Now, she was about to meet Vera. She had thought about Vera most of that morning. Vera was her only peer at the museum in San Francisco. Vera usually had a pile of eviscerated employees and vendors at her office door by the end of each day but Vera had never been a problem for her. Linda had quickly learned that Vera had no skill for small talk in the office, but outside the office she was a different woman.

Her friendship with Vera started after about year of working together in a familiar but business-centric manner. They had run into each other at Cole Haan one rainy Saturday and Vera had suggested a late lunch at the Four Seasons. Lunch had turned into tea and then many cocktails before Brett had to pick both of them up and drive them home. The next week, a formal invitation came in the mail for dinner at Vera's home with her partner, Alice, who had never been mentioned prior to the spontaneous lunch. The difference between the black clad and severe work Vera and the domestic one was startling. Her office at the museum was an astounding collection of acquisitions and personal gifts from galleries, all arranged to intimidate and impress. Linda had assumed incorrectly that she would have similar tastes in her home and had braced Brett for an uncomfortable evening, insisting that he dress his best.

Vera and Alice lived in a Mission-style town home with a view of the Golden Gate Bridge. The interior was warm and inviting and the food was home-cooked, plentiful and delicious. Alice had suggested that Brett lose the tie and coat and it wasn't long before Linda found Brett and Vera on the patio, shoes off, and drinking beer from bottles. Linda quietly left her prized pair of Chanel slingbacks at the front door and joined them on the patio. Dinner was served casually, almost as if it were an afterthought, with Alice keeping them in easy company with truly funny stories and quips from her work as a trauma nurse. When Vera dropped a buttered dinner roll on the floor, she simply laughed it off and said it would be an edible cat toy before dinner was over. Sure enough, to the table's delight, two aged and clearly well loved cats found it and, before devouring it, batted it a few times like kittens.

Linda entered the sunny atmosphere of the restaurant and checked her watch. She was ten minutes early, which was punctual in Central Vera Time. She skipped a primping session in the downstairs bathroom. It was just Vera, after all, why was she so nervous? Because she might bail out the sinking ship that is your career, she told herself. Scanning the restaurant for Vera, she saw her sitting alone in a large booth with a heap of papers in front of her.

Vera didn't look good. She had lost weight and the black and white play that had worked between her skin and her jet-black hair was lost as her hair looked flat and her skin had gone from alabaster to ashen. Was she sick? Don't stare Linda, just get to the table, she thought, as has she walked across the restaurant under the many pieces of suspended art that doubled as light fixtures. She could just imagine what Vera thought of the suspended art given her minimalist tendencies.

She made eye contact with Vera a few yards from the table and Vera stood and welcomed her. After a firm hug, she sat down and found that Vera had already ordered her an iced tea.

"I'm not sick," Vera said to Linda, not making eye contact. "I just look it. I get away from Alice for more than a day and I age thirty years. I think she cast a spell on me; she always has been the spiritual one. Good thing I love her aside from the fact that she apparently holds my vitality in the palm of her hand."

"You do look a bit off your game," Linda said, reaching

across the table and whisking a large piece of lint off Vera's shoulder. "How is Alice?" Linda asked, remembering that both she and Vera had routinely crucified co-workers for not having manners.

"She's good and sends her regards to you and Brett. She wanted to come up this trip but I told her that I was in full bitch-mode and that's not something I want her to see, if at all possible. How is Brett? I liked that he sent Alice a picture of his grill, without a message. It was like a ransom note. Alice has grill envy now, which makes me feel oddly inadequate."

"Mr. Grill is fine. He sends his regards and, of course, an invitation for some outdoor cooking. Don't worry about playing second to a grill; it's inevitable at some point in every relationship."

Vera handed Linda a thick binder and got down to business, including relaying messages from the staff at the museum.

Linda was missed and her second replacement had been fired in record time, much to Linda's enjoyment. Not to mention the woman's entire acquisition portfolio was utter crap, according to Vera.

"Total crap," Vera had muttered twice before reaching for the wine menu and pausing.

"First work and then wine," Vera said, putting down the wine list. She waved away the waiter with her other hand and a glare.

Some things don't change, Linda thought, taking solace that, while a total bitch, Vera tipped exceedingly well those that tolerated her.

"Let me give you the facts and the offer in detail before you ask questions or have comments." Vera outlined the proposal without stop, for more than 15 minutes. The offer was more than Linda was expecting and the size of the project was impressive. As she had mentioned, the collection was to be funded by two local billionaires and was largely specific in what was to be acquired. While the two funding partners were highly public figures, this project was to be private until they heard otherwise.

About ten percent of the acquisitions list was not specific and that would be the challenge. Some of the art may be lost to war or in the shuffle of time. They would be proving some negatives by the end of it, Vera said in her final remarks.

The commission was huge and their combined skill set covered most of what Vera outlined. Vera's final comment was that after expenses, she was willing to split 55/45, with Vera taking the bigger slice since she had landed the deal.

Linda sat back, pretending to think it over. She smiled at Vera, who warmly smiled back. "This makes SF look like child's play," she said with a mischievous grin. "When do we start?"

They toasted with their water glasses and sat in a pleasant silence before the waiter came over.

"Too early for champagne?" Vera asked, trying to look innocent.

"I don't think that's possible, certainly not under the circumstances."

Vera ordered a bottle of Taittinger. She also ordered, by memory, Linda's favorite salad. Linda would have normally been put off by someone ordering for her, but with Vera, it was all a matter of efficiency.

"I do need to ask Brett, of course, but he will be as excited as I am. Can you come by the house on this trip? He'd love to see you."

"Tomorrow after I get back from Bellevue I'm free. I tried to find your Queen Anne address on the map, but it looked a bit confusing. How about you pick me up here at the hotel tomorrow at six? That would give me enough time to change into something less formal. I also have a few bottles of California red up in my hotel room from Alice for Brett since he mentioned once that there is no good wine readily available up here."

Linda laughed. "Yes, that is his constant rant and now it's a chorus. The man that was at many of our parties, Edison Archer, has moved up here. You remember, he and Alice would always discuss death as a statistic and no one else would join their conversation until the topic changed."

"I do remember him. Handsome, quiet guy ... Alice was asking about him a few months ago. He's up here too?"

"Yes. Sadly, his parents both died recently. It was far too early for them to go and it has been tough on all of us. We were close to them too. It's worse since the coroner hasn't yet declared an exact cause of death. If Edison had found out, I imagine he would have told us. Brett is going to ask sometime soon, when the time is right. It's not an easy topic to bring up."

"I can imagine," Vera said, taking a drink of water. "Alice sees death every day at the hospital, but I think that's where she draws some of her peace. I didn't think it was possible in this age for there to be mysteries when it came to death, especially two deaths." Vera nodded to the champagne the waiter presented.

"Perhaps a better topic now that the champagne has arrived," Linda said, not wanting to think of the police tape and the dark days after Paul and Ellie passed.

"Agreed." Vera glared at the waiter until he was gone. Her warm smile was back when she turned to Linda. "Well, partner, it looks like old times again. Can you start next week?" Vera asked with a smile as she reached into her attaché, pulled out a large binder and opened it.

"Absolutely," Linda replied.

"Let's save the niceties for when we're at your place with Brett. It's a three-year project with a bonus clause for early delivery, so time is money."

Linda reached into her purse and pulled out her reading glasses and a highlighter, both of which she hadn't used since San Francisco. The highlighter worked perfectly and after a quick dusting, the glasses brought the contract to clarity. A contract with its own table of authorities; nice, Linda thought.

"Let's start with the schedule," Vera said, with a mouthful of corn bread muffin.

"It's on page 37," Linda said, pleased that she still could slice through a contract and faster than Vera.

FORTY-ONE

Cherie tossed the spare invitations onto the passenger seat of her SUV with one hand so as not to spill the quadruple espresso on her latest indulgence from Max Mara. The older man at the print shop had always come through for her and a few winks had scored additional invitations and a generous discount. She had no doubt that the little number she was wearing helped seal the deal. She loved how men were so easy to manipulate, and that was just what those horrid feminists couldn't get through their dowdy little heads. God had given her these looks and she was going to use them. No questions asked.

Once in the driver's seat, she checked her makeup in the vanity mirror and admired her new cut and color. She had turned up the volume on her blonde hair and it radiated. The Merkel event was this weekend and after months of planning, she wasn't going to let something critical like her hair or nails ruin the event. "No, sir. Not at all," she said aloud to her diamond bracelet as she admired its glitter in the strong sunlight. There would be more of this when she sold the Merkel Mansion, she thought.

She intended to close this sale fast, before the bottom feeders started nipping at the asking price. The structure was excellent and the interiors were flawless but empty. She had read that a British real estate agent had once restocked a castle with period pieces and had used the publicity to spark a bidding war. Adopting the Brit's idea, she had convinced the two museums who were the recipients of the Merkel art collection to loan the pieces back to the Merkel heirs under the pretext of making the collection whole again, and in its original home, if only for a week. Cherie repeatedly feigned enthusiasm in the collection and had even learned enough detail to sound knowledgeable. A little charade that was thankfully going to be over soon.

She hadn't invited many members of the arts community to the event. Judging from their clothes and cars, none of them would be buying a mansion anytime soon. Instead, she had focused on the toast of Seattle. Invitations to the "Merkel Mansion Open House and Art Exhibition" were numbered and, Cherie hoped, had an air of exclusivity that most people couldn't resist. She had checked each address on the list herself to ensure that only the right people were invited. Also, she had limited the east side trash since they could taint a real estate discussion with their suburban notions.

She used the notes from Edison's house as a coaster to rest the lid of the espresso cup so she could use a straw to drink the caffeinated brew. That fruit's home would have been a good notch in her belt, but clearly he had flaked and the note she had stabbed into the pillow didn't seem to be having its desired effect. Couldn't he take a hint? she wondered. Well, at least the Merkel Mansion was a go. It was much larger than the Fruit's house and sans curse, thank you very much. The mansion had amazing views and an expansive lawn and gardens. The Merkel Mansion was *the* Queen Anne address and it was going to be *her* sale.

She had never lost a client before Edison Archer. Well, she reasoned, it's not as if they had anything on paper, so he didn't really count. His handsome friend had flaked on her too. Perhaps Edison and Brett were *special friends*, because no red-blooded man had ever turned down a direct flirtation from her. That would also explain the Hippo. She must be the *fag hag*, she thought, priding herself on knowing the hip terminology. Well, their modern marriage was an insult to what she valued, but she wouldn't kick Brett out of bed, assuming he hadn't tasted the fruit of sin.

She didn't have time for these little gay intrigues, she decided, opening the glove compartment and selecting two of the eight pill bottles. A double dose of the new anti-depressant and a four pour of espresso would get her back on track. Once she washed the pills down, she felt the familiar warmth in her mid-section and she relaxed. She looked at her faux Cartier watch and frowned, just after two o'clock. Well, she didn't want to return to the Merkel Mansion just yet. The art people were still there doing the installations and lighting. She would prefer to avoid them and their nasty fashions. She looked at her new ensemble hanging in the suit bag in the backseat. The side of the bag was open so she could see the flawless green silk that made up the dress. She was going to look fabulous at the opening and the best of Seattle would see her in all of her Hermes glory.

She decided to use her spare time to stop by Metropolitan Market and make sure the catering was still in order and perhaps snag a sample of the menu and call it lunch. She couldn't live on espresso alone, she thought, as she pulled out of her parking spot and then quickly cut through the light Belltown traffic.

After a drive by Brett's house, since it was almost on the way, she justified, she circled back to Metropolitan Market. As she eased through the lot, she saw Brett's F-150 with its distinctive Sierra Club sticker on the back window. Cherie took pride in her eye for detail. Well, perhaps she would be a very lucky lady today, she thought. Smiling, she eased her SUV behind his truck and blocked his exit.

She took time to sip the last of the espresso and to pop a breath mint. Her lipstick was always flawless and a quick look in the vanity mirror confirmed this.

She heard a gentle rap on her window and turned to it with a high wattage smile, expecting to see Brett's handsome mug and muscled man frame. The wattage dimmed to a brownout when she saw the Hippo. She recovered, but not nearly to the previous wattage, and lowered her window.

"Oh my, I am sorry," she said. "I thought you were Brett." She heard his name come out of her mouth before she could stop herself. She tried to recover, "I didn't mean to block you in with all your groceries."

"Oh, you know my husband?" the woman asked with a politeness Cherie could not discern. "I'm his wife, Linda. And you are …?"

"Cherie Cahill, Amsted Reality. Pleased to meet you. Are you a friend of Edison's as well?"

"Yes, Brett and I knew Edison back in San Francisco before we moved up here and we knew his late parents as well."

"San Francisco?" Cherie caught herself frowning as Frisco to her was a godless place that needed a good dose of Revelations as she had told the women of the Ladies' Auxiliary just last month.

"Yes, Brett received a job offer we couldn't refuse and we moved up here. I was a curator at the SFMOMA at the time, but I'm a house frau up here," Linda said, smiling at Cherie in a manner Cherie still could not decipher.

"So, you were in art?"

"Yes," Linda said, shifting her full grocery bags.

Honey, you cannot hide that hippo fat with just a couple bags of groceries, Cherie thought, as she continued to force a smile and reached over to the passenger's seat.

"Here are a couple of invitations to a showing just down the street from your place. It's this Saturday. I know it's short notice to find something decent to wear," she said, looking down at Linda's stretch pants. "And bring that handsome husband too. Hell, bring Edison to show him there are no hard feelings for him changing his mind on the house sale. All his people will be there to see the art, and at least they know how to dress, so why am I complaining?"

"His people?"

"You know, the fruits." She looked Linda in the eye and lowered her voice to a conspiratorial tenor. "Listen, honey, you were in San Sodom Frisco so there's no need to explain the loss of good men to another gal. I need to dash. Just wear something black and you'll be fine." Before Linda could respond, Cherie slipped the SUV into drive and waved to Linda as she drove deeper into the lot.

Once parked and with the keys out of the ignition, she couldn't remember if she had taken her anti-depressants or not. "Well, better safe than sorry," she said to herself as she reached in the glove compartment. A minute and some Diet Coke later she admired her hair and smiled into the mirror to see if she needed any whitening gum. No, they were brilliant. And what was that hippo smiling about? With the vanity mirror flipped back up, she frowned and reached for her purse. She hated a mystery.

FORTY-TWO

"No problem," Adam said into the receiver of his ancient cordless phone. "I'll go over tomorrow to get the keys and call at seven from the apartment. Edison, it's not a problem. In fact, I'm over in your neighborhood all the time when I go to Whole Foods." He listened to the voice on the other end, with relaxed attention.

"Edison," Adam, paused, "I'm glad you called. I'll call tomorrow. Bye."

Adam hung up the phone and stretched, hoping the red marks from the chair that had pressed into his side would fade by afternoon. He looked past his temporary stripes and noted how clean the phone was since he had attacked it with Windex. The fact that his phone had been coated with dust was a commentary on his social life that he didn't need to advertise.

He crossed the room and sat on his well-used futon couch. The late morning sun came in the three windows of his studio's main room. Edison Archer had called him and asked for a favor. He had also extended an invite for a road trip and had offered a spare bedroom if he wanted to visit Seattle. The hour-long conversation had been the stuff of Adam's persistent fantasies.

While Edison was, in Adam's rational mind, forever unattainable, he also knew that he had something with Ben that was taking root. All of Adam's deal breakers, or "ship sinkers," as his father would say, had been dismissed by Ben's easy laugh and non-judgmental manner. Ben's open life was refreshing and his apartment showed no signs of anything scary. Adam had braced himself for Ben dealing the freak card from the bottom of the deck. He had waited for it that first night at Ben's apartment. Would it be meth? Gender confusion? Closeted? Boyfriend? The card never came and he doubted, now, that there was one.

Even Ben had laughed at the mention of the one warning sign, his unique ear and nipple piercings. Adam had cautiously asked about them and what attracted Ben to the look. Ben called the piercings his non-conformist failure. Every fag in the Castro had started sporting similar-style piercings about the same time he had his done, Ben had joked. Adam noticed that the nipple rings and earrings were gone on the next date. He decided he didn't want to question a good thing, and enjoyed being able to kiss Ben's earlobe without interference.

He liked kissing Ben, and for the first two real dates, they spent a lot of time kissing. While both of their bodies clearly were up for more, it was Ben who blurted out while slipping his hands free from under Adam's shirt that he didn't want to mess up something good with quick and easy sex. Adam liked the idea and decided that there was no hurry even if every cell in his body protested the denial of nature.

As with Edison, talking with Ben was very easy and he found himself being more open with Ben than he had been with anyone in a long time. He privately accepted the fact that he would probably have a crush on Edison for the rest of his life. Regardless, he was not going to let something as good as Ben be sacrificed for an unrequited crush. Still, Edison Archer had called him and they had talked for an hour.

The favor Edison had asked did come with some sad news. Edison was moving to Seattle. The silver lining was the option to drive back up to Seattle with Edison and his friend, Brett, via Lassen National Park. That bitch David would get his resignation if he stood in the way of a vacation to Seattle that would fit his budget.

He'd given into Edison's insistence to accept a check for the inconvenience of taking out his trash and empting and cleaning Edison's kitchen of the rotting food he had left behind in his sudden departure. He would check on the apartment until Edison could come down and move his possessions up to his new Seattle address.

Funny, Adam thought, he was suddenly a cleaning maven both at his apartment and now at Edison's place. His long held standard of cleaning only enough to thwart the bugs was abandoned quickly when he realized he would have to have Ben over at some point. His aversion to cleaning solvents was out the window when he ventured to Walgreens and bought sixty dollars worth of cleaning supplies and standard household items for a long overdue cleaning session. It had taken most of a weekend and the place was still a dump, but a clean dump. Ben had been kind when first seeing it, and since he had a bigger place, they usually went there and the topic of Adam's studio hadn't come up again. Adam's stumbled confession of his lie about his position at work had not, thankfully, come up again either.

Adam put a stray sock over his eyes to block the sun as he lay on the couch. He enjoyed the feeling of the sun's heat on his bare chest and pulled off his shorts to create his own nude beach. So, Val had taken refuge at Edison's after falling on her ass in San Francisco, he thought. That explains the fiscal rape he had endured at Boulevard. Not the classy power chick he had thought she was. He could forget and forgive. It had been a good week. He had a friend in Edison Archer and a real possibility that Ben was going to be someone he would want to date seriously. If Edison was the cake and Ben the icing, then the candle was Bitch One's absence from work. David was "working from home," whatever that meant, and Tony, one of the sane senior partners, had asked Adam to change cubes and work with him on a case that had gone from being a small client issue to the largest billing in the firm's history. Tony's request to Adam had come in front of Bitch Two, Julie.

While most of the staff liked Tony since he was decent to work for, the bonus had been the quiet doublewide cube with a window looking out toward Market Street. Julie wouldn't speak to him now, especially after Christina had claimed "medical issues" when Julie told her to take over Adam's reception duties. The hate Adam had felt from Julie was nearly palpable when he had walked in from lunch with Tony while she was signing for a stack of UPS boxes. Rodney had been giving Julie the cold treatment, only to turn on the high-volume hello to Adam and Tony.

Since working with Tony, Adam had surprised himself by checking his work voicemail from home, and he was taking a bit more care of his wardrobe. Tony, who did much of his own legal writing and editing, handled most of his own technical issues too. Adam had been shocked when Tony changed a toner cartridge in the printer rather than asking Adam or IT to do it. Tony's comment about never relying on the kindness of strangers in a law firm had forced Adam to laugh openly at work, which was rare.

The sun was starting to leave the couch for the barren wall and Adam realized he needed to find something to wear to his unusual outing. Ben, being one of the rare native San Franciscans, had suggested a progressive picnic—one that his parents had taken him on many times and that accommodated the San Francisco summer. They would start at Lafayette Park for a bite to eat and, if it was warm enough, continue to Alta Vista Park for cheese and olives. If the weather held, to the Presidio eucalyptus grove for salad, followed by the Golden Gate for a sip of hearty red wine in a flask. Finally, if fog free, dessert on the Marin Headlands or Baker Beach. Neither one of them knew the tide table and the beach had a nasty habit of disappearing. The Headlands would be a climb, but the privacy they provided had crossed Adam's mind.

Adam looked at his meager clothing options. He had been able to deduce that both he and Ben were in about the same fiscal boat. Ben dressed a bit more hip, but the clothing was not pricey so much as well chosen to highlight Ben's natural physical assets.

Per usual, he tried on all the obvious choices and ended up with his first choice. It was warm in the apartment so he went with his well-worn Helly Hansen T-shirt and a pair of comfortable shorts that had enough blue in them to complement the inevitable olive the sun brought out in his skin. He'd take a sweatshirt with him just in case the fog snuck up on them.

He looked in the mirror and saw a smile nervously cross his lips. He grabbed his keys and wallet and headed for the door, knowing he would be early, but a few more minutes in the sun would be nice. Adam was down the six flights of stairs and on the sidewalk before he realized he was whistling, hands in his pockets, sporting the faintest of smiles.

FORTY-THREE

Cherie stepped out of her SUV with her purse on her shoulder and a bag of groceries in hand. She normally made a point to avoid Fag Hill, as she liked to call the Capitol Hill neighborhood of Seattle, because so many gays lived there. But Janet, who was sick with a nasty cold, had asked Cherie to pick her up some groceries. Cherie knew Janet must genuinely be in need since she rarely invited her over, claiming her apartment was too small for company. It was true, as Cherie recalled, that it was a small one-bedroom, but it was also in one of those nicely appointed, old brick buildings that gave Capitol Hill its distinctive architectural charm.

Cherie resented the fact that the gays had infiltrated one of Seattle's nicer neighborhoods, but then they thought they deserved the best of everything, even special rights like marriage. She was so tired of the minorities always playing the victim card, but no one was going to make her feel guilty for being white, heterosexual and gorgeous. She had asked Janet how she could stand living in Little Gomorrah, but Janet had said there were many kinds of sinners throughout the city and she wasn't about to give up her tranquil little apartment with its leafy view.

Cherie couldn't help smiling at the irony that Janet, who prided herself on never getting sick, had come down with a cold in the middle of the summer. She had sounded awful on the phone, her normally low voice, raspy and broken. Cherie had picked up everything from the store that Janet had requested including juice, several kinds of soup, herbal tea, toilet paper, tissues and honey. Of course, Janet had wanted a special type of soup that was compatible with her diet, but Cherie hadn't seen it at Safeway, so she'd just grabbed some cans at random. They would have to do, since she really didn't have time to be Janet's "little angel of mercy," as Janet had referred to her on the telephone. With the art exhibition at the Merkel Mansion only two days away, it was all she could do not to be a nervous wreck, and it annoyed her that Janet had chosen this week to get sick. Still, she could hardly refuse her friend.

Walking up the sidewalk toward Janet's building, she caught the scent of flowers from a nearby garden. Looking up at the giant sycamores that lined the street, she could almost believe she was in a forest. She was brought back to reality as she spotted two fruits walking toward her hand in hand. One of them, the manlier of the two, could nearly pass for normal and she guessed he must be the *butch*. The other one was a wispy little thing and she figured he must be the *fem*. She wondered how in the world she had become so fluent in their sick little lingo. While she couldn't deny the manly one was easy on the eyes, she bet they both were big AIDS bags. She knew she wasn't supposed to hate the sinner, only the sin, and all that crap, but ever since her first sweetheart had turned out to be a big homo, she had never had anything but contempt for the whole damned lot of them. Of course, she had gotten her revenge, making certain that everyone at school found out about his little tear-soaked confession.

As the two fruits passed by her, they must have noticed her scowl because the fem of the pair called out, "Look at Ms. Ritz with the fake tits. She thinks she's so special in her little red harlot outfit."

Cherie hurried past them, not in the mood to engage the local wildlife, but not before hearing the other one say something about her looking like the Sears version of the Whore of Babylon. She was relieved to see Janet's building just ahead, and upon reaching the front door, she buzzed Janet's apartment.

"Hello," Janet answered in a low rasp.

"Hi, Janet. It's Cherie."

"Come on up, sweetie." The buzzer rang and she entered

through the doorway into the lobby. She heard her heels click loudly as she walked across the white marble floor toward the curved banister of the staircase. She climbed the stairs, surprised that she was so winded when she reached the third floor. Thirty minutes on the stair climber used to be such a breeze for her but now, after climbing a couple flights, she felt as if she had just completed a marathon. Well, she resolved, she would certainly get some R&R after the Merkel Mansion gala.

Cherie knocked on the door and heard a shuffling sound from within. The door opened and she saw Janet was dressed — If one could call it that — in an oversized T-shirt and boxers. She rarely saw Janet's legs, and the sight of her pale calves, which were strangely large and obviously hadn't seen a razor in a while, repelled her. She tried not to look at them, remembering that Janet was like a much older sister to her and she shouldn't be judging her in her time of need.

"Come on in, my red angel of mercy," Janet said in a grated whisper, looking her up and down.

Right away, Cherie smelled the distinct odor of sickness mixed with stale air. She also detected something rancid in the mix that reminded her of the stench that had pervaded her guest bedroom until Carlotta had found the offending Chinese food. She saw that Janet, who was normally an oil slick, was even oilier than usual and, with her disheveled hair and hairy legs, brought to mind the image of a well-fed cave woman.

"Oh, Janet," Cherie said, smiling in sympathy and gently patting her arm, "you don't look so well."

"I've been better," Janet said in a tired voice. "You know how healthy I usually am. I can't remember when I last used any of my sick days."

"Well, I'm sure the line at the post office will be suffering for it," Cherie teased.

"It must have come from staying out all night in front of the state prison, but at least they ended up executing the low-life."

Janet coughed and Cherie could hear the rattle of the phlegm in her throat.

"What a world we live in where people want to save convicted murderers from the death penalty, but sanction murder in abortion clinics."

"It sure is a crazy one," Cherie agreed. "But before you save the world, Janet, you need to take care of yourself."

"I know, I know, but spreading the Lord's word has always come first with me. The only way one can lead is by setting a good example." Janet cleared her throat loudly. "I've always tried to lead a righteous life, and while it hasn't been easy, I figure as long as I stay on the straight and narrow, I can show others the way."

Cherie sensed a sermon coming and decided to derail it as she was in no mood for one today. "I brought you some goodies," she said, lifting up the bag to show her. "Have you eaten recently?"

"No, I've been in bed most of the day. I'm trying to starve the fever so all I had was a piece of dry toast for breakfast."

"Well, you really should eat something, but you're obviously in no state to be up and about. Why don't you go lie down and I'll fix you some soup."

"You don't have to, honey," Janet said, drawing in some mucus from her nose.

"I insist. You just go and rest." Cherie had an ulterior motive for shooing Janet away; while she wanted to be there for her friend, she would rather not have to look at her.

Janet shuffled back to her bedroom and Cherie went to the kitchen and took the groceries from the bag, putting the juice in the refrigerator and placing the non-perishable items on the counter. She now noticed that the selection of soup she had quickly grabbed wasn't the most appropriate for a sick person: cream of broccoli, clam chowder, and several cans of vegetable soup with pasta in alphabet shapes that were more fitting for kids. She decided to go with the vegetable alphabet, reasoning that cream-based soups might be too heavy for Janet right now. She knew that vegetables existed back in biblical times and, if they didn't have alphabet-shaped pasta, they at least had wheat.

She chose to ignore the long paragraph of other ingredients listed on the can. Beggars can't be choosers, she rationalized.

She washed off the top of the can, as she always did, ever since one of the ladies from church had sent her an email about someone who had been poisoned to death by the rat droppings that accumulate on canned foods. She had learned from the email that all canned food is at risk since it is stored in rat-infested warehouses in Mexico. She had done her good deed that day by forwarding the email on to all her friends and family as the original sender had urged in the message.

After searching through several drawers, she found the can opener. Now she needed to find a pan. She was going to call out to Janet to ask her where she kept them, but decided not to disturb her. She searched through the lower cabinets, as that's where she kept her pots and pans, and found them in a cabinet under the silverware drawer. She poked her head into the cabinet to search for the right size pan and was surprised to see that the back of the cabinet was lined with what looked like identical packages of cookies. There were at least twenty or thirty packages, all stacked in neat rows. What was Janet doing with all these cookies? she wondered. She reached for one of the packages and immediately recognized it as the generic cream-filled chocolate cookies from church. How odd, she thought. She knew that Janet ordered all the food and supplies for the church. Perhaps these were intended for the church and she was just storing them. Yet, she knew the supplies came directly to the church, having signed for deliveries on more than one occasion.

She now recalled how Janet was always so protective of the church supply room and kept it locked. She couldn't help but think back to all those times Janet had so abstemiously resisted the cookies during the meetings. Was she going home and binging on her stolen stash? This would explain the dark crumbs on her clothes and the layer of crumbs in her car. Still, she knew she shouldn't be so quick to condemn her friend, since there was probably a logical explanation.

She opened the soup and poured it into the pan, setting the

flame on medium. She rinsed out the can, and while searching for where Janet kept her recycling, she opened the cabinet underneath the sink and instantly knew she had found the source of the rancid smell. She took out the garbage can and pulled out the bag. She was about to seal it shut when she noticed a McDonald's bag inside along with a brown speckled banana skin. Despite the smell, she couldn't resist shaking the bag a bit and, as the contents shifted, she saw the telltale plastic package of the generic cookies, which were sitting aside an empty family size bag of M&M's. Well, so much for giving her the benefit of the doubt, Cherie thought. She quickly closed the bag, not wanting to witness any more of Janet's indiscretions and placed a fresh bag in the bin. She now felt silly for having worried about buying soups that were incompatible with Janet's special diet. Apparently, anything was allowed on the *Hypocrite's Diet*, including stealing.

Cherie was appalled that her friend had repeatedly lied to her and placed herself on a pedestal of dietary purity. She sat down on the sofa, still reeling in disbelief over her discovery. While the soup simmered, she decided to flip through the channels on the TV to avoid talking to Janet. She scanned the room for the remote, but didn't see it. She could try to figure out how to use the buttons on the TV, but that just seemed barbaric. She opened up the cabinet underneath the TV and was pleased to find the remotes were lined neatly inside, right above Janet's DVD collection. She grabbed the TV remote and browsed the collection, mostly a mix of Christian, Disney and some PG fare. As she pushed aside *Beauty and the Beast*, she caught sight of a few DVDs that had fallen to the back of the cabinet. She pulled one of the DVDs out and what she saw stunned her. The title read *Homecumming Pussy Sluts on Parade* and showed scantily clad and generously endowed women in compromising poses on top of a breast-shaped float. She pulled out the other two DVDs, feeling strangely compelled to see them, and was similarly appalled: *Bound to Obey: Biker Chick Bondage* and *Lipstick Lesbian Power Suit Panty Party*. The last DVD especially unnerved her, as the woman who was pictured on the cover in a scanty power suit was a dead ringer for herself. "Oh my God!" she gasped, dropping the DVDs. Her sense of shock was interrupted by the sound of Janet shifting in bed, causing it to creak loudly.

Cherie felt a surge of panic and wanted nothing more than to get the hell out of there. She headed toward the kitchen to get her purse, but then she heard Janet's bed creak again.

"Honey, is everything okay out there?" Janet whined.

"Everything's fine, Janet. I'll be right in with your soup." As much as she wanted to leave, she realized she needed to play it cool. She would bring Janet the soup and then make up some excuse to leave.

She tried to calm herself down as she turned off the burner and grabbed a bowl and plate from the cabinet. She poured the soup into the bowl and placed the hot bowl onto the plate along with a spoon. When she brought the soup into the room, she saw that Janet was sitting up in bed, resting against a pillow, partially covered by a wool throw, which was woven with a repeating pattern of black and white sheep.

"Honey, you're so sweet to be helping sick little me. I can almost taste your sweetness."

Cherie winced, not able to look Janet directly in the face; instead, she looked down at Janet's hairy calves that were partially exposed from under the wool throw. It was then that a verse from Matthew popped into her head with surprising clarity: *Beware of false prophets who come to you in sheep's clothing, but inwardly are ravening wolves.* Wolf in sheep's clothing, she reflected, as she stared at Janet's legs. Her hands started to tremble uncontrollably and the soup bowl and spoon rattled against the plate.

"Is everything okay, honey?" Janet asked, eyeing her curiously.

She approached Janet, not able to get the verse out of her mind. *Wolf in sheep's clothing, wolf in sheep's clothing* …. She looked down at the bowl of soup, trying to steady her trembling hands, and saw that right in the middle of the bowl, separate from all the others, were the letters GGG, but then she saw the true meaning of her vision. It was 666, the sign of the beast. At that moment, everything became clear to her.

The end of days was near and the signs were all around her. She remembered the red laser of the gun scope that had been targeted on her. She recalled the vision she'd had in Edison's bedroom of the angels descending from heaven. She now understood that there were dark forces at work, some of them in the guise of friends. She absorbed the full implications of her epiphany, realizing that her trusted friend was not who she pretended to be, but was aligned with the Antichrist. Her hands were trembling violently now and the rattling of the china grew louder and louder. She looked at Janet straight on, who now appeared wide-eyed and frightened.

"What's gotten into you, sweetheart?"

Cherie didn't know if she threw the bowl or if it simply slipped out of her hands, but what she saw next was soup splattering all over Janet. Janet screamed in pain, like a demon doused with holy water, and Cherie dropped the plate and rushed out of the bedroom. Pausing only to grab her purse from the kitchen counter, she ran for her life.

FORTY-FOUR

Edison stretched out on the porch swing wearing what he and Val had decided was a "summer formal" suit and tie. Summer formal was the term used on Cherie's invitation and after searching the Internet in vain for a definition, he decided on a pale linen suit that was on sale at J. Crew. He assumed he could always wear it to an earthy lesbian wedding that would no doubt be on a beach.

The days of physical labor from putting his new home in order had left a tired soreness in his muscles, and it was an effort to find a comfortable position among his mother's bevy of worn and fussy pillows on the porch swing. He knew this was Stella's domain but Stella didn't seem too upset and had moved to the porch rail to lord over the lawn. Edison was aware of a gentle nag from the past in his mother's voice about wrinkling his suit, but having found a comfortable spot, and with Val in the house primping, he drifted in and out of a shallow sleep.

He remembered his father resting his head in his mother's lap after dinner on this same porch swing when it was at his childhood home. That summer—he must have been eight—before he joined Little League with Greg and Pauli, every night seemed the same. He could remember his mother's laugh and the murmur of their voices. His father would be awake, but his eyes closed, and would smile from time to time as his mother toyed with his hair. Edison would sit at his father's feet with a book and eventually fall asleep in the deep twilight. He'd wake slightly when his father carried him up to his bedroom later in the cool evening air.

The sound of Val's heels clicking on the foyer floor woke him as she approached. The few minutes of sleep left him refreshed. Stella was gone and there was a subtle change in the air as the afternoon shadows had lengthened. He straightened his clothes and the stiff invitation in his coat pocket reminded him of the evening's events. Val stepped through the open front door with his mother's silver cocktail tray, which was loaded with glasses and all the items needed for gin and tonics.

"Brett called a few minutes ago," Val said, carefully putting the tray on the wide porch rail. "They're running a little late and I said they should come over here since you were asleep on the front porch. I referred to you as Sleeping Beauty and now that I see you in your suit, I think I was right. You clean up pretty well. Gin and tonic?"

"Sure, I'll take a weak one. You look nice, very classy, and your haircut looks great too."

"Why thank you, Mr. Edison. Funny, I have never dressed and lived so well," she said, nodding toward the house, "and been so damn poor. Monday, by the way, this girl is calling some temporary agencies and putting her stuff out on the market. I thought I would reserve mornings for job search and afternoons for helping you get this place in order."

"Sounds good," Edison said, stretching again, frustrated that his dress shirt slid out of his pants every time he stretched. He tucked it back in discreetly since Val was there.

"Brett is a friendly guy," Val said, changing the topic and handing him a gin and tonic.

"You call this a weak drink?" Edison asked, feeling the gin overwhelm his mouth after a sip. "Where did you learn to mix a drink? The Garland School of Bartending?"

"It's always Judy, Judy, Judy with you people, isn't it?" Val asked in faux condemnation.

"But you're right," Edison said, "Brett is a genuinely nice guy. He and Linda leaving SF created a bit of a vacuum in my life that I guess I filled with work and Russell's drama. "Brett, though," he searched for words, "well, he is what he is and I think Linda appreciates that too. He gives me faith that straight men are good at heart."

"How Anne Frank of you. These are a bit strong," Val said reaching for the tonic water. She continued, "I look at Linda and see that she has some of the things I want in life. A solid partner for one, and a passion for something is the other. I think if I had those two things the rest would fall into place."

"I didn't hear you mention kids," Edison said without adding a viewpoint.

"I know," Val replied, rolling her eyes. "*That* I'll miss about 3Γ. No one there pressures you about kids because most San Franciscans can think beyond Ozzie and Harriet role models. I don't know about kids, to be truthful. I don't think about them that much unless someone brings them up. I'll be happy just being the aunt that accidentally leaves the kids at the mall overnight."

"I wouldn't mind them," Edison said. "But I don't want to do it alone. I had hoped Brett and Linda would have a brood so I could be the peculiar uncle who takes them to all the fun places."

"You'd be a great father, Edison."

"And you a great mother." He winked at her. "Too bad it seems the people that would make the best parents don't have kids and the trailer set has them in six packs."

"True," Val said looking out over the porch rail. "Brett and Linda are crossing the street. I'll mix them two short drinks so we can stick to our plan of eating and drinking Cherie out of her commission."

"You and Linda have been plotting?"

"Oh, you have no idea. And Linda is territorial. Good thing Brett is decidedly heterosexual or she would have skewered you a long time ago."

"You think I'm interested in Brett?" he asked, thinking of Brett, shirtless, professing his love, bedside ... a recent fantasy, but a classic.

"Compared to Russell, he is a god," she joked.

"So is Stella," Edison said, picking up the returning Stella, who licked his nose before jumping out of his arms to claim his position among the pillows on the porch swing.

Val finished making the two short drinks and further diluted hers and Edison's with tonic.

"Sleeping Beauty rises," Brett said, stepping up on the porch and taking the offered drink from Val.

"Edison, you look nice," Linda said accepting a drink from Val. "You too, Val. Is that Dior?"

"Yes, it's vintage, but it's for the summer season so I thought this would be a good occasion since my only other option might be to wear it mowing the lawn. I do really need to get some summer clothes. Some woman recognized a blouse of Ellie's I was wearing at the market yesterday. I felt like a thief or imposter. Then the poor woman thought I was Edison's wife when he came up and started putting his items in my cart."

"You two do make a cute couple," Brett teased. "Edison, she could make you an honest man and she already helped you reel in one date. Mr. Tinkle, wasn't it?"

"No offense, Val, but you're going to have to do better than Mr. Tinkle," Edison said, moving to her side and giving her arm a squeeze.

"Hey, what have you done for me recently besides saving me from myself?" she asked.

"Old lady clothes," Edison offered, finishing his drink. "So," Edison said, stretching again but mindful of his shirt. "What is our game plan?"

"Eat, drink and defeat," Linda and Brett said in practiced unison.

"Sounds like they are organized," Val laughed, setting her finished drink on the tray after taking Edison's empty glass from him.

"Brett and I can focus on the food and you two can keep the drinks going," Edison suggested.

Linda spoke clearly from behind her glass, "I'll take a look at the art and, if it's bad, drop comments on it. If it's good, we'll enjoy it but leave a lot of plates and half-empty cocktail glasses around to clutter up the place. She had to pay for food regardless, but she is being dinged for the alcohol, so let's drink her to fiscal despair."

"Oh," Val said, "let's make sure Brett is unapproachable. All three of us need to be on guard so he is never available to her."

"We can hide in the men's room if need be," Brett said to Edison.

"I don't think Cherie considers the men's room off limits," Edison said, "more of an invitation."

"Good point," Brett conceded, finishing his drink and placing it on the tray.

After locking up, they made their way down the front steps led by Linda.

"Brett and I were wondering if you two are up for some music later tonight. We moved out the furniture in our main room this week so the floors could be waxed. We were thinking now that the floors are done, we could have a post-party sock hop and crank up the music."

"Sounds like fun," Val said with audible excitement. "I haven't danced in ages."

"I'm in," Edison added as they went past the front gate and turned right to the Merkel Mansion.

Edison paused and turned back, stopping the group.

"Hold on, I need to put an end to something once and for all."

It was the familiar black Audi that had been doing slow drive-bys and parking in front of the house. Checking the license plate to be sure, he walked over to the driver's window that was open, as were all the others. Inside was a man, who looked to be of his father's generation, holding a camera pointed toward the front porch. Edison heard the shutter snap and felt the anger rise inside of him. He only modulated it slightly when he rapped on the roof with his knuckles rather than pound with his fist.

"Excuse me," Edison said to the man, hostility in his voice. "Why are you taking pictures of my house?"

The man seemed unfazed at Edison's tone, much to Edison's chagrin.

"Oh, they're for the Missis. We're interested in purchasing the house but she didn't want to take the car ride all the way from Everett. You're the owner?"

"Yes, and the house isn't for sale."

"Not for sale? So it's already been sold?"

"No. It's not for sale, period."

"But, it's been listed on the website for weeks. I thought it wasn't selling because of that curse nonsense."

Edison looked to Val, who had come to the car along with Brett and Linda. They all seemed equally perplexed.

Edison turned back to the man. "What do you mean it's listed on the website?"

"It's on the Amstead Reality website with instructions to contact Ms. Cahill and not the owner by the owner's request. Frankly, I'm tired of dealing with that woman."

Brett chuckled, "You and everyone else."

"So you're looking at the house too?" the man asked Brett with frustration in his voice.

"Oh, no, we live down the street, but Ms. Cahill has quite the reputation on the block."

"Apparently, she doesn't understand when a hot piece of property is not on the market," Linda added, leaning briefly against Brett.

"I'll be damned. It's been one excuse after another with that screwball and now it's all starting to make sense." He turned to Edison. "So, you're being straight with me when you say it's not for sale?"

"As straight as I know how," Edison said with a wry smile. "Ms. Cahill and reality don't always intersect; she listed the house without my knowledge or consent. I inherited it from my parents this summer and she was hoping I would sell."

"That's just not right. I'm going to call Amstead Realty first thing Monday morning and speak to her boss. I haven't been driving all the way down from Everett for my health."

"Well, I'm sorry for your inconvenience, sir. Her boss will get an earful from me as well."

"Here's my card," the man offered. "If you ever change your mind about the house, let me know. She's a beauty."

"She certainly is," Edison said, accepting the card, knowing he would never call.

"I had better let you folks get to your party or wherever you're all going."

Edison waved as the man drove off and then turned back to his group to see Linda glaring at the departing car.

"I cannot believe that bitch!" Linda fumed.

They turned and, in pairs, walked toward the Merkel Mansion.

"You probably could get her fired," Val offered, breathlessly, trying to keep up with them in her heels.

Linda stopped and took Brett's hand. Brett hadn't spoken since the man had driven off and Edison knew that he went silent when he was angry.

"This is going to be one hell of party," Linda said. "We need to make her uncomfortable on her own turf, just like she tried to do with you, Edison."

"So, we're going to stab her pillows, bash her hens and drip blood all over the place?" Edison asked with a half smile.

"No, sweet pea, I was thinking about eating her food, drinking her booze and general sabotage." Linda turned to Val while reaching into her purse. "Smoke indoors." She handed a pack of cigarettes to Val with a lighter rubber-banded to the pack. "I planned, just a bit," she said, causing Brett and then the others to laugh.

Linda turned to Edison, handing him a green bottle of Polo cologne. "You need to spray this while near the art or the food."

"Hey, that's my cologne," Brett said.

"From when, 1985?" Edison joked, as he put the cologne in his coat pocket.

"Well," Brett said, motioning for them all to move forward, "it is a bit old and the lady frowns on such things now."

"Lily is going to be there too," Linda said, as they neared the back of a van from a local television station.

"How did she get an invite?" Brett asked. "I thought Crazy only gave you two invitations."

"Oh, she has her own," Linda said, as they all stepped onto the sidewalk before the block long mansion lawn. "She's on the invitation list of the Pan Asian Art Museum. She's up to something tonight," Linda continued as they entered the iron gates of the Merkel property. "She wouldn't tell me what, but keep an eye on her. I think it could be amusing."

They were silent as they came up behind a group of older people in formal attire who all seemed to know each other. The wait in the late afternoon sun was short. Soon they were at the head of the line and the cool air rushing out of the open double doors of the mansion was refreshing. At first, Edison thought he would have to ask Val what she and the handsome greeter had discussed, but when he saw Val slip a card discreetly into her purse, he decided that it would be better to let Val tell him rather than have her suffer a public interrogation.

FORTY-FIVE

Cherie slowly descended the grand staircase of the Merkel Mansion, surveying the culmination of all her efforts. From her elevated vantage point, she had a clear view of the wide foyer and could see that her guests were arriving on time and that they were all the right people. The guests had taken the formal attire request seriously and their chatter competed with *Bewitched, Bothered and Bewildered* coming from the grand piano in the ballroom. To her, it was the sweet sound of success.

After months of groveling to the museums, the Merkel art collection was complete for the first time in decades. The mansion was shining from stem to stern in all its glory due to Carlotta and sisters, whom she had hired for the massive cleaning job. The ballroom, quickly filling up with Seattle's elite, reeked of money and it was she who had made this happen. If her classmates at Yakima High could only see her now—"Most Ditzy," my ass, she thought, recalling her yearbook nomination.

Everything had come together perfectly and she treasured the view for one last moment. One day she would own a mansion like this. Perhaps it would be this very one, she fancied.

Not only were the house and art collection masterpieces, but she was as well. She had purchased an emerald-colored Hermes gown for the event. The gown was long, but the slit up the side allowed her to show off her legs to great advantage. Of course, she knew the true focal point of her dress was the scandalous plunge of the neckline, and resting between her two best assets was a stunning emerald pendant, which had been given to her by a wealthy older gentleman years earlier.

This morning, her hair had been coifed and her makeup applied to perfection by Fausto at the salon. Fausto was a fruit, but he was also an artiste, and after years of hair don'ts rather than hairdos, she had felt lucky to find such an artiste. She overlooked his sinful lifestyle, reasoning that, as a talented hairdresser, he was at least contributing to Christian society. He had styled her hair in bouffant fashion and had likened it to an exquisitely woven bird's nest. With his relentless eye for detail, Fausto had even color coordinated her glitter eye shadow to match the emerald of her dress and pendant.

She descended the final steps and made her way to Marco, who was receiving guests at the front entrance. Marco was dressed like a butler, but he was actually a bouncer and aspiring actor whom she called when she felt lonely. He was built like an ox and was as dumb and horny as one too, but he was handsome and looked the part. He had taken his role of butler to heart, rehearsing for it as if it represented his big break. She had promised him $250 for the evening and a special bonus to be cashed in at a later time.

Besides Marco, there were two security personnel on the floor, one female and one male, posing as guests. Although there was priceless art to guard, Cherie wanted to be discreet with security and not give her guests the impression they were being scrutinized like potential shoplifters. Most of the first floor was open to all attendees, and prospective buyers could see the two upper floors as part of guided tours.

She sidled up to Marco, who was standing near the open front door, and in a low but firm voice said in his ear, "Remember, no one gets in without an invitation."

He nodded with a smile, shamelessly appraising her breasts. She smiled knowingly upon seeing his obvious lust, but quickly morphed her smile into a greeting as she saw an older couple entering the mansion. They looked important, the woman having a regal air about her, and it was only upon seeing their name on the invitation the woman handed to Marco that Cherie remembered who they were.

"Hello, Mr. and Mrs. O'Hara, so glad you could make it."

"Wouldn't miss this for the world," bellowed Mr. O'Hara. "Free booze and pretty ladies such as yourself."

Cherie waved the flush-faced geezer off with pretend modesty, and thought she actually felt a momentary chill in the air upon catching Mrs. O'Hara cast an icy look at her husband.

"This isn't Vegas, Peter," Mrs. O'Hara said reproachfully.

With that, Mrs. O'Hara headed to the ballroom. Her husband shrugged in resignation and followed her. Mrs. O'Hara, Cherie knew, viewed herself as the reigning socialite of Seattle. Cherie doubted anyone much cared for her, but over the years she had become an institution in her own right—by the sheer fact of having outlived most of her critics—and her presence confirmed the importance of any function.

Cherie followed the O'Haras into the ballroom, watching as Mrs. O'Hara joined a group of older women, leaving her husband to fend for himself. The ballroom was certainly grand with its twenty-foot high gilded ceiling that was original to the mansion. The art hung impressively on the walls, both the portable ones the museum had installed and on the mansion's walls, with the ballroom housing the largest pieces of the collection. The gleaming parquet floors sparkled and although it had taken several reprimands, Cherie was glad that she had finally impressed upon Carlotta what a mirror-quality shine looked like.

A server passing in front of Cherie caught her eye. He was carrying a silver platter of Vietnamese summer rolls but without the requisite dipping sauce. She hurried over to him and in a scolding tone asked, "Where's the dipping sauce for these?"

He stared at her blankly.

"The summer rolls need to be served with the sweet and spicy dipping sauce," she scolded him. "Go back into the kitchen ASAP and ask Nelson for the sauce. And tell him, I hold his ass responsible for every dish that leaves that kitchen."

The server hurried back to the kitchen looking flustered, and she glowered, thinking how she hated having to deal with these dimwits when a man with a camera approached her. From his press badge, she recognized him as a photographer from a local paper.

"Ms. Cahill, how about a picture for the newspaper?"

"Certainly," Cherie said, pasting on a practiced smile.

"Why don't we take it over there in front of the large tapestry?"

"Can you take it here?" Cherie asked, feeling a sudden trepidation.

"Nah, the lighting's better there and I think that magnificent tapestry is a more fitting backdrop for such a lovely lady."

"Okay," Cherie reluctantly agreed.

The tapestry was the centerpiece of the Merkel's medieval collection. Woven in the Late Middle Ages of dyed wool and silk, the tapestry took up half the wall and showed the Four Horsemen of the Apocalypse riding on Judgment Day.

It was a rather ghastly work, the Four Horsemen representing the various ills that would befall humanity during the apocalypse: war, pestilence, famine and death. Each horseman rode a different color steed and she knew from her Bible studies that it was the rider of the white horse that was traditionally believed to represent the Antichrist. The near life-sized dimensions of the horsemen made it appear as though they were leaping out of the tapestry.

The shocking incident had happened when she had been alone in the ballroom one night. She had been making certain everything was in order, when she felt the sudden compulsion to look at the tapestry and saw the horseman on the white horse turn to her with a grisly smile, his white steed seeming to snarl silently at her. Very clearly, she heard a voice beckon, "Come to me." This had all occurred in the briefest of moments and then the tapestry was back to normal. But she knew what she had witnessed. The Antichrist himself had contacted her and it was just one more sign that the end of days was imminent. If she hadn't taken enough Xanax to mellow a football team, she would have lost it.

She started taking Xanax to calm her nerves after the incident at Janet's apartment. Janet had repeatedly called her since then, leaving several desperate-sounding voicemails, but Cherie wasn't fooled by Janet's pretense of bewilderment. Ignorance was always the refuge of the guilty. Janet had been her rock and to find out instead she was the Antichrist's welcome wagon had been more than she could bear.

If it wasn't for the Xanax, she knew she couldn't have been functional at the party. She'd taken no chances, swallowing a double dose just before the party along with her double dose of antidepressants and some caffeine pills to keep her sharp. She kept some Xanax handy, just in case she started feeling anxious.

She hoped her premonitions would take the night off, but the tapestry was by far the largest piece of art in the room and it commanded one's attention. Even now, she could feel herself oddly drawn to it, but since her close encounter last night, she was trying her best not to look at it.

"Ms. Cahill, are you okay?" the photographer asked, breaking her out of her thoughts. "You looked like you were in a trance there for a minute."

"Oh, no, I'm fine," Cherie said, donning a tight smile.

"Well then show me those pearly whites," he cajoled.

Cherie forced a smile, knowing she had to rally for the press.

"Thatta girl," he said giving her a quick wink.

With the picture taken, he left her and she saw him head toward one of the local billionaires.

Cherie moved away from the tapestry quickly, but the eerie voice still haunted her. Why had the Antichrist asked her to come to him? Why was she being targeted? She realized she didn't have the luxury to ponder this right now. Instead, she looked about, focusing on the cheery groups of people viewing the art with drinks and hors d'oeuvres in hand. The open bar was certainly busy and the line at the food table was long, though she could see that the servers were handling the guests efficiently. She was glad she had communicated to the staff her zero tolerance for slackers.

Gazing straight across the room, Cherie spotted an older Asian woman who was standing between a ninth century statue of Buddha and a potted palm. The woman was sipping a drink and seemed to be staring at her. Cherie thought the woman looked familiar, but she couldn't place her. She wore a long, silky black dress and matching brocade coat embossed with a fire-breathing dragon print. Ugh, Cherie lamented to herself. She knew those invites she'd had to give to the Pan Asian Art Museum would come back to bite her. Oh well, she considered, since half the Merkel collection was from the Orient, at least the dragon lady fit into the general theme of the evening. As long as she had the decency to stay there in the corner, she supposed there wasn't much harm. But why was she staring at her like that?

Cherie turned her head in disgust, not wanting to focus on the trash, and peeked back to the foyer and saw a different sort of trash enter the front door. It was Linda Gale. So, the Hippo actually had a backbone underneath all that fat and decided to show up. Perhaps, Cherie mused, she had spent all day reciting some affirmations she'd learned at Jenny Craig, or her plus-size support group had given her a delusional moment of confidence. At least she had taken her advice and worn black. A man entered directly behind Linda, looking very debonair in his suit, and she was momentarily taken aback when she realized it was *her* Brett. She had never seen him in formal attire and could not help but mourn the fact that he wasn't on her arm tonight. She winced as she saw the Fruit appear next with what she guessed was his Rent-a-Hag. At least they had dressed appropriately, she grudgingly admitted, and thought they could almost pass for a normal couple to anyone unaware of their depraved ruse.

As if by sheer animal magnetism, Cherie saw Brett turn toward her, staring at her for a palpable few seconds before turning away. Was that the fire of desire she had seen in his eyes, she wondered, because she knew she had been singed by it. She looked at Linda and wondered if she was the type of hippo that would charge when jilted.

FORTY-SIX

The front doors of the mansion were painted a glossy white, and the paint looked fresh. Linda was tempted to touch them but she resisted. Once inside, she took in the formal entrance hall of the mansion. To either side, large rooms were open and art was hung, on both the mansion's walls and the short temporary walls that divided each room. Ahead of her was a large and broad staircase that slowly turned between the first and second floors. The interiors were beautiful and the harmony of the soft colors complimented the airy and vast entryway.

The view wasn't perfect, though, as Linda saw Cherie almost immediately. She was like a cat, eyeing the entrance from what might have been a large dining room converted into a ballroom. Linda gave her a cold stare and a quick disapproving scan, an immature technique that she had learned from Russell. Well, she mused, if she was going to be a bitch, then Russell had the credentials to teach a master class.

She turned to her little group as they made their way to the center of the foyer. "Whore at 11:00," she said in a stage whisper.

"Don't get too close," Edison said, stepping between them and Cherie. "She might have the new super virulent herpes that comes with each diploma from Trampolina Tech."

Cherie had turned to speak to an attractive couple, her realtor smile on full, but her eyes were dark, shooting daggers at Edison.

"Did you say the house has dry rot or she has dry rot?" Brett asked Linda in a voice suited for the near deaf.

"One for our team," Val squealed as they all watched Cherie move from the attractive couple to the central staircase that dominated the foyer. Cherie avoided their group entirely. Halfway up she seemed to speak to someone, but no one was near her. Perhaps she had a communications wire on her, Linda thought.

Cherie continued up the steps and spoke to a young woman, whom they all could see, stationed at a red velvet rope that blocked access to the upper floors. Before Linda could get in another comment, Cherie spun around and put something from her hand into her mouth, and then started down the wide staircase, diagonally.

Every man, even Brett, couldn't help but follow her form although Edison was looking at a passing food tray. She looked back at Cherie, who was now halfway down the great staircase. She was in a beautiful green dress that shimmered discreetly while screaming money at the same time. As Cherie sauntered down the stairs, it was a toss up for what was coming at you faster, her breasts or the scissor of leg that flashed from the slit in the dress.

Val shrieked, "That hair!" pointing openly at Cherie and drawing attention to the vortex of hair that topped Cherie's head. "It's not in Kansas anymore!"

"And that eye shadow!" Linda howled. "My God, did she apply it with a glitter gun?"

Brett laughed, and in full view of Cherie, pulled Linda close and kissed her openly on the forehead, leaving a wet mark she didn't wipe away.

"*Whore Descending a Staircase*, isn't that a painting from 1913?" Val said, again loud enough for nearby couples to hear.

"Good art memory," Linda said to Val, honestly impressed with both the art reference and the correct date of the *Nude Descending a Staircase* controversy.

A man near Val laughed despite himself and an older woman in front of them turned to Val and said sternly, "Young lady, if you do not have anything nice to say, come stand by me."

Linda smiled and the stern-looking woman in front of them broke into a bright smile that belonged to a maiden more than a matron.

Including the older couple, Brett asked if he could get them all drinks. After collecting the requests, Brett and Edison walked toward the caterer's bar, Brett's hand on Edison's back as they cut through the thick crowd. Linda wondered what it took for Brett to be comfortable with someone other than her and why with Edison he was relaxed. It had always bothered her that she couldn't understand the world of men.

She turned to see Val drifting to the palm lined entrance hall with the older couple. She caught up in time to hear the older woman explain that she was a close friend of the late Mrs. Merkel and then introduced herself as Edith Burke, and the quiet man she introduced simply as Jack. She went on to explain that she had no time for the likes of Ms. Cahill, since Ms. Cahill had tried to rescind her invitation after she had sent her RSVP.

"Such poor form," Linda said, nodding and loving that Cherie appeared to be a classless bimbo as well as a tramp.

"Well, it took a call to Robert Merkel, III to get me back on the list. He was so nice to send a limo for us tonight because of the gaffe. I hope he charges it to that stupid woman. I suppose I shouldn't tell Robert that I remember sitting on those very stairs with him on my knee and letting him play with my long blonde hair. Funny, he eventually married a blonde." She patted her thin white hair and laughed. "It seems like yesterday," she mused, smiling and clearly seeing a different room than the one in which they all stood.

Edith broke the silence with a softer voice, "The art is exactly as Pat, I mean Mrs. Merkel, had it. Ms. Cahill was smart enough to work from pictures, clearly."

"Probably can't read," Val quipped before covering her mouth.

"Such a sharp tongue. Remind me never to cross you," Edith said to Val, touching the padded shoulder of Val's dress. "I remember that tapestry of the Four Horseman. It is in the right place and no worse for wear. Pat and I always thought the horses looked like they would have been happier on a merry-go-round rather than riding into the apocalypse."

"I can see that," Val said, "or perhaps a nice green pasture."

"It is an excellent piece. The Merkels were in the right time and place to demonstrate their good taste," Linda said. "This collection would be nearly impossible to acquire privately these days."

Before Edith could respond, Brett and Edison came up to them holding several glasses and passed them around.

"Good food over there?" Val asked Edison.

"Excellent from the looks of it."

Linda watched the vortex of hair that was Cherie move around their circle, keeping her distance. Cherie seemed to wear the same fake smile regardless of whether she was facing a potted palm or the mayor.

"Oh," Val said, clearly forgetting that two outsiders were part of their group. "I have Sharpies if we want to write, 'For a good time, call Cherie Cahill, Amstead Reality' near any of the art."

Jack spoke up, "I'll take one of those, young lady, and I'll make sure it gets a prominent position in the men's restroom. With your permission," he said politely to Edith.

"Just don't use cursive, Jack; they will know that you shop with Dot."

"Relic," he said to Edith as he left.

"Sissy," she yelled back.

"Is that us in a few years?" Edison asked Val.

"You should be so lucky," Val said, reaching in her purse and handing Linda a Sharpie. "You are familiar with the concept of graffiti as social commentary, yes?" Val asked with a quick smile. "Why don't we give it a try while the boys eat and drink Cahill out of her commission."

"May I join you two gals?" Edith asked. "With this dress, I can provide cover." She put her arms out and the material fell like a superhero's cloak.

"I was just going to invite you," Linda said, taking Edith by the elbow and exchanging her empty champagne flute for Brett's nearly full bourbon and Coke. She knew she was leaving her husband alone in the den of the lioness but she trusted him now, more than ever, not to step in Cherie's cat box.

FORTY-SEVEN

"Do you think the gals are out of line?" Brett asked, pulling his tie off and stuffing it in his coat pocket. He had seen a few other men do the same thing as the summer heat and the crowd taxed the air conditioning. Brett noted with a smile that Edison had followed suit and had also unbuttoned the top two buttons on his shirt. Not to be outdone, Brett did the same.

"Oh, a bit," Edison replied. "Being here is feeling more and more like a mistake, but that won't keep me away from the food and drink."

"I hear you. I think this is cheap therapy for Linda. Wearing a tie on a summer afternoon is never my first choice. Hey, next weekend, let's make up for this with a trip to the San Juans on the boat. A couple of beers and some cannonballs off the back will make this all seem like a bad dream."

"Perfect. That would be a nice change. Did you intend to bring the womenfolk?" Edison asked.

"Nah, how about just us? Linda has her hands full with Vera and maybe Val could use the time alone rather than play-ing 'kept woman' to your lord of the manor." Brett positioned them in line for the food and used his height advantage to scope out what the long line of caterers were placing on the plates of the passing guests.

"Well, she may be nuts," he said to Edison, "but this is a good spread. It couldn't have been cheap."

"Her commission, if she sells this place, will more than com-pensate her," Edison said, taking a mini bottle of champagne from the giant ice swan whose back was crammed with pricey bottles. Brett took a bottle as well and after popping the corks, they knocked the bottles against each other and downed the champagne.

The food did look good, and as they approached the main table, a small army of caterers stood ready to prepare each guest's plate. Brett could feel the champagne's effect almost immediately since it had been hours since he last ate.

Within a few minutes, they were both through the line and with heaping plates, headed to the open bar. After a bar order, they moved carefully to the cluster of small tables and chairs where people were eating and talking in the view of the gardens beyond the large windows. They spotted an open table and as they approached, Brett heard a shrill giggle in his ear and felt a hand slip deep into his shirt before tugging at the hair on his chest.

"There is more of this to come, I promise," Cherie said in a husky whisper. He felt her tongue in his ear about the time his food hit his shoe.

"Cherie," he said looking to Edison for help, "get the hell away from me."

Several people were staring at him and Cherie. He tossed his empty china plate toward the open table. Edison caught it and gave Brett a signal to hand him his drink. With his hands free, Brett firmly pulled Cherie's hand from his shirt, popping a button, which went flying and hit Edison on the chin before bouncing into his drink. Her fingers had dug into his skin when he had pulled her hand up and out of his shirt, leaving a burning sensation.

When he let go of her hand, it went right back into his shirt, and her other hand went into his pants pocket and tugged on his briefs. Edison moved to pull her away, but she stopped Edison with hissing words and moved both her hands to the front of Brett's shirt.

"Bet you have dreamed about being right where I am, Edison Archer. Such a nice chest and so warm. A real man. I know you want that night and day, but he's only for a real woman, the way the Lord meant it."

Brett saw Edison put his drink down calmly, his face flush and he moved toward Cherie with a tense gait that made Brett suddenly uneasy that things were going to go from bad to worse.

"Eds, I'll take care of this." Turning to Cherie, he said loudly, looking into her wild eyes, "This real man has had enough." Not caring what the right thing to do was, he took hold of Cherie's wrists and squeezed them hard, driving her bracelets deep into her flesh until she let go of his shirt. She fought him and either she was stronger than most or he needed to get to the gym more.

She moved closer to him and he decided he had given this crackpot enough options to do the right thing. He leaned back slightly, and in an easy barroom maneuver, elbowed Cherie hard in the diaphragm, which should have knocked the air out of most men and certainly any woman.

Instead, like some sort of vixen robot, she whispered calmly, "Nice try, handsome man, I'm a Yakima girl. We don't fall for the urban cowboy moves. My brothers taught me better. If you know what's good for you, join me in the master bedroom and I'll show you what a real woman can give her man."

"Syphilis?" Linda asked, pushing between Brett and Cherie. Brett saw Edison relax and step back and take position near the edge of the open table. Edison folded his arms but Brett had the sense that he was ready to intervene on either Linda's or his behalf. He was still oddly red.

"Listen, bitch," Linda said in an icy voice, "you have a pretty party here, and if you don't want me to go Joan Collins on your ass, then you had better keep away from my husband and stop pretending that you are the Reaping Widow of Queen Anne."

Brett heard the crowd collectively inhale at the mention of the Reaping Widow and he was shocked that people actually believed in such crap. He was quickly drawn back to the pending catfight, ready to have any excuse to punch Cherie hard in order to protect Linda.

"You and whose army, you undeserving fat bitch? I have the Lord Jesus on my team and who do you have? Not your husband, that's for sure. What do you have, Fat Linda?" Cherie shrieked, stepping back. "What do you have? The army of lost souls, the damned?" she yelled, pointing at Edison.

Cherie stepped back again, the crowd parting behind her. Turning to Edison, she spoke loudly and in a tone best fit for cheap biblical remakes, "Your end of days are coming, Edison Archer, and it will be people like me and Brett who will have our union in the Rapture."

Her body was shaking and Brett noticed that one breast was nearly out of her dress. He scolded himself for noticing but it seemed to be par for the course when it came to all things Cahill. The pills popping from her cleavage and bouncing wildly on the shiny floor distracted everyone.

Cherie had backed up nearly to the door that led to what he assumed was the kitchen. She became silent and pointed to something about ten feet above the caterers. He then heard her mutter the words "the horseman" before turning and quickly disappearing between the double doors that led to the back of the house.

"Shall we go?" Edison asked, coming up to the two of them.

"Why are you so red, Edison?" Linda asked.

"Delayed rage," Edison offered.

"You look like a lobster, Edison," Brett said, teasing Edison as he made lobster claws with his hands. Speaking of which, I never got my food. How about we get some more food and drink while we wait for Val? We should at least get something out of this folly."

A man to his left knelt down, picked up one of the pills on the floor and looked at it. "Xanax," he said, "looks like she forgot to take it." He tossed it under the table and gave Brett a polite nod before walking to the bar.

"I'll get Val," Linda said, "and run the food line with her and meet you two here."

"Sounds good." He kissed Linda, holding her tight and pressed hard into her, not caring what other people could see. She yielded and he felt the warmth of her body against his and she responded with her lips and gently grazed his ear in the special way he liked.

He pulled back before he became a public nuisance. "We'll meet back here in a few," he said, noting with pride he could still make the color in Linda's cheeks flame and, apparently, he could do the same to Edison. Perhaps Edison was a bit more protective of his friends than his cool exterior let on. He had always known he had a brother in Edison, it was good to see it validated even if it meant engaging Crazy Cahill.

"I'll be here with lobster boy," he said to Linda, putting his hand on Edison's shoulder as they returned to the ice swan to lighten its load.

FORTY-EIGHT

Finishing his third helping of food, Edison was pleased that he had stayed at the mansion even though he was a bit apprehensive that Crazy Cahill might show up for an encore. With Linda and Val at the table and Brett showing no signs of being sated, Edison decided to make his way to the restroom and splash some water on his face. Even Val had commented that he was still red and wondered aloud if he was allergic to the cologne that Linda had given him to strategically taint the air. Brett had winced at her comment and Edison was amused that his alpha male friend was sensitive to such a small barb.

After leaving the table, he decided to detour to the bar for a fresh drink. Not another bourbon and Coke, he thought, perhaps a scotch. At least he would have a reason for a red face if he were holding a scotch. While waiting at the bar, he drained the last of his drink and the button from Brett's shirt hit his front teeth.

His face reddened further, knowing that he had firmly stepped into teenage girl crush territory by holding Brett's button in his mouth. Even so, he didn't spit it out. He touched his cheek while waiting in line at the bar and decided to make it a double. When he placed his order, the bartender, who looked like a young Greta Garbo, yelled to her fellow bartender in a perfect Darrin Stephens imitation, "Sam, you'd better make it a double." Edison smiled and she winked.

"Parties like this one require doubles," she said, tugging at her tie.

"Be sure to pour yourself a double, too," Edison said, not knowing exactly how to respond.

"Already have, believe me, we all have," she said, tilting her head toward the other bartender. "Husband and I have been nipping ever since our hostess, Martha Frigging Stewart, came by earlier with a pair of white gloves."

"I'm so sorry," Edison said. "She is a nutcase."

"Speaking of which," the Garbo look-alike nodded toward the glitter and hairspray nightmare that was visible and nearing.

"Good luck," Edison said, making a hasty exit in the opposite direction, drink in hand.

He made his way through the crowd, which had thickened since he'd gone to get food. Several couples stood on the grand staircase waiting for tours of the upper floors that were being given by the Amstead Realty drones. He cut across the entryway and made for the large room containing most of the art. Earlier, he had seen a sign indicating restrooms in this direction. He did like the art in the mansion and realized that at some point he would need to start making his new house reflect his tastes rather than that of his parents.

He passed a line of potted palms which were hiding some baroque-style furniture that was likely the Merkel's private property. He rounded the palms and first smelled and then saw cigarette smoke rising from the second to last palm. The brocade sleeve and ancient hand holding the cigarette were familiar, and between the fronds he saw Lily. His first instinct was to avoid her, but when he saw the waiter with a tray of full champagne glasses, he decided to give peace a chance. He was willing to try to reconcile his parents' high regard for Lily with his experiences one last time.

He got the waiter's attention with a polite wave and he took a glass of champagne for Lily and kept his scotch. He went over to Lily and was about to hand her the champagne glass when he realized that what he thought was her free hand held something.

It looked like a silver pen and then he saw the unmistakable red glint of laser light hit a palm frond. Without speaking, he turned to follow the angle of the laser pointer and had no problem finding Lily's target, the cleavage of Cherie's dress as she stood alone, her back to a large tapestry. He turned back to Lily and she tossed her cigarette, still lit, into the potted palm. She took the offered drink from Edison.

"You have your father's manners."

"What would my father say about your laser show?" Edison asked, grinning, thinking his father would be without words.

"Paul," Lily focused for a second, and with a rare smile turned to Edison and said, "he would have something to say. He would have suggested rechargeable batteries. He was always easy on the environment, you know. That is why you inherited cars, of, how can I be polite, cars of a certain age and make."

They both laughed thinking of the Prius and the older Volvo.

"You had good parents, proud parents. I hope you know that."

"I do, Lily. I miss them too."

Lily raised her glass. Edison mirrored the motion and they both drank deep.

"Have you been out in the sun?" Lily asked. "You're red."

"No, Brett, Linda and I had a run in with our hostess, the Reaping Widow. I think I'm still a bit angry."

"Understandable. I take it Brett and Linda are doing well after the encounter."

"Yes, Linda was triumphant. Brett was fondled a bit but no worse for wear."

Edison moved the button around in his mouth. He hoped Brett had not figured out that Cherie's words had hit a chord with him. He was comfortable with his secret and futile desire and enjoyed the bittersweet closeness of his friendship with Brett. In his heart, though, he knew he was being dishonest with himself and with Brett.

Lily interrupted his thoughts, "I'm glad Linda prevailed. Brett seems like a man immune to the indignity of a Cahill grope."

Edison felt a change in Lily's tone in this conversation so he decided to continue the carrot rather than the stick approach. "That's a nice outfit, Lily. The dragons look like they knew Mr. Escher."

"It's one of my favorites. As dark and formal as it looks, it's very comfortable and light. It doesn't show Stella hair, either."

"About Stella," Edison cleared his throat, "I know he responded to my father but not my mother. Now he responds to you but not me. Do I need to start dropping off envelopes of cash to keep you stocked in cat food?"

"No, no, he is heaven. My day would not be complete without sitting in the sun with him." Lily sipped her drink and looked at Edison fully for the first time in his memory.

Edison lowered his voice. "I worry about him. I have been assuming he's at your place when I cannot find him, but then I end up roaming the streets looking just in case. So, is there any chance you're in the market for a used cat named Stella?"

"I would be pleased to take Stella as long as he wants to stay."

"Good, I think Stella will be relieved."

They paused and looked out at the crowd, which was looking more formal as afternoon faded into evening.

"Perhaps another glass, Lily?" Edison asked.

"That would be lovely. I'll stay here with my palm."

Edison took Lily's empty glass. He turned and stepped away from the palm and heard the distinctive click of her lighter over the piano music, which was now a jazzy version of *Some Enchanted Evening*. As he rounded the group of palms, he felt a firm grip on his upper arm and before he could turn, he was up against the wall on the far side of the palms. He swallowed the button in his mouth when he saw that it was Allen who had grabbed him.

"Allen, I mean David. What is your name today?" Edison asked, setting the empty glasses at the base of the potted palm.

"You think you're so smart, you little homo. I waited in that park for you. You know there are going to be consequences. I saw you here with your wife. I think she's going to get the facts about the man she's wasting her life with," David hissed.

"Consequences? Are you going to pee on this floor or head back to my place to piddle?" Edison asked, wiping his face of David's hissing spray.

David glared at him. "I don't know what you're talking about, but you need to learn your place in a man's world."

"No, David, I know my place and it's far from you. If you want to start something, I'd be mighty pleased to finish it, right here, right now." Edison glanced down at David's fists, which even in their current clinched state looked a bit femmy. He also noted David had clearly started drinking early, given his wobbly stance and slightly slurred words. Behind David, Val stood silently watching, tapping her cocktail class with her fingernail looking bemused.

"Honey, dear, sweetums," Val's voice came from behind David. "I have been looking all over for you. Well, not really, I had one too many drinks and have been floating about." Val moved toward Edison from behind David, giving Edison a private wink.

"Who is your friend, Edison? You never introduce me to your friends." Val extended her hand to David, who was clearly caught off guard. Val's voice was higher in pitch and slightly needy sounding. "Hi, I'm Val, the old ball and chain. And you are?"

"Allen, I mean David."

"Oh, nice to meet both of you. So, what were you two boys talking about? The Mariners or the Seahawks, I bet. You men are all the same."

"Well, I was talking to your husband about his indiscretions, Val," David said.

"Really," Val said, looking concerned. "Did you drink too much again, Edison?"

"No, a bit more serious than that," David replied for Edison.

Edison saw Brett and Linda come around the side of the palm behind Val and, almost simultaneously, Lily lurched out from behind the fronds. She stood beside David, staring at him with a disapproving expression as if he were a mess someone else's child had made.

Edison had the distinct feeling of being cornered but was oddly relaxed, as David appeared to be on track to making a fool of himself. Edison squashed the smile that was starting to spread over his lips so as not to give David any hint of his disastrous course.

Val turned to Edison, "What does this man know, Edison? You know I love you even if you are a ..." she looked at David, then back at Edison in a pause best suited for Vaudeville. "A San Franciscan?" She inhaled and covered her mouth with her hand, keeping her eyes wide open as if she were Little Orphan Annie.

"No, it's not that, you stupid bitch," David snarled.

Behind David, Edison could see Brett with a knowing smile next to Linda, who had a thin-lipped look of contempt, one hand in Brett's and the other resting on her hip. Lily seemed fully engaged for what might have been the first time in the new millennium, her cockeyed expression worthy of a Bette Davis honorary mention.

David pointed at Edison with what appeared to be a mixture of satisfaction and hate. "Your husband is a ..." David said, pausing for effect.

"Fag," Val said, looking directly at David.

"Queer," Brett volunteered loudly from behind David, startling him.

"Homo?" asked Linda.

"Nancy boy?" asked Lily, exhaling smoke directly into David's face.

Val spun David around by his shoulder so they were nearly eye-to-eye and growled. "Listen, you little queen, you should know better than to demote the hag. I am not his wife, Mr. Tinkle, and I have your note right here." She padded her purse, to

Edison's surprise, since he knew he had put the note in the recycling.

"And if you weren't so busy pissing yourself and cruising parks you would know the difference between the wife and the hag." Stepping closer to David, she raised her voice and asked, "What about your wife? Eh? Does your wife know that you are the queen of denial, and apparently," Val said as she scanned him from top to bottom, "well past your salad days?"

"We are off point," Linda said, pushing between Val and David. "Edison is my fag, and I am his hag." She reached back and grabbed Edison by his shirt in mock toughness that was surprisingly firm.

"Wait a minute here, he's not part of a fag and hag combo platter. He's my best boy." With that, Brett stepped forward, grabbed Edison by the front of his belt and pulled him tight to his body, wrapping an arm around Edison's shoulder and muttering soft words to the top of his head as if he were a pet.

David was clearly fuming and confused as he looked at Edison and back to Brett. He then said something about "not needing this shit" and turned to leave when Lily blocked his way.

"Remember me, Mr. Tinkle? You left the lady's question unanswered. Does your wife know you are a big old queen of denial?"

"Get out of my way," he said, stepping forward to push past Lily.

"Let's ask her," Lily said crisply.

David froze. "Don't you dare," he said, looking like he would hit Lily.

"Oh, Miyuki dear." Lily quickly stepped over to a group of people who had moved near to look at a large stone Buddha.

"Miyuki, sorry to grab you like that but we need your intimate knowledge of a certain something."

The startled Asian woman was rubbing her arm where Lily had gripped it as she looked around their small circle. She was an attractive woman with too many years to be pretty and enough to be beautiful. Lily picked up the scotch glass that Edison had placed on the lip of the pot that held the massive palm. She tossed the ice into the pot's soil and then threw the glass down near David's feet before he said anything to his wife. The noise the glass made when it shattered on the parquet floor was loud enough that the people near their group hushed and turned to see what was going on. Lily cleared her throat and spoke loudly to Miyuki.

"Miyuki, this is Edison Archer, son of Ellie and Paul. Your husband has been trying to get in his pants, repeatedly, and now has resorted to blackmail." Pointing to David, Lily said in ringing tones, "He is your closet case, how should we deal with this?"

The room was deathly quiet after Lily spoke.

Miyuki was frozen, silent, glaring at David. Lily was about to say something when a heavyset man, well past sixty, pushed into their circle between Linda and David.

"David, what is going on here?" the man asked.

"Nothing that concerns you, Mr. O'Hara."

Lily interjected, "We have a situation here and I expect some answers."

Val, stepping forward, spoke out, "As a fag hag I have a duty and an oath to both Edison and the dramatic."

Edison noticed for the first time that Val was drunk. She tossed her drink, ice and lime wedge at David. "Don't mess with my fag," Val hissed. "And stay off Queen Anne."

"I don't need to put up with this from people like you, especially the likes of you," he said turning to Edison. David moved to push Edison against the wall but Edison reacted without thinking, grabbing David's right hand and twisting it, spinning David around so he now faced the wall. His hand was twisted high on his back causing him to yelp before he lost his footing on the slippery parquet floor and fell to his knees.

"On your knees again, David?" Linda asked coldly from behind Edison.

"Nice form, Edison," Brett volunteered.

"Well, Miyuki, he is your problem now," Lily said, taking

Brett's drink from him and handing it to Miyuki. "Oh, and Miyuki, please know that you are always welcome on my little corner of Queen Anne," Lily added, patting the dazed Miyuki on the arm.

"Thank you, Lily," Miyuki said, her voice sounding resigned.

Edison suddenly regretted embarrassing this woman in his eagerness to hurt David.

"I am sorry," he offered to Miyuki, his voice trailing off as David stood.

Miyuki ignored him and focused on her husband.

"I may be quiet but I'm not stupid. I've put up with this damage for too long," Miyuki said, glancing at Lily and then to Mr. O'Hara.

"Give me the car keys, David. Now. You have embarrassed me enough. And don't come back to Mercer Island tonight, either. You're not welcome at the house. I'll have Mother's attorney contact you at your office."

"About that, David," Mr. O'Hara said, stepping forward and patting Mrs. O'Hara's plump hand that held his wrist in what appeared to be terror. "David, this is unacceptable behavior from a member of a firm with high-profile clients, many of whom are here tonight. Tarleton, Wilkes and I will need to meet with you first thing on Monday. Do you understand?"

David, for the first time, looked like a threat. His eyes bulged and perspiration showed on his forehead. He reached into his coat pocket and, for a second, Edison feared he might have a gun. He noticed that Lily moved in parallel to David's motion and reached into her brocade coat. Edison tensed and stepped back toward the palm. David pulled out the keys and threw them at Miyuki's midsection.

"Maybe they will unlock your barren loins," he said savagely to his wife before turning to Mr. O'Hara. "You sir, can fuck yourself. It would be better than this old bag of shit," David said, pointing to Mrs. O'Hara. He stormed past them, only to trip on the Merkel crest inlay in the parquet floor. He recovered with an obscenity and disappeared into the crowd.

"I have seen enough," Mrs. O'Hara said as she stormed off in the direction of the grand staircase with her husband in tow.

"Miyuki, dear, are you okay?" Lily asked.

"Better than ever, actually, thank you," Miyuki said, smoothing her perfect hair. "If you will excuse me, I'm going to freshen up and have some food. I'm in the mood for champagne, too. Imagine that?" Without waiting for a response, she turned and headed in the direction of the bar.

Their small circle closed and was silent for a moment before Edison spoke. "Thanks for all your fine acting." Now that his friends surrounded him, of which he included Lily for the first time, he felt his face fade from crimson to pink.

"Who was acting?" Brett asked, pulling Edison by his belt again and giving him a wet kiss on the forehead.

"Look at him blush," Val said to Linda. "Damn, it's like he's thirteen and he forgot to wear underwear to pom-pom tryouts."

"Another cheerleading flashback?" Linda asked Val.

"No," Val said, "I should have tried the panty-free cheer, I never made the squad."

"Dears, Mr. Archer was about to get me a fresh drink, so stop embarrassing him, and Brett, stop molesting him."

"Oh, all right," Brett said giving one last tug on his belt.

"Lily," Edison said, scavenging for composure, as he turned to leave their circle, "I'll make it a double."

"Of course you will, Edison," she said.

They made eye contact as she had called him by his given name for the first time.

FORTY-NINE

"Shall we blow this joint?" Brett asked the group gathered near the entrance to the ballroom.

"I want to check with Lily before we leave," Linda said, scanning the room. She saw Lily standing near the potted palm again, sipping a scotch. "She seems to have an affinity for that palm. She's been there most of the night, though I've never seen her without a drink."

"Well, it has been quite a night, perhaps she's enjoying being a spectator rather than a spectacle," Val offered.

"It has been eventful," Linda said. "Mr.Tinkle's been outed and that Hellfire Harlot's suffering no end to her *daze*." Linda motioned to the giant tapestry where Cherie stood, staring. "I would say mission accomplished. How about we have a quick drink with Lily and then head back?"

"I'll pass," Edison said, sounding a bit tired. "I've had enough of this place. I think I'll head home."

"Do you want me to go with you?" asked Val.

"No, please stay and have some more booze and food for me. If you can take over cologne duty, I'd appreciate it," he said, taking out the bottle of Polo cologne from his coat pocket and handing it to Val. "Perhaps you can use it as mace in case Ms. Thing acts up again."

"I get first dibs," snapped Linda, territorially.

"We'll divvy her up," Val replied diplomatically. "I'll take her hair and you can have the rest."

"Well, on that civilized note, I best be going before I turn into a pumpkin," Edison said, eyeing his watch.

"Okay, buddy, we'll see you a little later then," Brett said, giving Edison a pat on the shoulder. "Nice handiwork with your stalker."

"I just hope his little fatal attraction is over. I don't want to go home to find Stella simmering on the stove."

"Yuck," Linda said, grimacing. "And to think I was going to hug you goodbye."

"Sorry, bad joke," Edison said. "Actually, I officially gave Stella to Lily earlier—that is assuming he's mine to give. Stella obviously made his choice already."

"Oh, that's so sweet," Linda said. "I will give you that hug now."

"Thanks," he said, returning her embrace. "And I will leave you kids to your evil."

He waved goodbye and headed toward the front entrance. Once he was out of sight, Linda turned to Brett.

"Do you think he's okay? He seemed a bit down."

"Yeah, I think he's fine. Probably a little overwhelmed from all the excitement."

"I'll call him in a few and check on him," Val said as she crumpled up one of Cherie's "No Cell Phone Use Area" signs that was taped to a nearby wall.

"Well, I'm going to get a plate of appetizers for Lily. Val, will you give me a holler if old Cinderslut over there throws herself at my Prince Charming again?"

"Not a problem," assured Val with a wave of her hand. "I have the vocal cords of a big angry crow."

Linda went over to the food table and selected a mix of appetizers. She had not seen Lily eat all evening and she wondered how such a petite woman could handle so much alcohol.

"Thought you could use a little nourishment," she said, coming up next to Lily and offering her the plate.

"Why thank you, dear," Lily said, accepting. "Was that Edison I just saw leaving?"

"Yes, I think he was a bit frazzled by all the low budget theatrics."

"What a shame, the night's just getting started."

"Oh, I think he's had more than enough excitement for one night. So, I hear you have a new addition to your family."

"Really?" said Lily, appearing genuinely surprised. "Is my daughter knocked up again?"

"No, Lily," said Linda, laughing despite herself, "I mean, Stella."

"Oh yes. That cat is very dear to me. So nice of Edison to formalize it."

Linda watched Lily take a sip of her drink and decided to broach something that had been on her mind.

"These last several weeks have been hard on Edison and I worry about him. I'm hoping you two can have a fresh start?"

"Paul and Ellie's deaths have been hard on all of us, dear, but you're right, I have been a little stern with him. It's just that every time I saw him in that house, it was a reminder that they were no longer with us. I do miss them terribly."

"I do too, Lily."

"Then when I found out he wanted to sell the house, I knew he didn't understand all that his parents had done for him."

"I'm sure he appreciates everything they did. His life was in San Francisco, though."

"Well, that boy needs to know more about his parents and perhaps when I'm ready, I'll tell him."

"That's nice," said Linda, not quite certain she understood. "They were such wonderful people and I'm sure you have a lot of great stories to share about them."

"That's not the half of it, dear."

Linda was about to question Lily, but then caught sight of Brett and Val who, by their arm gyrations and shimmying, appeared to be dancing to '60's music no one else could hear. She motioned with her head to Lily. "Look at those two, doing The Twist to *You Do Something to Me*."

Lily peered over at them disinterestedly. "I suppose the children are still wound up from all the excitement."

"You seem unfazed by the evening's drama."

"Oh, I have a feeling there's more drama to come," Lily said with a knowing smile.

"Well, personally, I have had enough of that bitch realtor." Linda gazed across the room at Cherie who was still standing in front of the large tapestry. "I cannot believe she threw herself at Brett like that. It's all I can do to stay on the high road."

"No need for that, dear. Would you hold my plate for a moment?" Lily asked, taking out a pen like object from her purse.

"What's that?"

"It's a laser pointer. I've had good luck with it in the past," she said, pointing to Cherie.

"What are you going to do with it?" Linda asked.

"Oh, you'll see."

Lily moved closer to the palm. Holding her scotch in her left hand, she turned on the laser, discreetly putting her right hand under a large palm frond and then pointed it toward Cherie. Linda saw a red dot appear on Cherie's back, between the two spaghetti straps that held up her dress.

"That's not strong enough to burn her, is it?" Linda asked, trying not to sound too eager.

"Oh no, dear. Something much better usually happens."

"She's been staring at that tapestry for a while now. It's like she's doing a bad imitation of Kim Novak in *Vertigo*."

"She got the dye job and knockers right, but my bet is she's praying to that wrathful god of hers."

Lily continued moving the red dot across Cherie's backside. Cherie seemed truly possessed by the tapestry, which she was viewing with rapt attention. Lily moved the laser off Cherie and onto the tapestry, inches above Cherie's head. All of a sudden, Cherie turned around, wide-eyed, her mouth gaping open in alarm. She then grabbed a large silver tray from a passing server. Linda saw appetizers fly everywhere as Cherie held up the platter in front of herself as a shield. "They're trying to kill me!" she screamed as she ran out of the room, shielding herself with the platter. The music stopped and the whole room hushed, as people turned in the direction Cherie had run.

"What was that all about?" Linda asked.

"I think Crazy is finally having a long overdue meltdown. Can you hand me my plate, dear?" Lily asked, dropping the laser pointer into her purse.

Linda handed her the plate and they watched as the other guests looked around with a mixture of shock and then growing amusement, judging by the scattered bursts of laughter echoing about the room. She saw a man and a woman, dressed very nicely, both speaking on wireless headsets run out the way Cherie had gone.

"Who the hell are they?" Linda asked.

"Let's hope they're the nice people from the funny farm who have come to collect her," Lily said, popping a mini-quiche into her mouth.

Suddenly, Brett and Val were upon them, laughing like drunken teenagers.

"Did you see that?" Brett asked Linda, choking out the words between his laughter.

"I don't think Helen Keller could have missed it," Linda replied, enjoying Brett's laughter.

"What happened to her?" asked Val.

"Oh," said Linda, looking at Lily with a sly smile, "let's just say the hand of fate gave her a slight push over the edge."

"Hmm," said Val, narrowing her eyes and looking at them questioningly. "I have a sneaking suspicion fate had no hand in this."

"Val, show them the picture you took with your cell phone camera," Brett interrupted.

"Oh yeah, I was just about to call Edison," Val explained, "when that bitch flipped and I snapped a shot. Take a look."

"Wow," Linda said, examining the slightly blurry image of a crazed Cherie running out of the room with the platter. "Honey, maybe we can use these for our Christmas cards this year?"

"I was thinking more on the line of blowing it up for target practice," Brett said, gesturing as if were shooting a gun.

"Dear, be sure to email me a copy," Lily said to Val.

All of a sudden, they heard the sound of glass shattering from the far side of the house.

"Sounds like someone in catering dropped a rack of glasses," guessed Linda.

"I have a bad feeling about this place," Brett said, looking up warily at the large chandelier hanging from the ceiling. "If we were on a luxury liner, I'd be scrambling for the lifeboats right about now."

"Well," said Val, "if the guy on the piano starts playing *Nearer, My God, to Thee*, I'm outta here."

"Such a lovely party," said Lily. "Such a lovely house too," she added, looking around the room.

"It is a very nice mansion," Linda agreed, "but it has a white elephant feel about it. I prefer our cozy home," she said smiling at Brett.

"So, now our home is cozy?" asked Brett, feigning insult.

"I'd take this place in a New York minute," said Val, looking up at the gilded ceiling, "sans tonight's drama."

At that moment, there was a huge roar from outside and Linda heard and then saw the large two-story windows rattle, appearing as if they would shatter. Looking up, she saw the chandelier glitter as it swayed from the shock wave.

"What in the hell was that?" asked Brett.

"Okay, now I'm out of here," Val said, slipping her cell phone in her purse.

"These coconut shrimp are divine," Lily said, looking down at her plate, apparently unaware of the commotion.

People started exiting the ballroom and Linda heard someone say that there had been a huge explosion down the street. They started to follow the crowd out of the room when Linda realized Lily wasn't with them.

"Wait a second," she said to Brett and Val. She turned around to see Lily rummaging for something near the now empty bar. "Are you coming, Lily?" she called.

"Oh, you go ahead, dear. I want to grab a few souvenirs," Lily replied, dropping a bottle of scotch into her purse.

FIFTY

Val hurried down the street trailing behind Brett and Linda. She felt awkward half walking, half running in a dress whose delicate seams and stylish cut were designed for a more genteel gait. She had taken off her heels, as had Linda, and could feel the pleasant warmth of the sidewalk on her feet.

As they neared Lily's house, she saw a crowd of people—a mix of neighbors and attendees from the party—gathered on the sidewalk in front of Edison's house. The air was heavy with a smell that reminded Val of the inside of a laser printer. Various-sized debris were scattered about Edison's lawn and the neighboring properties. Val saw Linda and Brett look to each other in stunned silence after they stopped in front of a large piece of smoldering wood from what had been a garage door.

When they reached Edison's property, Val was able to see the full extent of the damage. The garage had been blown apart, its remains still in flames. Smoke was also rising from the back of the house and ash littered the sky as if from a volcano. The windows on the first story of the house were blown out. The porch swing swayed gently in the evening breeze, deaf to the competing smoke and security alarms blaring from within the house. The front of the house seemed unharmed and she guessed the explosion must have occurred in the garage, which was toward the side and rear of the house. Gazing at the lesser plume of smoke rising from the back of the house, she wondered whether there was a separate fire in the kitchen. She panicked, for a moment, trying to recall if she had left the stove on, but then she remembered that neither she nor Edison had cooked that day due to the heat.

She heard several sirens approaching in the distance.

"Where's Edison?" she asked the others, putting her shoes back on so as not to step directly on the debris. "Do you see him anywhere?" she said, scanning the crowd.

Brett headed to the front porch and she and Linda were close behind.

"No, I don't see him," said Linda. "Do you think he could be inside?"

"I hope not," said Brett trying the front door. "It's locked."

"I can run back home and get the spare or maybe we can just enter through there," Linda said, pointing to the window nearest her whose frame was void of its usual glass except for some jagged shards.

"No need for that. I have a key," Val said, stepping up behind them.

At that moment, Val heard a police car pull up in front of the house. She turned around and, within a matter of seconds, another police car pulled up as well as two fire trucks and an ambulance. She saw the crowd near the sidewalk was gawking at the three of them on the front porch as well as the various emergency personnel who were now getting out of their vehicles. One family was licking their ice cream cones as they watched and she suddenly felt resentful that Edison's misfortune was once again the neighborhood entertainment.

"You three, step away from the house!" she heard an approaching officer shout.

"We think someone is inside," Brett said, ignoring the officer's directive.

"Sir, you need to step away from the house. You too ladies."

"Excuse me, I live here," said Val "and I'm not going anywhere until I find out whether or not my friend is inside."

"Ma'am, it's too dangerous," he said, beckoning her with his hand. "They need to control the situation."

"If you people aren't willing to do your job, I'll go inside myself," she said, turning around and taking her keys out of her purse.

The policeman grabbed her. "Ma'am, you need to step away."

"Get your nasty hooves off me, you pig," she said, struggling to get free.

"Hey, hey, there's no need to grab her," said Brett looking squarely at the police officer, freeing Val from his grip. "She, all of us, are concerned about our friend."

"Then step away, sir, and let the fire personnel do their job," he said, gesturing to a group of firefighters approaching the front porch.

"Stand aside!" shouted the lead fireman, who was wielding an axe.

"No need for your macho theatrics," Val said, raising her key. "Allow me." Val opened the door and out from a cloud of hot, smoky air ran Stella. The fireman with the axe leapt back as Stella hissed and ran past them.

"Just a little pussy," Val said to the firefighter. "No need to be frightened."

The firefighter gave Val a look as if he wanted to use the axe on her and then went inside with the others.

Linda turned to Brett. "Stella was out of there in a hurry. Not quite Lassie leading the rescue party."

"Folks, step away from the house," the police officer directed them again.

They descended the stairs of the porch and took a place at the end of the lawn, slightly removed from the crowd who had been cordoned off to the sidewalk. Val heard murmurs from the crowd about the Reaping Widow striking again. While she had never believed in the curse, she had to admit that Edison's house didn't seem particularly blessed with good luck.

She shivered in the evening heat as it occurred to her that Edison could be gone. Her buzz from the party faded with her growing sense of dread. During the past few weeks, they had grown closer than they'd ever been in San Francisco. And, just like that, she could lose her best friend and once again be homeless. Where would she go? Back home? After everything she had been through, did all roads inevitably lead back to the room above her parents' garage? She quickly pushed that thought out of her mind. Wherever she ended up, it didn't matter as long as Edison was okay.

Her thoughts were interrupted by the sound of Linda's voice. "How in the hell could something like this happen?" she asked no one in particular, staring at the firefighters who were dousing the remains of the garage.

"I don't know, but I smell foul play," answered Brett.

"Do you think it could have been Mr. Tinkle?" Linda asked him.

"Well, we know he's capable of illegal entry and blackmail, so arson isn't a big leap."

"Let's not forget about the Dial for Jesus Whore," piped in Val. "She was all about fire and brimstone and maybe she meant it literally. After all, she did run out of the party early."

"That makes perfect sense," Linda said, sounding eager to convict Cherie. "We already know her fondness for knives and guns. For all we know, that whack job carries around explosives."

Val turned back to the firefighters and watched as they hosed down what was left of the garage. There was still a thick cloud of smoke and the fumes now smelled like a mix of burnt plastic, rubber and wood. She could see the Volvo in its parking spot where the garage used to stand, blackened and damaged beyond repair, but still recognizable. She was surprised it hadn't exploded, but then she supposed it was only in the movies that vehicles blew up with the slightest provocation. At least the Prius, she noted, was safely parked in the driveway, which confirmed Edison hadn't driven anywhere.

"I'm going to call Edison's cell," Val said to Brett and Linda who looked on hopefully.

After several rings, the call rolled over to voicemail.

"Just voicemail," Val said, not hiding her disappointment.

Some firefighters had gone around to the back of the house and were spraying it with water, though the smoke back there seemed to her more residual than an active blaze. When she looked up at the house, she was startled to see someone peering out from Edison's second-story bedroom. Her heart skipped a beat as she thought it was Edison, but she quickly realized it was a firefighter and she felt her spirits plummet.

Then it entered her mind. What if Edison had been in the garage when it exploded? She dismissed the thought almost as soon as it had entered, not willing to go down such a dark path, but it was powerful enough to cause her upper lip to tremble.

"Where could Edison be?" Val asked aloud, sounding helpless to her own ears. "He was going straight home. Both cars are here. You don't think he could have been in the garage when the explosion happened or that someone deliberately trapped him inside and …." She choked on her words and was unable to continue, putting a hand to her face to wipe away the tears.

"Honey, it will be okay," said Linda, gently rubbing Val's shoulder.

"Edison's too smart to get trapped like that," Brett said, putting his arm around her reassuringly, but the unevenness in his voice betrayed his efforts to calm her.

The policeman, who had forced them away from the house earlier, now approached Brett and started asking him questions about what he knew of the explosion and their relation to the owner of the house. Brett answered for all of them and Val was thankful for this, as she felt her temper was prone to erupt if the policeman provoked her again.

She continued to watch the firefighters, who had stopped hosing the garage and were now searching around the property. Val guessed this was the most excitement the Queen Anne branch of the Seattle Fire Department had seen in a long time. Since arriving in the neighborhood, she wasn't certain she had even heard a siren, much less seen a fire truck.

She looked across the street at the crowd of onlookers who,

while still quite large, seemed to be diminishing. Now that the fire was out, she assumed the partygoers were anxious to get back to the comfort of their own homes, where they could tune into the local news to catch all the shameless speculation as to whether the Reaping Widow had struck again. As if on cue, a news helicopter flew over and started to circle like a vulture.

Turning back toward the house, Val saw the firefighter with the axe come down the front porch steps and approach them.

"The good news is that most of the house is undamaged," he started abruptly, as if they were continuing a previous conversation. "We searched all the rooms and we didn't find anyone inside. The bad news is that there was a fire in the basement and there's significant blast damage down there. There was also an explosion in the garage, which I'm guessing was related to the fire in the basement."

"Do you know what caused the explosions?" Linda asked.

"Witnesses reported seeing a bright flash before the explosion, so that coupled with the burn pattern would suggest a gas leak. This is only speculation since we haven't found the source, though we know it wasn't the gas line since the meter is still intact. We do an investigation as part of the standard report."

Upon hearing this, they looked at one another and Val guessed that they were thinking what she was thinking—that Paul and Ellie's mysterious deaths in the basement media room were caused by a similar gas leak.

"What if Edison is down in the basement?" Linda exclaimed.

"Ma'am, we're going to search through it as soon as we can. Do you know for certain that your friend was home at the time of the explosion?"

"No, but this is where he was headed when he left the party."

Linda wiped some tears from her eyes and Val saw that even Brett looked shaken. She guessed that they had collectively hit upon the fear that Edison was another victim of the house.

Val wiped her eyes with her sleeve and when she looked

down the street, she caught sight of two men approaching in the distance. One appeared to be dressed formally and the other one was simply in red jogging shorts. Red Shorts, she instantly thought, squinting to get a better look.

"It's Edison!" she cried out, pointing in his direction. Brett and Linda turned toward the street and immediately seemed to recognize him as well. They left the fireman in their excitement and ran toward Edison. As they drew close, Val saw that it was definitely Red Shorts walking with him. Edison had a puzzled look on his face upon seeing the three of them running toward him. They converged near Lily Ling's house.

"What's going on?" he asked, looking at them and then to the fire trucks and crowd of people down the street.

"Buddy, you're okay!" Brett yelled, giving him a hug and lifting him off the ground. Val and Linda were quick to embrace him as well, each claiming a side of him. Val could see that Edison looked confused by the unexpected show of affection.

"Where have you been and why didn't you answer your phone?" Val asked, not hiding the accusation in her tone.

"I guess I didn't turn my phone back on after I left the party. I went for a walk to Parsons Garden with John," Edison said, gesturing to Red Shorts who was standing shirtless beside him, hands placed on his hips.

Val saw he was undeniably attractive, but looked to her as if he were posing for an Abercrombie and Fitch photo shoot for which he was ten years late.

"We ran into each other shortly after I left the party," Edison continued. "John, these are my friends, Val, Linda and Brett."

John nodded. "We heard a loud boom and saw the smoke all the way from Parsons Garden."

Brett turned to Edison. "Buddy, your garage is toast."

"What happened?" Edison asked, moving toward his house.

"They think it was some sort of gas leak," said Linda, following him with the others.

"A gas leak?" he asked, picking up his pace.

Once Edison reached the sidewalk near his house, he stopped

and stared at the remains of the garage. "I never should have gone to that stupid party tonight."

"Better you were there than here," said Brett.

"The fireman said it wasn't a natural gas leak," said Linda, "so there may have been no way of detecting it. You would never have known anything was wrong."

Edison seemed to ponder this and looked silently at the house for a moment. "Has anyone seen Stella?"

"He's fine," replied Brett. "We saw him run out of the house. A little shook up, that's all."

"Poor cat," Edison mumbled. He turned toward John. "John, I'm sorry but I need to deal with this. Can we chat another time when my garage hasn't exploded?"

"Of course," he smiled. "Is there anything I can do?"

"Thanks, but no. I've got your number so how about I call you after I sort this all out."

"I'd like that," he said.

"Just so you know," Val said touching John's wrist lightly, "I'm the housemate, so it helps to get on my good side."

"I'll keep that in mind," John said, looking to Val slightly appalled.

"Bye, Edison. Nice meeting all of you," he said with a wave of the hand to everyone before departing.

Val watched as he walked away, happy that Edison had snagged such a hot number. She turned back to see Brett giving Edison a knowing smile.

"Here we are worried sick about you and you're making nice with the Soloflex guy."

"Oh Eds, I'm just so happy you're okay," Linda said, stroking the back of his head.

"Thank you," he said, smiling weakly, his mind obviously somewhere else.

He was staring at the wreckage of the garage and Val noticed for the first time there were tears in his eyes.

"Man, this place is cursed," he said. "I wish my parents had never moved here."

FIFTY-ONE

Cherie heard the spray of gravel as she made a hard right off the narrow mountain road. Her cabin was a mile up the drive and one of several that surrounded the lake. Now that she had nearly arrived, she wasn't entirely certain how she had made it there. She guessed she had been in full fight or flight mode, and she had apparently chosen flight.

What she did clearly remember was the voice from the tapestry beckoning to her, "Come to me" and seeing the leer of the horseman and the snarl of his white steed. She had used all her willpower to resist the Antichrist, repeatedly praying to God to give her strength. It was only upon seeing the red dot of the laser gun sight on the tapestry, above her head, that she had realized she was in mortal danger. Turning away from the tapestry, she had grabbed a silver platter from a passing waiter. She remembered seeing Swedish meatballs fly everywhere as she held up the tray vertically to use as cover as she ran out of the room. She recalled, in her haste to leave, driving into a Jaguar convertible as she roared down the mansion's driveway. Then, as she drove past the Fruit's house, she saw a blue and orange flame light up his property and heard a loud boom. It was at that moment she realized the full extent to which the dark forces were after her. They must have tried to hit her SUV with a rocket-propelled grenade and missed. Her last clear memory was of gunning the accelerator, quaking uncontrollably in fear as she turned onto West Highland Drive, her eyes a teary blur, knowing she had to escape to the safety of her mountain cabin.

She was thankful she had reached her destination, since she

had only the faintest recollection of driving down the freeway and exiting at the Indian casino, which marked the halfway point to her cabin. In past trips, the casino had been her guilty little respite. She knew gambling was a sin but, in truth, she'd never met a slot machine she didn't like. Gorging at the low-quality buffet afterwards was normally the pinnacle of her tacky and taboo detour. This time, however, she knew there would be no carpal tunnel shame from hours spent at the slot machines.

As she proceeded toward the lake, she saw the grassy clearing that bordered both sides of the gravel road. The sky opened up as she drove out from under the tree canopy. She could see the sun had already made its grand exit for the day, leaving behind a lingering curtain of red and purple in the western sky. She wasn't certain when she had left the party, but sensed she had made it up to the cabin in record time.

Pulling in front of her cabin, she was thankful for her foresight in buying the place and stocking it with enough food and supplies to survive in seclusion for quite some time. The cabin was two stories with two bedrooms, two bathrooms and log sides, which gave it an authentic charm. She'd seen plenty of dwellings labeled "cabins" in her line of work, though many were nothing more than cheap drywall nightmares that were located nowhere desirable. Hers had a stone foundation, heavy fir walls and a cedar shingle roof. Inside, she had furnished the place lavishly with all the modern amenities. She was on the power grid, but also had her own generator if it became necessary. Her lot was several acres in size, mostly wooded with a small patch of lakefront that afforded her relative privacy. Her closest neighbor was an upscale lodge about half a mile down the road. As she peered down the hill toward the lodge, she could see its lights burning in the distance and guessed it was full since it was high season. The lake, hardly a stone's throw away, was tranquil tonight and she saw numerous cabin lights dotting its shore.

Once at the front door, she dug her keys out of her purse and located the infrequently used cabin key. She then pulled out her Ruger SP101 revolver, making certain it was fully loaded, and released the safety. This was one of her favorite models due to its excellent design, combining the compactness of a small gun with the power of a larger firearm, along with a mild recoil. She unlocked the front door and kicked it open, gun in hand, ready to shoot, but was greeted only by warm stale air. Everything seemed quiet and she reached in to turn on the lights. She saw the place was in good order, just as she'd left it, though she noted a fine layer of dust had settled on all the surfaces. She closed the door behind her and engaged the dead bolt. If she had been followed, she wasn't going to make it easy for anyone to get her. After all, Janet had been up to the cabin before and who knew what evil that Sapphic sinner could summon.

She looked straight ahead into the large open main room. This room had been one of the cabin's major selling points with its full two-story high ceiling, exposed polished wood support beams and stone fireplace. She put her keys back in her purse, which hung on her shoulder. With gun in hand, she walked toward the kitchen, feeling a light grittiness under her heels as she traversed the hardwood floors. Recognizing the need for some fresh air, she reached up over the kitchen sink and opened the window. She knew that the kitchen window was secure as it was too small for anyone to climb through and high off the ground.

Back in the main room, she made sure the two sets of large windows on either side of the room were locked. Now, more than ever, she was thankful that she had custom-ordered the triple-glazed panes for the added security, and she pulled shut the two-ply silk drapes.

Both bedrooms were upstairs, and as she climbed the wooden staircase, she looked up at the reinforced skylight and could already see the first stars of the evening. She pressed a button on the wall in order to vent the skylight, letting the stale air and heat escape. She would close it back up before she went to bed.

Once upstairs, she went past the balcony ledge that overlooked the main room and turned left into the hallway that led to the bedrooms and bathroom. She ducked into the first bedroom, gun ahead of her, turning on the light switch. She kicked off her heels before kneeling down to look underneath the bed, which was empty save for a heavy layer of dust on the carpeting. She then opened up the closet, pleased to see it only contained the familiar storage boxes and empty hangers. She looked out the window at the lights of the lodge shining brightly against the darkening sky and made certain the window was locked before pulling the heavy curtains shut.

The upstairs bathroom was between the two bedrooms, and as she turned on the light and then pulled back the shower curtain, the famous murder scene from *Psycho* entered her mind, but she was happy to see that the shower was Janet Leigh-free.

She stepped into the other bedroom, turned on the lights and looked under the bed to make certain it was clear. As this was the master bedroom, she had installed a lock on the walk-in closet to store her survival gear. She pulled out the keys from her purse and unlocked the door of the closet, relieved to see her semi-automatic rifle hanging on the back wall. She waved away the musty scent, noting the sets of clothes and shoes she kept up here were just as she had left them. Kneeling in front of the trunk on the floor, she unlocked it and pulled open the top. Inside, there was a stockpile of ammo, her survivalist supplies and some favorite back issues of *Gun Totin' Ladies* magazine.

She picked up some extra ammo for her revolver, placed it in her purse and relocked the closet door. After making certain the window was secure, she went back to the bathroom and relieved her bladder for the first time since before the party. Once finished, she looked at herself in the mirror. Her mascara had run down her face, making two dark trails from her eyes to her chin from when she had been sobbing in terror. Her elaborate hairdo, which Fausto had likened to an exquisite bird's nest, was in disarray, as if a raccoon had made a wreck of it in search of an easy meal. Her glitter eye shadow still sparkled like the stars she'd seen through the skylight, but it had spread across her face in its own version of the big bang. She rinsed off her face, though after she dried it, she saw she had only managed to smear the glitter and mascara more. She'd take care of it later, she thought dejectedly. Taking out the remaining pins from her hair, she let it all down and brushed her hands through it several times.

Much to her chagrin, she spotted a rip on the left side of her gown at her hip. She had looked stunning earlier, she reflected, as she gazed in the mirror at her gown's low neckline, seeing the tops of her full breasts exposed in all their glory. It had been her moment to shine, her evening to triumph, and the forces of evil had taken it all away.

She turned off the upstairs lights and, with gun in hand, went back downstairs, remembering to inspect the first floor bathroom. Seeing there was no one lurking inside, she walked to the laundry room and pantry just off the kitchen. She opened up the large freezer and was happy to see it was fully stocked with all the essentials: meat of all kinds, vodka, vacuum packed bricks of coffee and pounds of her favorite chocolate, which she'd triple-wrapped in freezer bags. She then opened up the washer and dryer and checked inside, just in case, she told herself, because she knew she was dealing with a relentless and clever enemy, but she was glad to see they were both empty.

Perusing the shelves in the pantry, she saw the many jars of fruit preserves her mother had sent her from last year's crop. On the next shelf were dehydrated foods of all sorts, and dozens of cans of tuna and wild salmon. The middle shelves housed large cans of soup, tomato sauce and commercial size boxes of pasta. On the bottom, there were two twenty-pound sacks of rice, a ten-pound sack of both black and pinto beans, a large canister of olive oil, large sacks of flour, sugar and enough maple syrup and honey to send a family of bears comfortably into hibernation. In the corner were numerous five-gallon containers of spring water, neatly stacked on top of one another in a pyramid. A nearby stack of diet cola cases towered over the pyramid.

Feeling a little more relaxed now that she'd seen the place

was in good order and secure, she walked back through the kitchen, placing her gun in her purse. Once in the dining room, she went to the mahogany wine cabinet that rested against the wall. She fished out a wineglass and her best bottle of cabernet, figuring she might as well enjoy the earthly pleasures while they lasted. She uncorked the wine and brought the bottle and the glass back to the main room, setting them down on the table in front of the suede couch. She sank down onto the couch, tossing her purse near the throw pillow beside her. Her medications, she now realized, were still in the glove compartment of her SUV, but never mind, she thought. She was tired of the endless pill popping and she wouldn't need them anymore where she was going. Besides, she had all the medication she needed right here, she considered, pouring herself a glass of wine which she quickly drank down.

Who had focused the laser gun sight on her during the party? she pondered as she poured herself another glass. And who had fired the grenade at her SUV? She was the one who had controlled the invitation list and she'd made certain that only Seattle's elite had attended. Perhaps they had infiltrated the party via the caterers or those sketchy art people, she speculated, as she drained the glass of wine. If Janet had aligned herself with the Antichrist, surely no one was beyond suspicion. She had obviously miscalculated by inviting the Hungry Hungry Hippo and company. The Hippo certainly had it out for her, probably blaming her for her own failure as a woman and her sham marriage. Maybe the whole damned lot of them were aligned with the Antichrist. She couldn't trust anyone now. She would camp out here until the start of the Rapture, which, judging from all the signs, was imminent. She was confident that all her years of living righteously had provided her with a one-way ticket up to the holy place before all hell broke loose.

She sat there for a while, enjoying the effects of the exceptional wine. Nothing seemed important to her now other than her personal salvation. The Merkel Mansion sale, the Fruit and his now damaged home, the Hippo and her whipped husband could all burn with the rest of the damned. She guessed that one's destiny only become clear when faced with death. Nevertheless, she still didn't understand why the darkness seemed to be after her with a personal vengeance. "Why me, God?" she asked aloud, turning her head up to the support beams of the ceiling. "Why am I so special that the dark forces are after me? Have I been chosen for a reason?" she asked the skylight. "Are you there, God?" But there was only silence.

She was thinking of getting another bottle from the cabinet when a powerful drowsiness overcame her. With her eyes closed, she imagined herself ascending to heaven. She was a heavenly vision, resplendent in glorious white. The Baby Jesus was showing her the way to the light and she was about to enter it when a loud noise jolted her out of her dream with a fright. She opened her eyes, hearing several shots in rapid succession, and realized it was the unmistakable sound of gunfire, and nearby. She immediately rolled off the couch onto the floor, feeling her heart race, wondering how they had found her so quickly. She reached for her purse and grabbed the revolver from inside it. She lay frozen for a moment, on her stomach, but everything was still. She heard more discharges and noticed flashes of color appear through the skylight. It took her a moment, but she realized that it wasn't the sound of gunfire but of fireworks.

She waited on the floor a while longer until she heard the discharges again and felt more confident that they were indeed fireworks. Lifting herself up, she climbed the stairs, feeling rather dizzy, and went into the first bedroom. She pulled back the curtain and opened the window. As she peered out, a soft and cedar-smelling waft of nighttime air caressed her face. She saw the stars in their brilliance twinkling above and was momentarily startled when she heard the fireworks once again, and saw red and green blossoms briefly illuminate the sky over the lake.

In the distance, she could see a crowd of people standing on the lawn behind the lodge. There was clapping and laughter carried by the breeze and she thought she heard a speech of some kind, but she couldn't make sense of the words. Now she heard music playing, an ancient sounding tune, right out of biblical times. So it has begun, she determined. This was the sign for which she had been waiting. They were celebrating the coming Rapture, the end of days! She knew at once that she was meant to join them. She grabbed her heels from where she'd left them near the bed and rushed back to the staircase, feeling lightheaded as she navigated the stairs to the first floor.

She put her gun back into her purse and hung it on her shoulder, just in case the dark forces were lurking nearby. Once outside, she locked the front door and went around her cabin to the road that led downhill to the lodge. As she walked alongside the road, she suddenly felt clumsy in her heels, and looking down at the green sequins that covered her shoes, she thought it must be due to the unevenness of the ground.

As she approached the well-lit lodge, she no longer felt scared, rather a sense of giddiness overcame her. She saw a gathering of people celebrating on the grassy area between the lodge and the lakeshore. There were several tables of food and the people were gathered in small groups about the lawn. Some of them were wearing old-fashioned-looking costumes, while others were dressed in modern clothes. She noticed that many women wore colorful robes of silk, some looking as if they'd been spun of silver and gold. A number of men were dressed in suits while others wore long collarless shirts with slacks. She especially noted the men dressed in white and wondered if they were angels.

Scanning the crowd, she saw the source of the music was coming from a group of men who were seated at one end of the lawn. They were playing funny-looking guitar like instruments, long flutes as well as drums. The whole ensemble appeared to be right out of ancient Jerusalem. One woman was dressed in white and wearing a veil and a garland of flowers around her neck. Cherie recalled from her Bible studies that the dead were supposed to be resurrected for a great wedding supper during the Rapture and she felt overjoyed as she realized this was what they were celebrating.

She saw there were flowers everywhere and there was a buffet of food set upon the tables: fruits of all kinds, roasted lamb, vegetable and rice dishes, pastries, and a towering cake. The people seemed joyous. She did notice they were a little more ethnic than the average Seattleite, but they were well dressed and she guessed this is how people out of the Bible would look.

As she approached the tables of food, some of the people seemed to take notice of her. A nearby group of men and women gave her curious looks and she felt like Cinderella arriving late for the ball, her perfect blend of beauty and purity stunning them into a silent wonderment.

Seeing all of the heavenly-looking food, she realized she hadn't eaten anything in hours and grabbed a plate from the table and filled it up with some fruit and pastries.

A matronly woman dressed in an antique looking silk robe approached her, gazing at her inquisitively and Cherie gave her a wide smile of delight.

"Who, may I ask, are you, dear?" the woman inquired in an accented voice.

"I'm Cherie Cahill. I came from the cabin up the hill," she replied pointing to it. "This is the wedding supper, isn't it?"

"Yes, I'm the mother of the bride. Are you a guest of the groom's?" she asked, looking her over.

"It's such an honor to meet you," Cherie said, reaching out and taking her hand. "I suppose you can say I am a guest of the groom." She remembered that Jesus was the groom of what she had always figured was a metaphorical wedding ceremony of the Rapture. "The Lord Jesus Christ is my savior," she added. "Is he here?"

The way the woman looked at her made Cherie think that she might not be fluent in English. Cherie bit into the flaky crust of a pastry, tasting a burst of honey mixed with finely chopped nuts. She had never tasted anything so good.

"Like manna from heaven," she said to the matron, holding the pastry up in appreciation.

The woman smiled vaguely, but still appeared concerned. "Are you all right, dear? It looks as if you've been crying."

"Oh that," Cherie said, touching her face. "They were trying to kill me earlier, but now that I'm here I'll be safe."

The woman opened her mouth, looking alarmed.

"Speaking of death," Cherie continued as she gazed at the woman's antiquated garment, "you must be very happy to be alive again. How long were you dead?"

"Pardon me?" the woman asked looking aghast.

Cherie tried to make the woman understand. "YOU LOOK LIKE YOU HAVE BEEN DEAD FOR A LONG TIME," she said loudly, carefully stressing each word. She grabbed the woman's robe for emphasis. "I can tell by your strange costume."

The woman suddenly moved away. Cherie watched her as she disappeared into the crowd, appearing to search for someone. The woman turned back one more time and Cherie waved to her. Maybe she's still disoriented from the resurrection, she considered.

Cherie wolfed down the rest of her pastry and listened as a new melody started, sounding beautifully sensuous to her ears, and she suddenly felt compelled to join the dancing. She put down her plate and started swaying back and forth to the music, waving her arms, never having felt so carefree. She put her hands through her hair and swung around happily and the others started to pay attention to her, marveling at her moves. Gradually, as she moved about the dance area, it seemed as if the others had stopped dancing and that all attention was focused on her, the newest soul, she thought. This must be some kind of initiation ceremony, she guessed, a test of sorts.

She was up for the challenge, and as she started to dance, she caught sight of a man in a long white shirt with fancy gold embroidery on it. His shirt was unbuttoned to his sternum, and she could see the dark hair on his prominent chest. He was wearing white slacks and shoes and with his long, dark wavy hair, he looked angelic. He must be an angel, she decided. True, his features were different from how she had pictured angels ever since she was a girl and had a nightlight in the form of a flaxen-haired cherub; nonetheless, he was exquisite. She waved to him. At first, he didn't acknowledge her, but then she kept on waving enthusiastically and finally he smiled and hesitantly waved back. "A shy angel. How absolutely delicious," she said aloud, laughing to herself. She now felt ecstatic and started twirling around slowly and then faster. It was hard to balance on her heels, but somehow she was managing, and she saw people gather in appreciation. She caught sight of some children pointing at her and guessed they'd never seen a true Caucasian before—especially a blonde beauty such as herself—and was happy she was bringing so much joy to these ancient and dark-skinned people.

Suddenly, everything started spinning wildly, even when she thought she had stopped moving. Her heel twisted underneath her and she felt a stab of pain in her ankle as she fell, not knowing if she was falling up or down. Is it happening? she wondered. Is this the ascension?

"Are you okay?" she heard a man's voice ask.

Opening her eyes, she saw a blurry image of the angel who had waved to her earlier. He seemed to be bending over her, but she couldn't focus since he kept on moving. Then it hit her. This was no angel. This was the guest of honor, the Lord Jesus Christ!

"Why, you're no angel," she said.

He chuckled. "I've been called many things, but never an angel."

"You're my savior and you've come to rescue me."

"I've hardly done anything to deserve such praise," he said, smiling.

"Is it time to go up there?" she asked, pointing up to the sky, inadvertently belching near his face. "Oops. Silly me," she said, reddening.

"You've had a little bit to drink tonight, no?"

"Oh, just my own version of Holy Communion," Cherie replied, wondering if he could read her thoughts.

"My aunty says you live in the cabin up there," he said, pointing up the hill.

Your aunty? Cherie thought, not understanding. "But when do we get to go up there?" she asked, pointing up to the sky.

"Don't worry, I'll take you there. Can you walk?"

"No, I hurt my ankle. Besides, I want to fly with you." She made a fluttering motion with her hands.

"Okay, then I'll carry you. Is this your bag?" he asked, picking it up.

"Yes, but I won't be needing that any longer."

"Why don't you hold onto it, just in case," he said, handing it to her.

She now saw that a crowd of people had gathered around them. She heard a mix of voices, some talking in English, others in their ancient tongues. One of them directed a question to the Savior in an archaic-sounding language and she heard him respond in kind. I bet he's fluent in all tongues, she marveled.

She wrapped her arms around his neck as he lifted her up and watched the crowd disperse before him. Up close, she noticed how long and thick his eyelashes were. He was the most beautiful man she'd ever laid eyes upon and she couldn't help wondering if Jesus had any corporeal desires. As if reading her mind, she noticed him eyeing her breasts with seeming appreciation. A sweet peace-like sleep enveloped her and she gave into a feverish delirium, pressing into the firm body of her savior, letting him carry her on their ascent.

FIFTY-TWO

Julie never looked worse, Adam thought, breezing through the lobby doors of Wilkes, O'Hara & Tarleton. She had tied her long blonde hair into a tight bun that gave her face a mean look. The openly hostile glare she gave Adam was not flattering either. She was standing behind the reception desk tending to a large document mailing that, in the past, she had foisted on him.

"Adam," she snarled from behind the desk as he entered the code for the office door.

"Yes, Julie," he answered, trying to be civil. He didn't want to let her know that the contempt in her voice was music to his ears and the anger expressed in her body language was pure theater in his eyes. If this were a show at the Geary Theater, he would have purchased tickets, he mused, looking at Julie's ridged posture uncomfortably clad in a defeated looking Laura Ashley dress.

"Tony has been looking for you. He said it was important. I told him you were on one of your long lunches and I had no idea when you might honor us with your presence."

With that, she gave him one last glare and sat down in front of the small mountain of shipping labels. He thought about telling her he had a template that would easily deal with the labels, but it was payback to let her fill them out by hand with all the little angry letters that made up her penmanship.

"Thanks, Julie," he said, pushing through the glass door and into the interior of the office. "I know we can all rest easy when you're working reception," he added, not turning back to see her reaction.

His lunch had been a little over an hour, so he wasn't too worried about Tony. Working for Tony, so far, had been the best thing to happen to him at the firm. Tony was laid-back as long as the work was done right the first time and on schedule. As he walked to his cube, Adam started to worry that he had missed something in his work and he hoped Tony didn't have a dark side.

Once at his desk, Adam checked his voicemail, which was empty. There was nothing important in his email, just one red exclamation point next to a message sent from Julie to the support staff in all the offices. The Julie emails were always phrased in such a way as to suggest that all administrative staff reported to her. Adam had been amused to see that Christina and another woman, Beth, often put the Julie emails in the trash folder, unread.

He sensed someone come up from behind him on the plush carpet near the partners' offices where he was currently assigned. One of the things he hated about this side of the office was the deep carpet that caused him to be startled about once a week as well as to slip occasionally in his dress shoes.

"Adam, we need to talk. Please join me in my office."

Adam turned to see Tony, whose poker face told him nothing. He felt the dread of the unknown. He closed his email and followed Tony to his office. He made a mental inventory of his possessions in his cube and was cynically amused that after all these years he could fit his personal items easily into the small Banana Republic bag in his desk drawer. Even his email would not be a problem since he received his personal email on his Yahoo! account. He stiffened his back and his resolve as he prepared for what was probably a Julie-crafted dismissal.

Tony waited for him to enter his office before closing the door and gesturing to either of the chairs that sat in front of his desk. With Tony seated, Adam waited in the profoundly uncomfortable silence. Tony reached down behind his desk, opened a drawer and pulled out a bottle.

"Scotch?" he asked.

Adam smiled, the dread melting off him in sheets.

"I will, if you are."

"I will join you, but don't try to keep up with me. You were probably just a glimmer in your father's eye when I had my first hangover."

"I don't drink much, so this is a pleasant exception," Adam said, standing and retrieving the glasses from among the many binders and papers on the bookshelves.

"You really do know where everything is in the firm," Tony said with a chuckle.

Adam put the two clean glasses before Tony, who opened the bottle and poured the scotch before leaning back in the large chair behind the imposing desk.

"Adam," Tony cleared his throat. "David Touel has had some issues both related and unrelated to the firm. He is no longer an employee here."

Adam's imagination raced with the possibilities from the dark to the humorous. He also wondered if this had anything to do with David's racy online life.

Tony continued, oblivious of Adam's churning mind, "This isn't to be shared with others at the firm just yet. David's caseload was light but it spanned both Seattle and San Francisco. I met with O'Hara, Wilkes and Tarleton this morning. I will be dropping all my cases other than the big Anderson case to clean up the mess David left. Also, I will be the new managing attorney and joining the masthead, as Wilkes, Tarleton, O'Hara and Butler."

"Congratulations!" Adam said, surprising himself with the authentic enthusiasm in his voice. Tony accepted his handshake and then they both took a quiet drink of scotch. The scotch burned Adam's mouth, which followed by a pleasant warmth after he swallowed.

"So, it sounds like I will be finishing up and returning to my old duties," Adam said, putting the glass down on Tony's desk and imagining his first morning next to Julie. Perhaps he could wait tables, he thought, since the idea of going back to his old workspace seemed impossible. Tony filled both their glasses.

"Well, no, Adam. The venom Julie spits at you would be a Workers' Compensation issue in itself. I spoke with the trio of partners ...."

"Quartette," Adam interrupted.

"So it is," Tony said, with a broad smile, clearly basking in his own success.

"As I said, we spoke this morning, and we're all aware of your professionalism in dealing with David as well as the day-to-day stresses." Tony leaned forward, putting his elbows on the desk. He looked Adam in the eye and said quietly, "David's need to use company email to arrange his indiscretions is beyond me." Sitting back again, he went on, "You have made an especially good impression on Wilkes. You not hesitating to tell Wilkes that he had both his filing dates wrong and motions misplaced, regardless of his statements to the contrary, was a humbling moment for him and an amusing one for the rest of us." Tony chuckled and reached for his glass.

"To the point, Adam, the firm is in flux, which for you is an opportunity. I'd like you to accept a promotion to Case Manager for the Anderson case, and, assuming that goes well, become the Senior Case Manager for the firm when Anderson concludes at the end of the year. You'll need to be able to bounce back and forth between here and Seattle to do the job. There is a formal offer letter in HR with solid numbers waiting for your review. It has the compensation numbers but, as an incentive, I'd like to mention that it would include an office here in San Francisco."

"Tony, this is great news. Really great news," he repeated. "I'm really excited by this offer and to have the chance to work with you."

"Adam, I am flattered. The firm is lucky to have you. I enjoy working with you, not to mention that without you, the Anderson case would be a quagmire, and that is exactly what I told the partners this morning. Oh, Wilkes wants to give you the hard sell about a future at the firm, so why don't you join us for lunch tomorrow. He will do all the talking, imagine that, so you might as well get a lunch out of it. We're going to Aqua at one o'clock. I'll have Julie add you to the reservation."

"I'd be happy to join you, but will that be awkward for the partners?" Adam asked, tempted to back out as he thought of the firepower sitting at the table.

"It was their idea so I think you are more than welcome. Hold on, before I forget."

Adam finished his scotch as Tony picked up the phone and dialed an internal number.

"Julie, it's Tony."

"Fine, thank you. And you?"

"Good."

"I need you to add Adam to the reservation at Aqua that O'Hara asked you to make this morning. Thanks. Oh, one more thing, Adam is going to be moving into the office next to Mitchell as of next Monday. Please have it up and running. I think he'll need some assistance moving the Anderson documents in, so can you rustle up a crew to get it done?"

"Hello? That's a nasty cough, Julie."

"Thank you, Julie."

He hung up the phone. "Sounded as if she coughed up a hairball when I mentioned your office," Tony said, giving the phone a sideways glance.

"You never know," Adam said, not wanting to comment further in fear of becoming a different kind of catty.

"That leaves us with two issues. How about you finish things up here and then go down to HR and pick up your offer letter from Ellen? Then take the rest of the day off and see if you can have an answer for us by lunch tomorrow."

"Yes, sir. I can do that," Adam said, thinking he would call Ben before his shift to tell him the good news and coax him into a spur-of-the-moment celebration. "And the other issue," Adam asked?

Tony leaned back in his chair, interlacing his fingers and paused before leaning forward with a conspiratorial smile. "The wife and I want to know who that handsome young man you have lunch with is and just what he is saying that makes you smile like a fool all lunch hour."

Adam blushed, "That sir, requires a refill," he said, pouring Tony and himself a short glass.

FIFTY-THREE

Cherie opened her eyes and was momentarily blinded by the bright light. She saw a white cloth, like a robe, waving in front of her and she heard a disembodied voice speaking in a foreign language. She tried to lift her head, but it felt like she had a massive hangover. Slowly, her eyes adjusted to the light and she quickly realized that she wasn't in heaven. She was in her cabin bedroom and the white cloth was simply the curtain blowing in the breeze.

She saw a man appear near the doorway, talking on a cell phone and fragments of memory started coming back to her. "Jesus?" she called out, wondering why Jesus would have a cell phone. The man peeked into the bedroom, saying a few quick words into his phone before slipping it in his pocket.

"You're awake," he said, approaching her. "And how is the mystery lady feeling this morning? Or should I say this afternoon?" he added, looking at his watch.

"What time is it?" she asked.

"About two o'clock."

"Two o'clock? You mean I slept through the morning?"

"And all day yesterday. It's Monday."

"Monday!" She saw he was no longer wearing the white shirt and pants she recalled from before. Instead, he was dressed in an ordinary short-sleeved button-down shirt and khaki shorts. A heavy five o'clock shadow covered his formerly smooth face. "I, I don't understand. The last thing I remember was the wedding supper and ...."

"Yes, my cousin Farah's wedding reception," he interjected with a smile. "You made quite an impression."

"Cousin? What do you mean cousin?"

"Just what I said. It was my cousin Farah's wedding."

"You're not Jesus?" she asked, becoming alarmed.

"Jesus? No," he said, chuckling. "You've been calling out his name a lot. My aunty was convinced she'd seen you before hosting one of those programs on the local religious channel. I told her that was another lady who happened to have big blonde hair and wear lots of makeup. I thought that you probably just had a little too much to drink and were confused."

"I might have had a little something," she said defensively, "but who are you, then?"

"My name is Fazel Izadi."

Fuzzle? she thought, pegging the name and his slight accent as Hispanic. She noted that he had similar coloring to Carlotta's hunky brother Carlos, and she knew they were from Mexico, though as many times as Carlotta had told her she could never remember from which city.

"But what about the ancients? I know I saw them."

"Ancients?"

"The wedding guests were dressed in costumes right out of the Bible."

"Oh, that. It was a traditional Persian wedding, so many people dressed in the customary fashion."

"Persian? Isn't that …?"

"Iranian," he offered. "I'm originally from Iran. I moved to the U.S. eight years ago from France."

"Iran? France!" she said, feeling a sense of horror. Oh my God, oh my God, she thought, starting to panic. Her immediate instinct was to get out of bed, but when she tried, the pain of her ankle stopped her. "Ow!" she howled.

"You sprained it," Fazel said, approaching. "I was worried about your condition." His eyes seemed to convey a softness that contrasted with his manly form. "I've been walking up from the lodge to check on you every few hours. I hope you don't mind."

"You were watching me while I slept!?"

"No, just making sure you were okay, giving you fluids whenever you woke up and helping you to the bathroom. You don't remember any of this?"

Cherie tried to remember, but only hazy images of sitting on a jumbo jet that was bound for heaven came to her. She recalled Jesus was her captain, flying her to safety as she rested in first class, calling the angels who were serving as flight attendants whenever she needed anything.

"Vaguely," she answered.

"You were delirious and were tossing and turning as if you were going through a withdrawal of some kind. Your fever broke last night."

"Withdrawal? So are you a doctor now?"

"As a matter of fact, I am. You were certainly in no state to be left alone."

"So what kind of doctor are you?"

"I'm a surgeon by training, but I'm currently working as a researcher."

"I see," she said, trying not to show her suspicion that something was amiss. Then the verse from Matthew came back to her: *Beware of false prophets who come to you in sheep's clothing, but inwardly are ravening wolves.* Wolf in sheep's clothing, she reflected, looking him over. Her heart skipped a beat as she became utterly convinced that she was dealing with an agent of the Antichrist, if not *The Man* himself. While this wolf was certainly more attractive than Janet was, she knew she had to remain strong and resist all forms of temptation. Somehow, she had to take back the upper hand and she thought she knew how.

"Fuzzle, I have some medication in the glove compartment of my SUV. It's important I take it at regular times. Would you mind getting it for me?"

"Certainly," he said, seeming pleased to help.

"Would you hand me my purse, first? My keys are inside," she said, remembering that her revolver was there as well.

"Oh, I left your keys downstairs. I've been using them since the night I brought you back from the party. I'll go get your medication."

"Thank you, Fuzzle," she said, angry that her ploy had failed, but she now knew she was dealing with a clever enemy.

"By the way, it's pronounced FAR-ZEL."

"Uh huh," she replied, not up for small talk.

He looked as if he were bothered by something, but then simply said, "I'll be right back," and disappeared through the doorway.

She knew her only option was to get her gun from her purse before he returned. If only she hadn't locked her bedroom closet, she chastised herself, she could have grabbed the semi-automatic rifle she stored there and had a nice surprise waiting for him upon his return.

She quickly slid out of bed, being careful with her left foot. She saw her ankle was swollen and it hurt just to slide it out from the sheets. She was still in her dress, and looking down at it she thought that at least he hadn't taken advantage of her condition and ravaged her.

She hopped on her good foot from the bedroom, using the wall for support, and made her way down the hallway, feeling her head pound in complaint with each lurch forward. Once she reached the top of the stairs, she looked down and saw that he had left the front door partially open. She knew she had only moments to find her purse and get the gun. As she hobbled down the stairs, she imagined herself heroically capturing the agent of evil. She was certain her compelling story of heroism would earn her a several-page spread in *Gun Totin' Ladies* magazine where they would highlight her act of bravery in their "Profiles in Courage" section.

Once she reached the first floor, she scanned the room and saw her purse was on the couch. She quickly hopped to it. When she pulled out the gun, she heard the door of the SUV close. She sat down in a hurry, hiding the gun under a silk throw pillow she placed on her lap.

"What are you doing out of bed?" Fazel asked upon entering the cabin. He was cradling several of her prescription bottles in his arms, and he closed the door behind him with his foot and approached the couch.

"The question, Fuzzle, is what are you doing here?" she said, pulling the gun from under the pillow and pointing it at him.

He dropped the pill bottles to the floor. "What are you doing with that?!"

"I'm tired of running and I want answers. Who sent you here? Was it the Antichrist? Are *you* the Antichrist?"

He stared at her incredulously. "First you think I'm Jesus Christ and now you think I'm the Antichrist?"

"Notice how you haven't answered the question, Fuzzle," she said, feeling the advantage was hers.

"Originally, I thought it was just the alcohol making you loony and then sick, but now I see I was wrong. It must be all these medications." He pointed to the pill bottles on the floor. "Do you actually take all of these?"

"Stop trying to change the subject."

"There are no less than three different kinds of antidepressants, a cholesterol-lowering drug, two blood pressure medications, birth control, an anti-anxiety drug, caffeine pills … I'm surprised you're not dead from the drug interactions alone."

"I asked you for my medication, not a commentary. Anyway, my doctor prescribed them."

"One doctor prescribed all of these? Then he should have his license revoked."

"Well, it wasn't just one doctor," she said, knowing she had two of them, plus her shrink.

"Ah, so you're playing the system."

"I'm not playing anything. People take these all the time," she said, getting annoyed.

"Perhaps, but not all at the same time. These medications

aren't candy. They have serious side effects and interactions."

"Stop using your trickery on me. I know what you're trying to do."

"Ask yourself," he continued undeterred, "has it always been your habit to crash wedding parties and hold people at gunpoint? Then again, for all I know, maybe it is."

She thought about this for a moment. "I guess I have been feeling off lately," she said, slumping into the couch, reflecting back on all her sleepless nights and caffeinated days, her declining health, not to mention the visions and her Queen Anne adventures. "So, hypothetically speaking, if I did happen to take a few too many pills, you're saying it could cause hallucinations and perhaps bad judgment?"

"Such as thinking I'm Jesus Christ one moment and the Antichrist the next?" he asked with a wry smile.

"Something like that," she said, lowering her eyes.

"I think hallucinations are very possible. Cherie, if I may call you that," he said, stepping forward with open palms, "I'm only trying to help you."

Cherie didn't know what to believe anymore. She didn't know if he was telling the truth or if this was simply more devilish trickery. She rested the gun on the pillow, holding onto it loosely.

"Now why don't you hand me the gun," he said.

"No, I won't. You might be lying to me like all the others."

"You do know the gun isn't loaded, don't you?"

"What?!" she asked, opening up the chambers and seeing they were empty.

"I saw the gun when I got the keys out of your purse the night of the party. I was worried about someone in your condition being near a loaded gun so I took out the ammo. If I was working for this Antichrist, as you call him, I would have had ample time to complete my mission while you were unconscious for the last 36 hours, would I not?"

Cherie stared at him speechless. She saw his logic, but more importantly, she couldn't help but notice again how attractive he was. Something about his voice, its calm authority, made him all the more desirable to her. It had been so long since she'd met a real man, a man who might be equal to her womanhood.

"I have been awfully rude to you," she said, playing with the emerald pendant on her neck. "After all the kindness you've shown me." She moved her hand lower, just above her breasts, and watched his eyes follow its movement.

"It was nothing. I'm sure you would have done the same."

Cherie reflected on this, thinking how little he knew of her. "I suppose you need to get back to your family."

"I'm in no hurry. Most of them went back to Seattle yesterday."

"So you live in Seattle?" she asked hopefully.

"Yes, in the University District. How about you?"

"Belltown." At that moment, Cherie heard a chime and realized it was coming from her purse. "Oh, that's my cell. I must have an urgent email," she said, recognizing the distinct tone and taking her cell from inside her bag.

She retrieved the email, seeing it was from Alyssa, her assistant at work. In the message, Alyssa first expressed her concern at Cherie's sudden and "bizarre" exit from the party and seemed to think she had been on a "bad trip" of some sort. Cherie frowned at Alyssa's familiarity, but what could she expect from a rave regular, she thought. Alyssa commented on how it had been such a strange evening between the events at the party and the explosion at the Archer house, which they thought was due to a gas leak. The good news, she wrote, was that the Merkel Mansion had sold. Cherie would get her commission, though Mr. Merkel had been so outraged by her behavior at the party that he had banned her from the property and had chewed out Mr. Amstead. Mr. Amstead had also received an angry phone call from a man who claimed Cherie had been listing the Archer house on the website, unlawfully. Mr. Amstead wanted Cherie to call him immediately. Alyssa ended the message by telling Cherie not to worry about the details of the closing, as she was assisting Mr. Amstead personally.

Cherie shut off her phone and tossed it by her purse.

"Was it something important?" Fazel asked.

"Oh, it was nothing," she said, surprised that the sale of the mansion, which had seemed so crucial to her these last few months, could now seem so inconsequential. Even the fact that she would probably be fired didn't faze her. "I should wash up," she said, suddenly feeling self-conscious about her appearance. "I must look like a wreck."

"Actually, you look very pretty," he said eyeing her openly.

She laughed appreciatively, rising from the couch, but winced when she inadvertently placed weight on her left foot.

"Here, let me help you," he said, moving toward her and then easily picking her up.

She was mesmerized by the view of his muscled and hairy chest that was showing through the top of his shirt.

"Which bathroom?" he asked. "Upstairs or downstairs?"

"Upstairs please," she said, using her best Marilyn Monroe voice.

He carried her up the stairs with seeming effortlessness, as if she were only the weight of her dress. Her lips were near his face and, on impulse, she kissed him on the cheek, liking the coarse feel of his whiskers. He looked surprised, but pleased. Once upstairs, he took her to the bathroom.

"Can you stay nearby in case I need help?" Cherie asked.

"Of course, I'll be right here if you need anything."

"There's a club chair in my bedroom, so make yourself at home. But, if you could get me a Diet Coke out of the refrigerator, that would be super."

"My pleasure, mon cher."

"With crushed ice, please. I'll be right back," she said as she limped into the bathroom.

Once she closed the door, she looked at her face in the mirror, expecting the worst, but he must have cleaned it at some point because her makeup smears were gone and she saw a hint of the farm girl she used to be. Her hair was matted, but not too bad, considering. She took off her emerald pendant and clothes and then eased into the shower, thinking of the man who was waiting in her bedroom. She knew he wasn't a keeper; she could just picture her parents' horror if she brought him home to Yakima. She didn't care about any of this now, though, and would have thoroughly lost herself in her warm water fantasies had she not been so conscious of her bad ankle.

Once out, she dried herself off and then slipped the towel around her body like a tight mini dress. She hobbled to her bedroom where she saw Fazel sitting in the chair next to the vanity, browsing a *Gun Totin' Ladies* magazine with a perplexed look on his face.

"Thirsty?" he asked, offering her the glass of cola upon seeing her.

The glass was cold to the touch and she surprised herself by gulping down all the liquid. Already, she could feel her headache diminishing.

"Would you like some more, or perhaps something to eat?" he asked.

"No, I'm not quite ready for food," she said, giving him a knowing look. "Will you help me back to the bed?"

He obliged with his arm and gently eased her onto the bed.

"Oh, Fuzzle," she called, alluringly. "It's been so long since I've felt the touch of a man. Would you mind holding me for just a little while?"

He looked at her as if he were pondering something. "From the moment I laid eyes on you, I knew you were special. Trouble," he continued, "but special."

It was music to her ears and she beckoned him to come to her.

He bent down and held her gently, keeping most of his weight off her, but she grabbed him and started kissing him fiercely, locking her right leg around his body.

He pulled away. "Easy," he said. "There's no rush."

He rose from the bed and after unbuttoning his shirt, he folded it neatly and placed it on the dresser. He then lowered his shorts and boxers and she felt herself get even more aroused.

He bent down and unwrapped her towel and they were finally body-to-body, naked, like Adam and Eve, she thought.

He kissed her all over sensuously as if he were sampling a great feast. As exquisite as this felt to her, she was ravenous for the main course and pulled him toward her greedily.

He obliged readily, and as he pressed into her, she moaned and called out his name. "Oh, Fuzzle."

"It's FAR-ZEL," he whispered into her ear and then nibbled on the lobe, teasing the interior with his tongue.

"Oh, I'll never remember that," she said, laughing in pleasure. "I'll just call you Fuzzy."

He smiled and continued to press himself into her with a deliberation and skill she had never before experienced.

Perhaps, she worried, this was part of the Antichrist's elaborate plan to impregnate her with his demon seed. She didn't know what was true, anymore, and she didn't care. She'd worry about the repercussions later, as right now, he was taking her to a state of bliss. As he continued to thrust, all she could think was, sweet Jesus, the Rapture was finally coming.

FIFTY-FOUR

Adam heard Edison's footsteps on the other end of the phone line. They faded and he was left with just the faint sound of birds chirping. Then Edison's voice, distant, "It's Adam, I'm going to take the call from the kitchen. Can you hang up the extension in my bedroom?"

"Sure," was Val's reply, sounding a million miles away. After another bird intermission a voice came over the phone, female and feline, "Baby, what are you wearing?" it purred, heavy with solicitation.

Not missing a beat, he responded in the best Latin lover voice that he could muster, "It's hot here, baby. I'm burning up in this red Speedo, and you're going to make me boil over, again. You just make me so hot, baby, you gonna give me some sugar?"

The voice on the other end of the line giggled and even snorted before breaking into a laugh. Then the feline voice was back just as Adam heard Edison pick up the extension and saw Ben stick his head out from under the comforter. Adam pressed the speakerphone button and Ben slid on top of him, his heat welcome as the cold summer fog pressed against the windows.

"It's hot here too, baby. My bra fell off and I'm bending over to pick it up. Whoops! My miniskirt fell off too and I'm here in just my panties and heels! What ever shall I do?"

Adam, growled, "Baby, you make me so hot, I'm going to need a tissue."

"Tissue?" The voice on the other end echoed flatly.

"I mean paper towel. Oh hell," Adam said in exasperation.

"Take away the boy and send me a man!" Val shouted into the phone, regal voice ringing.

Edison hooted from the other extension. "Damn, Adam, you just don't have a phone sex future ahead of you, but you, Val, might. And if you start walking around here in just panties and heels I'm going to get you a French maid's outfit and see if we can get you a corner on Aurora Avenue."

"Have her put her hair up like Chrissy on *Three's Company*," Ben said to the speakerphone.

"Adam! You aren't alone!" Val shouted through the line.

"I put you on speaker so Ben would know with whom I'm whoring."

"I gotta keep track of my boyfriend. If he's working the phones, I want a cut," Ben said directly to the speakerphone as Adam felt his sweatpants being pulled off his hips.

Adam turned and flipped Ben off his back. Playfully pinning the naked Ben beneath him, he whispered, "Boyfriend?"

"I think it fits. You?" Ben asked, holding Adam with his gaze.

He moved closer and gently rubbed the tip of his nose against Ben's before brushing his lips against Ben's. He breathed his answer in a single utterance, "Yes."

"Shall we call back?" Edison asked, sounding patrician from the cheap speakerphone's distortion.

"No, we're here. And damn, we're queer," Adam answered.

"I miss San Francisco," Val whined. "It's just so goddamn dramatic."

"I hear you sister," Edison said. "I think we need to see ourselves here at Archer Haus as missionaries who refuse to let go of our San Francisco way of life."

"We will be the mad dogs and Englishmen of Queen Anne Hill!" Val burst onto the line defiantly. "We will never let our traditions go, even in the contrary face of reason."

"Yes, we will be like the imperialists who drank hot tea in India while ironing their shirts," Edison said from his extension.

"That will be us," Val said, "crazy and proud to the end.

Whether it be at the temp job making copies of copies or shooing all those goddamn strollers off the sidewalks into the mud where they belong. I feel like Norma Damn Rae without the Sally Field aftertaste."

"Nothing worse than a Sally Field aftertaste," Ben said as Adam felt Ben slide his sweatpants from his ankles.

"Amen," Edison offered.

"So, I'm hearing anger issues on the other end of the line?" Ben asked as much to the speakerphone as to Adam's thigh, where he rested his head now that he had successfully maneuvered Adam's gym shorts around his knees.

"Nah, we're just having minor transition blues. It's actually very nice up here and the quality of life is off the scale," Edison said.

"I wake up to birds each morning," Val added. "It's nice but I wish they came with a snooze beak."

"Speaking of birds, I liked the magnetic macramé geese on your refrigerator, Edison. I was surprised to see you have such an arts and crafts side," Adam said, trying to bring the call back to its original topic.

"Oh, that's from my mother. There's a matching goose up here to cover the toaster. When you visit, your guestroom will have duck-themed linens. Val got the bunny-themed hand towels, in case you were wondering."

"I was just going to ask," Adam said sarcastically. "I got your check. It was much more than you needed to send, Edison; I would do this for free, really."

"It's the least I could do. It must not have smelled too nice when you opened the refrigerator."

"The refrigerator smells like bleach now. All the laundry is done and I left it folded on the bed. We went to that office supply store on Van Ness and picked up some boxes too. I felt like I should spend some of that check on getting you ready so you and Brett can hit the ground running when you get into town. Did I read your email right and you two are driving down here in a rental?"

"Yeah," Edison said. "Brett and I have good memories of past road trips. You bought boxes with my check?" Edison asked, changing the subject.

"Yes, it was too generous so I used some of the money for boxes."

"Adam," Edison's voice came over the speakerphone loud enough to cause the phone to squeal. "That money is for your time and for cleaning up my place. Damn kids today," Edison fumed from the other end. "Well then, I am taking you and Ben out for dinner and that's final."

"Take them to Boulevard, Edison," Val suggested. "It will clear Adam's traumatic relationship with the restaurant so perhaps he will eventually forget our dark interlude."

"Oh, Val, you know how you can make it up to me," Adam said, switching to his husky faux predator voice. "Just wear those heels, a bottle of Windex and …."

"I cannot handle this," Edison interrupted. "Adam, I will email you the details of the drive down after I speak to Brett. Val, you should consider a future in phone sex, just don't use the house phones, thank you very much."

Edison hung up and Ben padded off naked to the kitchen only to return with some olive oil, bread and salt, which was his usual precursor to sex.

"So, tell me about the fireworks," Adam asked Val, taking the phone off speaker.

"Sounds like you have your own brand of fireworks down there, Mr. Adam," Val teased. "The fireworks up here looked worse than they actually were, but it was really bad timing for Edison. The coroner had just reported the official cause of death and then the explosion removed the mystery behind how it happened."

"So what caused the explosion?" Adam asked, trying to mask the impatience in his voice.

"It was a huge septic system from ages ago that was still connected to the house. The tank itself was out in the lawn originally and then a previous owner built a garage over it. Actually, the family that first died in the house built the garage. The large septic pipe would then leak methane into the house from time to time as pressure built up and the tank deteriorated. It must have leaked again in the 1970's because that's when the Reaping Widow earned her name. It killed the widower whose crazy wife had died, according to Edison, after publicly cursing her husband. He was dead a month later. Edison's parents unfortunately made a media room right where the pipe went into the house. The unsealed pipe was just behind some drywall. It leaked methane; they dozed off and never woke again. The gas then dissipated leaving the coroner with a mystery."

"And the pipe now? Is the house safe?" Adam asked, fascinated by Val's Reaping Widow story.

"Blown to bits, as was the garage. The house was dinged, but not much more."

"Wow. No wonder Edison said he was looking forward to going back to work. But why didn't the tank explode before this if it was leaking gas?" Adam asked, not holding back his curiosity anymore.

"Aren't you just fishing for an Agatha Christie angle. I guess the previous leaks were either too small or never reached the gas water heater, which is in a closet that is usually closed. Edison had left the closet door open after the security alarm people were here to install a smoke detector in the closet and upgrade the system. Gotta love the irony of that one. Oh, am I off speaker?"

"Yep, just you and me, kid."

"So, it sounds like you are nearing the trifecta."

"What do you mean?" Adam asked.

"The Maupin three."

"You mean Armistead Maupin, the literary icon?" Adam asked, amused and confused.

"You know, silly, what Edison always quoted back at Trident. If you have a boyfriend, a good job and a decent place to live, then you have it all in San Francisco. It's just nearly impossible to have all three at once."

"Well, the job has certainly been upgraded," Adam said,

eyeing the new work clothes in the closet that were largely paid for by Edison's check. He felt olive oil being rubbed on his calf and moving up his leg. There is number two of the Maupin three, he thought, smiling down at Ben. "Perhaps two of three," he said to Val. "I live in a dump and Ben pointed out last night that the peeling paint in the apartment might be lead-based."

"Just another ploy to get you into my bed," Ben said loud enough for the Seattle end of the line to hear.

"Not bad," Val said. "A man with a plan."

"And you, how are you doing up there with the Maupin three?"

"I fail all three, but Edison's home is nice, even though I'm just a guest. As bad as it all is, I'm actually optimistic. I have no idea why, but I think I'm in a good place. Allow me to change that answer after a few days temping for some stooge, like the corporate bitch I used to be."

"I've walked in those temp shoes more than once," Adam said. "The only good thing is that word, *temporary*." So, is our Mr. Edison going to be okay?"

"Yeah, I think so. You know how he was at Trident; no one could read him worth a damn. He's still like that, but from what I can tell, he's determined to get on with his life, his new life. I guess I'm parallel to him in a much shallower way, looking forward to starting anew."

"I'm happy for you, Val. It will be good to see this new Val when I'm up there in a few weeks."

"Will Mr. Man be with you?" Val asked. "I'd like to meet the man who melted Adam Sirna's heart."

"It was frozen?" Adam asked, surprised. He looked down and saw his tan legs were glowing with oil and Ben, with a leer, took purchase to Adam's very personal real estate.

"A bit," Val answered. "But hey, better than swimming around in denial like I was. Oh," Val purred, "Edison is waving a tray of blueberry muffins at me."

"You should prioritize," Adam said with authority. "And when I say prioritize, I mean muffins. Talk to you next week?"

With a muffin in her mouth, Val agreed and hung up.

Tossing the phone to the end of the futon, he heard a lusty animal growl from Ben.

"Less chat, more sex," Ben mumbled from between Adam's legs.

Adam looked up at the peeling paint on his ceiling, two out of three ain't bad, he thought.

FIFTY-FIVE

"Lemons to lemonade," Edison said, walking out onto the porch through the new front doors. He knelt down and picked up a splinter of burnt wood from the destroyed garage. After breaking it in two, he tossed it over the porch rail. The porch in its fresh coat of paint looked crisp and the new windows and doors gleamed in the afternoon light. It all reminded Edison of the New England homes he saw in paint commercials as a child.

It had been a few weeks since he rolled out the ancient looking house blueprints. Being out of his element, he had asked Brett and Linda for help in updating the damaged interiors as well as finding the army of contractors. The most obvious change to the house had been returning the front door to its original state. His parents had gone along with the single front door with a matching faux twin that wasn't functional but provided symmetry. Edison had decided to go back to the original design, two doors, both functional and solid.

Today had started early, with Brett, Linda, Val and Carlos sorting the debris Edison had picked up from the neighbors' yards in the days following the explosion. The industrial garbage collectors would arrive today to collect the sorted piles of debris, as well as a handsome check.

Leaning against a porch pillar, he felt the soreness in his back from the morning's work. The temperature was still rising and the early afternoon sun was strong but the pillar, while warm, felt nice against his skin. He had taken off his shirt by 10:00 and now he didn't even know where it was. He had been working with Carlos at the time, stacking the broken cross-beams from the garage roof. Carlos took off his shirt about five minutes later. The tight muscles of Carlos' lean body had caught Edison's eye. He was very shy, Edison concluded, and chose his few words carefully. Carlos certainly didn't mind getting into the work, and while moving the timbers under the hot sun, he calmly whistled, never short of breath.

Edison had been confused when Carlos had shown up with Brett and Linda and thought he was there to work rather than to lend a hand. Carlos made it clear, though, that he had just come to help. After lunch, Val went upstairs to change for an interview with a temporary agency, which she constantly described with the f-word. Linda went back to her house to prepare a dinner for Vera and her partner as well as to review the lease for office space near Edison's office in the old Washington Mutual Tower. Vera had changed her mind at the last minute and vetoed the Bellevue office location, the most logical choice since both clients lived on the east side of Lake Washington. Linda had summarized Vera's panicked change of location with the phrase, "big lakes make good neighbors." Brett had wandered off after lunch and Edison had assumed he was firing up the grill for Linda's feast.

It felt nice to be alone. Edison eased down the pillar and sat on the front step. The street was quiet, and while the boughs swayed, he only felt hot, still air. Although tired, sleep was not an option. His mind was still racing, chasing details. Even today's productive start unleashed more details to corral. The explosion had been an excuse, perhaps, to make his mark on the house. Also, he was considering inviting the runner in red shorts, John, over to dinner at some point and wanted the house to look like his own.

The rooms of the lower floor had been stripped of furniture and cleaned. He had then hired painters to freshen the soot-stained rooms. It had been hectic and expensive. When it came time to place his parents' small items back on the shelves and bookcases, Edison carefully stored the macramé and knickknacks in boxes and went to Pacific Place to buy items to fill the open spaces. The change in the rooms was perhaps small to others, but to him it was necessary and bittersweet.

He stood up, feeling weariness in his legs, and headed for the porch swing that invited him with its easy sway. There he could relax and, with its recessed position, it offered a surprising amount of privacy from the street. He turned and looked through the open double doors at the bottom of the dark chandelier, the new doors contrasting with the familiar chandelier. He shivered in the heat as he thought of his parents and their senseless deaths. He knew there was no one to blame and no greater truth that would come from their passing. When it came down to it, Edison thought, it just sucked. He sighed and stepped inside the double doors and pulled them closed in a gesture that felt symbolic but empty. Walking over to the porch swing, he sought an escape from reality.

Edison stepped back suddenly from the porch swing. Brett hadn't gone far when he disappeared. He lay before Edison on the porch swing among the many pillows. An empty plate balanced precariously on a pillow. Edison quietly stepped forward, rescued the plate and managed not to wake Brett. He went back to the rail and put the plate down. Brett's shorts rode low on his waist and Edison noticed that Brett had lost a few pounds. The golden hairs on his tan skin triggered a familiar response in Edison.

If nothing more, I am predictable and a tramp, Edison thought with resignation as he leaned against the rail of the porch. He drank in the view of Brett shamelessly. He knew he needed to date again. Russell had been a mistake and David a freak, but that was no reason not to date. The longer he waited or spent desiring the unobtainable that lay before him, the more of his life he wasted. There were no guarantees, he thought, looking over at the closed double doors. His thoughts were interrupted by the sound of footsteps bounding up the porch stairs.

"I forgot my shirt," Carlos said from the top of the steps.

Edison put a finger to his lips to signal silence and with a big smile waved Carlos over.

"He's no Snow White," Edison whispered, enjoying the closeness of Carlos' bare skin.

"All it takes is one bad apple," Brett said, not turning to face them or opening his eyes.

They both laughed and Edison noticed that Carlos hadn't pulled away from his side.

"We'll leave our gender-challenged Snow White alone," Edison said, "and if she is hungry, there are cookies in the freezer."

"She has risen," Brett said, rubbing his eyes and stretching.

"Your shirt must be out back. Oh, now I remember, I put both of them on the bridal wreath bush to dry." Edison motioned Carlos in the direction of the newly repaired side porch.

Once around back, he asked if Carlos wanted seconds on lunch.

"No, I'd need to go to the gym if I ate like you or Brett," he teased, slapping his flat stomach and pulling up his jeans.

Walking around the back of the house, they passed his mother's overflowing herb garden and came to the unruly bridal wreath bush.

"Here they are," Edison said, pulling their two shirts from the bush. "Sorry, they're still wet. I thought they would dry in this heat."

"No problem, it's one of my favorite shirts." He flipped the shirt over and showed Edison the logo. "Oakland A's. You gotta love them. You especially, since you used to live across the Bay from them. Did you catch the home games?" Carlos asked.

"Too far from San Francisco and the Giants had the nice new stadium," Edison replied, hoping Carlos would not peer too deeply into his laughably shallow baseball knowledge. He'd hate to admit he had only gone to the Giants Stadium to look at the architecture. "Not a Mariners fan?"

"No, it's all about the A's."

"You'll have to meet my friends, Greg and Pauli; they are devout Mariners fans. They might try to convert you." Edison exchanged the A's shirt with his so he could look at it and pull the splinters from it. He wondered why Carlos had worn his favorite shirt to move charred wood and debris.

"I don't think there's any chance of that. I tend to stick with what I like," Carlos said, for the first time making sustained eye contact with Edison. "Would you like to come over to my place for dinner Wednesday night?"

Edison wondered if this was a date or simply Carlos making a space at his table for the pitiful orphan.

"I'd like that," Edison said, holding eye contact, trying not to look at the naked torso in front of him.

"I'll email you my address, then," Carlos said with a smile of a man who had accomplished something. "Carlotta has your email. She will be there too. She wants to cook for you but she won't stay long. We can have dinner without all my sisters chattering and maybe a DVD afterwards."

"That sounds like fun. Email me and I will be there. Can I bring anything?" Edison asked.

"No, nothing," Carlos said, looking shocked. "Carlotta would raise holy hell if you brought something to one of her meals. It's cultural, not personal," he said, smiling but a hint of inflexibility crept into his face.

After a pause, Edison felt himself getting tense.

"I'll email you when I get home," Carlos said, turning and walking away.

Edison relaxed some and wondered what Carlos' intent was. He mounted the steps to the side porch and, in the distance, he saw Carlos slip on his shirt with a big smile on his face and then jump into his truck.

"I guess I know the intent," Edison said to himself. He stepped into the cool kitchen and went to the refrigerator for a drink. He felt sweat drip down his sides, cooling his body dramatically in the shady kitchen.

"Boy, you have men coming and going and here Linda and I were worried about you."

Edison jumped, startled. "You heard all that?" Edison asked, somewhat shocked that Brett would listen.

"Of course I did. You don't have a television in here any-more. I needed some sort of entertainment."

Brett was eating ice cream from the half-gallon container and wearing one of Edison's gym shirts, which was a little tight on him but flattering. Edison was amused that Brett was com-fortable enough to go to his bedroom and borrow clothing.

"So," Brett said, pointing with his spoon. "Let's get this straight, so to speak," he said, chuckling. "You meet some loser married guy off the Internet only to have him go berserk at a party. You leave same party and pick up a man on the way home, and now the hot Hispanic guy invites you over after his doting sisters pre-approved you. That's a lot of action. Inciden-tally, you are having quite a meal Wednesday; Carlotta ran the menu by Linda last weekend."

"You knew about this and you didn't warn me?" Edison asked, a little peeved that his best friend would not clue him in on the intrigue.

"I was going to tell you but Linda nixed it. She doesn't think you can act worth a damn so she wanted you in your natural state. And buddy, if you don't pull up your shorts soon, you're going to be in your natural state," Brett said, motioning with the ice cream carton to Edison's midsection. "No wonder you were getting Carlos all flustered."

Edison looked down and saw that he too had lost a little weight and was showing the world a bit too much skin.

"He did seem a bit distracted," Edison said, pulling up his shorts. "He must have thought I was advertising."

"Or a whore," Brett said walking over to the freezer, replac-ing the ice cream and taking out the bag of homemade cookies. "Time to get back into the game for real, Eds," Brett said, offer-ing him the open bag of cookies.

He took three and looked back at Brett. "You know," Edison

said, biting into a cookie, "you are right. I guess I need to think past recent trash to future treasure. You think he's interested in me?" he asked, cocking his head in the direction of the street.

"If he's over here asking you to dinner with his family, then he wants to get to know you better, I imagine." Brett grabbed a chair and straddled it. "But what I want to know is what it is in you, Edison, that makes you my best friend and my wife's confidant, but you rarely venture out into the social world, and when you do, you play games on the Internet and come up with garbage like David or that fool Russell? And don't tell me it's a gay thing," Brett said before Edison could reply. "Sex is sex and love is love. Why are you acting like a clueless Vestal Virgin when you have two solid options like John and Carlos before you? Something is wrong, guy, what is it?"

"I don't know. It's been this way since high school. I'm always about a day late when it comes to expressing what I feel with a guy. With Russell, it was easy; he didn't listen so it didn't matter.

"Well buddy, you need to work on it. You're not alone, though. We want you to be happy. Consider Val, Linda and me as your board of advisors."

"Lucky me," Edison said, breaking into a smile.

"So, you going to play both of them at the same time or date serially like I did when I was a strapping young man?"

"I guess, since everyone seems to be watching, I can't let it die on the vine like I usually do," Edison sighed.

"Not a chance. So what is your game plan?"

The front doorbell rang, startling both of them.

"Ah, saved by the bell," Edison said, turning to the front door. As he walked through the parlor, he put on his shirt. When he pushed his head through the shirt, he realized that he had never given Carlos his shirt back. The scent, not in the least unpleasant, was not his own. Carlos' smile at his truck must have been when he realized he had the wrong shirt.

The doorbell rang again and Edison sprinted the last way hoping that it wasn't Carlos at the door, knowing he would see him in the shirt. Before opening the door, he ran a hand through his longish hair. He opened the door to see Lily standing stiffly on the porch holding a large blue box.

"Lily, I thought you had the new key."

"I do, dear," she said, shifting the box to her left side. She wore an expensive-looking suit that seemed out of place in the hot and sunny summer day. "But who knows what a lady might see in a bachelor's house without giving proper warning?" She eyed Brett, who had followed behind Edison, and said with a smile, staring at Brett's groin, "Or a married man's home for that matter."

"Ms. Lily," Brett said formally.

"Need help with that, Lily?" Edison asked.

"Oh, it's for you, dear. Just put it on the center table," she said as she handed the box to Edison.

Edison walked over to the table and could feel Brett hovering over his shoulder. He wondered if Linda ever tired of his looming curiosity. It would be like having a large and curious stork around the house peering over your shoulder as you went about your day.

"Should I open it now?" Edison asked as he turned to Lily, remembering his manners rather than ripping into it like he normally would.

Lily looked around, first to the dining room and then to the parlor and finally up the stairs. Edison braced for the rage Lily would no doubt be spewing about the changes to the interior of the house.

"Edison, I like what you did with the house. The new doors and trim look wonderful. They will give the house a nice sparkle when the rainy season arrives." She looked around again. "Yes, you have a distinct sense of style. I like it."

"Really?" Edison asked, not hiding his shock.

"I like it," Lily said again. "I am a minimalist too, and while I loved your mother's sense of style, you cannot maintain it. You need to go with your strengths." Lily nodded to Brett as if to confirm her statement.

"It is nice in here," Brett said, "although Linda could help with some of these bare walls."

"I'll ask her about that when she gets clear of all her Vera drama," Edison said, noticing for the first time the large expanses of empty white wall.

"Open it, dear," Lily said, reminding him of the box in front of him.

He opened the box and saw the carefully wrapped bowl inside. "You found another bowl!" Edison exclaimed, lifting the bowl from the box, letting the wrap fall to the floor. Brett stepped in and pulled the box from under the large crystal bowl.

"Well, it's not something new," Lily said. "It's the twin of the one that Crazy shattered during her last tour of your home. Ellie and I bought them together when we were at Tiffany refreshing our silver patterns. Your pattern is Hampton, by the way, and if you look in the bottom left drawer of the dining room wall case, you will find it there. It was a good shopping day as I remember."

"I bet." Edison was surprised his mother shopped at Tiffany. He imagined her fitting in more with the arts and crafts crowd. It saddened him that he didn't know his parents as well as he thought he did.

"Should we fill it up with those little birds?" Brett asked, breaking the silence.

"You kept them?" Lily asked Edison with a warmth in her voice that surprised him.

Brett answered her question. "Yeah, Val and I rescued them that night and Edison cleaned them up and put them in a Nordstrom box. I visited them just today before I took a nap," Brett said, going to the foyer closet.

"Lily," Edison said, taking the box Brett offered him. "I had a chance to restock the bar and I think I may have some of your favorites on the shelf. Would you care for a drink?"

Lily looked at her watch. "Well," she feigned a moral struggle, "it is cocktail hour in Maine, so in the spirit of the Republic, yes, I'll have a scotch and soda."

"And you, Brett?" Edison asked, knowing that Brett would be happy to start after a long morning of dragging debris across the lawn. "A bourbon and Coke?"

Brett nodded as he straightened the crystal bowl on the table.

"I think I will have a gin and tonic," Edison said, putting down the box of hens and taking off the cover. Inside they were as he had left them, dozens of paper hens neatly arranged by color and all facing one direction.

"It looks as if they are attending a lecture," Brett said, peering into the box.

Picking up the lead hen, Edison volunteered, "Perhaps Flock Dynamics?"

"Or Edith Piaf: Friend of Fowl?" Brett offered.

"You two are dreadful. Clearly, they are reviewing Milton's Bird of Paradise Lost, you know, what went on in the Garden after we were all kicked out."

Edison rolled his eyes at the corny class concepts and put the paper hen back down in its makeshift lecture hall. "I'll get those drinks while you two break up the flock."

Edison heard the distant click of a cigarette lighter as he turned into the dining room and headed toward the bar. At the bar, with its small mirrored plates, he caught his reflection, the Oakland A's emblem on the shirt, and in the far background, he could see Lily dropping the colorful birds into the bowl. Beside her, Brett was aligning the table with the black circular tile in the floor. He set out the glasses and carefully made the drinks. Echoing off the foyer wall, he heard Lily exhale loudly and murmur to Brett, "He's just like his father when he's not like his mother. I may just like him after all."